For Jim

In memory of our two little angels in heaven
who we never got to meet. They will always
be a part of me and you x

A
Part of
Me
& You

Emma
Heatherington

A division of HarperCollins*Publishers*
www.harpercollins.co.uk

Harper*Impulse* an imprint of
HarperCollins*Publishers*
The News Building
1 London Bridge Street
London SE1 9GF

www.harpercollins.co.uk

This paperback edition 2018

1

First published in Great Britain in ebook format by
HarperCollins*Publishers* 2018

A catalogue record for this book
is available from the British Library

ISBN: 9780008281250

This novel is entirely a work of fiction.
The names, characters and incidents portrayed in it are
the work of the author's imagination. Any resemblance to
actual persons, living or dead, events or localities is
entirely coincidental.

Typeset in Birka by Palimpsest Book Production Ltd,
Falkirk, Stirlingshire

Printed and bound in Great Britain by CPI Group
(UK) Ltd, Croydon CR0 4YY

Chapter 1

Juliette

Queen Elizabeth Hospital, Birmingham, England

FRIDAY

I am just about getting used to the idea of turning forty when I'm told I am going to die pretty soon. Let's face it, you can't get much more ironic than that.

'So much for "life begins",' I mutter to my doctor Michael who looks at me with remorse as I give him a nervous smile and a '*shit happens*' style shrug. My face is telling a lie. My tongue is telling a lie. I am trying to pretend I am okay but of course I am not okay. Inside I am crying. I am forty and I am dying and I am not okay at all.

I stare at the floor until the pattern on the carpet makes my head spin and the ticking of the clock seems to get louder and louder as we both try to think of what to say next. The big loud hands of time, chasing each other in circles, taunting me as my life ticks away, hours, minutes, seconds ... stop.

Michael looks up at me like he might cry too, lost for words for once.

We've come quite a long way over the past three years since we were first paired up on this cancer journey and here we are now, reaching the end we had hoped we'd never have to face. The part where he tells me, as my consultant, that there's nothing more we can do except wait for the inevitable, for my share of the journey to end. The part where he tells me, as my friend, that all our battles through treatment, our suffering, our praying and positivity, all of it is now just a waiting game.

If only it was as simple as waiting – but I can't just sit around and wait. I have so much I still want to do in life and now, already, it's all about to end.

I go to the window and look out onto the city rooftops. I open the window and inhale the air, fearing that if I don't focus on something as simple as breathing I might faint, and we don't need to add to the drama, do we?

'Have you spoken to your family about this yet, Juliette?' Michael asks me. He is fidgeting with his pen as he speaks. 'I mean, I realise you didn't know for definite what the outcome was before today, but have you prepared them at all, for the worst?'

I know without having to look at him that he has taken his glasses off to wipe them for the third time since I got here, just to give his hands something to do.

He is such a fidget when he has to give bad news but this isn't just bad news. This is the very last piece of news he will ever have to deliver to me. This is the beginning of the end for me.

'My sister knows I'm here today, as does my mum, but they're still holding out hope. It will be a shock to them no matter what's going through their heads, no matter what they've been expecting, this will be the very worst, obviously,' I tell him.

'And Rosie?'

Oh God.

'Rosie thinks ... Rosie thinks I'm having a pamper day for my birthday at a spa with some friends today. She has no idea what's going on ... not yet.'

My voice cracks when I say my young daughter's name aloud. How am I going to tell her? *How?* She doesn't have anyone else to lean on. She's only ever had me.

'And Dan?'

Michael is really making sure this news is sinking in, I'll give him that much, as he lists the most important people in my life. My mouth dries up at the mention of Dan. I try to reply but I can't.

'You're going to have to tell him, for goodness sake, Juliette,' says Michael. 'The man must be going off his head with worry. He is still part of your family too, no matter what you've gone through.'

I turn to face him and lean on the windowsill with my arms folded.

'It's a bit more complicated than that, as you know,

Michael,' I say to him, unable to look him in the eye but I can tell he is raising an eyebrow. 'Oh you know it is, don't look at me like that!'

I am watching him now and just as I'd predicted, he is giving me a 'tough shit' glare.

'Dan and I have both accepted that he can't cope with me and my sickness,' I remind him. 'And I don't know that I can cope with him right now either. He has his own problems that he has to deal with, but I will tell him soon – just not yet. For his own good, not mine.'

Michael puts his head in his hands. He is almost as devastated as I am with this mess – and what a mess it really is when you realise you are going to leave behind everything you love. It's like you need to pack up to go somewhere, but you're going nowhere really; how the hell do you plan for that?

'You can't just block him out of this, Juliette,' Michael says. 'The man must be climbing the walls with worry. Do you even know where he is right now?'

I shrug.

'His mother's house, probably? Or with his sister?'

The truth is, I don't know at all. I don't have any idea where my husband is and right now it's better that way for me, for him, and for Rosie.

'And you really think that it's okay that you don't know?'

I nod. I shrug again. I don't know what to say.

'Today might change all that, obviously,' I tell him.

'And maybe it won't. I will have to think about it carefully as I'm sure you understand – I mean, you probably know me almost as well as he does by now.'

Dr Michael and I long ago ditched the doctor-patient formalities and admitted that we had actually become really good friends. We talk about everything from American rock music to favourite one-pot recipes (he's newly single) to our shared Irish roots, and I even gave him relationship advice once – though I'm the last person who should be doing so. The very, *very* last person. We've argued a lot too when the going got tough.

'You are the most annoying and stubborn person I have ever met,' he tells me, managing a light smile. 'And I mean that in the nicest possible way.'

'Yes, yes, you've told me that many times before,' I say, rolling my eyes. 'Look, I just need some time to get my head around this all and then I'll talk to Dan. I know I don't have the luxury of time but I need to just … I need to think about things. No matter how much I've dreaded this moment, and I knew that it might come soon, it's still a massive shock to hear my days are numbered. And the sickening thing is that I don't *feel* sick right now. I feel fine! How cruel and weird is that?'

We pause in silence.

'The sickness will come quite soon, unfortunately,' says Michael. 'So enjoy this time while it lasts. You will have the option of palliative care of course, when you feel you need it. And you will have to think about home versus hospice care just like we talked about before, plus your steroid management and what sort of pain control you want.'

The clock is ticking again, so loudly.

I don't have much time to do an awful lot and we both know it.

'What will I do now? I mean, next, Michael?' I ask him. 'What am I actually supposed to *do* right now? I'm so scared even though I'm trying to be brave. Please tell me what to do. Where do I go from here? How do I start preparing for my life to end?'

So many questions hang there in the air, like they are stuck in a cartoon speech bubble above my head. A series of questions that no one has the answers to.

Or so I thought.

'Are you asking me what you should do now as your friend, or as your doctor?' he asks me, the pain etched in his eyes.

'I'm asking you as ... I'm asking you as my friend, I guess.'

He gulps. He waits.

'As your friend,' he says. 'Okay, right now, as your friend, I think you should take a few days to yourself. Get away from it all before you get very sick.'

'What?'

This is not what I expected.

'Go somewhere nice where you've always wanted to go. I mean now. It's your birthday, Juliette. Go tomorrow if you can, but just do it,' he says. 'Pack up and go away somewhere for a couple of days, even a week if you can manage it. I really think you should do something just for you.'

I roll my eyes again.

'Oh Michael, that's a really sweet suggestion but as if I could,' I tell him. 'Somehow, I can't see myself mustering up the energy to jump on a plane to anywhere exotic with this time bomb ticking in my head. I mean the thought sounds good, thanks and all that, but I have the small matter of a teenage daughter to think of. Not to mention my job. I've a few features I need to write up. God, that sounds so unimportant in the wider scheme of things, doesn't it? A job? Who cares about their job when they're about to die?'

Michael takes his glasses off. This means he really is determined now. He stands up.

'I obviously wasn't thinking about jumping on a plane to anywhere exotic,' he replies. He has dropped his pen onto the table. 'I'm not talking about New York or the Bahamas or a trip to Niagara Falls, Juliette. I'm merely suggesting you just go somewhere quieter … well, quieter than *here* for a little while. Away from questions and worry and watching the clock tick your time away. Somewhere to reflect, to think, to savour your own well-being, to get your head around all of this … somewhere not too far away, but away from all of *this*. I am suggesting this as your friend, not your doctor. You should do it for just a few days. Just go.'

'Just go …' I repeat after him and those two simple words echo around my head.

I know he means well but going away somewhere is seriously the last thing on my mind today after what I have just been told. I still have to explain all of this mess to Rosie, not to mention planning the poor child's future without me, I have a big sister who is tearing her hair out with frantic worry, a devastated mother and father who will be totally inconsolable and Dan, my husband who ... well, he is the one I worry about the most, apart from Rosie. Dan, my true love, my best friend and the person who knows me the best in the whole world. I don't know if I will be able to tell him at all. I can't imagine saying the words to him. I just can't bear to hurt him so much all over again as I know exactly what he will do to cope and it's something I can't begin to think about right now.

'How about a few days in Ireland?' asks Michael, with a deep breath. 'Take the ferry. Go to that place you told me about ... what's it called, Killarry? You said it's beautiful there. That would be nice, no? Three days? A weekend even?'

Jesus, did he just say Ireland? The very suggestion of going back there fills my stomach with butterflies and my heart flutters at the thought of it.

'You mean Killara,' I correct him and I close my eyes. 'God, Michael, that would be like going to heaven, pardon the pun. The sea, the quiet, the peace ... never mind the memories ... ah, what did you have to mention that place for?'

'Sorry, I just thought it was somewhere you spoke so

fondly of,' says Michael. 'It's accessible. Not a million miles away but far enough away to get away if you know what I mean?'

Killara. I bite my lip. My sweet, dear Killara where some of my fondest, maddest, most life changing memories were made. Now, contrary to my initial dismissal of his suggestion of a short getaway, I'm beginning to consider it.

'Do you really think I could manage a trip there?' I ask him. 'It would be really strange to relive all those memories ... but maybe it would be just what I need to distract me from what's about to happen. Do you think I could?'

Michael's excitement leaves his face for a second.

'Ah okay. Maybe not there then,' he says, knowing exactly what memories I am referring to.

I raise an eyebrow.

'Maybe that's not the ideal place,' he retorts. 'Forget I suggested it. How about somewhere like Barry Island? Or Weston-super-Mare? Caroline and I spent a great weekend there at Easter. Or Blackpool even?'

'Too late, you've planted the seed of Killara,' I tell him and his eyes are full of regret. 'I've always wanted to go back, you know I have. Maybe now *is* the right time.'

'I shouldn't have said it,' he replies. 'What was I thinking? Tenby has a beautiful beach and I know how you love the sea.'

'Look, I won't be chasing any memories, Michael, I'm not that stupid,' I tell him. 'That would not be on my agenda even if I *was* to go to Killara and let's face it, it's a bit late for all that now. I wouldn't dare to look him up.'

He rubs his temples. 'Juliette?'

'Well, you suggested it!' I tell him. 'Come on, Michael of *course* it would be on my agenda. How could I go back there and not wonder where he is? Wouldn't you? It's something I've never faced up to, never told anyone about apart from my sister and obviously Dan knows a little about it, but now might be the right time. It makes sense actually. Imagine if—'

'Juliette, please no!' he interrupts me. 'Your timing to go looking for him is ... I can't think of the word ... you don't need that sort of pressure I am saying *that* to you as your doctor.'

'It wouldn't be *top* of my agenda to find him, I promise,' I explain. 'But you have to agree, it would be so good to put a few old ghosts to bed, not to mention the obvious answers for Rosie. Physically, do you really think I could go there? Even after what you've told me today?'

Michael knows what I am asking.

'Well, what I told you earlier is the unavoidable truth, unfortunately,' he explains. 'The brain tumour is like a ticking time bomb, but you're not going to kick the bucket overnight. You're feeling good right now so a week away won't make any difference.'

We both can't help but laugh at his choice of words. 'Kicking the bucket' sounds like something that old people do, not a forty-year-old woman like me who should have the world at my feet.

'I know exactly what I'll do,' I say, as a brainwave hits my good-for-nothing, wasting away skull. 'I'll take Rosie with me. Her school holidays start soon ... I could take her and we could spend some quality time together away from reality and it might help her, you know, find some sort of closure or understanding of what's ahead of us both.'

'Are you sure?' he replies. 'I never thought of that, taking Rosie. That could be good as long as you're not going to go looking for old skeletons in closets. This is not the right time to tell the child about her—'

'Oh God, Michael, what *am* I going to tell her about all of this crap?' I ask him, my head now in my hands. 'She's just fifteen years old for crying out loud. She wants to be thinking about boys and makeup tutorials on YouTube and the best way to get tickets to see Ed Sheeran – not her dying mother. My poor baby. What am I going to tell her?'

'Take her away with you for a rest,' says Michael, trying to keep me focused. 'Go and spend some quality time with her as you said, wherever it is you choose to go, and give her some more precious memories to hold on to.'

'But how do I tell her that I'm going to die?'

Michael pauses. The word 'die' hangs in the air.

'It will come to you when the time is right,' he whispers to me.

'You think?' I frown, squeezing my eyes tight so that I don't dare cry. I don't have time to cry.

11

'I think, yes,' he says gently. 'Do things you can't do with her here and ... chill out and relax with her.'

'Oh, Michael.'

'Talk to her, read to her, walk with her, give her some last amazing memories to cling on to,' he says. 'Take pictures, make videos, paint, eat, relax ... take her somewhere nice, Juliette. That's about the best thing you can do for her – give her your time. You do know how children spell love?'

'T – I – M – E!' I say to him. 'I gave you that line, thief.'

He shrugs at me. But he is right. His suggestion, as casual as I first thought it might be, has actually helped and I will leave this dreary hospital office with a purpose, something to cling on to and to make happen as soon as possible. I like his thinking. I will start to make plans. I'm good at making plans.

'Will you miss me when I go?' I ask him as I gather my handbag and coat from the back of the chair.

He looks at me and lets out a deep sigh, then shakes his head and laughs in disbelief, knowing that my question has two very different meanings. Will he miss me when I go on my break, and will he miss me when I go forever?

'Only you would ask such a question, Juliette Fox. Only you,' he replies. 'I can't bear to think of it and I'm trying not to think about it. We're good buddies now, me and you. I miss you when you go home after your appointments, never mind ...' He leaves the rest unsaid.

I close my eyes.

'Well, I'm going to miss you, that's for sure,' I tell him and a huge whoosh of nerves fills my tummy. We shuffle towards the door, not knowing what else there is to say in this sterile, hospital office where bad news is delivered on a daily basis.

'I won't miss this office or that carpet,' I tell him, trying to lighten the mood. 'And for goodness' sake change that horrible painting above your desk. You really need to brighten this place up, pronto.'

We both look up at the painting. It's not that bad really, but I'm trying to make a point.

'Caroline thought she was quite the artist, didn't she?' Michael says to me, and then he reaches up to the painting, takes it down and leans it on the wall with its back to us. 'There you go. Done.'

'I bet you feel better already,' I say to him, folding my arms.

He smiles at me and I wonder why on earth his ex, the free-spirited Caroline could ever have thought she would find better than the gorgeous, gentle being before me.

'I'm going to miss you. Call me when you need a chat,' he says when we get to the door of his office. 'Or when you get back from Ireland if you do decide to go?'

'I will. I promise ...'

His eyes fill up and he bites his lip.

'I'm so sorry, Juliette. I wish there was more I could do.'

'Ssh or you'll have me started,' I tell him, trying to keep things light in the most impossible of circumstances. I don't want him to cry but I know that the minute I close this door and walk away from him, he will bawl his eyes out. I know, because as he's admitted to me before, he's done that many times before when he has tried his hardest to make things work for his patients against all the odds.

'Enjoy your break,' he tells me, and I hear his voice crack under the strain of sorrow. 'Make sure it's the best of the best from here on in because that's exactly what you deserve and nothing less. Oh, and Juliette?'

'What?'

I know what's coming. I know exactly what he is going to say next.

'Find Dan, for goodness' sake,' he tells me. 'Find him and tell him you still love him before it's too ... you know what I mean.'

'Before it's too late?' I suggest.

His face crumples and he nods his head. He actually is crying now. My doctor, my good old buddy Michael, is crying.

'Oh my God,' I whisper, putting my hand to my mouth and closing my eyes to push away the pain.

The reality of this is like a deep blow to my gut and the butterflies return again to my insides. I nod and my bottom lip starts to wobble. My eyes sting like hell.

So, this is really it then. This really, really is it.

I am actually going to die.

Chapter 2

Shelley

Killara, County Galway, Ireland

FRIDAY

The apple tree sways in our garden and I stare at it through the window until it blurs, unable to decide if its three-year growth heals or hurts me more. Right now, it scoops out my very core just to see it standing there, alive and proud, oblivious to what it represents and so ignorant to the agony I am still going through since I first planted it there in her memory.

Matt's arms snuggle around my waist from behind and I feel his soft stubble on my neck, his familiar smell easing the hurt just a little as I close my eyes tight and fight back the tsunami of tears building inside me.

'Breathe,' he whispers, doing it for me as he speaks. 'You aren't breathing properly, Shelley. Let it out if you have to. Cry hard if you have to. I'm here. I'm right here.'

He rocks me gently before I push him away, and when I finally let go the release of tears is overwhelming, stronger than ever as I recall this time three years ago.

'It's just so unfair,' I manage to say to my husband between choking sobs but he doesn't reply because he too is broken still. I can tell by his own breathing that this is killing him. The cruelty of it all, the deep-rooted pain that will never go away as we struggle to come to terms with the loss that has ruined our lives.

'At least you had her for three precious years,' they said.

'At least you got to hold her and say goodbye …'

'At least … at least … at least …'

But there is no *'at least'* when it comes to loss.

There will never be an *at least*. Tomorrow we should be celebrating her sixth birthday with balloons and bouncy castles and princesses, but instead all I have is an empty house, boxes of stowed away photos that I can't bear to look at and a tree in the garden that is supposed to remind me of her. There is no *at least*.

'Fancy a walk on the beach before I go?' asks Matt, turning me round and wiping my eyes with his thumbs. We hold eye contact for a few seconds then he leans in and kisses my forehead so softly and somewhere within, I find the strength to thank God for this glorious man I've been blessed with. I lean on Matt's chest and let him hold me close just one more time, feeling his warmth and the sound of his heartbeat, which reminds me that we both are still alive. And then as always, just before it makes me feel better, I let him go – because I don't deserve to feel anything but pain.

'I'd like that,' I reply to him.

He always knows what's best when we find the clutches of grief becoming too much to bear. Or when *I* am too much to bear, I should say. I know that the cracks in our marriage are slowly starting to show, no matter how much I deny it and no matter how patient Matt tries to be. I fear I may be running out of time and I will push him away once too often.

Moments later, we are walking along the sandy Killara beach in silence, with nothing but the lapping of the waves for company and the splashing of our golden retriever, Merlin, as he bounds in and out of the water alongside us.

This place truly is heaven on earth. It is absolute paradise, with the village harbour dotted in the distance and the white sandy beach that our house, Ard na Mara, looks directly upon. We designed it, we built it and we named it carefully, choosing 'Ard' as the Gaelic for height and 'Mara' which means ocean or sea. It sits overlooking Galway Bay on a hilltop that only Matt could have secured with his planning contacts and skills that came from years in his profession.

The coloured shop fronts of the village sit like a smiling rainbow in the distance and seagulls swoop above us as the evening sun sets on the sea. It is paradise indeed and it is home, but for me, it's now a home with no heart or soul. It is empty and so am I.

I close my eyes as we walk, leaning on Matt for guidance and wanting to cling to his body just in case I fall again, or worse, in case he finally lets me go.

'I do still love you, Shelley,' he tells me and the rush I get from his perfect timing almost stops my heart from beating. 'I know this is a nightmare, but I love you so much no matter what we are going through.'

I inhale a smile and but inside I feel nothing. I wish I could say the same back.

'I don't know how you put up with me sometimes,' is all I can tell him and I take his warm hand in mine. We have a private joke between us, one we have repeated often throughout our ten-year marriage when the going gets tough, and his answer is always the same.

'You put up with me too, so we're even,' he replies and kisses my forehead, but we both know that is far from true. Nonetheless, it makes me feel better already. But ... I do know that his love has been tested to the very depths in the past few years as I have gone through every emotion known to mankind and lashed out at him when he didn't deserve it. Our marriage has survived so far and sometimes I don't understand how.

'Do you think this will ever get any easier?' I ask him with a scrunched face, and he shakes his head.

'We have to make it so,' he says to me. 'Yes, she was our whole world and we will always miss that, but we have to learn to live again, Shelley. We still have a lot to live for and I want my wife back. I need my wife back.'

And he is right. He does need his wife back and I so

want to be his wife again. I want to be his lover, his girl who laughs with him until I am almost sick with giggles, the one who feels like home to him, who is fun and interesting and who loves jazz, who runs a book club, who is a bit of a hippy and who cooks up a storm and hosts the best parties at any excuse. The one who dances barefoot in our kitchen with him when we are tipsy and feeling in love, the one who curls up to him when we watch a scary movie, the one who would suggest at the drop of a hat that we book a holiday or convince one of our sailor friends to take us on a boat trip or throw a party just because it's Saturday and life is so good. I want to be that person again, but she is gone and I can't seem to figure out how to find her again.

I think of my business, the vintage boutique near the waterfront that attracts locals and tourists all year round and the one thing that has stopped me from tipping over the edge in recent times. I named it *Lily Loves* long before our daughter was conceived. Lily has always been my favourite girl's name – it was the name of my maternal grandmother who was the most stylish woman I have ever known, so I always felt like I knew our own Lily before we even met her. Harry is the boy I never had. Harry or Jack. I often imagine life with the babies I lost through miscarriage before we were blessed with Lily and it soothes me to just picture their little faces. Who would they have looked like? I hoped they would look like Matt. He hoped they would look like me.

I think of Matt's talent, the talent that has made him

one of the country's most sought after architects. We only get to see so much of the world because of his job. In fact, he travelled the world for years before we met, researching and studying his art, and when he popped the question just months after we found each other, we knew that this was where we wanted to live and bring up our family. Matt has designed skyscrapers in the Netherlands, hotels in London and homes in some of Ireland's most prestigious locations and I am lucky enough to get to travel with him sometimes to see the fruits of his labour. I am so lucky in so many ways and sometimes I need to remind myself of that.

We have a beautiful life here by the sea on Ireland's famous Wild Atlantic Way, but it still kills me inside that I can't give my husband the one thing we both want the most – a family.

'Are you sure you're going to be okay when I'm gone this time?' Matt asks, just as Merlin jumps up on me, his wet paws covering my top in muddy sand. 'I could ask Mum to come and—'

'No, please, Matt, don't even go there,' I reply with a pinch. 'You know I'd rather be alone.'

'But, Shelley—'

'No buts, Matt. I don't want your mother here,' I say to him, my voice sharp with purpose. 'I don't want Mary or Sarah or Jack or flipping Jill, or whoever it is you're going to suggest next, to pop in and check on me, or take me out to lunch or go shopping with me. I don't want anyone, okay. Now, please don't go behind my back arranging things. I will be perfectly fine and much happier left alone, just as I like it.'

The tears are coming, I can feel them. Matt takes a deep breath and kicks the sand.

'I'm only trying to make sure you'll be alright,' he says again, and I can hear the hurt in his voice. I have nothing to give him back.

'I'm fine,' is all I can say.

'But I'll be gone for a week this time and what are you going to do for seven whole days while I'm away? Mope around here on your own in that empty shell of a house and cry until you're sick again?'

I can feel my lip tremble at the thought of how ill I can make myself since Lily died.

'Stop it Matt, please. I just want to be on my own,' I tell him again. 'It's better that way, please.'

Matt's face crumples with worry but he knows I won't change my mind. I have developed a routine to get through this heartache; it centres around working at my boutique shop during the day, where I partake only in small talk about clothes or the weather with customers, and then preparing and cooking my evening meal, with which I might have a glass of wine to fill the void I constantly feel. I might then read for a while or take a walk on the beach before bed but I don't mingle, I don't mix and I don't want to. Not yet.

The sun drifts down in the distance and the orange and gold light shines on my husband's face as he looks at me with despair.

'We'd better get back home or you'll miss your flight,' I tell Matt, ruffling the dog's head as he obliviously bounces around in excitement. 'I know you mean well, but I'd rather be alone, Matt. Please don't worry. Plus, I have this big guy to look after me, don't I, Merlin?'

The dog barks and jumps higher at the sound of his own name. Matt just shrugs.

'Sorry for losing it,' I say to him.

'Again,' he says. 'You mean sorry, for losing it *again*.'

And *again* I know I am pushing it. I can see in his face that he is weary and tired of trying so hard, only to be always told no. God, I dread if day when he has had enough of tiptoeing around me.

'Yes, I'm sorry, *again*,' I say, but we both know it won't be the last time I turn down his offers of help, or the last time I will push him away.

I may have figured out how to exist without Lily, but I have a long, long way to go before I can learn to live without her and my marriage is crumbling under all the pressure and pain that her loss has left behind. I don't want to live like this anymore.

But least we're still clinging on.

Chapter 3

Juliette

As the sun sets in the evening sky, I can't bring myself to go home just yet. I drive to Cannon Hill Park after leaving the hospital and spend the best part of half an hour trying to eat a ham sandwich that tastes like grit on my tongue, before I end up throwing it to the ducks in the lake. This place, this little slice of heaven is often the only piece of tranquillity I can find in my bustling day-to-day existence and I often wonder, now more than ever, why I settled for city life when the silence of nature has always appealed to me so much more.

Growing up on an inner-city housing estate, I always longed to live by the coast where I could walk by the sea, bake my own bread and grow my own vegetables and maybe have my own ducks in a pond in the garden. One day, I'd hoped to live a totally self-sustainable life, and I could read books and listen to loud music and no one would tell me not to because no one would be close enough to hear. That was my plan for my future, but my future isn't happening now, is it? It's too late. I have left it too late thinking I had all the time in the world. Christ.

It hurts my head to reflect too much, but I guess I'm going to have to get used to recalling my past as my days here come to an end. I remember telling Birgit, my Danish one-time travel companion, about my ten-year life plan and how she encouraged me to follow my dreams to travel the world.

'Always stop and savour the simple things,' was her advice back then, and even though I didn't ever get to be that globetrotter (unless you count package holidays to Spain or an annual weekend camping at Pontins), I have always remembered her words and promised myself that one day I would do just that. I would slow down and be present, I'd take in and appreciate everything I had instead of always looking out for tomorrow ... but I don't have too many tomorrows left now, do I?

It is July, my favourite time of year; when daisies bow and sway in what looks like a yellow and white sea below me, and the tree I carved my name in when I was a teenager is just in the distance, looking a bit more solemn despite its summer bloom. Maybe it knows what's going on today too. Maybe everyone knew this was going to happen. Everyone that is, apart from me.

I pick at my nails, my weak, brittle nails that haven't seen a good manicure in months and then I close my eyes and breathe. Sometimes it's good to just breathe.

My mind races and I battle with my thoughts, trying

desperately not to think of all the things I am going to really miss when I go. I count the months forward in my head. Michael couldn't give me a specific timeframe on my life but I know in my heart that at a big stretch I'll make Christmas. I'd give anything to see a white Christmas this year and, just one more time, to sit around the tree with my family and snuggle up with them as the snow falls, in front of a blazing fire.

I hold my head in my hands and try to fight off the wave of panic and breathlessness that I know is just around the corner. Rosie. What the hell is going to happen to my beautiful, innocent Rosie who has no idea what is going on and what life has laid out in front of her? And then the guilt ... my God, the guilt for the life I brought her into; no father in her life, and now I am set to leave her all by herself with absolutely no one to call her own. Yes, she has my sister and her grandparents, and Dan for what it's worth, but it's not the same.

Who will take her to the cinema like I do, where we stuff our faces with nachos and popcorn and fizzy drinks and then complain about feeling sick all the way home? Who will know that when she gets a headache, it's a sign of her time of the month and to get her a hot water bottle for her stomach cramps? Who will know that if you blend the vegetables in homemade soup she will eat it and love it with no idea that it's laced with more greens and garlic than she could ever turn her nose up at? Who will drive her to her latest boyband's gigs and wait for her as she tries to get a selfie with them afterwards and then who will mop up her tears when she is broken-hearted because they didn't have time to stop to say hello? Who will hug her and wipe away very different tears when she has her heart broken for the first time in real life?

My phone bleeps for the third time since I got here, disturbing my train of thought, and I give in and read my messages despite my need to switch off and absorb what I have just been told.

'I still love you, today and every day,' says the first one, sent earlier this morning and I bite my lip, knowing that it's from Dan. De's changed his number because of our 'break' but despite our agreement of no contact until I'm ready, or until he does what he needs to do, he can't resist sending a message – so I have his number just in case I need him. Despite his troubles I sometimes think I don't deserve him. I never did.

'Are you okay? Please text me Juliette,' is the next one, from my sister Helen who is undoubtedly sick with worry as she waits on me to give her news. She wanted to come with me to the hospital but I wouldn't hear of it. Michael was right when he said I was stubborn but I can't face breaking any more hearts just yet. I want her to stay ignorant for as long as possible, even if that's just for another hour or so.

'Hope you enjoyed your pamper day, Mum!' says the last one and on reading this I burst into tears. I had genuinely forgotten it was my birthday today.

Rosie has been planning something, I just know she

has. I didn't have the heart to tell her not to bother, that all this turning forty nonsense wasn't really on my mind. This time last year I had so many plans for how I would celebrate this milestone and I suppose I still should. I'm still here, aren't I? I'm not dead yet.

I'd better get home.

I pretend that I had no idea there would be any big fuss and smile through my touched up lipstick when I am met with a small, but perfectly formed, surprise gathering in my kitchen.

The duck egg blue cupboards and the fridge which is covered in pictures, drawings and memories from Rosie's playgroup days through to her secondary school life, now greet me like a warm hug. It's so good to be home.

'You little rascal!' I say to my teenage daughter. 'How on earth did you do this without me knowing?'

To be fair, she has done a pretty good job as I take in the banners and the show stopping cake. Wow. I guess this really is quite a surprise.

'Aunty Helen helped me,' says Rosie and I hug her close again, closing my eyes and praying for the tears to stay put. When I open my eyes I see my sister staring at me, that old familiar look of fear bursting from her soul. I can't react. Not now.

The party consists of my sister, her three boys and my daughter. I want to ask where my mother is but my sister beats me to it with an explanation.

'Mum couldn't face it,' she whispers to me as soon as the kids are distracted with phones and other gadgets. 'She has a migraine and has gone to bed. She's crippled with worry, Jules.'

I shake my head.

'It doesn't matter,' I tell Helen. 'I'll call her later. It's probably for the best that she rests. The less fuss we have today, the better.'

My sister gulps back her biggest fears when I say that.

'So, what's on the menu?' I ask, sniffing the air. 'Don't tell me? Is it Helen's famous fish pie?'

'You got it in one!' says my oldest nephew George as the children now wrestle for seats around my kitchen table, eyeing up the cake that sits as its centrepiece. It has my name on it and a big '40' candle. Shit, this is too much.

'I hope you're hungry, Mum,' says Rosie with wide eyes. 'This is just the beginning of the celebrations. We have your favourite sweets for after *and* prosecco *and* chilli crisps and I even made Aunty Helen get ice cream though we already have cake – but my teacher told me that life begins at forty so we've pulled out all the stops. This is going to be your best birthday ever and you deserve it after all you've been through with that horrible chemo.'

Ouch.

'It's not every day you turn forty,' says Helen, still trying to catch my eye but I just can't look at her. I keep smiling and wowing and making other over-exaggerated sounds of enthusiasm to my daughter and my three young nephews but I know that Helen can see straight through me. I dare not catch her eye.

She just nods and stares as I touch my synthetic wig and when the kids have settled in front of a movie later and I break the news to her, she slowly shakes her head in disbelief and shock.

'There has to be something we can try.'

If anyone looked through the window right now and saw us with our prosecco and cake, they'd think we really were celebrating.

'There are no more somethings, Helen,' I tell my only sister. 'I could try and fight on and spend the rest of my days vomiting and pumping my organs with chemo and radiotherapy but I'd rather spend them with you and Rosie doing nice things. I want to go out of this world with a bit of grace and dignity, if you can understand that. At home, preferably.'

Helen, of course, is having none of that and her eyes are filled with fear. My God, the agony I have caused her ...

'But there has to be some—'

'There isn't,' I remind her. 'There is nothing. I know, I know. It sucks, big time but please don't cry, Helen. I can't cope with any more tears and this mascara goes to shit when I sneeze, never mind coping with tears.'

But it's too late. She is sobbing and finding it hard to breathe so just like I did with Michael earlier, I get up to comfort her.

'I don't want you to be sad, Hel,' I say into her hair that smells, as always, of apple shampoo. I raise my eyes towards the ceiling and swallow hard. 'I had a quiet suspicion, no matter how much I denied it to myself that this might be the news I'd get today. Yes, it's crap and it's unfair and it's not what we want but we need to accept it because there's absolutely nothing I can do about it. Nothing. I'm so sorry, Helen. I'm sorry.'

It's as much as I can say to her as she tries to digest this latest blow because I think I may be in shock too. She gets up, wiping her nose on the back of her hand and tries to get busy.

'But you were doing so well,' she sniffles. 'How can it be so far advanced? How?'

'It's called cancer,' I say, and the very word makes me so angry but I will never let it show. 'I am trying to make sense of it all too but I don't really have time to contemplate or analyse so it's time for me to take action and do the things I should have done years ago. I'm going to make some really nice plans.'

Now, Helen shakes her head.

'Juliette, you don't need to make any more plans!' she says. 'Your life has been one big long plan that never got completed.'

'I beg your pardon?'

'The thirty things to do before you're thirty plan? I think you managed to do five? The list of life plans you decided to make for Rosie when she turned thirteen but didn't finish? Dan's most magical book of wedding surprises?'

30

She starts to laugh and I can't help but laugh too. She does have a point.

'Michael says I should go away for a few days to reflect, you know, a change of scenery,' I tell her. 'Somewhere quiet, away from reality if you like just to let this all sink in.'

'What? Away where to?' she asks. 'Is he ... is he sure you won't ...?'

'He is pretty sure I won't die in the next week or so,' I say with a nervous laugh. 'I'm thinking of going to Ireland, me and Rosie, what do you think? I want to go there and stay by the sea for a few days and think about ... life and well, death I suppose.'

But there's no pulling the wool over my sister's eyes. She knows exactly what Ireland means to me.

'No, Juliette, you just stop right there,' is her adamant reply as she opens and closes my kitchen cupboards and drawers, but then I didn't expect her reaction to be any different. 'Don't say that. You're not thinking straight, Juliette. You're in shock. Just stop.'

'But I *am* thinking straight,' I say to her. 'Even Michael said it would be good for me.'

'Michael doesn't know your history there!'

'No, well, yes, but actually he knows a lot more than you think he does,' I try to explain. 'But that's not why I want to go back. It's a spectacular place, Helen. It's my favourite place in the world.'

'Cornwall is a spectacular place,' says Helen. 'Scotland is a spectacular place. It has scenery and the sea and good food and it's—'

'Yes, and so does Barry Island and Weston-super-Mare and bloody Blackpool but it's not where I want to go, Helen,' I say. 'I want to show Rosie the one place in this world I loved the most and I want to tell her how special it was and how it still is for us both. I want to go there and switch off, and if anything else happens, then that's a huge bonus, but that's not the only reason why I'm going, believe me.'

My big sister is going to take a lot more convincing than that, but I was expecting this. I didn't think for one second that she would be helping me pack my bags and cheering me on my merry way to Killara, with Rosie in tow, to find a man who once sailed boats there – when here I am, back in the real world about to pop my clogs. No way.

'So, what are your other reasons then? I don't believe you for one second and have you thought about Dan in all of this?' Helen is still rifling through the kitchen drawers.

'Helen, Dan will understand,' I try to explain. 'I'll give him a call and tell him everything.'

'Juliette, you don't need any stress and you certainly don't need to be chasing unicorns and rainbows at this stage,' she says to me. 'At last, goodness, how can it be hard to find something to write on around here?'

She opens an old notebook of mine, and then licks her finger to flick through the pages until she finds a blank one.

'Why do you need something to write on?' I ask. 'I

just want to go there and spend quality time with Rosie. It will be great for us both, you know it will.'

She starts to write.

'You'll never find him,' she says, still writing. 'You hardly know anything about him. You said you don't even remember his proper name.'

She has a point. Except it's not that I don't *remember* his proper name. I never *knew* his proper name in the first place.

'I do remember the rest of him though,' I reply, and it's true. I remember his dark hair and his muscular back and the fumbling and laughing and urgency and the smell of alcohol – and the shame I felt when I woke up alone and the fear on the way home to Birmingham when sobriety kicked in and I realised how stupid we'd been not to have used any protection whatsoever.

I remember how I looked for him before I left the village the next day, just to see if he cared or wanted to see me again or would acknowledge what had happened between us but he had disappeared. I remember the hurt and shame I felt and then how Birgit and I had laughed and laughed at the very thought of me, a good Catholic girl from a convent school having a one night stand with a handsome Irishman when I didn't even get his real name, never mind his number.

But most of all, I remember the emptiness I felt when I got on the plane home to Birmingham without Birgit to laugh about it with, and the feeling that my life had just changed forever. And oh, how it had.

All of that, I can remember loud and clear.

'What are you doing?' I ask my sister who is still making notes in front of me while I daydream down memory lane.

'Nothing,' she says.

'You're writing nothing?'

'Okay, okay, I'm making *plans*,' she says. 'It's my turn to make some plans. It's not just you who makes plans in life, you know.'

I look across at my sister's notes and let out a loud sigh that makes her jump when I see the latest entry on her 'plan'.

'What?' she shouts, dropping the pen with panic. 'Are you in pain? What, Juliette?'

'No, I am not in pain,' I tell her. 'I'm just wondering why on earth you're writing that stupid stuff in front of me. *Make room for Rosie?* At least wait until I leave before you try and plan your life after me. Jesus, Helen, you have as much tact as our mother sometimes.'

'Don't exaggerate, I'm not that bad,' says Helen, tearing out then scrunching up the notepaper but it's too late, I already saw it. 'And don't try to change the subject. You are not going to Ireland to track down this *stranger* after all this time. You're not going. End of.'

I pull a funny face. She doesn't laugh.

'I think his nickname was Skipper,' I remind her. 'He was a captain on the boats so that sounds about right, doesn't it? Skipper. Or was it Skippy? Something like that. Or Skip ... No, it was Skipper. A captain. A boatman.'

'Yes, you said he was a sailor or something. You dirty rotten stop out.'

'A mighty fine sailor he was too,' I say with a cheeky grin but my sister is disgusted. 'I'm joking! Well, actually I'm not joking. Look, I swear, I don't even know if he was *from* Killara! He was probably just 'sailing' through like I was. He's not why I'm going back, I promise.'

But Helen has had enough of my jokes. She closes her eyes and then looks at me, not joking one bit right now.

'Please, Juliette,' she whispers. 'Oh my God, please think of Rosie right now. She was so excited today to arrange your party. I couldn't bear to watch her put the candles in the cake and wrap your presents. Did you like your presents? She was so proud of herself. And Dan? He left you a gift. Did you see it?'

I nod my head. A silver locket that he has known I've had my eye on for years sits on the worktop. It's too hard. All of this is too hard.

'I loved my presents,' I tell my sister. 'Thank you. You're the best sister in the world, you know that.'

'I'm your only sister,' she reminds me. 'You have to say that.'

'You're still the best, though.'

'That poor little girl has no idea,' she says to me. 'Her little face will ... oh, how are you going to tell her, Juliette? You're her whole world.'

Helen is at breaking point now as this all sinks in. I do not want to see this so I look away.

'Don't, Helen. Please don't say "poor Rosie" and don't

you dare cry again. I don't want you to be so sad.'

But she's off. It's hitting home with my sister that my life is about to end while hers and Rosie's and Dan's lives will all change dramatically.

'You do know I will look after her as best I can,' she sniffles. 'It won't be the same as you, I mean, it won't be as good as you, but I'll do my very best by her and Brian will help out too of course. I promise you we will do our best. We'll try and let her have her own room. My boys can bunk in together, it won't do them a bit of harm and—'

'We've had this conversation before, Helen. I know you will look after her for me,' I tell my sister. 'You've already told me all of this.'

'What I'm trying to say is that she doesn't need him, Juliette,' Helen tells me. 'She doesn't need a stranger entering her life with everything else that's going on. She's got me and Dan and Brian and the kids. Think about it. Think about Rosie. Please.'

'But what if I'm not her whole world?' I suggest to her. 'What if there is another world out there for her and just by bringing her there, it might give her some options? What if ...?'

I shrug and she squeezes my hand, wiping her eyes with the other and shaking her head. She is right, of course. My big sister Helen, mother of three, wife of one, and wise old owl, has always been right. She was not surprised when, sixteen years ago, I arrived back from a summer backpacking around Ireland with more baggage than I'd left home with. Not that I was ever overly promiscuous, but more that I was the careless sort who never thought anything would ever happen to me. Happy-go-lucky and carefree, I wouldn't have recognised trouble if it had stared me in the face. In fact, I still probably wouldn't.

'Gullible,' was my mother's way of putting it. 'Our Juliette would believe anything you told her and go back for more. She's as gullible as a fish.'

I've learned to shrug it off and accept that they might be right; but gullible, careless, silly or whatever way they wanted to look at me, I've managed very well, thank you very much, since my Emerald Isle vacation all those summers ago. Rosie has never wanted for anything, despite not having a father figure in her life ... well apart from Dan of course, but he was more like a friend to her. So why do I want to start picking at holes that aren't there, by digging into my sketchy past? Why am I potentially going to turn her whole world upside down and leave a terrible mess behind, when I could leave well alone safe in the knowledge that she will be just fine?

It's because I know that someday she will want to know who he is, and I'm the only one who can tell her.

It's because I do believe that there is another world waiting for her over there.

'I promise I will say nothing to Rosie until I know more about him,' I tell my sister and I can see her tongue twist into syllables and words she cannot get out quickly enough to stop me so I keep talking. 'It's what I've always thought I should do, you know, even though I've never mentioned it much. He might not be there anymore. I might not find him. I could have every door shut in my face, but imagine it was you. Imagine you had a child that you didn't know about. I don't think it's so wrong to tell someone the truth, do you?'

But Helen isn't listening to one word I say. She is miles away. She looks like she is already in a place where I don't exist anymore, where this seat I am on is empty already – where I'm gone.

'She writes to him, you know,' I tell my sister and her reaction is just as I thought it would be.

'No way,' she says, the sorrow etched in her saddened eyes. 'Does she really?'

'She's been doing it for a while now. She doesn't have a clue that I know so don't say anything to her. I didn't read a lot of it. No more than a few lines, but she's pining for a man she doesn't know one thing about. Please don't deny her the right to have this last chance of knowing where she came from, Helen.'

Helen twists her hands together and takes a deep breath, looks away and the tears threaten to spill again.

'She breaks my heart,' she says. 'You break my heart. You are so much braver than I could ever be, Juliette, you know that. I hope it works out for you both, I really do, but my hard, cynical knowledge of the world is just so frightened it will all go horribly wrong.'

'I want to go there to make some new memories with Rosie,' I try to reassure her. 'I want to awaken her senses to everything that this beautiful world has to offer – so that when I go she will remember all the positive things I have told her and shown her, and not just the darkness of sickness and death. Simple things over seven days, just Rosie and I, away from it all where I can teach her some of life's greatest lessons as I know them.'

For the first time in my life I think I have silenced my sister.

'That's a pretty amazing way to look at it,' she eventually says.

'I'll stay there for one week,' I promise my sister. 'We'll sail over on the ferry tomorrow at our leisure, stress-free, and it will be like a holiday for us both; our last holiday together. I will make a list of things for us to do, but this time I'll break my habit of making lists and not completing them. We will complete this one. We'll share some bonding time. Anything else that happens will be secondary, I promise.'

Helen takes a deep breath in and then out again. She rubs her eyebrows with her eyes closed.

'I just hope this works out for you because this is hard enough as it is,' she tells me. 'I don't want to see you make it worse. Please don't make it worse.'

'I won't make it worse, I swear to you,' I tell her. 'I'm going to take the ferry in the morning and spend seven days by the sea with my precious girl in the place where she came from. There's no time like the present and like you said, it's not every day you turn forty, is it?'

Helen wipes her eyes and smiles.

'You are the most determined, stubborn person I know,' she tells me.

'That's the second time I've heard that today,' I reply.

'Well, you go and do what you have to do in your favourite place in the world, sister,' she tells me. 'I will always be right behind you and I'll still be here if it all goes tits up. Now, let's go upstairs and I'll help you pack for your trip down memory lane you absolute ...'

I don't wait around for her to finish her sentence. I am already on my way up the stairs.

I agree to meet Dan at my favourite coffee shop, just around the corner from our family home, and when I see him walk past the window my stomach gives a leap. My hands are shaking as I lift my cup, and I take a small sip just to give myself something to do. I don'twant a coffee and I certainly don't want to be telling Dan what I am going to have to eventually.

'I got you an americano,' I say to him when he sits down opposite me. He is ashen with worry and his blue eyes look exhausted. This is exactly why I needed to give him some space from all my sickness and darkness. He hasn't been coping and when he can't cope, it makes all my problems multiply.

'You always know what's best for me,' he says. And I know I do. It's exactly why I had to ask him to leave,.

'You look tired,' I say to him, my maternal instinct and concern kicking in as usual. 'Have you been sleeping and eating okay?'

He rolls his eyes. 'I've been in better places,' he says. 'My sister's spare room is very comfortable but it's not home. Please tell me you brought me here to say you've changed your mind.'

I can't change my mind though. I need to stay strong and protect him from any more pain. If I create distance now, it might help in the long run when he has to deal with things after I go.

'I'm taking Rosie away for a few days,' I tell him, and his face falls.

'A holiday?' he asks and I hear the words in his head that follow – without me?

'Well, kind of,' I reply. He reaches across the table and puts his hand over mine, his coffee sits untouched. 'Quality time, just the two of us. I think it will be good for her and for me, to just get away from here for a short while.'

He looks out the window and puts his hand to his face, then breathes out in an obvious release of heartache and pain.

'That will be good for you both, yes,' he says to me, still looking away. 'It's your birthday today after all so you deserve to treat yourself.'

I stare at my coffee cup, unable to watch as his world comes crashing down. We both know why it has to be this way. His drinking lately has just been too hard to handle. It has been like having another child tugging and pulling at me, tearing me apart when I need him to be strong and deal with what's happening. Tough love, you might call it and believe me, it's tough on me too because I want nothing more than to wrap my arms around him and tell him to come home.

'This time out will be good for you too, Dan,' I whisper and at last our eyes meet. 'Make it work for you, make it work for us.'

'How can I do that? I'll do whatever it takes if you just tell me, Juliette.' He looks so desperate.

'I need you, Dan, just not like this and you know it,' I say to him firmly. 'I need the man I married and the man I love and I want to be by your side till death us do part, just like we promised when we took our vows. But we can't do that while you're the way you have been, I want you to be the man I know you can be again. I need you to put down the bottle and be there for me and Rosie, Dan. And I need you to do that now, more than ever.'

He breathes out again, then his face brightens up and my heart lights up

'I am going to do this, Juliette. I am going to be the man I want to be for you, I promise you and Rosie,' he says to me and I close my eyes and inhale his words. 'I am going to be with you the way you need me to be.'

I want to pull him close and hold him so tight so that our love squeezes all of this pain and illness away, and if only it was as simple as that. This is complicated. We are complicated, but somehow I believe him. I believe that soon I will have my husband back and it's what I want so, so badly.

Chapter 4

Shelley

SATURDAY

My Saturday, the day that would have been Lily's sixth birthday, starts off just as I'd dreaded it would. I wake up to be faced all over again with another day to stumble through, another day of dodging people and their sympathetic smiles and well-meaning ways, another day of being at work where I will try my best to muster up some enthusiasm for the business I built up for so long with such energy and passion. And on top of that, Matt has gone away for a week but perhaps that's a good thing.

I have drawn a solid line down my life and it helps me to deal with it all. There was my life when I had Lily and my life after I lost her – the lives of two very different people. No matter how much counselling or therapy I get, I just can't find that person I was before anymore.

On the outside I look more or less the same as I did before; a bit thinner, a few more lines and wrinkles and more gaunt in the face, but still the same Shelley physically. But inside I am screaming. Inside, I am so different that I don't recognise myself anymore. I am stone cold inside and if not for Matt, who tries to keep me sane and who sometimes manages to melt just a tiny corner of that ice-cold heart, I wouldn't believe that I have a heart left at all.

I feel very little emotion these days and it's a horrible existence. I am nothing more than an empty vessel lost at sea, just bobbing along and never to find any real direction. I am killing time. I sometimes wonder why I am still alive at all.

'You're like a boho princess,' one well-meaning customer told me yesterday as she admired the way I had matched up my long flowing dress with a headscarf, a chunky necklace and a long messy plait. 'You're the perfect advertisement for this shop. It's a real treasure trove. You must be so proud of it.'

And I used to be so proud of my business. If only I could get just a little spark of that energy and passion back that other people still can see in me.

I talk to Lily sometimes and it helps, it makes me smile. I close my eyes and I hear her little voice and I smell her skin and feel her hair on my face and I wonder where she is now. I hope and pray that she has found my own mother to look after her in heaven. I wonder what she would have looked like now, aged six in her blue school uniform. I wonder, would she still be friends with little Teigan from playgroup and would she have loved to read books and dance just like I used to do, and would she love to draw houses and big buildings like her daddy does?

'Mum, please look after her up there,' I whisper into the emptiness of my bedroom and a tear falls onto my pillow at the thought of the two of them together in heaven, at peace, happy. I really hope they are.

I need to get up and face the day.

So I do that; I cry as I brush my teeth, I cry as I fix my hair and I cry when I try and do my make-up. Eventually, I give up and lie on the sofa and let my exhausted body heave and shake and howl out noises in this giant, quiet empty house. I want my mother so badly.

'Why did you have to go too?' I plead at her photo that sits on the white marble mantelpiece across from me. It's the only photo I have kept on display in this house. All the pictures of me, Matt and Lily were packed away when I decided I wanted to move away from here and never come back – a decision I never followed through with because Matt managed to change my mind. 'Why is this house so sterile and cold and why did my baby have to die? I hate you God! Why did you take my baby and my mother so soon? I hate all of this!'

I curl my body up and hug my knees and tell myself that this too will pass. It's all part of the grieving process – the seven stages of grief that I have read so much about, that I have been familiar with for most of my adult life since I lost my mum when I was sixteen years old. I could write a book on bereavement and what to expect next and how to get through it all, day by day, one day at a time like my dad kept telling me then and he keeps telling me now. I don't care to know what stage I'm at right now, but I wish I could fast forward through them all and get rid of this feeling of hollow emptiness that follows me everywhere I go these days.

'She's the Jackson woman,' is what I hear from locals, whispering when I walk past them in the village. 'You know, the couple who—'

They all whisper and nudge and look on in pity.

It's like a label that I wear now, a label that replaced 'she's the northerner who came here after her mother died and never left' or 'she's the one that Matt Jackson, the architect, fell for the moment he saw her in the Beach House Café.'

I am used to the whispers of a small town and I always did like to overhear the one that connects me to Matt. He is the best thing that ever happened to me.

My aching cries turn into more gentle sobs and I stretch my legs out, knowing that my breathing will soon steady and the tears will stop. I make myself a mug of coffee to drink out on the balcony that looks over Galway Bay where I can feel the sun on my face. I know I will soon be almost okay again. I need to be okay again. I can't go on like this. I need my life back and I need to find the strength to move on.

It is raining outside, so I open the French doors and let the sea air soothe my soul. I focus on the lighthouse in the distance and stare at it. I sometimes pretend that Lily is there in my mother's arms, both of them waiting for me, and if I wave out to them they can see me. I wave across and blow a kiss then close the doors.

I try again with my make-up and I plait my hair just like I automatically do every day. Then I grab my coat and keys and make my way out of the house, reminding myself that every little step I take is an achievement and that I will get through this day no matter what it takes.

Juliette

When it rains in the West of Ireland, it really does creep under your skin – a fact that the other tourists who wander the colourful streets of my beloved Killara seem to have copped on to as they're all in waterproofs and branded umbrellas in comparison to my light blouse and floaty skirt. And as for the sandals I'm wearing – well my toes are floating in a sea of mud and rainwater and the smell of the sea, oh how much the smell of the sea takes me right back to the heady days of that youthful summer when I last walked the streets of this picturesque paradise.

We left home this morning and almost ten hours later, after a car journey to the ferry port with Helen, a ferry from Holyhead to Dublin and a bus journey across

Ireland, we are finally here. I don't yet believe this is real. Maybe it's because of Dan and our conversation this morning which I can't seem to shake off.

'You are killing me,' he said to me when I told him I was coming here. I couldn't bear to tell him how ironic his words were. It's not him who is dying, it is me and this is exactly the reason why I need to create some space between us. He can't cope with my illness, he never could and the more he drowns his sorrows in drink and self-pity, the more I feel the need to run. I love him, I need him, but right now I don't have the energy to prop him up when I need to focus on what will become of Rosie.

'So, what do you think?' I ask her as we stand in a puddle on the pavement.

'It looks boring,' she says. 'I don't understand why you wanted to come here to mark your birthday. Why couldn't we have gone to Spain or Paris or even London like you said we would? Somewhere exciting! You're such a weirdo.'

Weirdo I can live with. Boring I can definitely live with. I am just delighted I convinced her to come with me in the first place, because believe me, it wasn't easy. There were so many more important things to do at home like hang out with Josh and Sophie and the new kid on our block, Brandon whose father does security for some Disney pop princess whose name I can't remember. But I just know that Rosie will love it as much as I do, even if she never finds out the very important, but very much secondary, reason I decided on here over any other more exotic location.

Apart from the weather, I must admit that nothing seems very different about Killara from that summer all those years ago. I recognise the pubs of course – the bright pink exterior walls of O'Reilly's with the nightly Irish trad music sessions' the Beach House Café on the pier, that boasts the best seafood chowder in the country; and the bright blue Brannigan's Bar and B&B, the place I met Skipper on that hazy, drunken night when my daughter was conceived.

I'm not staying in Brannigan's this time but I decide I will pop in just for old times' sake while we wait on our check-in time at our cottage, a funky little rental right by the harbour which is the only thing that Rosie seems excited about.

'Aunty Helen has such good taste,' she said when my sister emailed us a link to the cottage rental website last night. We couldn't believe that it was available but the owner had had a last minute cancellation – a little whitewashed two bedroom cottage with a bright yellow door, fully equipped with surf boards and wet suits and the owner offers boat rides out to the famous Cliffs of Moher, which I've promised Rosie will be on our agenda. The very thought of doing even half of what I've planned to do here exhausts me but, as promised, my list is made and I can't wait to get stuck in and make some memories with my girl.

We stop outside Brannigan's and I take a deep breath and bite my lip.

'Do you mind if we pop in here, just for a look around?' I say to Rosie. 'We have half an hour until our cottage is ready.'

Rosie shrugs and shivers a little, then follows me inside to the steamy heat of the bar and it really is like stepping back in time. Its interior smells like home-cooked dinners and alcohol, there's a patterned navy and beige carpet on all the floors and despite being only just after lunchtime, there is already a crowd gathered in the poky bar, all glued to some sort of sport on the giant TV in the corner.

In my head it's the summer of sixteen years ago, and despite the noise in the bar I can hear *his* voice, I can see Birgit dancing, I can smell the booze and the sweat and his aftershave on my skin and—

'Sorry about the noise!'

'What? Sorry, I was miles away,' I tell the barman. 'I'm just thinking how ... it doesn't matter. What were you saying?'

'I was apologizing. About the noise. There's a big game on today,' he says to me with a smile. He's cute and if I wasn't so sick I might try and flirt with him. My sister would kill me if she could read my mind. He looks about twenty-five years old at the most.

'Who's playing?' asks Rosie, who all of a sudden has taken an interest in Irish sport and seems to have forgotten how dull this place just seemed to her. 'You'll have to forgive my ignorance, being English. Foreign and all that.'

The man-boy winks at her and then smiles at me. Oh,

how I wish I was in a position to flirt back – if my teenage daughter wasn't here to compete with me of course. And if I was fit enough to even contemplate having some fun. I am wearing my favourite blonde bobbed wig on this trip and apart from my bloated, puffy face and slightly podgy frame from the steroids, to the outside world it's not at all obvious that there's anything wrong with my riddled body. I almost feel sorry for the lad who definitely has a twinkle in his eye and doesn't realise the pitiful truth in front of him.

'Galway are playing Mayo,' he says but our faces tell him we're clueless. 'Gaelic football? A derby. A bit like Manchester United playing Liverpool, only a little bit rougher and tougher.'

'Ah, I get it now,' says Rosie. 'I hope you win. My great-grandad is from Waterford. Is that near here at all?'

He shakes his head and laughs, then whispers.

'I'm secretly cheering for Mayo, but don't tell anyone in here that. If you're around later, pop by and I'll explain the rules.'

She glances at me and smiles back at him in a way I have never seen before. My daughter is flirting with this young man and she doesn't care that I am standing here. She is growing up. Oh God, I am going to miss all of this and I won't be here for her to turn to when her crushes don't go her way. Who will be her first proper boyfriend? Who will break her heart? Who will she cry to when she doesn't know how to understand all the feelings that come with falling in love?

But I have witnessed this moment, yes. We have only arrived here on our little vacation and already I am seeing new things in her, and I hope she does so with me too over the next few days. I have seen with my own two eyes, my darling teenage daughter catch the eye of a boy she fancies and if I never get to see it again, at least this is something I can carry in my heart until the end of my life. We are making memories already, but every one of them is going to remind me that I don't have many left.

Damn you, sickness. This dying game is no fun at all.

Chapter 5

Shelley

'I've been calling you all morning, darling,' says Eliza, my mother-in-law, when I answer my phone on the way into the village after lunch. 'Are you driving? Can you talk?'

'I am driving but you're on loudspeaker,' I tell her. I've been avoiding her calls all morning but now that I hear her familiar voice I wish I'd answered earlier. Maybe I'd have avoided the meltdown that has caused me to be thirty minutes late to take over from Betty, my assistant, at *Lily Loves*.

'It's okay to cry today,' she tells me and I nod as I drive, feeling tears prick my eyes again. 'Cry every day if you feel like it. It's all part of your healing process. The colour blue is good for you today, darling, that's what I am feeling. Look out for it today. It will be good for you. Look out for someone connected to the colour blue who crosses your path.'

'I'm on my way to work,' I tell her. 'Did Matt tell you to call me? Please Eliza, I don't want any fuss today. I need to just try and get on with things and keep busy. It's the only way I can cope.'

I pass no remarks on the colour blue she refers to. Some of Eliza's mystic words of wisdom are of great comfort, but some can't get past the cynic in me and I push them away to the back of my mind.

'Do whatever you have to do,' says Eliza and she pauses for a few seconds. 'You're going to be okay, Shell. It's all going to be okay. I am praying for you every day and I am sending light and healing. Positive energy is coming your way and don't ever forget that.'

I roll my eyes and try not to give her a smart answer, but I don't feel like it's going to be okay no matter how much Eliza prays every day. No matter how many chakras she tries to clear or clean, no matter how much energy she sends, and no matter how many candles she lights for me, I don't think I will ever be okay again. Apart from Matt, I have no one and nothing in my life to live for and I sometimes worry that even he isn't enough.

'Thanks for the call,' I tell Eliza, wanting to end our conversation now as I approach the village. 'I really do appreciate it.'

'There are good things coming for you real soon,' she says and I take a deep breath.

'Do you really think so?' I ask her, before she can hang up. 'I hope there are, Eliza because I don't think I can cope with living like this anymore. I need some hope. I think I'm ready for some hope if I could only get a sign.'

'The colour blue, I tell you,' she says to me. 'You'll see the signs when you are ready, Shelley. Look, would you like me to pop by later? We could go to the Beach House for dinner?'

I know she means well and I know Matt means well but how many times do I have to tell them that I can't bear to face the world? I want to go to dinner, I want to walk with my head held high, but today I can just about manage to go to work, maybe visit the grocery store afterwards and go home, in that order.

'I don't think so, Eliza,' I reply, not wanting to sound ungrateful but I know she will understand. 'I'm not really up to much today but I do appreciate the offer, you know I do and I will keep looking for those signs. I'm ready to grasp any glimmer of hope that comes my way.'

'Okay, well when you're ready you know where I am,' she says. 'Now, keep those positive thoughts to the forefront. You've come such a long way, whether you feel like it or not. Your light will return soon, I just know it will. Your mother is close today. She is sending angels your way. And blue.'

'I'll try and stay positive,' I tell her. 'Have a nice day, Eliza. Goodbye.'

I hang up and sigh, but despite my nonchalance, I really do appreciate her call. Eliza may just be telling me what I need to hear when I need to hear it, but it all helps and at this stage of my deep grief I would try anything. Anything, that is, that doesn't involve leaving my shop or my home, which doesn't give me too many options, does it?

I park the car alongside the edge of the pier and the sight of the fishing boats all lined up in their usual places makes me smile a little inside. I like familiarity and after thirteen years in this little place, I can finally call it home – though a part of me will always long for my mother's embrace back north where I grew up, but that's no longer within my reach. I never meant to settle here, or to stay any longer than a summer break but then I met Matt and the rest is history.

I make my way to my shop, my safe place where I can distract my mind with idle small chat to customers and sorting out new stock and choosing items from flea markets and online distributors to meet the fashion demands of my colourful clients. Again, the smell of its interior – a faint hint of coffee mixed with frankincense (recommended by Eliza for its healing powers) – fills me up and gives me the strength to keep taking one day at a time.

Terence, my delivery man is running a day late which never happens but it only serves to distract me. Soon, I'm on my third coffee of the afternoon and I'm trying with all my might to concentrate on a celebrity magazine to take my mind off this day which is dragging despite my attempts to keep busy. Maybe I shouldn't have opened up this afternoon after all. I should have gone away for the day, somewhere new for a change of scenery, but I honestly can't remember the last time I ventured any further than where I am standing right now in my shop.

The bell rings as a customer enters and I bolt up and try to smile a hello at the lady who's just entered. She browses around the rails near the door like most people do when they come in to *Lily Loves*. It's a real treasure trove of colourful, retro pieces and I treat every item of clothing like it's made of gold. My customers are the only contact with the outside world I choose to have these days, apart from Matt.

This isn't a local though. She is a tourist for sure and I need to make sure she feels welcome.

'Hello there,' she says in a very distinctive brummie accent. 'What a day!'

'Is it still raining out there?' I ask her. She is my only customer of the afternoon so far and I'm glad to see her, but I'll stick to my small talk as usual. I feel safe talking about the weather, clothes and jewellery but I'd die if she struck up a real conversation outside of that.

She nods and shivers in reply and then gets on with her browsing, much to my relief, so I go back to my magazine where I'm now reading about a woman who shed nine stone, only for her husband to dump her. Nice.

'Do you have this dress in any other sizes?' the lady asks eventually and I spring back into business mode, eager to talk about what I know best. 'I seem to have forgotten how changeable the weather is here in Ireland and I packed all wrong.'

I can see that, I want to say, but of course it isn't my place to comment on her outfit.

She is around my age, maybe a little bit older, and has the most beautiful warm smile. I feel bad that I have to tell her that the dress she has chosen, made of a pale green, light wool with a high neck and long sleeves, is the last of only three sizes I took in for the summer collection. She doesn't seem as disappointed as I am though and goes back to the rail and continues to search.

'I'd really have loved that one but just my luck ...' she mumbles to herself as she flicks through the rows of dresses on the rails at the far end of the shop. 'Red is my colour, I'm told, yet I always choose green.'

'I have a similar one in yellow if that's any good?' I suggest, but then we both giggle as she points at her hair which is a few shades lighter than yellow. She shrugs.

'I'd look like Big Bird,' she says. 'I should've packed a different wig for my trip instead of trying to pretend I'm a sexy blonde. I've never been blonde in my life! In fact I've dyed my hair so many times down the years I don't even remember what my natural colour is now.'

I nod nervously when she tells me it's a wig, and go back to my stool and my magazine by the till, my out-of-practice social skills tripping me up at the idea of discussing anything other than my safe topics with this stranger.

Thankfully though, she isn't bothered by my non-answer but I turn up the background music in the shop just in case, and try and focus on the reality TV stars who now look up at me from my magazine.

My eyes dart across to her every now and then though

as she browses. She is holding a favourite of mine, a royal blue wrap-over jersey dress that skims the knee and I want to tell her that it would suit her very well, but I'm afraid of her indulging me with her own sad story. I need positive thinking today. I daren't open the flood gates and talk about Lily and I know that is exactly what would happen.

'Can I try this on?' asks the lady. 'I need something to wear that isn't shorts and a t-shirt or a floaty skirt that you could spit through. What on earth was I thinking? That's what I get for coming here in a hurry.'

I point her to the changing rooms and just as I'd predicted, the dress fits her like a glove and brightens up her pale face no end.

'It suits you. It really does.'

'I suppose it does,' she says, admiring her reflection in the mirror. 'How much is it?'

'Sixty euro,' I tell her. 'But I can do it for fifty-five?'

She is just about to reply when Terence arrives at the door, pushing it open with his backside like he always does, his hands laden with cardboard boxes full of delights that I can't wait to get my hands on.

'Sorry Shelley! Better late than never, love,' he says. 'I got stuck at the hospital yesterday. Did you get my text?'

I glance back at my customer but instead of responding to the price, she has disappeared back into the changing room so I focus on Terence and the delivery while I wait for her return.

'I didn't get your text, but not to worry,' I say to him.

'I thought you'd traded me in for the big game today.'

Terence sets the box of goodies on the floor and wipes his hands, damp from the drizzle outside, on his trusty black jacket.

'I'm going to try and catch some of the second half from my armchair at home,' he tells me, handing over the delivery receipt and pointing out where I need to sign. 'You're my last delivery. I always save the best to last.'

I look up and he gives me a wink and a knowing smile.

'I'm doing okay,' I say to him, wincing as I write the date on his copy of the receipt. 'Just don't talk to me too much about it. Talk about the football match. Or the weather. Horrible weather for July, isn't it? Where on earth is our summer?'

The lady with the blonde wig is out of the changing rooms now and without looking my way, she hangs the dress back where she got it, gives a casual wave in my direction and slips off out through the door. Strange. I was sure she was going to take it.

'Awful weather altogether,' says Terence. 'I have a bet on that Galway will do the business, but I think that's my heart more than my head talking. What do you think?'

'Eh?'

I look past him out on to the street where I see her scuttle away in the light drizzle, her handbag her only shelter from the rain.

'The match?' says Terence.

'Oh yeah. The match. Let's hope we can do it,' I mumble back at him.

'Look after yourself today, missy,' he tells me and since he knows me so well by now he leaves it at that. I walk him to the door, unable to resist a peep outside into the damp, drizzly day. I see the woman with the wig shuffling past a few diehard fans in Galway football jerseys out for their half-time smoke before she makes her way down the road past Brannigan's.

I see tourists every day, all year round here in this town but there's something about her that has caught me, in a good way and I wish I had engaged with her more. I wish I had the courage to talk to people, especially other women, properly. You know, make friends again. Socialise. But I always get stuck. I get too afraid of opening up to people who would rather not hear of my troubles. Everyone has troubles of their own, I suppose, and who would want to hear about mine?

Chapter 6

Juliette

'I forgot my purse,' I say to Rosie who has made herself at home on the sofa in the cottage that will be our home for the next seven days. 'How on earth could I do that? I got to the shop and tried on the most gorgeous dress then realised I didn't have my purse with me. Have you seen it anywhere?'

'The wi-fi here is so bad,' says Rosie, totally ignoring what I just said. 'I'm going to go off my head with boredom here. Where is this place anyhow? Bally-go-backwards or somewhere? I can't even find it on Google Maps.'

She is snapchatting or doing whatever it is that teenagers do on their phones, recording and sharing their every move, and her nonchalance to reality and the fact that I cannot find my purse is making me irritable.

'Rosie, have you seen my purse anywhere?' I ask more directly. 'I went to that nice vintage shop on the corner to buy something warm and it's not in my handbag. Rosie?'

She swings her long legs off the sofa and grunts as she walks to the sideboard in the living area and hands me my purse from inside her own handbag.

'Are you losing your memory or something?' she asks me. 'Like, duh! You gave it to me in that pub earlier to pay for the drinks and told me to keep it safe 'til we got to this place. You always forget stuff and then act like it's my fault! I don't want to be here! I am so bored already!'

I take the purse from her and put it in my bag, bewildered at what has just happened. I don't know what has shaken me more – the fact that I genuinely don't remember giving her the purse or the way she just spoke to me. Rosie never speaks to me like that, ever. We have never raised our voices to each other and I certainly don't want it to start happening now.

'Rosie, this is a beautiful place and I know it's raining and the wi-fi might not be what you are used to, but I want this to be special for us. We haven't had a holiday together in such a long time.'

'What are you on about? We went to Salou last year. And why do we even have to go on holiday in the first place? What's the big rush to go on holiday?'

'Yes, you, me and Dan went to Salou last year,' I reply. 'I mean just you and me. I have so much planned for us over the next few days and I really want us both to enjoy it. Please don't ruin it before it begins.'

She slumps down on the sofa and puts her nose into her phone, giggling at whatever her latest message is which stings me to the core. She is ignoring me and I don't like it one bit.

'Rosie?' I say to her. 'Rosie, will you listen to me? I've gone to a lot of effort to bring us here. I've made a—'

'Don't tell me, Mum, you've made more plans that you won't see through,' she mutters. At least she was half-listening but again, her words hurt. I'm really not used to this.

'I'm going to the shop to get my dress and I really do hope your attitude changes while I'm away, Rosie.'

It is on the tip of my tongue to tell her that I am trying to make our last days together perfect. That I'm not going to be here for much longer. That I am dying. That it's not just any holiday, but our very last holiday. But I bite my tongue and leave her to her snapchatting. I know exactly when and where I am going to break the news to her.

It's in my plan for the week ahead, of course.

Shelley

Matt calls me for the second time this afternoon just as I'm putting the finishing touches to the mannequin in the window. I've dressed it in the most beautiful, glitzy gold fringed dress that arrived in Terence's delivery. I cradle the phone under my ear to speak to him as I pin the waist in to fit my so-called size 10 model.

'The town must be buzzing today,' Matt suggests. 'You know, with the match? Any idea of the score? I thought I'd call you first to check in before I looked it up.'

'Sorry, I have no idea,' I tell my husband, only half-listening as I admire my efforts at dressing the window. This has always been one of my favourite parts of retail and I was told more than once that I had a flair for it. 'Hopefully we win.'

'You say that like you really care,' laughs Matt. 'Shelley, the football fan. Anyhow, I'd better get back to my client. He's a moody sod, old Bert. I was thinking if we do win, maybe you should go for a drink tonight to take your mind off things? Call one of the girls like you used to? Though I'd say there will be plenty of action around the village whichever way the result goes. It's not often we get so far in the Championship so we may as well join in. What do you think?'

I gulp at the very thought of it.

'What?'

'A drink? Tonight?'

'I ... I couldn't, Matt,' I stutter. 'You know that I couldn't go out tonight, not if Galway won the *world* championship. No way. Not tonight.'

His silence irritates me slightly.

'Are you still there?' I ask.

'Yes, of course I'm still here,' he says. 'Look, forget I mentioned it. I just think sometimes it's good to keep busy and distracted. I know it's working for me and you're doing well at work, aren't you?'

'Doing well?'

'Shelley, I'm trying my best here. I'm stuck in Belgium and missing you like crazy and this is killing me to be away today of all days but I hate the thought of you sitting at home alone tonight. Please do something. Don't be on your own. A drink with friends won't change things and crying at home on your own is never going to bring her back!'

That hurt. I know I shouldn't be sitting home alone all the time, I know he is right, but I am absolutely heartbroken at his suggestion that anything I do or don't do might make me think she is coming back. How could I celebrate a stupid football game today? How could he even think of such a thing?

'I have to go. Sorry. Chat to you later, bye Matt.'

'Shell?'

'Bye.'

I hang up and jump when the doorbell sounds as a customer enters. I look up, and just as I had anticipated, it is the lady with the wig again – only this time she doesn't look as glamorous as she did before.

'Is everything okay?' I ask her, breaking my own rules around overstepping the mark when it comes to conversation that doesn't involve fashion stock or clearance sales. 'You left in a hurry earlier.'

'I'd like to buy that dress, please,' she says to me, flustered. 'I can't believe I haven't brought proper clothes with me. I can't believe I'm here ... and I can't really afford to go shopping and let's face it, I won't get much wear out of it but just … I'll take the dress.'

And at that she bursts into tears.

Juliette

'I'm so sorry for all this,' I sniffle, handing over my debit card as the unaffected shop lady packs my new dress into a very fancy paper bag. 'It's not like it was a big row or anything, it's just the thoughts that it triggered, you know, it got to me and I haven't let anything get to me so far. Not this time. This time I was meant to be strong. That's why I'm here. To be strong. For her. To do the right thing. For her.'

I am rambling to a stranger and the poor woman is as white as a sheet behind the small counter as she hands me the very trendy bag.

'You know, I got some gorgeous new stock in just after you left,' she tells me, as if on autopilot. 'Some really nice stuff so if you want to come back again and try on more, you're very welcome. I can do discount so don't worry about price. No point you shivering on your holidays.'

'I can't come back again. There's no point me buying a lot of nice clothes, not now,' I tell her. 'I don't have time to wear them.'

Was she not listening to a word I said? Maybe it's a good thing she wasn't. Maybe that's how she was trained, you know, to be professional and not indulge in anything more than small talk with strangers. Just take the money and run and all that. Maybe I shouldn't be ranting and raving like this to someone who has no idea of why I am here or what little time I have left.

'Okay, well the dress you chose really suits you,' she says, tugging at her hair. 'I'm glad you came back for it. It's very you. It suits you. It suits your hair, I mean, your wig. Sorry! I'm not thinking straight. Thank you. For your custom.'

Apart from her annoying hair fiddling, she is almost robotic and I feel like shaking her by the shoulders. A dying woman has just broken down in front of her two eyes and she is too wrapped up in her new fucking stock to notice.

I open my mouth to let it all out but then I look into her eyes and I see they are totally glazed over with tears, and the agony in her eyes runs through me, sending shivers down my arms and into my fingertips.

'You're not okay yourself, are you?' I ask her and she hands me a tissue, again mechanically like she is trying to block me out. I wipe my nose and dab under my eyes. I wasn't stupid enough to wear that cursed mascara again this time.

She shakes her head and keeps glancing at the window, at the door, as if in fear of someone coming in and seeing her.

'I'm fine, but thank you,' she says to me. 'You said red was your colour. There's a lovely red—'

A stray couple of tears escape from her eyes, causing her to stop and take a breath. She doesn't wipe them. She tries again.

'There's a lovely size twelve—'

'Oh for goodness' sake,' I reply. 'Forget the size twelve red whatever it is you are trying to sell to me, please. You're not okay at all, are you?'

She shakes her head again but still purses her lips in defiance.

'Thank you very much ... for your custom.'

She nods and I'm waiting for her to say 'have a nice day' like it's rehearsed in her script but she doesn't so I leave her to it. She evidently isn't as prone to public breakdowns in front of strangers as I am.

'You are very welcome,' I reply and then I say it for her. 'Have a nice day.'

I slip off my sandals and damp shorts and lie on top of the bed in my room that overlooks the harbour of Killara, and I breathe in the sea air that creeps in through the open window of our cottage. The blue dress from the vintage boutique hangs on the wardrobe door at the far side of the room and I wrap a tartan blanket over me to lessen the chill of the breeze.

I close my eyes, listening to the sounds of the early evening in this little hidden gem of a place that once changed my life, and I wonder if he is out there, somewhere, walking the streets or on the boats, totally unaware that his own flesh and blood is so close to him, she too unmindful to the history of this village and her deep connection to it.

'You're way out of my league,' he told me on the night we met, looking up under dark wavy hair and I laughed in reply. There was no way I was out of his league. I knew well that he must have had women drooling over his every word. I remember his dark brown eyes, under knitted eyebrows that made me go weak at the knees ... though that may have had something to do with the cocktails and vodka Birgit and I had consumed before we bumped into him at the bar. If only he knew what he left behind when he walked away the next morning.

And speaking of the outcome of our very quick encounter, my reminiscing doesn't last long before I'm interrupted by a raging ball of hormones that knocks once on the door and then enters, hand on hip.

'I thought you said we were going for dinner soon?' she says, and I don't know whether to laugh or shout at her newfound stinking teenage attitude.

'We can go soon, yes, I was just about to get changed,' I tell her. 'Is it still raining?'

She rolls her eyes as if I have just asked her something as obvious as what my name is.

'Of course it is still raining. It's lashing out there. I really don't know why you brought me here. Is there a McDonald's nearby? I'm starving.'

'Starving?' I say to her in reply. 'Do you mean that in a literal sense because I highly doubt you are "starving"? You can't be starved after the lunch we had earlier.'

'Okay then, I'm just bored and I eat when I'm bored. Is there a McDonald's or even a Subway or a KFC?'

'No, Rosie, there is no McDonald's here, not one Big Mac in sight for miles and miles and isn't that wonderful?'

Her eyes screw up and her face twists and I swear I barely recognise this person in front of me. Who on earth kidnapped my darling daughter and left me with this devil child?

'How does anyone actually live here? It's like the middle of nowhere!' she pants. 'They don't have proper wi-fi and have you seen the TV? It's like something from the 1980s.'

Ancient history then, obviously.

'You haven't even seen the place properly yet,' I remind her. 'We've only just got here. Give it a chance.'

But Rosie is ready with her next complaint.

'And does it *always* rain in Ireland? Every time I look out that window it's pissing down. Does it rain *every* day?'

'No, not *every* day, Rosie.'

'I heard it does,' she says. 'I Googled it, after waiting ages for the page to load up and it said to expect four seasons in one day. So does that mean it might snow later tonight? Wonderful!'

'Well, it doesn't rain on Wednesdays,' I try to joke but again she looks at me like I'm the one from another planet. 'Look, give me twenty minutes and we'll go and explore and see if there is any part of this village that appeals to you at all, no matter about the rain. You seemed to like that young barman earlier?'

'Mum, don't be so gross. I just kind of liked his accent. Now, please, I'm starving.'

'Okay, okay, I will be twenty minutes,' I tell her again. 'Can you wait that long or will you die of boredom in the meantime?'

She lets out a deep sigh.

'Can I go for a walk while I'm waiting?'

'In the rain?'

'Yes, I can take an umbrella. There are two by the door. Or maybe I'd be safer in one of the wetsuits in this weather.'

I pause, wondering if I should let her go wandering alone and then I realise that we really are in the middle of nowhere and it is broad daylight and I suppose I should encourage any glimmer of enthusiasm that she shows for our stay.

'Be back in twenty and take your phone in case you get lost,' I say, knowing that this too might be the most ridiculous suggestion in the world to make. 'Don't go far. Just along the harbour.'

'I'll hardly get lost when there's nothing here!' she sulks back and at that she is gone, leaving me with the slam of not one door, but two, as she makes her way out onto the harbour pier.

I savour the silence when the door slams shut. She is so full of anger, I just know she is. I want to protect her so much but I am tired, too tired to talk too much about anything after such a long day. I need to keep going though; I came here to spend time with Rosie so no matter how much she is grating on me this evening, and as much as I would rather crawl under the duvet than go out for dinner, I need to keep going.

In the meantime, I rub my throbbing temples and relish in this moment I have to myself. Twenty minutes apart won't kill us. At least I hope not.

Chapter 7

Shelley

I arrive home around six and I'm so glad to see Merlin at the gate. He's wagging his tail and barking with joy now that he finally has some company after a long afternoon on his own. He is soaked through from the rain and when I get out of the car he makes sure I am too as he jumps up onto my clothes with his muddy paws.

'You're an eejit, Merlin,' I tell him. 'Why didn't you stay inside out of the rain? That's what we made you a dog flap for!'

He doesn't care what I say of course and is much more interested in what I have in my shopping bag, though I can assure him the contents aren't very exciting at all. I hate cooking for one but for the next few evenings I don't have a choice. Well, technically I do have a choice. I could take up Eliza's offer, or I could do as Matt suggested and call one of my ever-patient friends even though they are fed up making suggestions to help me get better. There is no getting better from grief. They say time heals but I'm not so sure of that anymore.

Merlin follows me to the front door, still barking and wagging, and when I reach the doorstep I see why he is so excited. I sometimes swear that dog could talk if he tried and he glances up at me and then down at a bouquet of flowers that sit on the sheltered porch and back up at me again, as if to gauge my reaction to this unexpected delivery.

'Gosh, I really wasn't expecting this,' I say to the dog. 'Who was here, Merlin? I wonder who these are from.'

The cerise pink, white and sap green flowers really are a sight to behold and I open the door and take them into the hall, followed of course by my trusty friend. Merlin waits and watches as I put them on the sideboard, take off my damp coat and leave my shopping on the floor, before opening the card attached to the flowers with anticipation.

I read the greeting, take a deep breath and exhale long and hard just like I was taught to do in therapy when I need to really release some nervous energy or stress. Then I fetch my phone in my handbag to text my friend Sarah for her kind thoughts.

Bless you for remembering, I say to her and then make my way to the kitchen to fetch a vase for the flowers and give them the attention they deserve. By the time I reach the sink she has messaged back.

I will never forget her, she replies. *Take it easy and call me if you need me. No pressure x*

I put the flowers on the dining room table and I do, to my surprise, get some comfort from how they brighten up the whiteness of the room. It was my part of the deal with Matt when he finally talked me round to staying in this house after Lily's death to keep everything totally white. I redecorated from top to bottom, all plain and neutral with no frills, no heaviness, no colour I suppose, and most of all, no heart. Bless him, he played along and has let me take everything at my own pace, but I was and still am numb. I need my surroundings at home where we lived with her to be dumbed down too, with no memories on the walls. I put all her little paintings from playgroup that decorated the fridge into a box, while all the framed photos of her firsts – her first haircut, first tricycle, her first Christmas and each of her three birthdays – are all boxed up and in her room upstairs.

It's the only room I didn't whitewash. I couldn't, but I have closed the door and I never, ever go in there. To do so would tear me apart in a way from which I could never recover. To me, part of her is still in that room where we shared bedtime stories and dress-up time, and where I'd slip in at night and watch her sleep under the yellow glow of her nightlight as tiny stars shone from it onto the walls and ceilings. That room was a precious place, a room full of night-time kisses, lullabies and songs and I just couldn't, and will never, change it from how it was on the morning that she left us. I have memories in there and I have closed the door on them in case they ever get lost. Her smell, her favourite cuddle toy, her shoes, everything is in that room and they will stay there for as long as I live.

There's something about the very thought of her shoes in particular that chokes me up. Her tiny, shiny shoes that she loved to put on and off all by herself, thinking she was such a big girl for doing so. But she was just a baby really; just a baby who couldn't be left alone, not even for seconds. Oh God, oh God, please help me ...

Our wedding photos are in there too tucked at the bottom of a wardrobe, our holiday snaps together with Lily, our photo albums and our home videos – they are all frozen in time because my life has ended and I have no idea how I am getting from one day to the next. No idea whatsoever.

'Fancy a walk?' I say to Merlin who is the one thing that keeps me going and functioning when Matt isn't around. He makes me put one foot in front of the other. He makes me talk as well, as I couldn't possibly not communicate with a face as friendly and warm as his and I swear he knows exactly when I need him. I have sat alone on many occasions on the sofa, trying to remember how to breathe, when he snuggles around my feet or puts his head on my knees in sympathy and I stroke his fur to awaken my senses and bring me back to life.

I fetch his lead, put on my raincoat, fix up my hood and change quickly into my trainers – within minutes we are on the beach and I just keep walking and walking as usual without realizing I am moving at all.

Juliette

There is nothing, and I mean nothing that irritates me more than trying to get a hairbrush through a wet wig when in a hurry.

I called this wig Marilyn Monroe when I bought her, but at the minute she is more like Marilyn Manson with her knots and tangles and I feel like flinging her across the floor in frustration.

I sit at the dressing table in my tiny adopted bedroom with the wig poised in my hand, just like the kind assistant, Dorinda from Lady Godiva's wig making shop showed me to do and after patting it down with a towel and combing it through with conditioner spray, I still have a battle on my hands to try and resemble a normal head of hair before I go out for dinner with Rosie.

Apart from my wig atrocities, I feel very comfortable and very bright in my new blue jersey wrap dress and not like a dying woman at all. It's a fine dress, one which I have decided could easily be glammed-up with some heels and jewellery, as well as dressed down in flat pumps like I have chosen for now. I have to say I am delighted with my new purchase.

I think of the lady in the shop and how she tried to hold a conversation but couldn't, how she stuttered and stammered instead and avoided any eye contact at all with me as I paid. She was a strange fish, but then I guess no one knows what others are going through and who am I to judge? I did feel sorry for her though. She

looked a troubled soul and nosiness did get the better
of me for a while as I wondered what on earth could be
distracting her so much from her work. A sick relative
perhaps, or a row with her husband, or maybe she had
had some bad news herself and seeing me prance about
in a wig and getting in a fluster over a hormonal outburst
from my teenage daughter, who still hasn't returned by
the way, was all too much for the poor woman who just
wanted to sell the bloody dress and not hear my life
story to go with it.

I call Rosie when I realise that she has gone over the
twenty minutes curfew we agreed and hold the earpiece
away from my ear in preparation from the tirade I will
get for fussing over her when she is only ten minutes
late, but she doesn't answer. Typical. I try again, but still
no answer so I leave a voicemail which I know will
irritate her even more, but then everything I do today
seems to irritate her. I wonder if it really is possible for
teenagers to transform into alien versions of themselves
in such a short space of time. Evidently, it is. My daughter
is living proof.

'Rosie, this is your mother,' I say to the phone. 'You
know, the one who is waiting for you to go for dinner
because you are apparently starved? Well, I'm ready now.
Almost. I'm ready apart from this stupid wig which just
won't sit properly so if you can make your way back or
I could meet you at the Beach House Café if you're across
that way? It's the little place on the pier, you can't miss
it. Oh and the address of this place, in case you have

ventured too far despite your insistence that you wouldn't get lost, is 25 Pier Head, so just ask someone and they'll help direct you back here, I'm sure. And hurry up, please. I'm starving now myself. Bye.'

I go back to my wig duties, waiting for the door to open or the phone to ring or at least a text to say she is on her way. But another five minutes pass and there's still no sign of her.

I place the wig on my head and adjust it and for a brief moment I admire my own reflection. I don't look so bad actually. Doesn't a bit of lippy and a new dress work wonders for the soul? Maybe Dr Michael has made a mistake with his diagnosis because physically I feel absolutely on top of the world, in my new attire and not to mention my new surroundings with the sea at my door and a delicious seafood meal to look forward to with my one and only child.

I spray some perfume and feel my tummy rumble as I rub my wrists together. It's forty-five minutes now since she left and still no reply from Rosie. Okay, so she hasn't been herself since we got here but this really is out of character for her. As cheeky as she was earlier, I don't think she would intentionally put any worry in my mind. We're a team, me and my Rosie. A team of two and, even with Dan in the mix, we've always had an unbreakable bond after so many years on our own.

My hunger turns to butterflies now and I leave the bedroom, go down the narrow hallway towards the sounds of the TV coming from the living room. My nerves are on edge. Maybe she's here after all? The TV ... I don't think she would have left it on.

'Rosie' I call ahead. 'For goodness' sake turn that volume down. I've been wondering where you've got to! I thought you were—'

I reach the living room door but the room is empty. I turn off the TV and notice my hands are shaking. It is really lashing down now outside and I don't know whether to leave the house to look for her, or stay here in case she comes back and I miss her. I try her phone again. Nothing. Oh God, what on earth should I do? I have no coat and it is pouring down outside. She's been gone almost an hour now. I should never have let her leave the house alone. This is all my fault. Children aren't meant to be left alone, not in strange places especially. She may be fifteen but she isn't streetwise which is my fault too for being so bloody over-protective. What should I do?

I need to go and find her.

The second umbrella she mentioned stands by the door but it snaps when I put it up so I duck my head and walk out into the rain, not knowing where on earth to look first. I begin to fear the worst.

It's peak season here and tourists travel and pass through constantly so what the hell was I thinking when I let her go wandering around on her own? If she was as hungry as she said she was, maybe she headed to the corner shop for some snacks? I really have no idea and I can't think straight. The streets suddenly seem quiet and eerie despite the heavy rain.

The bar from earlier? Maybe she went back there to see that bartender, after all. The fear I feel right now takes me right back to when she was just two years old and I lost her for what felt like hours, but was really less a minute, in a department store. The rush of heat to my fingertips, the perspiration, the blinding terror that someone may have hurt her or taken her away from me. I can't lose her yet, we still have time to do so much together. Where is she?

'Rosie?!' I shout into the empty evening air and out onto the pier. 'Rosie, where are you?'

A shiver runs through me and I feel sick. We aren't meant to be apart on this trip. Why did I let her go out alone? This is all my fault. I *am* stupid and forgetful just like she said I was. She hates me. She has never spoken to me the way she did earlier.

'Rosie!'

I feel dizzy and nauseous as I walk through the rain up and the winding street. Even though I have no idea where to start or who to ask, I need to find my daughter and take away her pain. And I will.

Chapter 8

Shelley

Merlin and I are approaching the end of the sand dunes about halfway up the beach, which normally tells him it's time to turn to go home, but to my surprise he darts off in a direction he never ventures, sniffing and yelping lightly as he climbs one of the sand dunes. For the first time in my many years of walking this beach, I can feel my heart flutter in fear of what may have got his attention.

Then I hear something, a whimper through the rain in the distance.

What on earth could it be? It's someone crying and it sounds like a child. Oh God. Am I hearing things in this awful rain?

'Lily?' I call out, then cover my mouth with my hand when I realise what I just did. I am losing my mind. I am hearing things. Oh God, help me. But the crying ... is real and it's coming from somewhere beyond Merlin.

Yet still I can only hear Lily. I hear her cry just like I did that day – close enough to hear her but far enough for me to be too late. It's not Lily, I know it's not her but I can hear and I can't bring myself to ignore it. I look back towards my house in the distance, the yellow lights coming from the kitchen window, and the lighthouse across the bay. Someone is in trouble and I can't just run and hide. I need to try and help.

I pull the strings tight on my hood as the rain comes down in buckets, drenching my hands and running down my face, and I cagily follow Merlin towards the sand dunes, calling his name to come back, hoping that I am imagining things, hearing things as I often do.

'Merlin! Merlin, come back here! Merlin!'

He darts on, up to the top of the sand dune, still barking, and I slip and slide in the mushy sand, balancing myself as I stumble up. I hear the sobbing more loudly now and it comes from underneath a large green golf umbrella. I freeze. I don't know who it is or what I should do and then I see a hand reach out for the dog and hear a young voice greet him amidst the sobs.

'Hello there, you!' the voice of what appears to be a little girl with an English accent says, so I approach her, coughing to announce my presence and trying to make some noise over the sounds of the rain so that I don't scare her.

'Excuse me? Are you okay?'

I walk around to the other side of the umbrella to find her huddled up with a sodden paper bag of chips by her side, which Merlin is now helping himself to but the girl doesn't seem to mind.

I look at her. My heart stops.

'Lily?' I say.

'What?'

Oh God. What am I saying? I'm seeing things again. Please don't let this happen again! I can't keep seeing Lily in every child I see.

'I'm so ... I'm so sorry if I frightened you,' I say to her over the rain. 'I thought you were someone else.'

My heart starts to beat faster. She looks up at me with familiar eyes and I stumble backwards, squinting to make sure what or who I am looking at is real.

I can't keep doing this. Eliza has tried to coach me through this and Matt has calmed me down when I have come home before convinced I saw her somewhere, or when I wake up in the night in cold sweats believing that it's all just a horrible nightmare and she is at home safe and sound and I go to her room calling her name to find an empty bed. And here I go again letting my mind wander. But this is not Lily. This is a teenage girl who looks nothing like Lily. It is not my dead daughter. My daughter was only three years old, for goodness' sake.

'It looks like you're the one who's frightened,' the girl replies in a choked-up voice that isn't as tough as she wants it to be. 'What did you call me?'

'Me?' I mutter.

'Yes, you,' she says. 'You look like you've seen a ghost. Oh, just leave me alone.'

She is about fifteen or sixteen, I guess, and her dark hair is tucked behind her ears but it's the familiar sadness in her young eyes, dripping black with mascara, that takes my breath away. The fear, the worry, the anger, the pain ... she looks away which allows me to compose myself.

'I'm sorry, I don't normally sneak up on people like this,' I say to her. I should really just do what she says and leave her alone but what if I do that and then hear later that something awful has happened to her out here.

'That's good,' she says with a snigger. 'You should try minding your own business. Everyone should.'

'It's just,' I try to explain. 'Well, my dog, Merlin, well, he never leaves my side for too long so I had to follow him and then I heard you and ... please just tell me, are you okay? Can I do anything?'

She looks at me like I've lost my mind. Maybe I have.

'Can I help you at all?' I try again. 'You're going to catch your death up here. It's pouring down.'

'Who are you, my mother?' she says with attitude and her words and tone take me back in time again. 'I *have* one of those, thank you very much, and *one* is quite enough.'

'No, no, I'm not your mother, no, but I'm sure your own mother is worried about you?' I realise that I must sound exactly like a mother, her mother.

'Look,' says the little English voice with the big dark eyes. 'Just take your lovely dog for a walk and leave me alone before you catch *your* death. And why is everything about death these days? You don't know anything about my mother so just leave it, will you?'

'Well, no I don't know your mother, but—'

'She thinks no one knows anything about her,' says the girl. 'But I know more than she thinks I do. I'm not stupid. I just don't know what the hell I'm doing here and I want to go home so she can die back there instead! No point dying here where no one knows her, is there?'

So, her mother is dying. Oh no. Oh, this poor little girl.

She cries openly now and wipes her face on the back of the sleeves of her sodden jacket. I sit down beside her. I don't think twice about it and I don't notice the rain anymore. I just sit.

'Just go away and mind your own business,' says the girl. 'You don't have to feel sorry for me. I seem to be doing a good enough job of that myself, thank you very much.'

I should really go and do what she says, but I don't. I wait. I stay.

'I don't want to go just yet, if you don't mind,' I tell her, not knowing where this urge to stay with her is coming from.

I normally walk straight past strangers these days. The old me would have stopped and helped a stranger, but not the me after Lily died. These days I normally don't take time to care. I don't take time to care because I usually *don't* care – but this time, I do.

'And you didn't scare me at all actually,' I continue.

'You remind me of someone that I know very well and it startled me, that's all.'

She looks at me like I've just sprouted two horns at the suggestion that she could possibly remind me of someone. Imagine.

'Well I don't know anyone around here so you must be seeing things,' she tells me and looks away, hugging her knees again. 'I can't possibly remind you of anyone you know.'

A cold shiver runs down my spine as I realise who she reminds me of, and it's not my Lily after all.

'It's not someone from here I was talking about,' I explain. 'It's someone who came here to live and who never went home, quite a few years ago. A young girl, just like you.'

'Who?' she asks. 'Someone from England? Don't tell me, it's the accent that gives me away.'

Her voice is dripping with sarcasm and I can't help but laugh just a little.

'My mind is a bit mixed up and I thought you were someone you couldn't possibly be, but now I realise – I realise you remind me of *me* actually,' I tell her and this seems to get her attention.

'Yeah, right,' she says. 'You have no idea who I am or what I'm like, so how can I remind you of yourself. That's stupid.'

'Believe me,' I tell her. 'When I was a lot younger. I was exactly like you are now in a lot of ways. Exactly.'

And it's true. She really is just like me twenty years

ago and it's like looking at my own reflection, not physically, but in her I see the same sense of deep despair and anger that she feels inside right now. The hopelessness. The fear that the one person who you need the most is going to leave you soon and that no one else in the whole world can understand what you are going through.

'My name is Shelley,' I say to her and her tear-filled eyes meet mine again. 'I live in the house over there on the hill, the one across from the lighthouse. I wonder ... would you like to come over and get dried off and call your mum from there? She must be worried sick.'

She doesn't look so hard around the edges now. Her lip trembles and I see she is just a little girl, really. She is a lot younger at heart than she looks, beneath the makeup and the attitude and the tears.

'You're scared, right?' I say to her and she nods, biting her lip. 'Is your mum sick?'

Her bottom lip trembles more and she breathes in stifled muffles, trying so hard not to let it all go.

'She is ... she is very sick,' she stutters. 'She's dying.'

'I'm so sorry,' I mumble.

'She's dying and I'm so afraid that she's going to die really soon and I don't know what I'm going to do without her. It's so unfair!'

I gasp inside. This is like looking in the mirror, like looking back in time.

'Of course, you're scared,' I say to her. 'Is that why you've run away from her? To lash out and cry here on your own.'

89

She nods again and I wait for a backlash from her but instead she leans forward to pat the dog who has settled at her feet, still feasting on her bag of chips.

'You're scared because there is nothing you can do and you're angry and frightened,' I continue. 'And you are so frightened you are going to be left on your own and it feels like no one understands what you are going through.'

She looks at me like I have read her mind, then tries to speak and her voice breaks when she does.

'She thinks I don't know the truth but I do know,' she sniffles. 'I heard her talking to Aunty Helen before we left and she said this would be our last holiday ever. Like, how am I meant to enjoy myself when I know it's our last holiday ever? I am so mad! She must think I'm stupid but I just don't know what to do. She could at least tell me instead of trying to pretend everything is okay when everything is just awful. I'm not a baby, I should know the truth!'

I put my arm around her and hold her close as her shoulders heave.

'Cry all you want,' I say to her. 'Cry and get it all out if that's what you came here to do.'

The rain mixes with my own tears as she sobs and gasps for breath in between sniffles and lets all her pain out. She grasps my coat as she cries and I squeeze her tight, wondering where on earth I have mustered up the courage to sit and empathise so much with someone I have never met, when I can barely hold a conversation with my own husband these days. I haven't spoken to my closest friends like this in such a long time but I want to help her. I need to help her.

'Do you want to come with me and Merlin and we'll call your mum before you really do get sick out here?' I ask her when she begins to settle. 'I don't have my phone with me but we can contact her or I can take you to her?'

She shakes her head.

'I have my own phone here in my pocket,' she says. 'But thanks anyway. I can call her and make my way back. She'll be so worried. I need to go back.'

'Yes, that's a good idea,' I tell her.

'Why do you care?' she asks me. 'How do you know what I am going through?'

'Unfortunately, I know all too well,' I explain. 'I know you are feeling so many things right now but your mum is only doing her best for you.'

'I didn't want to come here.'

'I'm sure she knows why she brought you,' I say. 'She will tell you everything in her own time, believe me. Imagine how hard this must be for her too. You need each other. You need to make this time special even though you are confused and angry right now. Your mum is still here and you need each other.'

She pauses, hesitant.

'I should get back to her,' she says, standing up, sobbing now. 'I shouldn't have stayed out so long. We were meant to go for dinner and she was wearing her new dress that she bought today and now I've ruined the whole evening.'

Her face crumples and I want to just take away all her pain and make everything alright for her, but I know I can't. It's not as simple as that, unfortunately.

'Your mum will understand,' I say to her. 'Mums always do, believe me. Now, go and give her a big hug and tell her you are sorry for worrying her. You may not think it, but I know exactly how mad and frightened you are right now.'

'You can't possibly know,' she asks. 'No one does.'

'I do,' I explain, standing up to meet her, 'I know because I was once a young girl like you and the same thing happened to me and I ran away from it all too, but I had to go back and face up to what was happening, no matter how horrible it was. My mum got very sick too, just like yours is now.'

'She did?' she says, and she lifts the umbrella and we stand beneath it together. 'And did she get better or did she die in the end?'

I wish I could tell her different. I look out to the sea, then back at her and I take a deep breath.

'I was sixteen when she died,' I explain to this beautiful, inquisitive child. 'Her name was Rosie and she died after a short illness and I only wish that I got to have one last holiday with her, just like you are doing now.'

The little girl's eyes widen.

'Rosie? That's my name,' she says and for the first time, she smiles slightly. 'I'm Rosie too. How weird is that?'

For some reason I am not surprised that she shares a

name with my dear mother. I have a feeling that we were meant to meet this evening, young Rose, me and Merlin.

'How did you – how did you cope without her?' she asks me and I take a deep breath because I honestly don't know.

'It's hard,' I tell her, not wanting to frighten her more but not wanting to shield her from the inevitable, heart-wrenching truth. 'We can talk about it more if you are around for a while, that's if your mum allows you and if you want to?'

'Really?' she squints back at me through the rain. I can feel her relax a little.

'Really,' I say to her. 'I know exactly what it feels like to have so much anger inside and that blinding fear of not knowing where to turn. You can talk to me anytime.'

'I don't mean to be angry with her,' says Rosie. 'But she's treating me like a baby and not telling me what everyone else already knows.'

'You're angry at the situation, not at your mum,' I try to explain to her. 'It's horrible and it hurts and it's not fair. You are right to be angry, but be angry at the illness, not at her.'

She sniffles and nods a bit.

'Go and find your mum, Rosie,' I tell her. 'Try and be brave though I know it's the hardest thing in the whole wide world right now. Be brave and you are going to have a lovely holiday with your mum, I just know you are.'

She smiles and pulls her damp sleeves down over her hands.

'Thank you,' she whispers. 'Thank you, Shelley. And you too, Merlin. He's a really sweet dog, aren't you Merlin?'

'You know where I am if you need me,' I tell her.

She pats Merlin's head goodbye then walks away from me, her head bowed down against the rain, and I put Merlin back on his lead and walk in the opposite direction, back home to my empty existence but feeling something like I haven't felt in such a long, long time.

I feel warmth inside, deep inside my broken heart that has been frozen for so long. I think I may have helped that little girl in some way.

At least I hope I have.

Juliette

'Rosie! Rosie, oh God, Rosie where were you? Look at you! You're soaked right through!'

I am out of my mind when I finally find my daughter wandering down the street in the lashing rain. She's so pale and cold that I want to pack my case and get on a plane back to Birmingham right now and pretend this whole stupid trip never happened in the first place.

'I'm so sorry, Mum,' she tells me as she falls into my arms and I kiss her forehead what seems like a thousand times in relief.

'I checked every shop, every bar and I have never been so frightened in all my life, do you hear me?'

'I'm sorry, I'm sorry,' she repeats in a chant. She is soaked through.

'Are you okay? Just tell me you're okay?'

'I am,' she says. 'Just cold and wet but I'm fine and I'm really sorry. I'm so sorry to have worried you.'

We walk arm in arm through puddles across the street and down past the harbour to our cottage, where I realise I have left the front door wide open, but to be honest I couldn't care less. Right now, I really want to go home.

'Just tell me nothing bad happened to you, Rosie,' I say through the rain. 'I want you to get dried off and warmed up and tell me exactly where you have been. I can't believe I was silly enough to let you go wandering alone when I don't actually know this place or the people in it at all. Do you know how precious you are to me? What the hell was I thinking?'

'Mum, it's not your fault,' she says to me. 'None of this is your fault. None of it.'

'It is my fault! I was here only once!' I tell her. 'Just once a lifetime ago and I seem to think it's some picture postcard different planet where nothing goes wrong ever! How the hell do I know that there aren't murderers and rapists lurking around each corner? How?'

'Mum, stop, please, nothing happened,' Rosie tells me when I finally stop ranting and try to listen to her as I catch my breath. I usher her inside the cottage and throw my soaking wet Marilyn stupid Monroe wig on the sofa and kick off my sodding pumps which I hate now with a vengeance and start to strip off the blue dress which now feels ridiculous since it's been soaked right through too. I am a crap mother. I never should have let her go walking round a strange village on her own. It looks like Dr Michael was right after all because right now I feel sicker than any cancer could ever make me. I'm sick of myself and the stupid risks that I have taken all my life.

'Get changed, quickly,' I tell my daughter who is standing in silence, staring at me with my pathetic fluffy mousey hair and my puffy steroid-filled body which is scarred inside and out.

'Can we still go for dinner?' asks Rosie. 'I'm sorry your new dress got ruined. I got chips but a dog ate them. Are you hungry, Mum?'

I think I'd be physically sick if I ate but I can see my baby girl is shaken and cold and I don't want to get angry with her. I don't have time to fight with her.

'Get into the shower quickly and warm up then we can order some takeaway,' I tell her with a forced smile. I am so bloody relieved that she is here and she is alright. 'There's a nice Chinese a few miles down the road and I'll see if they deliver.'

Then we both look at my sodden blue dress on the floor and start to laugh.

'Well you've nothing to wear to dinner now, have you?' says Rosie and I lift the dress up and swing it around so that the rain water splashes her face.

'Quick, shower and we'll have a pyjama party!' I tell her, and then I chase her down the hallway in my under-wear, shaking the water from the dress at her as she laughs heartily and closes the door on the bathroom and locks it, still laughing … and then I lean up against the door and slide down onto the floor, crying and laughing with relief that she is safe and well. I am so blessed to have this time with her.

I don't want to miss a second. I won't ever let her out of my sight again.

Chapter 9

Shelley

I scrape the leftovers from my boring lasagne meal for one into Merlin's food bowl, knowing that if Matt got a sniff of what I was doing I'd be in trouble. I give Merlin a knowing wink that tells him it's our secret as he laps it up with great delight. The lights in my kitchen are low and the surfaces are shiny and clean like they always are these days with no little fingers to smudge them, my laundry is up to date with no tiny milk-stained pyjamas to wash and there's nothing much on telly for a Saturday night so I stand and stare out the window at the sea in the distance which is now still and black, with only the light house for company.

I could have a bath. Or a shower. Wow, what a choice to have to make ... and then I could put on a face mask and a bath robe and fluffy slippers and watch soppy films that I don't normally get to watch when Matt is at home, but I've kind of run out of those. I used to enjoy my time alone when Matt travelled for work to the most exotic locations across the globe. I would pamper myself and enjoy the time and space and let Lily sleep in our bed and sometimes Merlin jumped onto the bottom too.

This house was my haven and I had made it so, designing the interior of every room exactly how I wanted it with memories of our travels in almost every possible space or corner I could find – a large wooden elephant from Africa used to stand in the hallway, much to Lily's delight and she would cover it with sticky hands and pull at its ears and try to climb on top of it as soon as she was on her feet. A large handmade patchwork rug once hung on the dining room wall, something I picked up when we were in New Delhi before Lily came along and it reminded me so much of those early romantic days when everything we did together was exciting and new. Then there were the two wine glasses we smuggled back from a 5-star hotel in London in our hand luggage on the plane and we couldn't believe they were still intact when we got to Dublin airport. We toasted Lily's first birthday with those glasses. Gosh. That was probably around this exact time five years ago in this very kitchen. What a different place this house was back then. It was a home, a proper home, bursting with life and love and noise and people, overflowing with coloured plastic toys and cuddly bears. When Lily discovered her artistic side, we were constantly wiping down walls and doorframes which she'd colour with crayons at every opportunity. The sound of children's TV programmes was sometimes still chiming out even after she was asleep at night – we'd realise we didn't actually have to listen to the theme tune of Balamory when it was well after 8pm and we'd laugh at how immune to it all we'd become. Her little plastic cutlery and plates and bowls spilled out of cupboards and I'd find her handiwork in the most unexpected places, like the time I found the sugar bowl on top of the washing powder box in the utility room. She thought they matched and I suppose to her little eyes they did. Both white, both powdery in texture ... she was such a clever girl.

And now all of that is gone. I live in a world of basics here. No personality. No heart, no soul, nothing to get attached to. This is not a home anymore, it's a shell. It's a place to hide away from reality, where I lock the doors and don't let the outside world in.

My phone rings, which is a welcome interruption to my wandering mind and I answer it with a smile. It is my dad and his Northern Irish accent makes me both teary and calm at the same time. His timing, as always, is perfect.

'Tough day, pet?' he says and when I just nod in reply, I know he can still hear me. 'You're doing really well. I'm proud of you, girl. We all are and you're in my thoughts all day, every day.'

I nod more and exhale until I find the words I am looking for and when they come out, they are not what I expected to greet him with.

'I met a little girl today, Dad,' I tell him. 'Well, a teenager really. I found her crying on the beach because her mum's dying and she was scared. How on earth did we get through it, Dad? How did we learn to live again without Mum?'

Now it's his turn to choke up at his little house over two hundred miles away, in the same kitchen my mum used to cook in and where they used to dance arm in arm after Sunday Mass to country songs, as roast beef cooked slowly in the oven and my favourite sounds and smells filled the air.

'One day at a time, I told you, Shell,' he reminds me. 'That's all you can do is take each day as it comes. That little girl will grow up to be a woman, just like you are now and she will have many more ups and downs ahead of her, just like you've had. Life can be pretty tough sometimes but we've all got to learn to live through it, if you know what I mean.'

'I know exactly what you mean,' I tell him. 'I just don't know how to make it better.'

'You'll get there,' he assures me. 'Look at me now compared to the wreck I was back then. I couldn't find the strength to get out of bed and do a day's work for two whole years after your mother died. I wanted to end it all, but I battled on and it was never easy but I learned to live again by taking it one step at a time. Now, I enjoy two holidays a year, I've a nice wee retirement fund in the bank from all those years of hard work and my house is my own with no mortgage to worry about. Life is good. It is absolutely horrible for you now, love, but you will get there some day when you're ready, I promise.'

'And you have Anne, Dad,' I remind him with a giggle. How on earth could he forget Anne?

'And top of the list is my darling Anne, of course,' he says and I can hear my stepmother cackle with laughter in the background at the very idea of him leaving her out in his 'life is good' speech.

Thank God my father is happy, I think to myself. We may live miles apart but it only takes a phone call from him to give me just a little glimmer of hope that I might find peace like he has some day.

'And how's the lovely Eliza?' he asks me, knowing that his asking after my mother-in-law will definitely raise a smile in me. 'Still talking to the fairies, is she?'

I shake my head.

'The angels, Dad,' I say to him. 'She talks to the angels. There's a big difference in talking to angels and talking to fairies, my goodness! She'd murder you if she heard you mock her like that.'

She'd laugh if the truth be told. Eliza knows my dad by now and they always share great banter on the rare times we all get together.

'What's her latest prediction, go on, give us a laugh?' he asks me and I can just picture him leaning on the kitchen counter with his weather-beaten face and big hearty smile, waiting to be entertained.

Eliza, with her mood stones, chakras and crystals just doesn't cut the ice with him at all. He really likes her and enjoys her company, but the cynic in him can't help but kick his heels up in laughter at some of the things she believes in.

'I can't think of anything,' I tell him, trying my best to recall our conversation from earlier today. 'Oh, wait a minute. Actually, she did tell me to look out for the colour blue today, something she said on the phone this afternoon when I was going to work. She said blue would be good for me today.'

My dad lets out a roar of laughter.

'I hope you told her you were surrounded by it when you looked up above,' he chuckles. 'The sky is blue and the sea is blue and you're surrounded by both every day! Holy mother of God, I never heard worse in all my life! Look out for blue! Blue! Blue *what* you should have asked her! A blue moon? Ha!'

I roll my eyes as my dad erupts into fits of laughter. He is old school, and as black and white as they come. It's either one way or another, right or wrong, up or down, long or short. No nonsense and nothing in between and he finds those who see those differently quite fascinating. Hilariously funny obviously, but fascinating all the same.

'Now that you say it, I didn't see anything blue that I don't see every day,' I tell him, retracing my afternoon in the shop and my trip to the grocery store then my brief stop at home to fetch Merlin for his walk, then the little English girl with the big umbrella on the beach who told me about her sick mother and then I remember ... actually, I remember there *was* something!

'Well, there you go,' says my father, still in kinks of giggles and before I get to fill him in, he decides it's time to go. 'I'll leave you to your evening there now, pet but remember what I said. One day at a time. You're playing a blinder and wee Lily and your own mother are looking after you every step of the way, do you hear me?'

'I hear you, Dad,' I say to him. No matter how cynical he might be, my father still very much believes in heaven and the angels when he needs to. 'Big love to Anne and I'll chat to you very soon. Thanks so much for the call, it really cheered me up. Night night, Daddy.'

'God bless, Shelley, night night love,' he says, just like he always does. I hang up the phone and sit down on the kitchen sofa, staring out at the lighthouse as I realise that Eliza, for once, may have been right on the mark with her colour predictions.

The English lady who was sick, she bought a blue dress from me today. The little girl, Rosie, whose mother is dying said that her mum bought a new dress today. That warmth I felt when I walked away from Rosie was a feeling I really haven't experienced since, well, since Lily's death I suppose. I totally believe that they are all connected, but then I suppose when you're wrapped up in grief, you'll cling onto any little sign at all, won't you?

Juliette

'And who was this lady? Did she tell you her name?'

Rosie and I are snuggled up in our pyjamas, dry and warm at last with a steaming bowl of noodles and prawn crackers on each of our laps and I am quizzing her on her travels earlier. She seems a lot more settled now, much more like the daughter I know and adore and a lot less edgy and defensive than she was when we first got here this morning.

'Her name was Shelley and she lives in the big house that overlooks the beach, across from the lighthouse,' she tells me. 'I was so upset but she made me feel a lot better and told me to give you a big hug. Her mother ... well, her own mother got sick too, just like you, when she was around my age so she kind of understood why I was so upset and afraid.'

'Oh, you poor baby,' I say to my darling girl and my instinct is to go to that kind lady's house right now and hug *her* and thank her for looking after Rosie and sending her back to me.

'Mum, you should see the dog she has,' says Rosie, her eyes widening in excitement. 'His name's Merlin and he ate my chips and though his fur was soaked in the rain he was so nice to touch and he let me pat his head and didn't even bark. I'd love a dog like him. He's cool.'

'Really? What type of dog is he?' I ask her, knowing that no matter what type he is, there's no way she could ever have a pet where we live. It's too close to the middle of the city and there's hardly room for the two of us never mind an animal. Plus, I'm hardly in a position to make any big plans for the future right now, am I?

'A golden retriever,' she says. 'Or something like that. He's big and sandy and I bet when he's all dried he's really cuddly and fluffy. I think he liked me.'

'I bet he did,' I tell Rosie. She always did have a connection with animals and again, my 'future' dream was always that we would live in the countryside or better still, by the coast and she could fill the place with dogs, cats, chickens, the works. Even a pony if she wanted one. I always dreamed of her owning her own pony, but instead I could only ever afford that tiny terraced house where there wasn't room to swing a cat, never mind own one.

'Maybe this place *is* nice after all, Mum,' Rosie announces, her young innocent mind full of dogs and kind ladies on the beach. Whatever or whoever it was who changed her mind, I will be forever grateful.

'I really hope we can have a nice time,' I say to her, wanting so badly to tell her the whole truth about my now terminal diagnosis right from the horse's mouth and how precious this time really is, but she is smiling and eating and she looks so content, so I daren't rock her world, not yet. 'Maybe tomorrow we will quickly drop by and say thank you to Shelley for her little chat with you?'

Rosie nods and smiles more.

'I'd love that,' she says. 'I could maybe see Merlin again, too. I'd love to see him when he's all dry and snuggly and cuddly. Do you think I could get a dog someday, Mum? Maybe when we move to a bigger house like you said we would?'

I pause at the mention of the future and I honestly don't know what to say.

'Never mind,' she says. 'It's not the most important thing in the world right now. I'll go get some chocolate. Do you want a glass of wine?'

I sometimes think I gave birth to a mind reader. I would bloody love a glass of wine.

'That would be just perfect,' I tell her and my heart glows as I watch her walk out of the room in her fluffy pink robe and slippers, so much more content and happy than I've seen her all day.

How on earth am I going to leave her behind in this world without me?

Chapter 10

Shelley

SUNDAY

Sundays are the longest days when Matt isn't here to share them with me. We normally start the day with breakfast, then Eliza joins us for Sunday lunch, which Matt has mastered, and then we chill out for the afternoon in front of an old movie and the Sunday papers. We used to go for a swim just before dinner, but that hasn't happened in three years, not for me anyhow, and in the evenings Matt joins the lads in the local for a few pints while I browse online for bargains for the shop or read or have an early night.

I used to have so much to do, it felt like there weren't enough hours in the day. I was always coming and going, folding laundry, washing dishes, vacuuming up bits of spaghetti, lifting toys, washing her face and hands, making sure she got to the loo on time, getting her a drink, finding a lost sock, negotiating between Peppa Pig or Paw Patrol or whatever movie she had her eye on at that time. It was always Matilda. I catch my breath at the memory. And we'd eat together and we'd chat about nursery and her friends. How she loved making friends.

Today, I make poached eggs for breakfast and eat them on my lap, hurriedly, barely tasting them, eating only because I should. I don't know when I last tasted anything or made an effort with food. I used to set the table for breakfast, even amongst all the madness with a toddler, with such precision and pride – a glass of freshly squeezed orange juice, some salt and pepper, a mug for my coffee, some milk, some toast and I'd turn the radio down low and let the sounds of my youth fill the kitchen as country music filled my soul and took me right back to my childhood, when my mum and dad would enjoy it so much as they cooked and laughed together. I'd flick through Sunday magazines at my leisure while Lily ate breakfast beside me or played with Merlin on the floor and I'd love the fact that Sundays dragged on and on and we never had anything important to do – just eat and sleep and enjoy each other's company.

But everything has changed since then.

I don't cook much at all these days, not like I used to anyhow. Dinner parties were once my speciality and I'd invite the mums from Lily's playgroup round at any excuse and we'd eat our fill and drink wine and chat about men and children and politics and celebrities.

We'd have pizza parties in the summertime and invite

the neighbours over and Matt might get out his guitar and entertain our guests with a few James Taylor songs and after a few drinks he'd be rocking out to AC/DC with his biggest fan, old Harry from up the road, on 'air drums' and Harry's wife would beg them to 'stop that racket' as she plugged her fingers with her ears.

I have so many brilliant memories of our life as it used to be, but now, the very thought of having so many people in our home makes me feel panicky and full of guilt. How could I laugh and entertain like that again when Lily is gone?

Oh, how I long to feel good on the inside and the outside, to get excited at things, to laugh with friends until my sides are sore.

My doorbell rings and I look at the clock, startled as to who it might be and I feel my heart race and anxiety rush through my veins. It's certainly not Eliza. She knows not to call before midday on my day off and it can't be the postman on a Sunday. I hesitate. My first instinct as always when this happens is to stay put, not to answer and wish any callers away, but Merlin races to the front door barking in excitement and blows my cover. My stomach is gripped with nerves that gnaw at my insides and I look around the kitchen, trying to figure out what to do. The bell rings again. Shit. I gulp. I breathe out. I don't want to talk to anyone.

No. I need to stop this. I close my eyes, take a deep breath and I walk through the kitchen and into the hallway and open the front door. I am trying, I really am.

Juliette

'There's no one here, love. Come on. We'll try again later.'

I am just about to give up when the dog that Rosie told me about runs up to the glass panel on the door, barking excitedly, and Rosie kneels down to his level, calling his name as he wags his tail and jumps around on the other side.

This really is a magnificent house. It is modern, yet tasteful with its gleaming white exterior, landscaped driveway and black front door with potted spider plants outside, but behind it is the real magic because you look right out onto the magnificent sights of Galway Bay.

'I really think we should just—'

My urge to give up and leave is interrupted when the lady of the house opens the door and we recognise each other instantly. It is her from the shop where I bought the dress, but I can see her properly now that she isn't stuck behind a counter and she resembles a little doll; frail and small and pretty with that look of fear and worry still lingering on her face. She looks annoyed at first that we have disturbed her but then she speaks.

'Rosie!' she says, her face softening. 'Gosh and you must be Mum? Well, it looks like we have met before after all.'

She holds the door with one hand and her dog's collar with the other and already Rosie is reaching across to pat the dog's head. I really do get the idea we have inter-rupted her morning and I am highly embarrassed that we have done so. I only came here to say thank you, but it's Sunday and we probably shouldn't have called unannounced like this. I feel my face burning.

'I am so sorry to spring ourselves on you on a Sunday morning,' I try to explain. 'Rosie, well actually me, not Rosie, well ... I just wanted to say thank you for yesterday for talking to her on the beach and for sending her back to me feeling so much better than she was when you found her. I was worried sick, as you can imagine.'

The lady nods and smiles at me in fleeting glances but it is Rosie who she is really looking at, her head tilted in sorrow.

'That's very nice of you,' she says to me, still holding the door and the dog, still looking at Rosie. 'I hope you are a bit better today.'

I hand her a gift bag, wondering which she will let go of first to take it from me, the door or the dog. She lets go of the door and looks back at me in bewilderment like I have done something wrong.

'Really, you had no need to bring me a gift,' she says. 'Sorry, I didn't get your name? I'm Shelley.'

'Yes, yes of course, Shelley, Rosie told me that. I'm Juliette, Juliette Fox. I bought the blue dress from you yesterday? It's just a book and a bottle of wine, some chocolates in there too. I hope you like chocolates. And reading.'

She nods at me and smiles a little.

'I love both. It's very kind of you to pop by,' she says, but she still doesn't move from the door or invite us in.

I can't wait to get away from here. I really shouldn't have come at all but at least I know I did my bit to thank her.

'Well, we'll not keep you, I'm sure you're busy,' I say to her, taking Rosie's arm as a cue to go but she is engrossed in the dog.

'I told you he was cute, Mum,' she says. 'Oh, I'd so love a dog like this, wouldn't I Merlin? Wouldn't I love a dog like you?!'

My eyes meet the woman in front of me for a split second.

'Erm ... would you like to come in for a coffee?' she asks. 'I don't have much more to offer you, but I definitely do have coffee. I think.'

My gut instinct is to turn down her offer and get on with our plans which include a beach walk and then Sunday lunch on the pier to start with, but something tells me that this lady, Shelley, hasn't invited anyone in for coffee in a long, long time and that as hard as it is for her, part of her would like us to stay.

'Are you sure we aren't interrupting your morning?' I ask her. 'We really only intended on saying a quick hello and thank you. You don't have to—'

'No, no, I insist. Please come in. I hope Merlin behaves. He really does get excited when someone comes to the door.'

She opens the door wide and lets the dog go, then puts her gift bag on a sideboard in the hallway and allows us into her beautiful home. Everything is white or cream and there is nothing on the walls – no pictures, no mirrors, no rugs on the floor, no ornaments, no lamps. It really is very bare, like she has just moved in.

'This is such an amazing house!' says Rosie as we follow Shelley down the hallway, our voices echoing off the cream marble floors and blank white walls. 'Do you have a gym? I bet you have a gym and a pool and everything! It's like a hotel, isn't in Mum?'

I get the feeling either this lady has either definitely just moved in or she is about to move out. A messy divorce perhaps? It doesn't feel lived in at all.

'It is beautiful,' I say to my daughter who probably has never been in a house like this before. I feel like Lloyd Grossman from that Through the Keyhole programme, looking round me in awe and trying to guess as much as I can about the occupants.

'Have a seat,' says Shelley, signalling us to some high stools around a shiny black marble topped island in the vast kitchen. I look out of the window as she boils the kettle and wonder if I'm drooling down my chin at the view. A lighthouse sits in the near distance, tall and white with black and red trimmings, and the sea, a mid-blue blanket of tranquillity, looks almost close enough to touch on the other side of the hilltop garden where an apple tree stands alone. A dining room table takes up most of the far side of the kitchen and double doors lead out onto a small balcony with a small table and two chairs. Whoever designed this house at this location ... well, they were onto something.

'So, are you here on holiday?' asks Shelley, taking me out of my dream-like stance where I was imagining living here for even just one day.

'Yes, yes we are,' I say, realizing that we haven't really spoken much yet. 'I was too busy admiring your view there, sorry. I don't think I've ever been in a home with such a spectacular view.'

'Yes,' says Shelley. 'We are very lucky indeed. I guess it's easy to take such things for granted when you look at it every day but I agree, it's a top location. My husband worked his heart out to raise the money to buy it.'

The kettle clicks off and she suggests tea or coffee.

'Tea, please for me,' I reply and look at Rosie who is, like me, drinking in the surroundings so much that she can hardly speak. 'Rosie?'

'Oh, sorry, what?' she asks and I laugh and shake my head.

'Shelley was asking if you'd like tea or coffee?'

'Thanks, but I'm okay,' she says. 'Is that a real balcony out there?'

Both Shelley and I laugh at her innocence.

'I don't think it's an optical illusion,' I say. 'That would be just unfair to tease us like that, wouldn't it?'

'It's very safe and there's loads of room out there if you'd like to go outside for a look, Rosie? Thank goodness the rain has stopped. Yesterday was like the end of the world!' says Shelley.

She is slowly beginning to relax. Slowly. For someone who owns such an original and stylish shop, not to mention the funky clothes she wears, I can't understand why Shelley has such stilted communication skills and such an empty home – it all feels so incongruous.

'Yes, you must have been soaked through,' I say to her. 'It wasn't exactly the welcome to Killara I was expecting. The last time I was here, the sun was splitting the trees.'

'Do you have wi-fi?' Rosie asks and I can't believe she just asked that.

'Rosie! Oh, please ignore that, Shelley. Rosie, you don't need a wi-fi code everywhere you go.'

Rosie doesn't seem embarrassed, and Shelley just laughs graciously.

'Of course I have wi-fi,' she says and she calls out the code to Rosie who taps it into her phone, then makes her way out to the balcony with Merlin by her side while Shelley pours the tea.

'I'm so sorry about that. Teenagers and their addiction to technology!' I say to her. 'It always makes me feel so old to say this, but what happened to the art of conversation? My daughter is always stuck to some sort of device and it drives me insane sometimes.'

'You're very lucky to have her,' says Shelley without turning towards me, and then she brings the cups to the table with a slight smile.

'Oh, I know I am,' I say to her, sensing there is a reason why she is reminding me so. I want to ask her if she has any children, but there certainly doesn't seem any sign of them around. The house is clinical, *she* is clinical, yet her warmth to Rosie yesterday tells me that if the surface was rubbed ever so slightly there is a very different person bursting to get out from under her cool exterior.

'She was very taken by you yesterday,' I say to Shelley. 'I honestly don't know what sort of magic you shared with her but she is a much brighter little girl today.'

'Oh, I wouldn't say it was magic but just a shared sense of fear,' says Shelley. 'I have offered to lend an ear if she ever needs it, I hope you don't mind. Gosh, I sound like a counsellor and I am really the least likely person to be counselling anyone right now.'

She gulps, like something has caught her breath. I don't want to probe too much as I can see this woman is walking on eggshells emotionally. I don't ask what exactly she said to Rosie yesterday for fear it might make her crumble and I'm glad when she changes the subject.

'So, you've been here before then?' she says. 'Was it recently?'

I laugh a little as the exact date rolls off my tongue.

'21st to the 23rd of August, sixteen years ago,' I tell her.

Well, it's not like I could ever forget the dates, could I?

'I was only meant to stay one night but we loved it so much we stayed a second,' I explain. 'It was the last stop of a six-week backpacking trip around Ireland which I began alone and finished off with a Scandinavian girl I met called Birgit, and we had a ball here, we really did. Young, carefree and single. It was great fun.'

Shelley sets the tea down in front of me and I glance

out onto the balcony to where Rosie and her new best friend Merlin are making acquaintances, taking selfies, of course. Then she'll be sending them across to her friends back at home, fishing for likes, isn't that what they call it?

'I moved here a year after you then,' says Shelley, climbing onto a stool across from me. 'I came here the first time when I was sixteen to stay with my aunt just after my mum died. I needed to get away for a while and I spent the entire summer here. The second time I came to visit, four or five years later, I met my husband and fell madly in love, as you do, and never went home. Oh, to be so young and in love once more ... to have known what was ahead of me.'

A divorce. I knew it.

She twiddles her long, plaited hair as she speaks about her past and it's the perfect opening for me to really explain how much her talk meant to Rosie yesterday.

'Rosie has just turned fifteen,' I tell her, my eyes darting back and forward to Rosie as I talk. '... I am terminally ill, Shelley, and I want this holiday to be perfect for Rosie. I don't want us to have to deal with my impending death just yet.'

'I'm so, so sorry for you,' says Shelley, biting her lip, still twiddling her hair. 'I can only imagine how frightened you must be, knowing that you'll be leaving such a beautiful child behind. I'm so sorry ... How are you feeling?'

'Well, I'm hardly tap dancing on top of the world,' I

say with a tired smile. 'But there is something strangely peaceful about it all. I've accepted it and I'm determined to make the most of the short time I have left.'

She looks like she doesn't believe me. I don't blame her.

'Aren't you angry?'

'I've already been there,' I tell her. 'I've been through every emotion known to mankind since I was first diagnosed. The treatments, the sickness, the dependency on others to do the things I used to find so easy, then the hope and the glimmer of light when it seemed the treatments had been successful, then its blasted return, more chemo, same all over again and now here we are.'

'That sounds like a living nightmare.'

'Oh, it has been tough but even a warhorse like me knows when I'm beat and I intend to make the most of every second I have left,' I say to her. 'It's back and I can't fight it anymore but my only concern now is for Rosie and making the most of my time with her before I go. This is my last chance to give her some wonderful memories and I want to make every day special for her.'

Shelley shakes her head and shivers.

'She's got a lot ahead of her, poor thing,' she says to me. 'And a lot to get her head around right now. I would love to tell you she is going to be okay but it's not an easy path for anyone to have to travel so young. We always miss our mum, no matter what age we are. It's a sad club that no one wants to belong to, and I'm in it too, I'm afraid.'

We both look out at Rosie who is in another world with her phone and her new canine companion on the balcony. This is hard for me to hear but it's straight from the horse's mouth, from someone who has been through it all and if it comforted Rosie to hear that she isn't the only one who lost their mum in their teens, then surely I should be comforted by that too?

'I sometimes wonder if she had a brother or a sister, would it be easier on her, you know?' I say to Shelley. 'Did you have anyone to lean on when you lost your own mum?'

Shelley shakes her head knowingly.

'I would have given my right arm to have a sibling, but no, I'm an only child too and it was horrendous. I think you are doing exactly the right thing by taking her on this holiday, Juliette,' she says. 'You have made a very conscious decision to give her the very best of you before you go and I don't think there is anything more you can do than that. I wish I'd had that time with my mother.'

I feel a lump in my throat at the reminder that this is all really happening. I am here, in a stranger's house in Ireland, asking for advice on how to prepare my daughter for my death.

'And after I go?' I manage to whisper.

Shelley's eyes are glazed now and I'm afraid I may be probing too much.

'Make sure she is with the people who love her most,' she tells me. 'Make sure she has someone to watch over her every step of the way – an aunt, a friend her own age, a father figure, anyone you can trust to make sure she has someone to turn to when she needs to. That's really all you can do.'

I look out at Rosie as my heart breaks into millions of pieces.

'And I suppose,' says Shelley, 'depending on whether you believe in it all, I think a reassurance that you will be with her in spirit, as clichéd as that may sound might help more than you know.'

Oh God.

'I do believe in that,' I tell her. 'I have so much I want to do and say to her and I just hope that I have time to pack it all in.'

'Do you know how long?' she asks me.

I shake my head.

'I don't have a specific timeframe, but I know I don't have long left,' I tell her. 'Weeks, maybe. Who knows? A few months, if I'm lucky.'

Shelley looks me in the eye and then looks away again.

'Oh my goodness, I don't know what to say to you,' she whispers. 'That is just heart-breaking for you both.'

'Sorry, I didn't mean to burden you with all this on a Sunday morning,' I tell her, remembering that we have totally interrupted her morning with my doom and gloom. 'I'm sure you are used to much more jolly visitors than us! We really should be making tracks and leaving you to get on with your day.'

I go to stand up.

'No, it's okay, honestly,' Shelley tells me. That pain

again on her face. That deep, deep pain. Desperation, almost.

'We should go. I'm sorry.'

'No. Look,' she says. 'Yesterday was a tough day for me and I wasn't expecting to have that kind of conversation with anyone, so I hoped that I had helped Rosie just a little, and to see that I have means a lot to me. You have no idea what it means to me, actually. It's really nice of you to pop by. I'm glad you did and you really don't have to go yet, not on my account anyway.'

She looks at my seat and I sit down again.

'I'm glad we called too,' I say to Shelley. 'You've been through it all yourself so I guess you really do understand.'

I want to ask her what it is that she is going through now though, not out of nosiness, but out of concern. This young woman is in turmoil and full of angst and I have no doubt that she has not had a visitor in this beautiful cold house in a long, long time. I try to lighten the mood.

'On a more positive note,' I say, straightening up in my seat, 'we are going to have a lovely time here in Killara. The best time, ever. I've always meant to come back here and never did, so when my doctor suggested some quality time out from city life, I knew I'd have to do exactly what I was told and come here again to see what I've been missing.'

Shelley takes a sip from her tea, holding the cup with both hands.

'There's something about this place, isn't there?' she says to me, her eyes filled with wonder. 'A lot of people don't ever leave when they come here. It gets under their skin so much – the food, the sea, the art, the music, the friendly locals, not to mention the pubs. There is always something happening to cater for all tastes. I love it here, I really do. I can't see Matt and I ever living anywhere else but here. I wanted to move away from this house, but when it came to it, how could I? How could I leave something that we put so much of ourselves into?'

And I can see exactly what she means. Shelley is like a young woman who has it all with her big house and her own business, yet her eyes are vacant and I really do get the impression that she is only living life in first gear right now. I'm obviously wrong in my divorce assumptions. Oh, what I'd give to be in her shoes with her whole life ahead of her. She speaks fondly of her husband, she has the most magnificent home and works in that gorgeous, quirky shop, so what on earth more does she want in life? What is she missing at such a young age?

'Look, I know you haven't lived around here forever,' I say to her, not knowing where I am finding the courage to actually ask this question or how it has entered my head out of the blue. 'But can I ask you something?'

My bold streak that has run through my veins since I was just a young girl has sprung to the surface and I can't help myself from asking her my burning question.

'Of course,' she replies. 'Go ahead.'

I want to stop myself but I can't.

'I wanted to ask you ...' I begin, then pause. 'Look, I'm going to just cut to the chase. Do you know of a man who might live around here, well, he might not live around here at all but – oh actually, just forget it. I sometimes think I'm losing my mind going down this road at all and—'

'Tell me,' says Shelley, shifting on her seat. 'Are you looking for someone?'

I pause.

'Not actively, no,' I manage. 'I'm just being curious and opportunistic of your local knowledge since you've lived here a while, but ignore me. I could be asking for trouble.'

But Shelley isn't letting me away at that.

'If I don't know of him I can guarantee that my husband will as he has lived here most of his life,' she says to me. 'Is it someone you have a history with? An old flame? Oh, is it an ex-lover?'

She looks excited, but I can feel my face flush slightly and I shrug, trying to play it down though I can't help but smile at the thought of those hazy drunken days here all those years ago.

'Oh please, go on!' she says, and her face is suddenly, dare I say, animated, like she has forgotten for just a moment what it is that is constantly on her mind and preventing her from smiling these days.

'I can't believe I'm asking you this,' I say, putting my hands to my cheeks like an embarrassed teenager and my voice drops to a whisper. 'You see ... I'm looking for someone I haven't seen since we met here all those summers ago, way back in 2003. I don't know if he lived here or if he was just passing through like I was back then, and I don't have a proper name for him but I would so love to get some closure. I'd just like to know where he is, or even better, let him know about Rosie if the vibe from him was right. You see ... Rosie is his. I must be losing my mind to be telling you this. It's a secret I've kept from almost everyone since the day she was born.'

Now, Shelley is *really* interested.

'About Rosie?' she says in a whisper. 'Oh my goodness, Juliette, that's a lot more serious than I thought. Tell me what you know of him and I'll ask Matt or Eliza if I can't help you myself. That's if you definitely want to find him. It's a big decision under the circumstances, isn't it?'

She waits in anticipation for his name and my urge to say it lingers in the air. She has stopped twiddling her hair and doesn't seem so robotic now that I have given her this information. It is pretty serious when you think about it, that somewhere nearby might be a man who has the same flesh and blood and genes as my daughter and whom I have never yet told of her existence – but here I am, fifteen years after her conception, when lo and behold, I am just about to die. It's serious alright. It's crazy perhaps. Me and my big mouth.

'Actually, just forget I ever mentioned it,' I say, sliding off my stool and lifting my purse. 'I shouldn't have told you that, Shelley. I'm really sorry. Rosie and I should be on our way – gosh, is that the time? I really wanted to get a long walk in and then take her for lunch. At least the sun is out today and I don't have to worry about clothes. Yesterday was a strange one. Thanks for the—'

'Please don't go.'

Shelley stands up as well and looks me in the eye.

'Please don't leave yet,' she says. 'I would really like you to stay and chat. Tell me about your mystery man. I may not have a clue who he is but I'm enjoying our conversation and you have no idea how long it has taken me to do this.'

I have no idea what she is talking about.

'Do what, Shelley?'

'This. *Talk*. Chat. Get excited. Have a conversation with someone about life and the ups and downs we all have to encounter and how the world doesn't just revolve around me and this empty house and my misery and grief. I never do this. I never let anyone in. Just talk to me about him. Please. It's exciting and it's new and I haven't been moved by anything in three years and I really don't want you to go. And if you decide when you leave here this morning that you want to keep our conversation top secret I can assure you my lips are sealed. I promise you, I really do. Would you have another cuppa?'

I am totally taken aback by Shelley's outburst and the plea on her face has melted my heart. She is a young woman living in a big empty shell of a house, wracked with the worries of the world when she surely has her whole life ahead of her and here she is, begging me, me on death's door, to stay and talk more about my whimsical dream of a man who I know nothing of. I am strangely honoured and let's face it, I don't have much to lose, so I sit back down on the stool and she does the same.

'His nickname was Skipper,' I whisper to her with a shrug and a smile. 'There, I said it out loud. Skipper. He was a boat man, and what a fine and handsome boat man he was. Skipper. And that's all I know.'

I wait.

'Do you know him?' I ask, wondering what on earth is going on in her mind. I wait and watch for her reaction as the name sinks in. And it does. Her mouth has dropped open.

'Oh my God,' she says, her hand slowly going to her mouth.

Is that a good *oh my God* or a bad *oh my God*? I can't tell.

'I do know him,' says Shelley and she swallows and gulps as if I have just delivered the worst news ever. 'Skipper the boat man ... I know Skipper for sure. Are you sure he's Rosie's father?'

I nod my head and look outside at Rosie.

'I'm totally sure,' I tell her. 'There's no way it could have been anyone else.'

Chapter 11

Shelley

I can't believe what I'm hearing from this stranger in front of me. Jesus, I do not know what to say.

Skipper?

I get up to make more tea as promised and I can feel my hands shaking as I do so.

'I knew I shouldn't have told you this,' says Juliette and I feel so bad for not being able to hide what I'm thinking. 'Maybe we should just leave, after all.'

'No,' I tell her. 'You don't have to.'

'Is it bad that it's him?' she asks me. 'Is he a bad person or is he someone I should avoid?'

'No, he's not a bad person.'

'Oh my God, is it your *husband*?'

'No!' I tell her quickly. 'God, no! It's not my husband.'

Her pale face relaxes just a little.

'Matt wouldn't know the first thing about working on boats,' I explain. 'But he *has* told me so much about

Skipper. Oh Juliette, I am so sorry to be the one to have to tell you but—'

'What then?'

'I'm sorry,' I tell her, glancing out at Rosie, then looking back at Juliette in pity. 'He's ... he's not here anymore.'

I can't say it. I really can't say it but then Juliette says it for me.

'He's dead, isn't he?'

I nod. She's right. Skipper is dead. Oh Christ, this is awful. She sits back down on her stool and puts her head in her hands and she starts to cry.

'Oh, Juliette I am so, so sorry,' I say to her. I go towards her and I want to touch her shoulder and make her feel better but I don't. 'I wish I had much better news for you and it was so brave of you to tell me but—'

'What the hell am I crying for?' she whispers and sniffles, glancing all the time out towards the balcony in case Rosie comes back in. 'I barely knew him. I don't know why I am getting so upset. I know nothing about him, only what I see every day through my daughter. Why am I so *upset*?'

'Of course you're upset,' I say and then I do something that until yesterday, I haven't done to anyone since Lily died, apart from Matt, or my dad when I see him. I reach out to her and I give her a hug, just like I did with Rosie yesterday evening on the beach. She hugs me back tightly and I try to squeeze away some of her pain and some of my own pain too.

'I swear to God I wasn't expecting him to be dead,'

she tells me when we part. 'I had myself all prepared for him being a married man who didn't want to know me or Rosie, or even someone who didn't remember me and denied it all and demanded some sort of DNA test to prove it. I had so many scenarios go through my head but never did I think he would be dead. He was only my age or thereabouts. Maybe a bit younger. How can he be dead? When?'

'Skipper, or Pete which was his real name, was only about twenty-five when he died, I think,' I tell her, trying to explain this as gently as I can. 'I didn't get the chance to ever meet him in person, but Matt speaks so fondly of him and his death was a big shock to everyone who knew him.'

She looks out the window, her face furrowed in pain. 'How did he ...?'

I swallow. I only ever heard this story second-hand through Matt but it's one of those stories that everyone around here knows.

'He was killed in an accident,' I tell her. 'A boating accident, which makes it even more tragic as he was one of the finest captains around here, or so they say. I'm ever so sorry.'

I can't bear to think what must be going through Juliette's head right now at the news of Rosie's biological father being dead all this time. The thought of leaving her child behind with no consolation of finally meeting her biological father must be truly devastating for her.

'I had so many silly hopes and dreams for what might

come out of this trip, even though I denied it to everyone, including myself,' Juliette says. 'I had hoped so much in my heart that Skipper would remember me instantly and would recognise Rosie as his own the moment he laid eyes on her, and even if he had a wife and family of his own, he would slowly welcome her into his life ... so that when I go, I would know that she at least got to meet him and that I'd done my bit instead of all these years of telling her that her father had never known I was still pregnant with her, and that I'd never been able to find him to tell him about her.'

'Oh you poor thing. Is that what you told her?'

She shrugs and nods. 'I'm not proud of it, but I had to come up with something to answer her questions,' she said. 'That worked until she was about ten and then I met Dan, my husband, and she forgot about what she didn't have for a while. But recently, well since Dan and I split up actually, she's been asking me about him again and I've found letters that she has been writing to him, telling him all about her life so far and it just tore me up inside when I saw her longing for him in black and white. I really hoped this would all be different, just for her sake, but my sister was right. I shouldn't have come here. I should have let sleeping dogs lie. I should have just gone to Scotland or Cornwall or somewhere that isn't here, somewhere with no memories.'

I want to phone Matt and ask him what I should do or say in this situation. He would know exactly what to do. He is so much better at this type of thing than I am, plus he would be able to tell her so many stories about Skipper and some of the funny times they spent together which would maybe ease Juliette's pain. He knew him so well and I know that when Matt hears there is a little girl alive in Skipper's memory, it will be bittersweet for him and all who knew the legendary Skipper around here.

'Look, I know there must be so many "what ifs" going through your head right now,' I say to Juliette, 'but I think you were right to come here. I do still think it was meant to be.'

'You really do think that?' she asks me, dabbing under her eyes with a tissue. 'Oh, I really hope you're right because right now I feel like such a failure, a romantic fool.'

'Yes, I really do think so,' I say, not knowing where or how I am finding the words. 'You have got answers. They may not be the answers you were hoping for, but at least you have closure in your own mind and you can tell Rosie the truth. Tell her that this is where you met her biological father all those years ago and about the fun you had and how this is the place she can come to when she wants to feel close to him. And maybe close to you too, after this time together here. This has always been a special place for you and it's now even more special for your daughter, Juliette. Focus on the days ahead with Rosie. In time, she may want to look up some of Skipper's relatives and who knows what she will discover, but you've made the move you always wanted to. You've come here and I don't think you've done so in vain, not for a second.'

Rosie and Merlin arrive back into the kitchen which is perfect timing as only moments before the situation may have been a little hard to explain, but Juliette has perked up now and she beams when her daughter enters the room.

'Do you have an iPhone charger by any chance?' she asks me, holding up her phone as if I need to see what an iPhone looks like. 'Mum, I swear I want to live here. There are even sockets to plug in your phone out on the balcony. This is *so* my dream house. I feel like Kendall Jenner hanging out here. My friends are so jealous.'

Juliette shoots me a glance and rolls her eyes and we all have a laugh at Rosie's observations.

She looks so different today with her hair tied up in a loose ponytail and a lot less make up on. Her skin is dewy and young and now I know why she looked so familiar to me when I first laid eyes on her. We have a connection. I may not have known Skipper, but he was one of Matt's best friends and a friend of Matt's is a friend of mine. Now here I am standing in front of the daughter he never knew he had. I may sound a bit like Eliza with all my belief in fate and signs, but I definitely did feel a connection when I looked into her eyes on the sand dunes yesterday and now I know why.

'I should have one somewhere,' I reply as Juliette tells off Rosie once again for speaking out of turn, but I honestly don't mind. What I would give for Lily to be here now asking for things or playing up or throwing a tantrum or being cheeky. I would give the world without hesitation.

I find Rosie a phone charger in one of the kitchen drawers and she thanks me then bounds back outside.

'I think my Merlin has a new best friend,' I say to Juliette who watches her daughter leave, her head tilted to the side and a look of pure love on her face.

'She sometimes seems like she hasn't a care in the world, like she doesn't have the worry of a dying mother and an absent father she never knew to deal with,' she says to me. 'I just wish she could be like that for a lot longer – young, innocent and carefree, but it's all going to come crashing down soon, isn't it? Her teenage years are going to be robbed and she'll have to grow up overnight. My poor little Rosie.'

I can't let the idea of how sad that is sink in right now.

'Look, if you want to find out any more about Skipper, you know, when Rosie is up for it, I can give you my details,' I tell her, trying to give her some direction to go from here.

'You will? Oh, Shelley that would mean the world to me.'

'Of course I will,' I reply. It's the very least I can offer. 'And she can talk to Matt and we will help her in any way we can. I don't know a lot about her father, only what my husband has told me, but Matt will be so delighted to look you both up and tell you what he can.

Oh, I wish he was here right now. He would have all the answers you're looking for.'

And I so know he would. Matt would be over the moon to meet Rosie and Juliette in honour of Skipper and I can't wait to tell him all of this. And wait till I tell Eliza! She'll be convinced that she is Mystic Meg after her prediction about the colour blue yesterday. I do feel strangely positive for having met Rosie, and now Juliette. Maybe some encounters in life are fateful after all, though my father would have a fit of hysterics if he heard this.

'Are Skipper's family local?' asks Juliette. 'Or is there a grave I could visit before I leave here?'

Oh no. I was hoping she wouldn't ask that question.

'I'm afraid not,' I tell her. 'He wasn't from here, you see. He was from County Waterford which is over three hours' travel from here. I guess he must have been a regular visitor here, but no, there is no family here and no grave locally. I'm sorry.'

To my great surprise this final bombshell doesn't seem to be as devastating to Juliette as I thought it might be. Instead she looks a little happier for hearing it.

'My grandparents are from Waterford,' she tells me, and I can totally understand why her spirits seem to have lifted at that. 'They're from a town called Dungarvan, do you know it?'

'Yes, I've heard of that place. Never been though,' I say to her.

'I have,' she says with delight. 'I visited there with Birgit that same summer and I can't believe that Skipper and

I didn't cover that when I met him in Brannigan's that night. Well, to be perfectly honest, I don't recall a lot of what we talked about, but I'm sure I would have mentioned that should he have said where he was from. Drink, eh? Oh, to be so young and naive. I should be ashamed of myself. No wonder I've kept it more or less to myself for all these years.'

I shrug my shoulders. 'We've all had fuzzy nights that we'd rather file away in the back of our minds,' I assure her. 'But no matter what you talked about to him, don't you feel better now knowing where he was from and that he was such a fun, talented person?'

Juliette nods. 'I do. Thank you so much,' she says. 'Plus, I can't believe we've been talking for an hour and I've told you my life story and you've barely told me one thing about yourself.'

I freeze at the idea of it. No, I can't go there, not right now when I am doing so well with this distraction. I don't want to talk about me, I am sick of my life story and all of my misery. Focusing on Juliette and Rosie and Skipper and all its mystery, not to mention the great feeling I get by knowing I may be able to help them, is what I need to hold on to.

'I have enjoyed it, really I have,' I tell Juliette. If only she knew how rare this scenario is for me to be chatting over tea, in my kitchen, with a virtual stranger. 'I am very glad you called and it looks like Rosie has enjoyed herself too. I know Merlin has.'

'They both certainly have,' says Juliette. 'She's like a

different child after meeting you yesterday, Shelley. Look, maybe we could meet up again before we leave Killara, would that be an idea? Let me buy you a tea next time and you get to tell me your deepest darkest secrets now that I've spilled mine out to you!'

Juliette laughs like it's the most natural thing in the world for her to simply return the favour by buying me a coffee, but the very thought of doing something so ... well, so normal and sociable and public, well it freaks me out, much to my own frustration.

My anxiety returns like a bolt out of the blue at the thought of meeting her somewhere other than here, but I really do *want* to see both of them again. I hate being like this. I hate feeling dizzy and sweaty and tingly all over with pins and needles as soon as someone suggests something like this to me. I need to rise above it. I wish I could.

'Or better still,' Juliette continues. 'Why don't you join us for Sunday lunch down on the pier in that cute little Beach House Café right now? Rosie must be hungry by now and there's no point you cooking for one – my treat? I'd love to chat more and we could bring the dog and sit outside now that the sun has decided to show its face.'

I freeze again. My mouth dries up. I don't know how to explain this to her. I want to go for lunch and I want to chat more down by the pier with Merlin, out in the sunshine and watching the world go by, but I don't know if I can. The guilt rises. The panic rises. So I do what my bereavement counsellor once told me to do when I feel such an attack coming on. I look for an object, something familiar. My wedding ring ... yes, that will do. I touch it. It's real. I breathe right into my diaphragm. I twist it around my finger. I breathe more.

'Shelley, are you okay?' Juliette asks me and I just manage a nod in reply. I look down on this feeling in my mind. It will not overpower me. I am in charge. I am in control. I want to go so I will go.

'I'm really sorry, but I can't, not today, but thank you,' I say to Juliette. Shit!

'Oh,' is her reply. 'Okay then, I totally understand that it's short notice for you. Some other time then, eh?'

I nod again and manage to stammer. 'Yes, yes, of course. Some other time.'

Some other time? Hardly sensitive of me to agree to that. Not like she has all the time in the world though, is it? But the fear ... why on earth do I have to be like this?

Rosie comes in with Merlin again and it's a welcome distraction.

'He really is the smartest dog I have ever met. Watch this, Mum.'

Rosie kneels down on the floor and Merlin lifts his two front paws up and places them on her shoulders which distracts me and I feel my pulse slowing down. *I* didn't even know he could do that.

'Good boy, Merlin!' I say to my dog, feeling calmer already at his familiarity. 'You must be something special,

Rosie, because I've never ever known him to do that to anyone.'

Juliette beams at this, as does Rosie.

'And he can give me his paw and he lies down when I tell him,' Rosie tells us. 'Oh, he is just the best, aren't you Merlin? You're the best dog in the whole world!'

My breathing slowly returns to normal and my heartrate slows to a regular beat as I watch this little girl work her magic on Merlin, who isn't really used to anyone but me or Matt these days. Why does she soothe me so much? Does she remind me of what my future could have been like with Lily? Why do I feel this sense of ease and contentment when I see her? A stranger's child, a young girl who I don't know, yet who I long to hold tight, to look after in this big bad world when her darling mother has to leave her all on her own. She is like me, that's why. She is about to go through exactly what I went through and I long to take that all away and give her the security she deserves ... but of course, I will never be able to do such a thing.

'We need to get going if we want to order lunch,' Juliette says to her daughter. 'Shelley, are you sure you won't join us?'

I want to, I want to, I so want to but I can't.

'I can't,' I say, squeezing my fingers. Juliette looks at my hands, then at me and then it looks like the penny has dropped.

'What are you afraid of?' she asks me. Rosie has busied

herself with the dog again, delighted to have stretched out some extra time with him.

'It's just ... I'm just afraid.'

'Of me? Of Rosie? Of being seen out with a stunner like me in public?'

I manage a tiny smile. 'No, well, I—'

My heart starts to race again.

'Would you feel better if you did come?' Juliette asks me. 'Would it make you feel like you've done something positive today?'

I nod. I can't speak. The thought of actually doing something nice for me, fills me with such—

'Guilt,' I spit out. 'I'd feel guilty if I went out and enjoyed myself.'

Juliette folds her arms.

'Oh no,' she says, shaking her head. 'Guilty if you enjoy yourself? If you have lunch out in your own home village? You can't live like this forever, Shelley. No way! You can't keep punishing yourself for whatever it is you feel you may have done wrong.'

Juliette is right, of course. I need to rise above this grief and fear once and for all and put another's needs in front of mine. I have only just met these wonderful people and I will not allow my anxiety to rule my heart for any longer. I will go. I will force myself, I will be strong for once and I will go.

'Can you give me five minutes to freshen up?' I ask Juliette, whose face instantly brightens at my turnaround. I am going to do this. I am going to believe in myself and take this all as a sign to help myself as much as I seem to have helped them.

'I don't mean to push you into anything you aren't comfortable with, but please don't ever feel guilty for enjoying yourself, Shelley,' she says to me. 'Life is way too short for that crap. Maybe you have other plans?'

'Unless you count reading the Sunday papers online, or having yet another bath, or walking Merlin on the beach which I do every day, I have absolutely no other plans.'

'Well, then put some lippy on and let's get out of here. I think I owe you at least a lunch, and believe me, Juliette Fox doesn't do lunch in halves. We will be having the works, just you wait and see.'

I don't think I am going to get out of this at all and I actually love that Juliette is pushing me. Normally people just give up when I say 'no' more than once but she is making me do this. She is pushing me to do something totally normal and as hard as I know it will be to go out and face the world socially, I know it's what I want to do deep down.

'Can you wait for five minutes?' I ask. 'Or I can meet you there?'

'We can wait for you of course,' she tells me. 'Now go quickly and don't you dare change your mind.'

'I won't change my mind,' I say with determination. 'Rosie, maybe you could fetch Merlin's lead from the hallway and help me get him ready?'

Rosie is already halfway down the hallway and Juliette flashes me a smile.

'You have no idea how much this means to me, to see her so full of life and energy, Shelley,' she says to me.

'I do have an idea,' I reply. 'I feel it too for some reason. She's a special girl, your Rosie.'

'Well forgive me for being biased, but I honestly think she is very special indeed,' says Juliette. 'I suppose I'm starting to see just how amazing she is as I'm absorbing everything so much more, now that I know it's all coming to an end.'

'I can't imagine.'

'Everything in me is heightened, Shelley,' she explains. 'Every hurt, every fear, every little bit of love that comes my way, I feel it all at its strongest and it can be very frightening, but also very rewarding.'

'Ready!' says Rosie, clutching onto Merlin's lead as he tries to take her for a walk around the kitchen already.

'I'll be as quick as I can,' I tell them both and I go quickly to the bathroom where I dab my pressure points on my neck, wrists and temples with cold water, look at my reflection for ten seconds, and say a quick prayer to Lily to help me make this step today. I know she would want me to get on with my life. I know my mother is cheering me on to forgive myself and laugh a little, to see the brighter side of life again and to believe in love again, not only with Matt but also with friends and strangers alike. I do feel like I am making a big change right now. My mother is close, just as Eliza told me on Lily's birthday yesterday.

I can do this. I know I can.

Chapter 12

Juliette

'Well, that was just to die for,' I say as I scrape the last mouthful of buttered seabass and pesto mash off my plate. We are sitting outside the Beach House Café just as planned and to our delight and very much to our surprise, the sun has stayed out to greet us and it reflects off the bay as we talk and chat at ease.

'I've never tasted crab claws before,' says Rosie. 'I can't wait to tell everyone at home that I actually ate the claws of a crab! They were delicious. I think I may have a new taste for seafood, Mum.'

I smile at my daughter. We are making memories already and she doesn't even realise it.

'This is the girl who I once had to bribe when she was three to eat fish fingers,' I remind her and Rosie rolls her eyes. 'And now she has developed taste buds for seafood. Who knew!'

'Mum, I don't think Shelley really wants to hear my

whole life history!' says Rosie. 'How boring to have to listen to what a teenager used to like and dislike when they were three, seriously!'

Oh, just when I thought I was getting away with daring to comment about her, the teenage Rosie with attitude is back in the room.

Shelley looks like her mind is in another world.

'Are you okay, love?' I ask her. 'Did you enjoy your food? This must be one of your favourite places here, just to sit and feel the sun on your face, the cool crisp wine on your tongue and to look out onto the sea as the world goes by.'

But I may as well be talking Japanese. Shelley is elsewhere. Totally distracted.

'My Lily always ...' she says.

Then she stops. She takes a deep breath.

'Go on?'

'My Lily ... my Lily always loved fish fingers,' says Shelley and I do a double take. 'She would have eaten them for breakfast, lunch and dinner if I'd let her. Ketchup too, of course, lots of ketch—'

At that her voice breaks, as if it took all her energy just to tell that one simple anecdote.

'Lily?' I ask gently. 'Is that ... is that your daughter, Shelley?'

I dread to think what I am about to hear, but suddenly this poor woman's nervous energy now is beginning to make sense.

'That's what you called me last night on the sand

dunes, isn't it?' says Rosie in a whisper. 'You thought I was Lily?'

Shelley nods in reply, already in a state of despair.

'I'm sorry about that Rosie, but you're not the first girl I've mistaken for Lily,' she says. 'I just can't help but see her everywhere I go and it's killing me inside.'

Her eyes fill up and they dart around, looking anywhere but at her present company. Oh God.

No one can speak. I honestly don't know what to say. I put my hand out to reach hers but she pulls away and puts it up to cover her mouth.

'I'd forgotten how much she loved some foods until you said it,' she whispers, the tears now streaming down her face. 'It's funny the little things you forget until something triggers off a memory and then I have to realise all over again that she's gone.'

'Shelley, I am so, so sorry!' I say to her. 'You poor darling. All this time I've been talking about my own tales of woe and you've been going through your own hell. I am so sorry.'

'I knew I shouldn't be here,' she says, standing up and gathering her belongings in a hurry. 'I really should get home and stay on my own where I don't cause a fuss. Thank you both, thank you for lunch. I knew this was a bad idea. I'm not ready. I knew it.'

'You don't have to go, Shelley,' says Rosie. 'We haven't finished yet. If I'm being brave then maybe you can too?'

Her eyes continue to skirt around us and I follow them to notice the stares of other diners watching us from all corners of the patio and then to my horror they start to whisper at the commotion, looking directly at poor Shelley.

I overhear one saying *that's the lady whose daughter died so tragically when—*

'What the hell are you all staring at?' Shelley yells at them, in a very uncharacteristic outburst. 'Do you know how long you've been staring at me now for? Three years! Three long lonely years of being stared at! Yes, it's *me*, the Jackson lady who left her daughter for seconds and it went terribly wrong! Yes, it's me! Stare and stare and stare like you always do and whisper your own conclusions! Stare all you want but it won't help me or my pain! Nothing will so you can all feck off because nothing is going to make this easier or harder on me. Nothing!'

She turns away from us all and marches off, Merlin catching up alongside her with his stray lead scraping along the ground.

'Come on, Merlin,' I hear her mutter. 'Let's go home now.'

'Mum, go after her please,' says Rosie. 'You always know what to say. Please help her.'

I push back my shoulders. My daughter thinks I always know what to say and that fills me with the courage and strength to help Shelley. If Rosie thinks I can, then I can and I will.

'Shelley, you don't have to leave!' I call out after her. 'You were doing nothing wrong by being here! Please just stop! Listen to me!'

To my surprise she stops, but I realise it's not because I asked her to. It is because she can't physically walk any further and she collapses into my arms when I catch up with her, sobbing uncontrollably as she clings to me.

'I only went to answer the phone,' she says through her streaming tears. 'I told her to be careful! I told her not to go near the water even though it was just a shallow pond but she fell and hit her head and within minutes she was gone. She drowned, Juliette! She drowned in a shallow pond at her own home and everyone blames me. They say I shouldn't have left her and I know it was my fault. They're right. It was my fault.'

I gulp and a lump forms in my throat, so big that I am not sure I can speak to her. I can't imagine what she has been going through. She has lost her own child and she blames herself ... I am about to lose mine and though we are on opposite sides of that loss right now, it chokes me up to believe that this has really happened to her. How cruel! How bloody cruel!

'Shelley, Shelley,' I say into her hair when I manage to find the strength to speak. 'Look at me, please.'

She looks into my eyes and I shake my head.

'You made a mistake,' I tell her. 'Surely you've been told that before? A mistake! It's something we all do. We aren't perfect, none of us are. You can't go on like this. You have to learn to live again, do you hear me?'

'I'm losing him now too,' Shelley whispers to me, her voice breathy and desperate. 'Matt hasn't called me all morning and he normally does as soon as he wakes up.

He's had enough of me. Everyone has. I'm a wreck, Juliette. I don't deserve to be here. It's all my fault.'

I look over her head and up the street to where the shopfront of *Lily Loves* sits proudly and I shake my head in defiance.

'You are not a wreck! Look, Shelley,' I tell her. 'I don't want to talk to you about this here, out on the street with those nosey parkers almost dropping their teeth into their chowders as they watch, because their own boring lives aren't enough to occupy their gossip hungry souls. I swear, their mouths are so far wide open you could park buses in there, and it's not an attractive sight at all.'

She smiles at that, but just a little.

'That's better, now come on. Lift that chin up,' I tell her.

She doesn't, so I do it for her.

'Up!' I say.

'I can't go back over there,' she whispers, wiping her eyes. 'They all think I'm nuts. Matt thinks I'm nuts. I'm even more nuts than my mother-in-law and that's saying something.'

I link her arm and turn her around towards the restaurant.

'Oh yes, you bloody well can go back over there,' I tell her. 'We haven't had dessert yet and I don't do lunch in half measures, didn't I tell you so? I don't have too many lunches left do I? Now walk and talk and don't look their way if you don't want to. You did nothing wrong.

We are all perfectly entitled to have a public meltdown as and when we feel it, especially when we're going through what we both are. Let them stare. Life is too short for that shit, believe me. Chin up, Shelley. Up!'

We walk together back towards the restaurant's vast patio which I notice Merlin has made his way to already, back into the comfort of Rosie's grasp, who smiles at me with great pride when Shelley and I return to the table. She pets Merlin protectively and hushes him like a baby and I fill up in wonder at how the human spirit can stand together when in need. I could be wallowing in my own self-pity right now, I suppose, and I would have every God given right to, but I refuse to do so when I see someone else going through so much unnecessary pain.

My days here may be numbered, but Shelley's aren't and I want to make very sure that before I leave this place, she realises that her life is still worth living and that every single day we have here is a gift – we should always try to make a difference, however small. I may be the one who is dying, but she needs a reminder how to live and I'm going to make sure she does just that.

'Excuse me,' I say to the waiter on his way past our table, just loud enough for the earwigs beside us to hear. 'We'll have a bottle of your very finest, coldest champagne with three glasses and your dessert menu when you have a second, please.'

'Of course, madam,' he says in reply. 'A day of celebration for you three beautiful ladies?'

He is a charmer and a handsome one at that so I give him my most flirtatious smile, much to the amusement of Shelley and the embarrassment of my daughter.

'Yes indeed,' I reply to him with a bat of my eyelids. 'We are celebrating something very special.'

He waits for more, as does my company – not to mention the gossips at the next table.

'We are celebrating this beautiful sunny day in this most magnificent place. We are celebrating being alive and all that life has to offer,' I announce. 'Nothing more, nothing less and I think that's as good a reason to celebrate as any, don't you?'

He tilts his head and nods. In fact, he actually bows. Ha!

'I like your style,' says the waiter and a few moments later, when he returns with our drinks, we are raising our glasses together.

'To today and the joy of being alive to enjoy it,' I say to my daughter and my new friend, Shelley. 'Every day is a disco. Every day is an adventure girls, and don't you ever forget it.'

We clink our glasses and wipe away tears as we toast.

'You're my hero, Mum,' says Rosie, sipping her very first taste of real bubbly here in front of me. 'When I grow up I want to be just like you.'

I close my eyes and try to picture my baby girl all grown up, something that I will never get to experience and my throat tightens again. When I open my eyes, Shelley gives me the biggest smile she can manage under the circumstances, and then she squeezes my leg under the table like she knows exactly what I'm thinking.

'I'll drink to that,' she says and my heart fills up with a rush of love as I savour this precious moment. Rosie takes a photo as I raise my glass.

To her, I am a hero. Now, that is one memory I will want to take with me forever.

Shelley

'I'm so sorry, love. You weren't banking on this drama queen taking over your holiday, were you?' I say to Rosie later when we are back at their cottage after lunch. We had dessert just as Juliette promised and it was truly magnificent. I had the finest strawberry cheesecake with my champagne, and even though the stares of the locals dropped off (they got bored when I stopped reacting, just as Juliette predicted) it took me a while to relax again, but I managed to do just that and it was a wonderful afternoon in the end.

For the first time in a long time, I realise, I actually tasted my food today. I savoured the flavours of a seafood linguine, marvelled at the different sensations that a good meal in good company can bring. Maybe it's the bubbles, maybe it's that I needed to get that outburst out of my system, but I feel like I have crossed a bridge of some sort. A small bridge, but certainly a step in the right direction. Matt will be thrilled to bits that I managed to find companionship through an act of kindness on my part, and that I was brave enough to go with it and that despite that one hiccup, it has done wonders for me from the inside out.

After lunch, Juliette insisted I come with them to their cottage for a coffee rather than go back to my house alone and I didn't dare argue. The lightness I feel right now is a very welcome feeling indeed. Juliette is a force alright, but in the best possible way – I feel like someone is really trying to kick my ass in the right direction. Tough love from a stranger. Who'd have guessed?

'I like it that you're here with us,' says Rosie. 'And not just because of your dog, if that's what you're thinking. I think you're really cool.'

I raise an eyebrow.

'I don't believe you for a second. It's all about the dog,' I say to her as her face protests. 'And as for me being cool, ha! Is my face a mess? I should probably go and fix it up when the bathroom is free, shouldn't I?'

Juliette had raced straight for the bathroom when we reached the cottage door, claiming she was dying to go and asking me to pardon her pun, so I can just imagine how my face must look after my crazy meltdown earlier. I don't really wear much makeup these days, for no other reason than that I've totally lost interest in my appearance, but what I did have on must have worn off by now.

'Can I please do your make up for you?' Rosie asks me, her eyes like saucers at the thought. She already has her kit by my side before I have time to answer and I am in awe at the collection she has in front of her. 'I love doing makeup for Mum sometimes and even though she goes on that I use too much, I think she secretly loves letting me practise.'

'How many brushes exactly do you have?' I ask her. 'I think I might own three at the most but your collection is insane!'

'Twenty-seven,' she says, proudly. 'I study YouTubers all the time for tips and products and for every birthday or occasion my family know exactly what to get me. Makeup and brushes. Or Shawn Mendes stuff but I think I'm up to date with him right now.'

She tilts my head back and puts some cool cleanser on my face with a cotton pad and oh boy, but it feels good – across my forehead, around my temples, onto my cheeks and nose and chin as my eyes drop with relief. I am exhausted, I realise. Mentally exhausted with the all-consuming obsession with all things Lily and what might have been. I am physically exhausted too, rooted in the past in a state of misery and it is draining the very life and soul out of me.

But as usual, no matter how much I try to fight it, my thoughts go back to her.

This could have been my own daughter someday, treating me to a makeover. Telling me about all her products and the things she has learned online. A tear falls from my eye but Rosie doesn't mention it, if she notices. She just moves on to some moisturiser and something she calls primer and I find myself relaxing more and more under her touch.

'You could do this for a living,' I tell her from my dream-like state. 'You definitely have a magic touch.'

'Nah,' she says. 'There are far too many teenage makeup artist wannabes around for my liking. You only have to look on Instagram for them. I'll wait until I'm properly qualified, if you don't mind. I just enjoy it for now. I don't even know if I want to do this for a living. I think I might want to be a vet or a zoo keeper or maybe a midwife. I might like to deliver babies, yes. I just can't decide if it's humans or animal babies I prefer. It's all too much to think about sometimes.'

I do admire Rosie's ambition, even if she is a little confused. At fifteen I didn't know what I wanted for dinner, never mind what I wanted to do when I was older. At least she's considering her options.

'Tough job but a very rewarding one,' I tell her.

'Which? A zoo keeper or a midwife?' she asks me and then she bursts out laughing. 'I'm sorry but I'm just picturing me delivering a baby hippo for some reason. Sorry, I'm a bit of a weirdo. Just ignore me.'

I open my eyes and the joy in her face at her own joke does that thing again to my weary heart. A glow. I close my eyes again so she can continue.

'Well, exactly. I'd imagine both are rewarding and tough at the same time,' I tell her. 'It's so good to have some idea of where you want to go, and even if life takes you in the completely opposite direction, I do think it's all meant to be. Could you deliver a baby hippo do you think?'

'O-M-G! I would so panic and I'd probably call my mum!' says Rosie and then she stops what she is doing, dead.

I open my eyes.

'Keep going,' I whisper.

'I won't be able to call my mum though, will I?'

'Rosie, come on. Keep focused. Job in hand. I can't wait to see what you can do with an old hag like me.'

I hear her take a deep breath. She is such a brave little girl.

'I bet she's laid down on the bed for a rest,' she says. 'I'd better just check that she has in case she's been kidnapped or something.'

Rosie skirts down the hallway and back again within seconds satisfied that, yes indeed, her mum has taken a sneaky lie down.

'She gets tired so easily,' she says to me. 'I think it's probably her age as well as her sickness. She turned forty on Friday you know.'

At that I burst out laughing. She is winding me up and I know it.

'What's it like to be older?' she asks with a smirk, moving on to her foundation application.

'I beg your pardon?'

She giggles and so do I.

'Not that you're old or anything, like, but my mum is forty and that's pretty old,' she says. 'You don't look forty, though. I mean, neither does my mum but then it's hard to judge without her own hair. She used to look totally different, before the 'you know what'. But you definitely must be younger.'

'I'm thirty-five,' I tell her, with a smile. She really is making me laugh with how she is digging a hole for herself on this age conversation. 'I'm a whopping twenty years older than you are, imagine? I can still remember when I was fifteen so very clearly and I can tell you, I didn't have the makeup collection that you do. We didn't know what fake eyelashes were and fake tan was a luxury and something we made a mess of. You are an expert in all of this, believe me!'

She takes another big breath again.

'Do you think she'll die soon?' Rosie asks me in a whisper and I shut my eyes a little tighter, a little too tight for makeup application though she has stopped now, either in deep thought or planning her next move.

'I think it's good that none of us know when we are going to die exactly,' is all I can think to say, with my eyes still closed. 'Sometimes though, when you do get a warning through illness it means that you can perhaps do nice things for as long as you are fit to, before your time runs out. You know, make some lasting memories while you still can or carry out ambitions.'

I hope I'm saying the right thing.

'You didn't get a warning with Lily though, did you?' she asks me, and this time I do open my eyes. She is looking in her makeup case, what for I do not know, and even though my fight or flight intuition is challenging me to the max right now, I am not going to run away from this question. I will not have another meltdown. I will answer the young girl. I will face up to my demons.

'I didn't get any warning, no,' I tell her, matter of fact. 'I shouldn't have left her when I did, but I did. I never in a million years thought she would go near the pond but she did. It happened in seconds. Time waits for no one. When I got to her, it was too late. We never know when our time is up. That's just the way it goes.'

I say it like it's a script I have rehearsed in my head, a script from my bereavement counselling days, but these are words that I have never said aloud until now. Rosie looks back at me and I can see her face is so full of questions. Part of me wants her to keep going, to keep asking questions, to keep talking about Lily. She doesn't though, so I do the talking anyway as she applies my eye make up with another one of her special brushes.

'She was just three years old when she died,' I tell her. 'Yesterday would have been her sixth birthday and I would give anything in the whole world to have spent that day with her. I miss her every single second of my life. Do you remember when you were six, Rosie? I'm trying to imagine what she would have been like.'

'I don't remember much, sorry,' says Rosie. 'Oh wait, I do, yes.'

She laughs at the memory.

'We went ice skating for my birthday but I couldn't

do it so I huffed and sat on the benches while my friends glided around like they were on Dancing On Ice or something and I was so jealous,' she says, talking at the speed of light. 'Plus I was mortified because David Clarke was there and he was the most popular boy in the class and I fell slap bang on my bum on the ice as he skated past me, *and* he was holding hands with Patti Smart. Not that I blame him. Who wants a girlfriend who can't ice skate after all?'

I can't help but snigger.

'A girlfriend at six? Are you serious?'

'Well, yes, of course I'm serious,' she tells me. 'Do you think I'd lie about such things? I don't remember my seventh or my eighth birthdays so well, but my sixth birthday with David Clarke and when I fell on that ice, well ... that will live with me forever. Damaged for life, I was. Mind you, he isn't much to look at now so it was all a big blessing in disguise.'

Rosie expertly moves the brushes across my eyes and asks me to open and close them periodically which I do so obediently and I can't honestly believe I am here, in this cottage, with a teenager chatting to me about her life on a Sunday evening, when I'd normally be cooped up alone in the house with only Merlin to stroke, Matt to argue with or Eliza to avoid. I feel, dare I say it, a tiny bit more alive for it.

'My mother always threw the best birthday parties for me,' I tell Rosie and she smiles as she listens. 'My favourite one was the time we all went horse-riding and everyone wanted this one beautiful silver-grey mare called Sixpence but I got to ride her because I was the birthday girl. I think that was my best birthday ever. I had a blast.'

'That sounds like a good one,' says Rosie. 'Do you still ride horses then?'

'I used to,' I tell her. 'I haven't done so since ...'

'Since Lily died?' she says as if it's the most natural thing in the world to ask about.

'Yes,' I reply, but I can't repeat what she said. *Since Lily died.* 'Yes, you're right, Rosie. Not since then.'

'Would you come horse-riding with me tomorrow?' Rosie asks me. 'Look up, please.'

She applies mascara as I look up to the ceiling.

'Who, me? Horse-riding? Tomorrow?' I ask her. I get that same flutter inside that I got earlier when Juliette asked me to go to lunch.

'Yes, you,' she says. 'Horse-riding tomorrow. I haven't done it since I was about six or seven and I'd love to go riding on the beach if there's such a thing round here.'

'Well, yes, there's a beach obviously,' I tell her, finding it hard to think of tomorrow. 'And there are pony trek-king places obviously, but ...'

She waits for my answer but I simply can't give it. I can't think that far ahead. I don't do social activities these days, and I have to work my usual afternoon shift, don't I? Yes, that's it. I have to work. There is no way I can do this. Lunch almost tore me in two until Juliette gave me the strength to get through it and though I feel stronger for it, I don't think that I could master horse-riding on the beach. Could I?

'So, will you come?' she asks me again, and I can feel my heart beat a little faster at the thought of committing to something, to making plans outside of my work and my big white empty shell of a house.

'Do this.' She makes a shape on her mouth for me to imitate so that she can apply some lipstick and I sit there like a mannequin, doing exactly what I am told.

She holds up a mirror to my face and when I see my reflection, I have to take a moment. My goodness, I swear I am unrecognizable, but only in the best possible way. Her touch was subtle, like she knew exactly what I needed. A natural look, some light gold around my brown eyes and a soft blush on my cheeks that hasn't been there in, yes, you've guessed it, three years.

To my great delight and surprise, I don't feel guilty though, like I usually do when I think of taking any tiny steps to move on in my life after Lily. I feel something different, something I just cannot put my finger on right now.

'So do you like it or not?' asks Rosie 'Because my hand is getting sore holding up this mirror. You don't have to say you do if you don't. My friend Melissa is probably better. She has—'

'I love it, Rosie,' I whisper, and then I look up at her and I smile – not just a forced smile that I use for customers when I tell them an outfit is beautiful on them, or for Matt when he asks me if I enjoyed dinner, or for Eliza when she asks if I'm okay, or even for my dad when he tries to make jokes on the phone.

This is a real smile. I know it is because it is touching that feeling that I couldn't put a name to a moment ago. For the first time in a long time I don't feel stuck or stagnant or numb. I feel something more real. I feel *present*. I am in the here-and-now and it feels quite overwhelming, but in the best possible way.

'Thank you, Rosie,' I say to my teenage makeup artist. 'Thank you so, so much. You made me look a little more alive and that really means a lot to me.'

Rosie shrugs and packs up her makeup bag like it's no big deal, but to me, it really is.

'I suppose I should go check on Mum,' she says, and my heart jumps when I think of how long we have been chatting. I had totally forgotten about Juliette and her whereabouts. 'I bet she's fallen asleep like she always does after a glass of wine with her lunch. I'll be right back. Don't leave without saying goodbye though or Mum will be gutted.'

This little girl ... this precious little girl who has made me feel pretty on the outside has no idea how she and her beautiful mum have made me feel on the inside today. I could have walked away from that restaurant in a drowning state of tears. I could have wallowed in my pity as I made my way back up to my house, all alone, waiting on Matt to call so I could tell him about how horrible it was having everyone staring at me, blaming me for what happened to our daughter when they had no idea how tired or stressed I was that day or how quickly it all happened. He would have told me, no, begged me, to stop and to try and move on which would have angered me more and I'd have hung up and fallen asleep on top of the bed, just as Juliette is doing now, only with my scars wide open and the world blocked out.

Instead, here I am, feeling a little bit more alive for having a champion by my side today. Juliette, this stranger, and her strong and beautiful daughter have taken me under their wing through an overwhelming act of kindness. She made me walk right back to my seat today instead of running away, she made me face up to my fears and do something as simple as eating a dessert and actually taking the time to taste it.

Maybe Eliza is right with her predictions.

Maybe angels do walk around us after all.

Chapter 13

Juliette

Rosie wakes me with her mutterings about makeup and horse-riding and Shelley this and Shelley that and I realise, much to my embarrassment that I have fallen asleep while our visitor has been sitting out in the living room. Sweet Lord above, I only came in here to change my shoes, and thought I'd have a five-minute rest on top of the bed, but here I am almost an hour later being woken from a deep slumber that I hadn't planned.

'Please, don't wake her up on my account,' I hear Shelley call from down the hallway. 'I'm going to slip off now anyhow. I can't thank you enough for such a wonderful day, Rosie. Tell your mum I will see her again when she's up to it.'

Rosie throws up her arms and leaves the bedroom to stop Shelley from making a quick exit.

'You don't have to go,' I hear her say as I try to gather my thoughts and wake up from my slumber. 'You can watch a movie with us and we could have some pizza later? Come on, please stay!'

Check out my daughter being 'hostess with the mostest!' Shelley should feel very privileged indeed as it's not everyone Rosie likes having around, especially during mother and daughter time.

'I'm awake now,' I call out to Shelley who must be terribly confused as to what is going on. 'Just give me a few seconds. Maybe stick on the kettle, will you? I might choke if I don't get a cup of tea quickly.'

And on that note, I'm not just being cheeky. Those bubbles have gone to my head from earlier and I'm really thirsty right now. Plus I'm really tired. I could sleep for a million years right now but I'll have plenty of time to sleep when I'm dead, won't I?

'I'll make the tea,' says Rosie. 'Shelley, will you stay? Please?'

I make my way out into the narrow hallway of the cottage to see Shelley standing at the living room door, her handbag on her shoulder and her dog at her feet. She looks like she needs me to rescue her from Rosie's insistence that she stay for a cuppa. She also looks different, a lot brighter than before.

'Rosie fixed my makeup,' she says which explains her appearance, but for the first time since I laid eyes on her, I see an innocence shine through when she makes that simple statement about having her make up done. I see before me a girl who lost her mum at a young age too, someone who is longing for love from someone who won't judge her, but will gently nudge her in the right direction through her sea of grief.

'Well, don't you look just like a movie star,' I say to her with a smile, trying in the most superficial way to make her feel better. I long to hug her and tell her she is stronger than she thinks, but she is like a fragile little bird before me and I know she is doing so well to take these baby steps, already so much better than the frail, pitiful creature who served me in the boutique only yesterday.

'I think I'll slip off home now,' she tells me in a whisper, looking at her watch. 'It's almost six in the evening and I need to get ready for work in the morning, and I'm sure Matt will be in touch soon and I can't wait to tell him all about you two. You've really made me smile today. Thank you, Juliette. It's been a while since I've smiled, believe me.'

'And you've made a little girl in there a lot more content, so I've a lot to thank you for as well, Shelley,' I say to her. 'I think you've got a fan there. A little friend if you want one.'

She seems genuinely touched as she shrugs off her modesty.

'Well, I am very honoured if that's the case,' she says to me, her beautiful face breaking into a smile.

'You deserve to smile a whole lot more,' I tell her. 'You deserve to love and be loved and experience all the good things in this world. Life is good, you know that, Shelley. I don't think I realised just how much more there is I want to do in this life until I was told that I can't, so I plan to pack in as much as I can until I, quite literally, drop. Don't stop living before your time is up.'

Shelley looks at the ground and then back at me.

'You're a remarkable woman, Juliette,' she says to me. 'I don't think I've ever met anyone like you before. You are one in a million, but I'm sure you've been told that before. If I only had half your strength and positivity.'

'Ah, stop,' I say to her, feeling my cheeks blushing. 'I have my meltdown moments too, don't you worry. Plus I've had more than a few hard lessons recently myself and I suppose it all depends on how we react to the crap we are dealt with. No one gets it easy. None of us are getting out of here alive, so we may as well grab it by the horns while we can.'

I walk towards her but then decide to keep my distance as I get the impression Shelley doesn't do hugs that often and I don't want to scare her off, even though I think a good strong hug would do her the world of good.

'I'll take Merlin home and keep working on getting my life back together,' she tells me, just as Rosie announces tea is ready in the kitchen. 'Thank you so much. You have moved mountains for me today.'

'Can you please stay for tea?' asks Rosie, but I do think that Shelley's time with us has come to an end, for today anyhow.

'I'll catch you both tomorrow maybe?' she says. 'I have to work in the shop but after that, you know where I am. In fact, I'll give you my number.'

She takes out a business card for *Lily Loves* from her handbag and her hand trembles as she gives it over. This is a big step for her, I can tell. Is this what it's like in life after death? Is this the empty shell I am going to leave behind in my daughter? I desperately hope not.

'We'll give you a call and you're more than welcome to join us anytime for breakfast, lunch, dinner, whatever,' I say to her, trying to lift her spirits by giving her something, anything, to take us up on. She looks like she might cry as she purses her lips and nods her head in response.

'And Merlin too, of course,' says Rosie. 'I'd love to go horse-riding someday this week like I mentioned before if you're up for it. Mum hates horses and it would be nice to have the company of someone who actually gets it.'

'I do not indeed hate horses!' I correct my daughter. 'My goodness, you're making me sound like Cruella de Vil! I am a bit *afraid* of horses, that's all, but I certainly don't hate them.'

Rosie rolls her eyes and mouths to Shelley. 'She hates them. She pretends she's allergic. Swear.'

'I'll text you my number now so you can give us a shout if you ever feel like witnessing my great hatred for horses,' I tell Shelley. 'Can I call you a taxi or are you okay to walk? At least it's nice out.'

'A taxi around here?' she laughs. 'I'd be home before you could explain the directions. It was such a lovely evening, seriously. You have no idea how much you have lifted my weary spirits.'

'And you mine,' says Rosie, and I gulp, wondering just exactly how much my daughter knows about my reason for choosing to come here to find her father without me telling her as yet. Maybe I will tell her tomorrow, the whole truth and nothing but the truth. But for tonight, it's movies and chilling with my girl after an interesting day. And for me, you can't get any better than that.

Shelley

I walk through the village of Killara with my dog by my side and my head tilted just a little bit higher than it has been in a long, long time. It's a gorgeous evening and I stop at the shop window of *Lily Loves* and take in all of its greatness, allowing myself just a little moment of glory on how far I have come.

Everyone thought I would close the shop after Lily died and I guess I would have had great reason to, but Eliza stepped in and found me an assistant in Betty – an eccentric older lady from Limerick who was looking for something to keep her mind active and her eye for fashion alive. I did all the ordering from home for a long time while Betty, who in the early days I rarely had to meet face to face, kept things ticking over on the shop front while I took my time getting back on my feet again after what happened.

I'm still easing myself in to my work and it has been a life saver really to be able to focus on delivering the very best in vintage bargains for my ever-growing fan base of customers.

I work a maximum of three hours a day in the shop itself, afternoons mainly. I couldn't dream of getting out of bed and organised any earlier than that now that I don't have my baby girl's sweet voice to cry out to me first thing, insisting that she wants her breakfast and that her favourite teddy, La, wants hers too. I have no idea where La ever came from but she was a humble little thing, just a pink ball of fluff with two ears and a cute nose that my daughter took everywhere with her every day for the short three years of her life. La of course is packed away in a zipped-up case, under Lily's bed and I don't think I will ever be able to look at her, or touch her or smell her again.

'Shelley! Oh my goodness I thought that was you! How good to see you!'

Oh no. I close my eyes. Oh please, no. Merlin stirs from beside me and I get him to sit at ease.

I inhale sharply and my vision blurs when I turn to meet the voice of one of my best friends, Sarah – the one who left me the flowers yesterday and the one who I so carefully avoid every day of the year in case I take a step backwards when I see her with her children. Her six-year-old daughter stands beside her and she is pushing a toddler boy, her son Toby in a stroller. I think I am going to be sick.

'Th-thank you for the flowers yesterday,' I say, but it doesn't even sound like my own voice when it finally comes out. 'How is – how are – I'm sorry I was just in a dream world there staring in at the shop window. How are you?'

Sarah tilts her head to the side and nods, placing her hand on my shoulder.

'I heard Matt's away,' she says to me, with genuine concern. 'Look, I know you're taking things at your own pace and you're quite right to do that, but is there anything I can do? Anything at all?'

I glance down at her daughter Teigan who was Lily's best friend since the day she was born. Teigan has no idea who I am of course, it has been so long since I dared set eyes on her and I don't think I am ready to do so yet. She is licking an ice cream that is almost bigger than her face and her little brother is covered in white also, both of them so far removed from life and all its cruelties which is exactly how they should be of course.

'There's nothing really,' I tell Sarah, but I can't meet her eye. 'I'm just heading home now to feed Merlin here and have an early night. I'm okay, I swear to you.'

'Oh, Shelley, are you sure?'

I nod unconvincingly, tucking a strand of hair behind my ear and still not looking her way.

'I'm actually a tiny bit better than I was yesterday,' I say to the pavement, 'and the day before and the day before that. One day at a time as my dad keeps reminding me. I'll get there, Sarah, but thank you.'

I glance at Sarah who looks like her own heart is breaking for me. I want to tell her about Juliette and

Rosie and their connection to Skipper but I don't think it's my place to say all of that. I am nearly sure that Sarah, a native of Killara and one of Matt's oldest friends long before we became close, once was a girlfriend of the enigma that is Skipper. I say enigma simply because his name seems to crop up so often and everyone who mentions him seems to have a story to tell about him though he died so young, but none more than my new friend Juliette who has a living piece of him all to herself.

'Call me when you're ready,' says Sarah when her children start to get fed up and the conversation, as usual with me these days, is going nowhere. 'No pressure, that's what I always say to you, but you know where I am. We could go out on the boat like we used to, just you, Matt, Tom and I?'

We really did used to have such fun sailing around the Atlantic coast when we hadn't a care in the world. Tom, Sarah's husband, was another of Matt's sailor friends and they always wound Matt up that he was the only person in Killara to never have found his sea legs. Matt is the first to admit that he prefers dry land to the wilds of the ocean, unlike most of the locals around here.

'Thanks, Sarah, maybe we will one day again,' I say to her, reaching into my purse. 'Here, Teigan, buy your little brother a treat someday soon but not right now as I can see you're busy with that ice cream. Get yourself something really nice for your—'

I hand the little girl a ten Euro note and I get that

choking feeling in my throat that tells me I'm about to forget how to breathe very soon.

'Get something for—'

Her birthday, I want to say. She was born only days after my Lily so I know it has to be soon but I can't say it. I just can't.

'Are you okay, Shelley? Honestly, you've gone a funny colour. Shelley?'

I can see Sarah, just about, but my vision is blurring even more now as an anxiety attack beckons. The money drops to the ground and I feel Sarah's hands on my shoulders, propping me up.

'Shelley,' says another familiar voice. 'Are you alright?'

I slide back into consciousness and then out of it again when I hear the unmistakable voice of Juliette calling me, or am I imagining it? Am I longing for it?

'Juliette?'

'Shelley, it's me! You forgot your phone. What happened?'

I focus on Juliette's friendly, warm face and I manage a smile but I notice how the two women in front of me share worried glances.

'What happened? Is she okay?' asks Juliette, and poor Sarah looks bewildered.

'I'm Sarah, her friend, an old friend, and I just stopped to say hello. I'm not sure what happened. One minute we were chatting, the next thing ...'

Juliette waits, as do I. Then Sarah whispers, covering her daughter's ears

'You called her Lily,' she says, her face crumpling in sorrow. 'You kind of ... you didn't hurt her, Shelley, it's okay.'

She holds her daughter close. Poor Teigan. Merlin whimpers at my feet.

'Don't worry, I'm sure it was all a bit of a misunderstanding,' says Juliette. 'I'll look after it from here, Sarah and like you said, I'm sure Shelley didn't mean any harm.'

I called her Lily and I grabbed her but I only wanted to give the child some money to treat herself and her brother, just like people used to do to me when I was out walking with my mother when I was little. I didn't mean any harm!

Sarah shakes her head in deep sadness and pity and nods at Juliette who links my arm and leads me away from my shop, further up the hill towards my house. I feel drunk but I know I'm not. I am so unsure of what just happened.

'I was going to suggest you stay with us tonight but I'll walk you home,' says Juliette. 'Your phone's been ringing – it was under Rosie's makeup bag of all places.'

I watch Sarah and her children scuttle down the hill into the village, her arm protectively around Teigan as she stoops down to whisper to her.

'Maybe when we get you tucked up in bed you can text your husband and tell him you are going to be okay, Shelley,' says Juliette. 'And you *are* going to be okay, Shelley, because I am going to make damn sure of it.'

Juliette

We walk, arm in arm along the coastal hill that leads up to Shelley's luxurious home in the distance, at the top of the little village with the still of the ocean to our left and green fields to our right. The lighthouse twinkles out on the sea and windy stone walls guide us along the busy little road that takes us out of the village and leads further south along the magnificent Wild Atlantic Way if we were to follow them that far.

I inhale the sea air, feeling like I am breathing in pure undiluted magic. How I wish I had more time to live in a place like this. If there is one thing that cancer has taught me, it's to appreciate absolutely everything I see, touch, hear and feel. The smell of the fish and chip shop; the cry of the gulls above our heads and the feeling of space and freedom and being on holiday. Heaven, pure heaven, but to Shelley, she is still going through hell.

'What happened?' she asks me and I can only tell her what I saw.

'You stumbled, that's all,' I tell her. 'You were giving the little girl something and you stumbled towards her and you – well, you must have mistaken her for Lily.'

'Money,' she says. 'I was just giving her money but all I could think of was Lily, all I could see was Lily. Teigan was Lily's best friend and it's her birthday in a few days' time. I must have frightened the life out of her. Poor Teigan.'

'That's enough,' I tell her. 'That lady was your friend, right?'

She nods. 'Yes. My best friend around here. We used to do so much together.'

'Well, she's bound to understand what you must be feeling right now,' I tell her. 'Anyhow, you needn't waste time worrying about such minor things. Send Sarah a quick sorry and it will all be over and done with. Time is too precious to beat yourself up over nothing. Life is too short for shit, that's my motto and don't you ever forget it. No shit from now on!'

At this, Shelley starts to giggle, and then she stops in her tracks. I let go of her.

'Why do you care so much about me, Juliette?' she asks me. 'And more to the point, why do I let you care? What is it about you that makes me let you in so easily?'

I have no idea how to reply. I have no idea why I care so I can't answer her.

'Well ... I don't know, you helped me by helping my daughter,' I say to Shelley in my bid to explain. 'Or maybe it's just human nature to want to look out for someone in distress? Maybe I'm just being human?'

Shelley isn't overly convinced.

'But I am letting you,' she says, her eyes wild and full of wonder. 'I haven't let anyone into my life in three years, never mind a stranger, and then you and your daughter come along and we're best buddies all of a sudden and I feel better than I have in such a long time. I'm not knocking it or pushing you away, I just think it's all a bit—'

'Wonderful?' I suggest. 'Believe me, when you don't have time to sweat the small stuff, you tend to focus on the positive acts of kindness rather than turning a blind eye or pushing someone away just because you can.'

She looks away from me and strands of her long, wavy hair blow in the breeze.

'I have pushed so, so many people away who tried to help me,' she confesses, her face full of worry. 'I've been deliberately pushing everyone away, even my husband.'

'I've been doing that too, so that's another thing we have in common.'

'You've been pushing away your husband?'

'Yes, my husband, Dan,' I tell her. 'My darling husband Dan turned to the comfort of booze when I first was diagnosed a few years ago. I couldn't bear to see him cry and beg for things to go back to how they used to be, so two weeks ago when I knew my dreaded next appointment was around the corner and the worst was yet to come, I asked him to leave.'

Shelley gasps. 'No, Juliette, you didn't?'

'I did,' I nod. 'I pushed him away because I can't watch him in so much pain, and he can't watch me in pain, but boy, I miss him every single day, Shelley. My heart is aching for him. Does that make me a hypocrite? I suppose it does, in a way.'

'How do you mean?' asks Shelley.

'Well, here I am telling you to live your life to the full while you still can and meanwhile back at the ranch I'm pushing away the man I love more than anyone just to make it easier on us both, when in reality it's not making it easy at all. It's making it worse, even though I am doing a good job of denying it to myself.'

'Maybe we just came along at the right time to teach each other a few good old life lessons then?' suggests Shelley. 'Maybe we both need to realise what's important before it's too late?'

'I think we have,' I say to this darling girl who is living each day swallowed up with grief and sadness, though she longs to live and to love again. There is hope for her though. I can see it and I am determined to make her see it too before I leave this place.

Shelley leans on the stone wall to gather herself and I don't wish to hurry her but I think of Rosie back in the cottage waiting on me to start our movie night.

'Are you sure you don't want to spend the evening with us rather than being on your own?' I ask her. 'You do know you are very welcome, but I think I've pushed you enough today, so don't feel pressurised.'

'Gosh, no,' she says, shaking her head and fixing her jacket. 'I can walk from here. I'll go home and ring Matt and I have old Merlin here to look after. Go back to your daughter and cherish every moment with her while you still can, Juliette. And maybe give your hubby a call?'

And in that moment as we stand in the evening breeze with the sea down below us, I realise the intense irony of each of our situations. Shelley would give everything to have what I have had – some time to cherish, albeit cut short, with my only child, and I would give everything to have what she has – a life to look forward to and all the time in the world to do it.

'We'll see you again,' I say to her, reaching out my hand and touching her arm. She smiles, just a little, but it's always good to see her smile.

'I hope so,' she says, and then I watch her walk away, a sad and lonely figure with so much to live for, but who feels she has nothing left to live for at the same time. I see a flicker out at the lighthouse in the distance and a gust of wind blows through my hair. Shelley stops and looks out towards it too and then walks away again, her head bowed and her heart sorry. I really hope I can make her see that her daughter up in heaven is urging her to smile again.

Chapter 14

Juliette

MONDAY

'Please, I swear Mum, just let me call them and see if they can fit us in. It will only be for one hour at the most. You can watch, you and Merlin. He'll keep you company and it's a gorgeous day outside. Come on. Please.'

Rosie sits on the edge of my bed and for the first time in my whole life , I want to gag my darling daughter.

'Five minutes,' I tell her. 'Five minutes of complete silence from you is all I ask and I will contemplate it. Please.'

She sighs from the very tips of her toes and makes a face that would turn milk sour but I don't react. It is 7am. She never sees 7am on a school morning, never mind on a holiday morning so there is no way I am going to jump to her every whim at the crack of dawn when we are meant to be on a relaxing break. She wants to go horse-riding, but I didn't manage to arrange it as today was all about taking the boat around the Cliffs of Moher. Apparently there is no better way to see them than from the sea itself, and maybe I am being selfish, but I really want to feel what it's like to be out there on that ocean, just like Skipper used to be every day.

My phone rings, disturbing my third minute of contemplation. Oh no, it's Dan. I can't answer. I tried to talk to him last night but there was no reply and now that he is calling me back I am afraid to hear his voice in case it sets me back. But I can't not answer. Shit.

'Hello?'

'At last, Juliette! God, it's good to hear your voice at long last. I left my phone in the car last night like a bloody idiot. Are you okay?'

Jesus.

'Hello Dan, yes, I'm okay. How are you?'

I don't need to ask how he is. It's 7am on a Monday morning so I know exactly how he is going to be. Hungover or still slightly drunk.

'Is it true?'

Is what true, I long to ask? Where on earth do I start with what is true these days? About my illness? About where I have run away to and not told him? What?

'What have you heard?' I ask him, hoping it isn't about my health. There is no way I am going to tell him my days are finally numbered first thing in the morning and certainly not on the phone.

I swallow. I can feel his pain from here. I can see him rock and squint as my admission to the extent of my illness hits him hard in the heart.

'Helen told me,' he says. 'I spoke with her yesterday and she told me the truth. What about Rosie? How is she? Did you tell her? I should be there with you when you do. Jesus, Juliette!'

I shake my head. Oh Lord, what am I *doing* here? Barry Island would never have raised such questions or caused such heartache for any of us. I feel so far away from him and I know he is right. I shouldn't have run away without telling him the full story.

'I wish I could tell you it isn't true,' I tell him. 'But it is, Dan, and I promise when I get back on Saturday we can have some time together. I want to make our last days the best days ever, love. We can see this through, me and you, I know we can.'

'Are you going to tell her about her father and his connections there?' he asks, his voice choked up with worry. 'Why Juliette? Why would you really think you need to leave her with the burden of a man who might not even want to know she exists when she has so much to deal with already?'

Where on earth do I start to explain to my recently estranged, darling, lovely, gentle, troubled husband that no matter what my intentions were when it comes to Rosie's biological father, I have hit a brick wall; that any slight glimmer of hope I may have had in the back of my mind, no matter how foolish it may seem, has come to nothing.

'He isn't here, Dan, so you don't need to worry about any of that,' I whisper. 'He never really was here after all, so it's one less thing for you to be concerned about. We will be home soon and we can have a good long chat about everything, about Rosie's future, and about yours too.'

I want to say 'and we'll all live happily ever after' but of course that is never going to happen.

'Please don't break her heart, Juliette by telling her about him now.'

He sobs down the phone and my lip trembles for the hurt I know he is feeling right now. I have been with this handsome, strong, magnificent man for many years and he devoted every inch of his heart to me and Rosie, so to think of me being here as I face my last days on this earth and not spending time with him must be the ultimate blow.

'Can I speak to Rosie?' he asks and my stomach leaps. I don't want her to hear him cry. Not now when she is in such good form.

'She's asleep,' I say to him. 'Maybe later?'

'She isn't asleep,' he says and he laughs at my attempt to brush him off. 'She sent me a text half an hour ago. Jesus, Jules what on earth are you playing at taking her there when you are so unwell? You should be here, with me so we can talk about what's going on. We could be making plans and just, just talking and – why can't things just be like they used to be? Why?'

Ah, shit, shit, shit. I am crying now and so is he.

'Why don't you come here to us, Dan,' I tell him. 'Sober up and come here and be with us and we'll try and make it like it used to be just the three of us against the world.'

'Go there? To Ireland?'

'Yes.'

'No, no, no, no no,' he rambles. 'No, I don't want to interfere on your holiday and I don't think I could stand being there, knowing that—'

He lets out a huge sigh and I can just see his hand-some smile in my mind when I close my eyes. Drunk or not, I freakin' love this man and as I spend my last days on this earth, I want to be with him and my daughter for every second but I need him to be straightened up for my last days. That may be selfish of me to insist on that, but it's the only thing I have left to insist on.

'This is killing me too, Juliette,' he says. 'But you don't need to hear that, sorry. I just want to see you. I want to touch you. I don't want you to die.'

He is sobbing heavily now, so I know we are on the wrong path with this conversation.

'Where are you?' I ask him. 'Are you still on Emily's couch? You should just go home and wait for us there. Go home to our own bed. I won't be long. I'll be home soon.'

'You don't need to care about me,' he says. 'You have enough to worry about. I know that's why you pushed me away in the first place. I'm not what you need. I'm a burden, an extra stress that you and Rosie don't need right now.'

'I didn't ever say that,' I say, as my hand automatically goes to my mouth and the tears roll down my face. 'I just wanted to protect you and I need you to be able to face up to me not being here. It's out of our hands, Dan. I don't have very long left.'

I picture him, the handsome, strong, decisive man I used to know and I long for him to show me that person again. How did it come to this? When did we drift so far apart that we lost sight of our sparkle and charm and strength and all the things that made us fall in love?

'I need you to try and be strong for us all,' I say to him. 'I need you Dan. I need you to be strong.'

'I'm going to get better and so are you,' he tells me. 'I promise. We are going to fix all of this. I am going to fix it all and we will have our old life back, just give me time, Juliette. Can you give me time? We'll build that big house by the sea and we'll take those holidays and Rosie can have a dog and a pony and anything she wants and ...'

I hear Rosie singing in the kitchen and I'm thankful that she is out of earshot for what I am about to say.

'But I don't have time anymore, Dan,' I whisper to him firmly. 'You have to understand that, babe. There is no time for all of that now. I wish there was, but my time is almost up.'

'Don't say that, Juliette,' he says. 'There's bound to be something—'

'There's nothing,' I tell him. 'We don't have a happily ever after, Dan but what we do have is the chance to

184

make our last days count and make those as happy as we can possibly be. Now, sort yourself out and I'll see you on Saturday when we get back. Please, get some sleep. Please, darling. You sound like you need it.'

I hang up the phone and lean back on my pillow, inhaling and exhaling slowly as I embrace this over-whelming sadness. Dan doesn't seem to be able to grasp the harsh reality of all this. We don't have a future anymore. My future is right here, right now so I don't have time to linger and mope. I need to make every second count instead of dwelling on my grief and allowing each day to be a waiting game. I will not wait for this to happen. I'm determined to enjoy every second for as long as I can.

Shelley

When a fifteen-year-old girl bounds into your shop, begging you to take her horse-riding because her dying mother is too tired, or too allergic, or too whatever to join her, what on earth are you supposed to say? I can't exactly say no to that, can I, no matter how much it petrifies me to even think about it?

'Didn't your mum say she wanted you to go out on the boat today?' I ask Rosie, whose face is perfectly made up just as mine was yesterday. She looks the least likely person I have ever seen to go horse-riding, with makeup like that plastered on her face.

'She was meant to but they can't take us today and all we've done all day is walk the beach! I've never walked so much in my entire life.'

'Does she know you're here?' I ask her. I look at the clock. It's just after four and I have only had two customers today so I suppose I could shut up shop early. It's a beautiful day outside and I tend to find that on those days, most tourists and locals like to flock to the sea rather than the shops, not that I blame them.

'She warned me under no circumstances to come here and ask you,' says Rosie, 'but to be honest, I can't sit in that cottage for any longer watching daytime TV or trying to get phone signal when it just isn't happening. So, what do you think? Horse-riding? Me and you? Date?'

She fingers through the rails of clothing as she talks to me, her head tilted to the side as she chews gum and again I get that awful flashback feeling to when I was her age, so innocent to the way my world was about to be tipped upside down around me, never to be the same again.

'Well, you aren't going to go horse-riding in those clothes?' I say to her, taking in her long loose sweater, shorts and flip flops. 'You'd better go home and get changed.'

She almost jumps out of her skin with excitement.

'So, we can go then? O-M-G you are like the coolest person ever! I actually love you right now! Thank you!'

'Meet me back here at five,' I tell her. 'I need to make

a phone call to make it happen but it shouldn't be a problem. Deal?'

'Deal, total deal!' she says, and she bounds out of the shop into the sunshine and I smile from the tips of my toes at the joy such a simple gesture has given her. That poor little girl. The happier she can be over the next few weeks, the better.

But before I can make that happen, I have to face another of my own fears. I have to step out of my comfort zone and reach out to the people of Killara who I have hidden from for so long; but as much as it frightens me, I don't think for a second that they will let me down.

Matt calls me when I am coming out of the shower, back at the house where I have laid out my jodhpurs and a t-shirt on the bed.

'You're going where?' he asks, and just like Rosie, the joy in his voice is tangible.

'I'm going horse-riding on the beach,' I tell him and I can't help but smile in return. 'I know, I know, don't die of shock. I am actually doing something that doesn't involve my work or you or this house or the dog.'

'Wow,' he says to me 'I am seriously, seriously over the moon with that! Fantastic! Amazing, Shell!'

He lets out a noise of celebration that sounds a bit like a 'woo hoo' and I tell him to calm down already. It's not really that big a deal. Okay, it is, but still.

'Who are these people?' he asks me. 'Where do I send them some champagne and flowers for making my wife do something fun at last? At last! Lunch yesterday, horse riding today?'

I sit on the edge of the bed and check the clock radio on my bedside locker and realise I only have ten minutes to get back to the shop and meet Rosie.

'I'll explain all to you later,' I say to him. 'It's a long story and I really have to rush but it'll be worth the wait. I've to meet Rosie at five and it's almost that already.'

'Ah Shell, you said that to me last night when you were too tired to talk,' he says and I feel so bad for not taking time to explain. 'Are they old friends of yours? Your long-lost family? Who?'

'It's all good,' I say to him, trying to put on my socks as I cradle the phone under my ear. 'I mean it, it's worth waiting on to hear the full story and you will never believe it. I'll call you straight after and fill you in. You are going to love it.'

'Alright, alright go and have some fun,' he tells me. 'And send some pics. I need to see the evidence of this, okay?'

I put the phone on loudspeaker and drop it on the bed as I squeeze into my jodhpurs. It has been a long time and thank goodness I haven't put on any weight. If anything, they're a bit loose on me but that's exactly what I expected.

'Did you have a good day?' I ask him. 'How's France?'

'I'll tell you all about that later too,' he replies. 'Now go quickly before you're stood up. I am so freaking happy right now. I love you Shell.'

I gulp as he says those words that he has been so patient with, waiting all the time for me to say it back to him but I can't know or feel if I love anyone when I don't even love myself anymore. I may be taking very tiny baby steps right now but I've a long way to go and I don't want to lie to him by saying it just for the sake of it. I want to learn to love him again like he deserves to be loved and I won't say it until I know that that's absolutely true. I want to feel it.

'I know you do,' I tell him. 'I'll call you later and I'll send you some evidence. Enjoy dinner with Bert! Tell him I said hi!'

The slight pause illustrates his disappointment and I want to kick myself for being so cold and so honest. I can't say 'I love you' back, I just can't. I try to but the words stick in my throat. I can't say it until I know I really mean it from my very core and although I am starting to finally 'feel' again, I still have quite a bit to go.

'I'll tell Bert you said hi,' Matt says to me. 'Have fun, babe. You deserve it more than anyone I know.'

And at that he is gone. I have shut him out once more.

I need to go quickly and meet Rosie.

Chapter 15

Juliette

'I'm sorry it didn't work out today for the boat trip, honey, but I've got it all arranged for tomorrow. We could maybe take a walk around the village and—'

'Mum, I do not want to walk around the village. I am so sick of walking, I'm sorry.'

Oh no, it's another one of those days when nothing, and I mean nothing, I say is going to be right.

'Well, how about if we go swimming?'

Rosie busies about the cottage, only half-listening to what I have to say.

'It's okay, Mum, I really have to go,' she tells me, pulling on a pair of boots that don't belong to her. 'Now do you want to come with us or what?'

'Where are you going? With whom? Who owns those boots?'

She shrugs. 'Dunno who owns them but they fit me perfectly. I found them amongst all that water-sports stuff by the back door. And I already told you, Mum! I'm going horse-riding. With Shelley. You coming? Come on, please. You will enjoy it!'

Wait a minute, wait a minute. I don't remember being told any of this. I remember it being suggested, but I didn't realise it was actually arranged.

'How on earth did this come about?' I ask my daughter.

'Mum! I told you!'

'Ah, Rosie are you sure Shelley's up for this?' I say to her. 'I know it would be good for her to go horse-riding but is she okay with it?'

Rosie stops what she's doing and lets out a deep sigh that I swear, sounds like it came from her ankles.

'Why do you *always* have to be so negative?' she asks me. 'It's only horse-riding for goodness sake! It's not like I asked her to go to the moon or anything. And I did tell you! You just weren't listening or else you forgot. You're always forgetting stuff these days.'

Well, I don't really have an answer to that, do I? Maybe she did tell me. Maybe I did forget. Michael did say that I would become more and more forgetful as the tumour in my brain grows.

I try to act normal which is never easy around a 'know-it-all' teenager, let alone when you have a terminal illness which makes you forgetful.

'As long as Shelley is happy to go along with you?' I say to her. 'I mean, who owns the horses? Are they Shelley's?'

I would not be one bit surprised if Shelley did keep

horses. The woman practically lives in a palace though I didn't see any stables when we were up at her house. Not that that means anything, she might keep them elsewhere.

'I have no idea how she pulled it off but she is meeting me at five at the shop so I'd better hurry. Come on, Mum! It will be fun!'

'Hmm, okay but—'

'Look,' she says to me. 'It's like this. You have about two minutes to move it and come with us or else sit here and look at these four walls and I don't know about you but I'm getting cabin fever sat here all day, so come on.'

I am being bossed around by a teenager and I actually quite like it, mad as it may seem. This is what so many people wish away – these hormone-fuelled, mood swing years of slamming doors, hiding in bedrooms and throwing tantrums; one minute she was a toddler with attitude, now I've fast forwarded to swear words and developing bodies and all the rest. I want to witness all of these magical, unpredictable moments from now on. I want to enjoy every single time she tells me she hates me, or that I'm a weirdo, or that I'm so not as cool as I think I am and any other insult she might throw my way. I want to see her on that horse, her face determined and bold, fearless with innocence as she gallops along the water front and most of all I want to hear her laugh and laugh and even if I can't be a part of that experience directly, I will happily sit on the side-lines and cheer her on every step of the way.

I take a picnic rug that is folded in a basket in the living room and grab my coat. The sun is still in the sky but as the evening sets in, I know how the weather can change in this part of the world. Rosie is already gone ahead of me, eager to beat the clock to meet Shelley in case she might miss this golden opportunity she has been so hoping for since she got here.

Shelley

Sarah meets us at the beach as promised with her horse box in tow and when I see her I don't have to say a word about what happened with Teigan yesterday. She puts her arm around me and squeezes me in, kissing my forehead and I close my eyes and drink in her familiarity, her perfume, the woman I used to turn to for every little question I had about motherhood or marriage or life in a village that I was still learning to call home.

'You're doing great,' she says to me. 'Now, introduce me to your friends, please?'

I can feel my shoulders straighten with pride as I introduce Sarah properly to Juliette and, of course, to Rosie who has eyes only for what is in the back of the horse box. Even poor Merlin, who I hold on a lead has to take a back seat to this excitement. There is a cool, light breeze in the air which is perfect riding weather and I can feel the adrenaline pumping through my veins at the thought of whisking along the coastline and letting the sea air blow my troubles away.

I was right about my friends rising to the challenge of making this happen for Rosie. It took just one quick call to Sarah who was only too glad to take time out of her own busy schedule and arrange for the horses and all the gear we're going to need here. Life in a small community can nourish you and prop you up when the chips are down and until now I have chosen to see only the other side of it; I have focused on the gossips, on the claustrophobic stares, on the smothering whispers from the shadows but from now on I choose to see the good in people and I feel much better for it already. I want to make this holiday as magical I can for Juliette and Rosie and I feel enriched that I can lean on my neighbours to make it happen.

'How long are you here for?' Sarah asks Juliette. It must be the most common ice breaker in the world when we meet a tourist or visitor.

'Seven days in total,' says Juliette. She looks tired today, a little darker under the eyes than she was when she first came into my shop on Saturday. 'I can't believe it's Monday already and we still have so much to do!'

'Well, if you need any advice or tips on what to do raound here when it rains, and it does rain here a lot, don't be afraid to call on me. I'm a born and bred Killarian, through and through.'

And Sarah is telling the truth. She is warm and friendly and spends most of her life outdoors, be it trekking with her ponies around the winding roads, or camping out with her kids under the stars, or spending time out on the sea with her husband, Tom. I take an inward breath, remembering the Skipper connection and how much she would know about him should Juliette wish to ask but I bite my tongue for now. It's not my place to bring it up and besides, this excursion is all about Rosie.

'You all set?' I ask her and her glowing cheeks and wide grin means she doesn't have to answer.

'You're a superstar for arranging this,' says Juliette, expertly taking Merlin's lead to allow me to help get the horses sorted. 'You are way ahead of me right now on brownie points with my daughter.'

My heart aches for her. It isn't a competition, I want to say to her, but I can tell that she is slightly pinched at how she can't get stuck in and do something as simple as horse-riding with her daughter. Once again, Juliette and I are on parallel levels of emotion as I think of how easily this would have become a way of life for me and Lily. We would have spent most of our time on this beach and probably taken it for granted. Knowing now what I do, and seeing Juliette long for more time with her daughter, I will never take anything in this life for granted again.

'I haven't done this in a few years,' I say to Juliette, trying to make her feel better, 'so I'll probably not live up to Rosie's expectations, but it's all just a bit of fun. Now, Rosie, which of these two fine beasts do you fancy?'

We all take a moment to admire Sarah's horses who,

next to her children, are her ultimate pride and joy.

'This is Neptune,' says Sarah, stroking the nose of her shiny brown mare who she has had for as long as I have known her. 'And this rascal is Dizzy. I think you'll like him, Rosie. He's full of fun and he much prefers young people to us oldies.'

'Speak for yourself,' I joke with Sarah and she shoots me a glance that is full of hope. To just be here, standing on the beach with her and my new friends, and to be doing something as simple as making conversation is so refreshing, yet something I have avoided doing. I feel once again the security of friendship, like someone outside of my little bubble has got my back. The power of a smile, the warmth of a hug, the comfort in a familiar voice. I have numbed myself to try and avoid any more pain but just by being here, I can feel a tiny, tiny flutter of hope as a spark of life is ignited from deep within. Why have I been punishing myself for so long when all I needed to do was accept the hand of friendship? Instead I've been hiding away, curled up in a world of darkness though it wasn't what I deserved. I see light and hope by just reaching out and seeing the good in human nature and acknowledging that kindness does exist if we find the right people and look in the right places.

'Dizzy, it is for me, please,' says Rosie. 'You're a fine fellow, you are, Dizzy! And you are lovely too, Neptune, but I agree with Sarah that Shelley is more your type.'

'I'm glad I'm not having to choose,' says Juliette. 'With

me being even older than you, Shelley, I definitely wouldn't be in Dizzy's club at my age.'

'Mum just turned forty,' says Rosie to Sarah as if it's the funniest thing ever. 'She's ancient.'

Sarah and I give a playful laugh as Juliette rolls her eyes to the heavens.

'Thank goodness with age I have also developed a thick skin,' she says.

'You're only a young thing,' says Sarah. 'Forty is the new thirty, isn't that what they say? You've your whole life ahead of you still.'

Rosie looks at me and then her mum and for a second no one really knows what to say. It's not Sarah's fault. She doesn't know what's going on with Juliette or why she's here. I try to change the subject quickly.

'Are you sure you won't give this a go?' I ask Juliette. 'Neptune is a very gentle pony and Sarah could walk alongside you both? I can have a go after you. What do you think?'

Juliette grips Merlin's lead a little tighter and shakes her head at the very idea.

'Come on, Mum! I bet you'll love it. Just try it out and if you don't like it then that's okay. Do it!'

'I'm wearing sandals and shorts,' Juliette says with a shrug but Sarah has an answer to that.

'I have boots and jodphurs in the boot of my car,' she announces. 'What size boots do you wear? Five?'

Juliette nods, her eyes widening in fear as she looks upon Neptune who stands in wait.

'I'd need about a size twelve in trousers though. Oh, I'm not sure about this at all. I was only coming along to watch you experts at work. I've never been on a horse in my life!'

'Well, today is a good day to start,' I say. 'What do you think? Come on! You can do this! If I can do it so can you!'

Juliette's face breaks into a smile.

'You know what, sod it,' she says. 'Why not? I'll give it a go for the laugh. No time like the present and all that.'

'You superstar!' says Rosie, who is already in the saddle and ready for action. 'You'll love it Mum, I'm telling you. I can't believe you're actually doing this! Amazing!'

She blows her mum a kiss and Juliette catches it, just like I used to do with Lily when she was a tiny little girl. When I see Juliette close her fist and put it to her heart, I want to press pause and savour this moment forever.

I wait with Rosie and the horses while Sarah sorts Juliette out with some riding gear and the look on the young girl's face is something that I have never seen in her before. Her eyes are bright and shiny as she takes in her surroundings with the light breeze in her hair, her mouth in a wide smile. As she sits up high on the horse waiting to share this experience with her mother, I realise that this is a memory that she will cling to for a long, long time. I get that feeling again, that glow inside and I allow myself to totally absorb the joy of others and the small part I have played in making this happen.

Juliette

Sarah helps my foot into the stirrup and on the count of three I mount the horse which looks and feels like a giant to me. His coat is soft and silky to touch which I notice when I wobble a bit in the saddle and put my hand on his neck when searching for the reins.

'You okay?' says Sarah and I nod, not knowing whether to laugh or cry. The waves lap only feet away from me and the feeling of fresh air on my face is both exhilarating and breath-taking from up high. I never had any sort of desire to ride horses, despite taking Rosie for lessons when she was younger, and the very thought of being on horseback is enough to make me fearful and dizzy. Yet here I am, on a beach in the West of Ireland with my daughter by my side and these wonderfully generous people giving us an experience to remember.

'I'm going to lead him along and I'll be walking beside you every step of the way,' says Sarah. 'Shell, will you do the same with Rosie and Dizzy just to make sure she gets a feel of it before we let her go it alone.'

'It's okay, I can manage by myself,' says Rosie, but I agree with Sarah. It's best to take this one step at a time. I, for one, can't stop shaking with nerves but Rosie is super confident as she takes to it like a duck to water. Shelley and Merlin walk alongside her just to be sure, which makes me feel better. I have enough to worry about with my own new buddy Neptune, without fearing for Rosie taking off into a gallop!

The horse starts to move along the shoreline and I tilt my head back and laugh out loud as the wind breathes on me and the sun shines on my face. This is so not me. I'm very much a feet firmly on the ground person and as much as I have denied it, I don't share the same passion for animals as my daughter does. I don't dislike them of course, but they were never really my thing; but here I am on a horse, walking slowly along the coast and I am absolutely loving it. This is what I came here for, like Dr Michael said, to do things that I would never do at home with Rosie, to do things that will feed my soul and enrich my senses, to push boundaries, to make memories and I had no idea what this day would bring which is what makes it all so wonderful.

And an extra bonus is that I am showing Shelley that if I can step out of my comfort zone then so can she.

I watch Rosie up front with Shelley, who walks alongside her looking up at her with such protection and care that I wonder how blessed we are to have met someone like her on this trip. How did this happen? How did I get to be here in this glorious place with such wonderful people who care so much about showing us a good time?

'Are you enjoying it?' Shelley calls back to me and I smile and take the chance of giving her the thumbs up while still holding on to the reins.

'It's like I'm on top of the world!' I shout down to her and Sarah looks up at me knowingly. She pats the side of the horse and whispers something to him then gives me a wink. What on earth is she up to now?

'Come on,' she says to the horse and she begins to run alongside us, bringing the horse into a gentle trot as she does. We overtake Rosie, Shelley and Merlin and as we up the pace I grip the reins and bob along as the horse moves up and down, up and down.

'Yee ha!' I shout to Rosie and she pretends to wave a lasso back at me.

'I'm coming to get you!' she calls after me and soon we are trotting alongside each other, laughing and smiling and pulling faces and I fill up inside with joy as this moment plays out in front of me. Right now, I don't care for tomorrow. I just want to stay like this, to hold onto this feeling of pure happiness and exhilaration as I share this precious moment in time with my girl. I absorb the present, I live for each second and right now there is no better feeling.

Shelley waves at me as she runs alongside Rosie and her pony, and I can see that she too is experiencing a rush of emotions. I feel so much gratitude, so much joy and happiness, and a sheer contentment so filling that I feel like I could burst.

'Thank you!' I mouth down to Shelley, who runs along so effortlessly. 'Thank you so, so much!'

Shelley shakes her head in response.

'No, thank *you*,' she says to me and I think I understand what she means.

Chapter 16

Shelley

I am lying on the sofa in our 'good' living room in my dressing gown, silently reflecting on what was such a wonderful evening on the beach with Juliette, Rosie, Merlin and my good friend Sarah.

I wonder just how much I have been missing as the world has kept going around me over the past three years.

Grief freezes you, I guess. It puts you into a different zone, one that doesn't relate to everyday things like going to the movies, or eating out in nice places, or planning around the weather, or taking the car to the garage, or making a dental appointment, or opening your mail. All of those things seem alien when you're bereaved, like they belong in some parallel universe because all you can think of when you lose someone is how cruel life is, and learning to function again can be almost be like learning to walk again. It is crippling.

Yes, I have functioned; I have kept going with the shop,

I have managed to get my hair coloured when it became unbearable on the eye (if Eliza hadn't nudged me in the direction of the hairdressers I might never have noticed, mind you). But I have never actually allowed myself to stop and *feel* anything until now. Well, not until Saturday I should say, when I found Rosie on the beach and from then began tiny flickers of movement in my heart and in my mind. It was like I was slowly waking up from the most horrific nightmare. The nightmare is real, but waking up isn't so frightening anymore.

Today, was the best though. Today I felt the rush of joy that comes with gratitude, the rush of satisfaction that comes with helping others, the rush of adrenaline to see Rosie and her mum experience that precious memory of something so simple as horse riding along the beach for the first time together.

I think of the last few weeks I spent with my own mother and how much I wished I had done things differently, but I was merely a child and I wasn't to know the years of regret and longing I had ahead of me, of how much we were both missing out on. If I was a child again I would laugh more with my mother, I would sing songs together, I would tell jokes, watch movies, go shopping, make her dinner, help more around the house, tell her about my boy crushes, my fears, my hopes and dreams and listen to hers because I wish now I had realised that she too was a person and not just my mother; she was a woman with a past, with memories and ambitions, and milestones that she too hoped one day to reach for her own satisfaction but of course never did.

But most of all, if I was a child again I would dance more with my mother. I would take her hands and turn the music up loud at every opportunity and we'd laugh and dance and dance and dance ...

I hope that Juliette and Rosie remember to dance.

The sound of their laughter today and the way Juliette glanced across to her daughter with such brightness and light and life in her eyes was something I wished I could have caught on camera, but it will be forever instilled now in Rosie's memory which has filled me up a little inside. Juliette may be cursed with a terminal illness that will eventually take her away from here, but today she was alive and she was loving every minute of it.

My living room is filled up too with the smell of a vanilla candle burning, a gift today from Juliette after our two hours of fun on the beach. We were soaked through, we were exhausted, we were starving but we were bursting with laughter, smiles and the great joy of the outdoors.

'This good old scent of vanilla, as bland and boring as its reputation may be, is a great aroma for bringing joy and relaxation,' Juliette said when she gave the candle to me as we walked through the village. 'You looked right at home there today with those horses and both you and Sarah made me feel so at ease. I loved it. You need to do things like that to relax you more Shelley and feel the joy that life can still bring you. Lily would want that and so would your mother.'

She had unexpectedly popped into the little gift shop which is just two doors down from *Lily Loves* and as Rosie and I waited outside, we were sure she had spotted some tacky souvenir like one of those back scratchers covered in shamrocks, or a tea towel with an Irish blessing – the sort of things that don most of the windows in those shops all down the coastline.

'I bet she gets a Guinness t-shirt for Dan,' says Rosie as we stood there waiting. 'Or rugby jerseys for Aunty Helen's boys. She said she would bring everyone back something that is unmistakeably Irish so goodness knows what she's up to. I wouldn't be surprised if she came out with a real leprechaun.'

But we were very wrong as when Juliette emerged from the shop only moments later, she handed me a little paper bag with the candle inside and a full explanation as to why she chose it.

'You are very kind,' I told her. 'But you don't need to be giving me gifts, you really don't. It's such a pleasure to be around you two and I mean it when I say it. Today was good for me too. It really was.'

'I bet it was nice to spend time with Sarah?' Juliette said to me and I smiled.

'It was like the good old days again,' I told her. 'Well, you know what I mean. Almost like the good old days when it was just me and her sometimes and we'd do stuff together and laugh about it for days. I've missed that a lot. I'm realizing now just how much I've missed having friends.'

Now, as I lie here in my fluffy robe, feeling clean after my shower and at peace in the quiet of the evening, I promise myself to make sure that Sarah and I meet up again soon. I believe I have turned a corner today and when the phone rings and I hear Matt's voice, I light up even more. I have so much to tell him which makes a big change from my usual downbeat tales of evenings spent alone in the house with nothing and no one but our dog for company and the doom and gloom and sorrow of white empty walls.

'You should have seen her face, Matt. Honestly it would have taken a tear from a stone,' I tell him when I'm in mid-flow about Rosie today. 'The pride when she saw her mum get up and face her fears to join her horse-riding. I could cry even thinking about it.'

Matt, as I predicted, is full of questions about my newfound friends.

'So, these people, this mum and daughter, they're from England did you say?'

'Yes, they're over for a week on a last-minute holiday. They're staying in the cottage by the pier. You know the one with the yellow door? It's really cute and—'

I haven't told him the link to Skipper yet. I'm saving that one for after I tell him all about our adventures today and yesterday.

'Yeah I know the one,' he says. 'It's normally booked up months in advance, though? That was a coup to get somewhere so nice to stay last minute.'

'I know, it's perfect.'

'And you met them when they came into the shop then on Saturday?' he continues. 'How the hell did you become friends? You said you can't do anything more than small talk with strangers? I've seen you in action, Shell. You freeze up.'

My husband should work for the FBI. So many questions ...

'I know, I know but this was different,' I explain to him. 'Well, as weird as it may sound I kind of got the feeling that something special was about to happen when Juliette came into the shop and bought a blue dress. Your mum had told me that morning to look out for someone associated with the colour blue.'

'Oh, here we go,' says Matt with a laugh. He is very much on my dad's side of the fence when it comes to his mother's predictions and interpretations.

'Anyhow, that's neither here nor there, Mr Cynical,' I tell him. 'It was really when I came across Rosie, her daughter, on the beach that evening that our paths properly crossed. She was so upset and I stopped to try and help her and that's when she told me about her mum being sick and how worried she was, and I related to her. I really felt her pain, Matt. It was only two days ago yet it feels like so much has happened and so much has changed already, in the best possible way.'

'That's beautiful, babe, I am so thrilled for you,' he says. 'And you went out for lunch with them? *Out* for lunch? Seriously?'

'Yes, I did,' I tell him, feeling really proud of myself

right now. 'We just went down to the Beach House, hardly the Ritz, but still.'

'And how was it? Was it easier than you thought? I actually can't believe this, Shelley. I really want to go and give that woman a medal, what did you say her name was?'

'*Juliette*,' I say to him for the third time. He never was great with names. 'As in Romeo and Juliet?'

'Oh.'

'I did feel a panic attack coming on when she suggested it,' I continue, 'and I tried to back out a few times, especially when we got there and I felt everyone staring but Juliette made me come back and eat dessert and we had a glass of bubbly, then went over to her cottage and Rosie, who loves Merlin by the way, did my makeup and honestly Matt, it is just so sad to think of what they have ahead of them. I only wish I could help them more.'

Matt takes a moment to let all of this sink in.

'And then horse-riding today?' he says. 'With Sarah. That's pretty big of you to arrange all that for them. I can't believe this. I've been trying to get you to hook up with Sarah for months and months now. How is she?'

'She is like my best friend, Matt, that's how she is,' I say to him, my voice softening now. I swallow. 'She is a breath of fresh air and just what I need right now. I've missed her more than I realised. Sarah was amazing today.'

'Yes, you have needed her,' he reminds me. 'She's a

good friend to you, love. You should let her be just that from now on.'

Mentioning Sarah just reminded me that I still have to tell him about Skipper. I take a deep breath. This is going to be quite the bombshell and the big moment I've been saving for when we finally have time to talk and my head is not all over the place.

'There is a pretty big reason why they chose to come to Killara,' I say to Matt, 'and I want to tell you all about it but I'm totally drained right now and it's a whole big story and I need to be in the right head space to even begin explaining it.'

'Is it bad or good?' he asks me.

'It's good,' I laugh. 'Well, it's sad but good. I'll tell you tomorrow, I promise. Where are you off to tonight? Anywhere nice?'

'Meeting clients for a drink in the lobby,' Matt explains. 'Hardly the Ritz like you just said, but Bert warned me not to be late. I suppose I should go and shower, babe. I am so, so proud of you and all you have done today and yesterday, you know that?'

I cradle the phone.

I really don't want him to go. I want to keep talking to him, to keep listening to his reassuring voice, to feel him close to me. The very thought of feeling like this stops me in my tracks. Matt has always been there, by my side, and I have never really worried about him not being there, or dare I say, noticed if he wasn't there but now I have this want, or need, to talk to him. I've been enjoying talking to him for the first time in a long time. I actually feel something for him and I don't want him to go. But he has to, of course.

'Thanks Matt, I'm kind of proud of me too today,' I whisper down the phone. 'Have a lovely evening with your clients.'

He laughs.

'You know I wish I was sat at home with you instead,' he says to me. 'I'm missing you tonight.'

'Me too,' I reply. 'I'm missing you too.'

My admission hangs for a moment in silence. We both take a deep breath.

'Chat to you tomorrow, love,' he says. 'Get an early night. You're amazing, you know that, don't you?'

Now it's my turn to laugh.

'Don't over-do it,' I say to him. 'I'm only human and sometimes it's nice to feel enough emotion to remind me of that. It's nice to just *feel* stuff. I think I'm slowly healing, whatever that means. Chat tomorrow, Matt. Have fun.'

We both linger before hanging up and I smile, thinking of the early days when we had just met and we'd do as most couples do, argue over who was going to hang up first, but then Matt remembers again that he is in a hurry.

'Shit I need to go. Okay, go, go, go,' he says.

I hug the phone against my ear to hear him closer.

'Bye, bye, bye ...'

And he is gone. And I sit there holding to the phone, enjoying the feeling of missing him. I have missed that feeling too.

Juliette

'Hashtag, best day ever!' says Rosie to Helen who has video called Rosie's phone. 'I swear, Aunty Helen, you would not have believed it, would you? Mum, on a beach, on a horse and actually loving it!'

'Never in a million years,' says my sister, who is beaming as much as we are, as we gawk into the screen, me leaning over Rosie's shoulder.

'It was what I can only describe as exhilarating,' I tell my sister who is shaking her head in disbelief. 'I'm serious! And the look on Rosie's face when she saw me overtake her was priceless.'

'Well, go you!' says Helen. 'Maybe we should all step out of our comfort zones a little bit more often and try things we don't think we'll enjoy. I've always wanted to have the courage to go up in a hot air balloon. Do you think I should try it?'

She makes what is supposed to be the sound of a hot air balloon rising and points slowly upwards as if going up into the sky.

'If it's good enough for Phineas Fogg, it's good enough for you?' I say to her and Rosie looks at me like I've sprouted a second head. 'Didn't he travel around the world in a hot air balloon or am I totally wrong on that one?'

'Who?' says Rosie and I make a face behind her back which of course she sees me do in the mini screen on her phone.

'How's Mum and Dad?' I ask Helen, knowing that there isn't an awful lot she is going to tell me, not in front of Rosie anyhow.

'Mum's still battling with her migraines and Dad is still insisting he's taking her to a specialist and Mum is still digging her heels in and saying no.'

'So, the usual?' I say and Helen nods in agreement. 'Any other news from home? How are the boys? And Brian?'

Helen thinks for a moment.

'Great. No news here,' she says. 'The boys are off school and I'm off school too and I must admit that life here is just ticking along. No horse-riding on the beach or eating crab claws in the sunshine or walking golden retrievers or visiting fancy pants houses for us. I wish we'd booked a foreign holiday now, but we didn't, so we're just ticking along. Nothing exciting I'm afraid. Or should I say, glad? Maybe it's a good thing. No drama.'

I know exactly what she means – but as lovely as it is to be just ticking along, I want to give my sister a shake up to do something just a little bit more exciting for a change. I want her to go up in a hot air balloon, I want her to book a holiday last minute, just do something instead of letting one day drift into another. She is young, she is brimming with energy and health and warmth and love and it's such a pity for her to just be ticking along.

'Why don't you surprise your husband with a night

out on the tiles this weekend?' I suggest to her and she bursts into laughter.

'Surprise him? Me and Brian? We are way past the stage of surprises, Juliette. I think he would die of shock and imagine the horror if I arranged something for the weekend that didn't involve watching football on a big screen or playing darts down the pub.'

'Surprise him, I dare you!' I tell her. 'Get dressed up, book a table somewhere nice, arrange a babysitter and let your hair down, just the two of you. Then book a flippin' holiday and go enjoy it. There's no point in just ticking along, Helen. Get busy living or get busy dying, that's my motto for as long as I can stick to it.'

I feel Rosie shift in her seat. Maybe I shouldn't have said that – the 'dying' bit.

'Mum's right,' says Rosie, much to my relief. 'There's a lot more to life than just ticking along. I know you mean there's no big news or no drama and that's fantastic, of course it is, but you should be enjoying yourself a lot more than you do. You should travel more. I can't wait to travel the world.'

Helen smiles at us and lets out a sigh.

'I have three very lively boys to keep me busy,' Helen reminds us. 'But yes, I get what you mean. I should be stepping out of my comfort zone a little bit more, just like you did today, Juliette and I should be tasting things like crab claws just like you did yesterday, Rosie. I'll get my thinking cap on and do something nice this weekend.'

'It doesn't have to break the bank,' I say to her, knowing

that with a mortgage and a family and a million other things on her mind when it comes to finances, it's not as simple for Helen to get up and go as we are insinuating.

'There is a movie I'd love to see on the big screen,' says Helen. 'Brian would probably rather pull his own teeth out than watch it but we could maybe go for a drink after I suppose, that might convince him to forego the darts league.'

'That's the spirit,' I tell her. 'And make sure to hold hands and snuggle up in the back row. Put on something nice, you know, underneath too.'

'Mum! Too much info!' says Rosie and I shrug.

'Nothing wrong with a bit of romance,' I reply.

'You know what ladies, I am just going to *make* him go,' says Helen. 'I'm actually looking forward to it now that you've said it. It's been a while since we went out together, just the two of us. Sunday lunch at the local with the boys has been my social life for too long and with sport of some sort on in the background it doesn't leave much room for romance. I'm going to make my husband take me on a date.'

'That's more like it!' I tell my sister. 'Now, on that note, we are going to leave you to your planning and go to bed as we've another big day lined up for tomorrow, haven't we Rosie?'

'Have we?' asks Rosie. 'That's news to me.'

I smile smugly and shrug my shoulders.

'You'll just have to wait until then to find out what

exactly I'm talking about, but it's going to be another good one, just you wait and see.'

'You can't leave me hanging like that,' says Helen. 'Tell me what you're up to so I can sit here pulling my hair out as the boys wreck the house tomorrow and be green with envy.'

'I'll text you,' I tell my sister. 'Now, babysitter, Brian, movies, booze and dancing. Get it sorted!'

'I love you both, you know that,' says Helen, just as we are about to sign off. I can see her lip wobble. Mine starts to tremble too.

'Right back at you, Aunty Helen,' says Rosie, but I can't speak. I just wave at her into the camera and hug Rosie a little tighter than I should.

'It's the cliffs tomorrow, isn't it, Mum?' says Rosie. 'You finally got someone to take us out on a boat, just like you've been wanting?'

I inhale her hair and close my eyes. I am so tired but I don't want her to see it.

'Let's get you to bed, missy,' I say to her and her arm goes around my waist and we sit there for what feels like forever. How am I ever going to leave her on her own? She gives me a squeeze as if she is reading my mind and despite my fears, I know that she is a strong, feisty lady like her mother and part of me knows that she will one day be okay.

Chapter 17

Shelley

TUESDAY

I wake up from the sweetest dream with a smile on my face and I open my eyes to a burst of sunlight that seeps in between the curtains, forming a sparkling line that falls right on to my bed. I have no idea where I was in my dream, or what I was doing or who I was with but something wonderful certainly did happen and now I am lying here with a smile on my face and a warm fuzzy glow inside.

And then it comes back to me. I saw Lily and she was smiling at me from the lighthouse in my mother's arms. She was wearing her favourite yellow coat and her bright pink wellington boots and it was raining so she had her hood up but she looked so happy and safe. She was waving at me and giving me a thumbs-up as my mother looked at her with such endearment.

It was beautiful.

I stretch slowly under the covers and check my phone from my bedside table and it's a lot earlier than when I normally wake up. As usual, there is an early morning greeting from Matt and another from Eliza which was sent only minutes before I woke. She says she is going to town and she is wondering if I need anything. Nothing new there in that the woman has the patience of a saint as I always tell her no and she still insists on asking every time she is passing through to do her own bits and pieces.

'Town' to us is thirty minutes away in Galway City and I haven't had any interest in going there for so long, even though I used to go at least once a week, if not on errands, then just for the experience. I used to adore walking the cobbles of Shop Street and listening to the buskers, or sitting on a bench eating a fish supper by the Claddagh basin and watching the swans sail up and down, or catching a play at the Town Hall or a gig at Monroe's or the Roisin Dubh and marvelling at the variety of live music on offer. That was a different me. That was me when I knew how to enjoy myself.

I have truly pressed pause on my life. I have stopped being me but I feel ever so slightly stronger with each day that has passed since Lily's birthday at the weekend and with her help, each day from now on I will try and fix that. No matter how hard it is to keep moving forward, it is what I have to do.

I read Eliza's message again.

'Do you need anything from town, love? I'll be passing through if so.'

I don't really need anything in town, just as I always don't, and I press reply to tell her so. What I do need to do is get up and shower ... and then I suppose I will cook the same breakfast that I won't even taste and watch the same daytime TV that is like chewing gum for my brain and then I'll worry and wonder and relive the same things that I do every day as I wait for 2pm to come round when I need to be in work and the clutching pain of grief will slowly ease off until I come back here again in the evening and battle through it until bedtime.

I close my eyes and I see Lily's little face again. Her hand waving at me from side to side like she used to – those chubby little dimpled hands that used to touch my face and melt my heart just by looking at them. My mother kisses her on her temple and she gives me the same thumbs-up again just like in my dream. Mum's smile is so radiant, so safe, so comforting and I find myself smiling back at them, hoping that they can see me ever so slowly getting better.

I don't need to do any of that mundane stuff again today, do I Lily? Tell me what I need to do, Mum.

And then I feel it.

What I need to do is hold on to this glimmer of positivity that has embraced me since Saturday, and which has come to me even stronger since I woke up only minutes ago.

What I need to do is grasp this opportunity, this spark

of life that has been ignited since I met Rosie and Juliette. What I need to do is try and live again.

So I'm going to make today matter, just as I did yesterday and the day before with Juliette and Rosie. And so I do something that I should have done ages ago. It's only a little gesture, but I'm going to push myself and make the effort. I send my mother-in-law a text that reads as follows:

'Fancy a passenger into Galway? I might need a few things after all and will tag along if you don't mind?'

I press send and a wave of shock overcomes me but I can't back out now.

She calls me straight away.

'Hello?'

'I'm just making sure I'm not imagining things,' she says in disbelief. 'I mean, I was just messaging on the off chance but I didn't even expect you to be awake yet? I hope I'm not imagining things! I'm on my way to you right now if you want to come? Please say you do?'

'You are not imagining things,' I tell her, sitting up on my bed. The stream of sunlight sits right on my lap now and I get a strange energy from the light of a new day, as if it's urging me on, encouraging me to get up and do this. 'I can be ready in fifteen minutes if you can pick me up then? I have to be at work at two o'clock, of course, so I'll go only if it doesn't make you have to rush back?'

'The morning is young, darling,' says Eliza. 'I will be there in fifteen and I will have you back at the shop for two on the button, fed, watered and feeling great for a change of scenery. Now go and get ready! Go, go, go!'

I hang up the phone and smile, then I close my eyes and say thank you. I don't know who or what I am thanking but something has shifted within me. I'm not on top of the world of course, I'm not even ten steps up a mountainside when it comes to living life to the full again, but I have one thing that I couldn't find within myself for too long now. I have hope. I now have found some sort of hope and faith and belief that I will soon, very slowly, be able to move on. With Lily's love in my heart and my mother's soothing voice in my ear, it is beginning, dare I say it, it's beginning to feel good.

I step into the shower and I feel a thin layer of the darkness of grief wash off my hair, down my back and I gulp back tears at the sheer relief of just a glimmer of hope.

Eliza toots the horn fifteen minutes later as promised but I'm already at the door, ready and waiting and I distract Merlin with a squeaky toy to let me get away. Five minutes in the shower, a quick lick of makeup (nothing compared to Rosie's masterpiece yesterday but enough to take away the ghostly pale look from my face), a spray of perfume and I'm ready to face the world again. It really is so different to the days when it would take me at least an hour to gather up Lily's belongings, put together a change of clothes just in case of any accidents, her drinking cup, her cuddle toy, her second 'flavour of the week' toy and then the time it took to dress her and convince her to get into her car seat. I'm not even going to think about that this morning. I don't have to punish myself. I've been punished enough.

'Look at you, Shelley! You look radiant,' says Eliza, lifting her sunglasses to get a better view. 'You look like a different person. Well, you look like you but in the best possible way and it's wonderful! What's going on?'

Eliza is driving her pale blue convertible Volkswagen Beetle which suits her personality to a tee, and her wavy, thick, auburn-dyed hair is coiffed to perfection. Matt's family don't do things by halves. Eliza totally believes in living life to the full and she has a great taste for the finer things in life, well, as much as she can afford, but she is also incredibly generous and charitable and a very warm and popular lady around the village of Killara and beyond.

'I do feel a little bit better, Eliza,' I admit to her, putting my handbag in the back seat and getting into the front beside her. 'A good bit better, actually. I didn't even allow myself to think twice earlier. When I saw your message, something clicked in me. I had the strangest dream, or maybe it wasn't even a dream, it was more like a feeling that pushed me on, a sign. Can we get signs in our sleep do you think? It's just that I woke this morning with what felt like a new sense of reassurance that everything was going to be okay? That it was okay to smile a little bit more? I saw Lily and she looked happy and I guess that's made me feel a bit happier. Is that stupid?'

Eliza steers the car down my driveway and out onto the winding road, taking a right for Killara village which we pass through before we take the main road for Galway City.

'Of course, it's not a bit stupid, it's very real, Shelley,' she explains to me softly. 'We get signs when we sleep as that's when we are at most vulnerable and at ease. We are wide open to receiving messages from loved ones or even simple spiritual guidance, and we wake up with, just like you have, a sense of reassurance to keep going forward. I'm not surprised that you feel better after sleeping if you think you may have had some sort of spiritual communication.'

'It really has spurred me on,' I tell her. 'Not only that, though. I've had an eventful few days, I suppose you might say.'

Eliza glances at me and then back to the road.

'I was wondering what was going on,' she says. 'I've called at the house and even Merlin wasn't there and I was beginning to think you'd fled the country? I didn't want to torture you with phone calls, but then today when I was heading into town I thought I'd left it long enough and would check in.'

I don't even know where to begin to explain all the wondrous things that have happened to me, so I start with Saturday afternoon, the day of Lily's birthday and the lady with the blue dress. Eliza doesn't make a fuss or say 'I told you so' when I mention the colour blue, just as she'd predicted. She just smiles and nods her head as I tell her all about Juliette and Rosie, why they're here and their connection to Matt's old friend Skipper.

'Oh Eliza, when the poor woman told me that the name of the man she was hoping to look up was Skipper, I didn't know how to break it to her. Imagine that feeling that your only child was going to be an orphan? Imagine, what she's been hanging on to as some sort of happy ending for her daughter has been destroyed. And wee Rosie, gosh she really would break your heart because she has no idea of the huge loss she is about to experience. I really felt something for her the moment I saw her on those sand dunes and then when I found out she was Matt's friend's biological daughter, it all made sense.'

Eliza seems to be in deep thought, like she is taking it all in. Eventually she responds.

'I don't think you feel that connection to little Rosie because of a man you have never met,' says Eliza. 'I'd doubt that's the case.'

'You don't?' I ask. Gosh. I thought she would be totally convinced that it was so fateful that I was to run into the long-lost daughter of my husband's deceased friend from yesteryear.

'No,' she says. 'I think there is more to it than that. I think Juliette and Rosie have been sent to you for much more personal reasons. You feel you have been helping them, yes?'

'Well, I suppose I have,' I tell her. 'It was by helping Rosie and listening to her that I first felt something change inside of me. And then when she encouraged me to have lunch on Sunday it was like I was actually tasting food for the first time in ages, and then I saw them together on the beach yesterday and the joy they felt from sharing that time on horseback together. It just moved me so much and I felt so much in my heart for them both.'

'Exactly,' says Eliza. 'We reap what we sow, Shelley. Sometimes when we take the emphasis off our own grief and troubles, and reach out to others, we get so much more from it without realizing it. Your friendship and kindness to those people in their time of need is paying dividends your way. I don't think it's anything to do with, what was his name again?'

'Skipper,' I remind her. My goodness she is as bad as her son when it comes to names.

'Skipper ... something to do with boats, then, I take it?'

'Yes, that's him. He used to sail in here from time to time. Do you remember him?' I ask her.

'No, I don't, sorry,' says Eliza. 'I can't say I remember him at all. Where did you say he was from?'

'I didn't,' I tell her. 'He's from Waterford. At least I think that's where Matt said. They were good friends about ... well, I suppose it's over fifteen years ago now.'

Eliza shakes her head.

'Hmm, Skipper ... it's not ringing a bell at all.'

We're driving more slowly now through Killara and the village is bright and bustling with tourists just as it always is at this time of year. I see Betty in the shop dealing with a customer and then further down the

224

village I spot Juliette and Rosie buying an ice cream from a van by the pier and I wave to them but they are too far away to see us.

'Are you sure you don't remember him?' I ask her. 'Skipper? I *think* his real name was Pete? Matt told me all about him one night when he was feeling all sentimental about people who touched his life who have been and gone. He was a sailor and he used to come here and hang out with Matt and his friends in the summer. People like Tom and Sarah and others round his age? No?'

Eliza shakes her head. 'Definitely not, darling,' she says to me. 'Mind you, I can't keep up with some of the people Matt has been friendly with down the years. His school-friends, his university friends, his work friends from his many different jobs. Did I ever tell you he once wanted to be a postman?'

'No,' I laugh. 'I don't think he has ever admitted that one to me, ha.'

'Well, I'm sure this man you are talking about was indeed a friend of Matthew's but I don't remember ever meeting him,' says Eliza. 'And you say this lady has a child to him and was here to find him?'

I look out onto the bay as we take our time behind a bus full of sightseeing tourists which is deliberately driving slowly to admire the view of the harbour.

'This was where she met him, yes,' I sigh. 'Poor lady. I feel for her so much to be in such a dreadful situation with her little girl.'

But Eliza is on a different wavelength altogether.

'That's sad indeed,' she says. 'Now, excuse me for changing the subject, but let's get back to this wonderful big step you have taken to leave this village today! What would you like to do when we get into town, love? How about we start with a nice brunch out in the sunshine and we take it from there? We will have a lovely time, I promise.'

My tummy rumbles at the very idea of a sumptuous brunch in the sunshine, and Eliza turns up her sound system with The Eagles blasting out, the music making heads turn as we leave the stone walls of the village and swing out on to the main open road.

'That would be just perfect,' I tell her, and I tilt my head back and look up to the sky, smiling with gratitude for this beautiful day and the new strength I am finding from within. This time I know exactly who I am thanking. I see her little hands again and the look in her eyes touches my heart and warms it up a little. Thank you, Lily. I feel you with me every day.

Juliette

I watch Rosie as she delves into the most indulgent whipped ice cream, complete with sprinkles, a flake, and the whole works. That's when Sarah, Shelley's friend from yesterday's horse-riding escapade spots us as she is leaving Brannigan's Bar across the road with her young daughter in tow.

'Hey there! How are you two today? That looks very good indeed,' she says and Rosie and I nod in agreement.

'It's the best ice cream ever,' says Rosie, who has had a complete turnaround on her opinion of Killara since Shelley came on the scene. Everything is now 'wonderful', 'amazing' and 'the best ever' and I have no intention of putting her off her notions as I totally agree. Even the 'crappy' wi-fi doesn't seem so big a deal anymore.

'Have you seen Shelley today?' she asks Sarah. 'I wonder what she's up to?'

I sigh and laugh lightly. Sarah saw Shelley for the first time properly in a long time only yesterday even though they both live in the same village and I don't want Sarah to be reminded of that as it was such a big deal for them both.

'Rosie, love, I told you that we can't expect Shelley to be our tour guide every day we are here. Sorry, Sarah,' I say to Shelley's friend. 'So this must be Teigan? Am I right? What a gorgeous girl you are.'

Sarah puts her hand on her daughter's shoulder and the little girl smiles a toothy grin up at me. She really is such a cutie with brown curls to die for, big green almond eyes like her mother and a dimple when she smiles. I can totally understand how looking at her must be heart-breaking for Shelley.

'I'm going to be a big six tomorrow,' Teigan announces and we all wow in amazement. 'And I've grown two inches since my last birthday. My daddy measured me.'

Sarah hugs her close with a proud smile.

'I only wish I was six tomorrow and that I could grow two inches taller,' I say to Teigan who shies now in to her mother's leg. 'But my days of being six and growing any taller are long gone.'

Sarah looks on at her daughter with great affection.

'As are mine,' says Sarah. 'Oh, to be carefree and six years old again!'

'I'm having a princess and ponies party,' whispers Teigan timidly and Rosie perks up at this.

'I would love to have a princess and ponies party,' she says. 'That's the best theme I've ever heard. Mum, I know I'm going to be sixteen next birthday but I am so having that theme for my next party. That's so cool, Teigan!'

I feel like someone has punched me in the stomach when I think of Rosie's birthday which will be in May of next year and which I won't be here for.

Sarah swiftly steps in.

'We sampled some of that delicious ice cream the other evening when we bumped into Shelley up the road a bit, just outside her shop, didn't we Teigan? Oh that's right,' says Sarah. 'You walked Shelley home of course. Sometimes my memory ... it must be old age creeping up on me!'

'You only think you're bad. Mum is the worst for forgetting things,' says Rosie. 'She forgets everything these days, don't you, Mum! You couldn't be as bad as she is!'

Sarah gives me a sympathetic smile and again swiftly changes the subject.

'So, what's on the agenda today, girlies?' she asks. 'Anything nice?'

'Well, actually,' I tell Sarah. 'We have a wonderful afternoon planned and you are very welcome to join us if it suits you. We are finally going out on a boat to view the famous Cliffs of Moher. Rosie has never been on a boat before. Well, she has been on a ferry obviously on the way here, but it's not the same thing, is it?'

Sarah breaks into a smile.

'No, it is definitely not the same thing,' she says. 'I would love to go out with you and thank you so much for the invitation, but I've my toddler to pick up at lunch time from crèche and Toby and speedboats are not a good mix. Teigan and I were just in there chatting to my mum to see if she could have him for even an hour as Teigan has a dental appointment but she's too busy. She runs the B&B at Brannigan's.'

I look behind Sarah to the infamous green building where my journey began in this village and my tummy gives a whoosh.

'Gosh, I didn't realise you had a family connection to Brannigan's?' I say to her. I don't want to sound over-curious or surprised, but I really didn't have any idea. 'Is that your mum's place?'

'Yes, that's my whole family,' Sarah explains. 'We are Brannigan, well I was before I was married. I grew up in that building. We have a family home to the rear and then the front rooms are all for tourists. I thought Shelley may have mentioned that to you but I'm sure you have had more important things to talk about than my family history.'

I look up to the windows of the B&B, and get flash-backs to the room I stayed in – the lady who tutted at me when I couldn't find the key to my room at such an ungodly hour and how Skipper didn't want her to recognise him and waited outside until the coast was clear before I could let him in to join me upstairs. Shit. That must have been Sarah's mother.

'I hope I don't get seasick when we go out on the boat,' says Rosie, bringing a welcome interruption to my awe at Sarah's home being where I first stayed and the possibility of her own mother being that very woman who we woke up so late at night. 'I hope Shelley can come. I bet she's working though.'

I can't help but let out a sigh again. 'Shelley is very popular right now, as are you too after your generosity yesterday,' I say.

'Well, that's not a bad thing to hear at all,' Sarah responds. 'I'm delighted to be popular. If only I was as popular with my own children sometimes!'

Teigan looks up at her, totally oblivious to what Sarah is getting at.

'Look, I know you've probably got a hundred and one things to do this morning,' I say to Sarah, 'but do you have time for a coffee and a bun across the road? My treat? I'd like to do something to thank you for going to all that trouble yesterday. We really did have such fun, didn't we Rosie?'

Rosie nibbles at the remainder of her ice cream cone and then responds.

'It was such fun, yes,' she says to Sarah. 'Thank you so much. Dizzy was the cutest horse—'

'Ever!' I say at the same time as her and we all have a giggle.

'Okay, I think we have time for a coffee and a bun,' says Sarah. 'Teigan, don't tell your brother and daddy that we were eating yummy stuff without them when we get home, will you?'

Teigan claps her hands with glee and we cross the road to the little coffee shop where we take our time to marvel at the range of delights on display. Chocolate éclairs bursting with fresh cream, zingy lemon tarts with juicy strawberry toppings, wedges of mint Aero cheesecake and a rainbow of cupcakes dance in front of us and even after tasting a little of Rosie's whipped ice cream, I can't resist sampling just a little something from the menu.

'You only live once so feck the diet,' I hear Sarah mutter, obviously trying to rid herself of any guilt associated with divulging in so many calories.

'You'd better believe it,' I whisper to her and she bursts out laughing at being caught out talking to herself.

'We women really are hard on ourselves when it comes to treats, aren't we?' she says.

'Everything in moderation,' I say to Sarah and she perks up at my thinking. 'Go for what you fancy, go on, and don't even think about it again except for how much you enjoyed it.'

I choose a hazelnut latte with lemon tart and Sarah has an americano with an éclair, while the girls slurp on milkshakes and carry cupcakes outside to the little terrace, to one of its dainty metal tables on which there is barely enough room to hold all of our treats.

'Teigan, shall we move over to the next table on our own?' asks Rosie. 'You can tell me all about your party and what it's like going out on the boat because I've never been before, and you can also tell me all about that little rascal Dizzy. I really loved meeting him yesterday.'

'Oh, that's a wonderful idea,' says Sarah as she helps them set up on the next table and they settle down with their treats. 'Teigan has been out sailing lots with her dad so she knows lots of tips and also how not to get seasick. Don't forget to tell Rosie how important it is to wear a life jacket, won't you Teigan?'

Teigan looks thrilled to bits to be given such a responsible task and I am so proud of Rosie for taking the little girl under her wing and including her in the conversation. She was always so good with little ones and I just know she would have loved a younger sister or brother, someone to share her life with, someone to call on unconditionally – someone like I have in Helen. Yes, she has her cousins, Helen's boys, but it's not the same. They are a tight unit of five in that family and I really don't know if Rosie will fit in when she goes to live with them. Maybe she'd be better off with my mum and dad, though with Mum's own health worries and they aren't getting any younger ... oh, I can't bear to think of that now.

'What a delightful young daughter you have there, Juliette,' Sarah says to me and I sit up a little straighter at the compliment. 'It's so kind and thoughtful of her to include Teigan and make her feel like a big girl. She's a special young lady, for sure. Shelley told me she was and I can already see why.'

'She really is,' I reply. I can't help but agree. 'I may be totally biased, but she's a real ray of sunshine in my life. I can't even imagine what I would have done had she not come along, and believe me, I had lots of plans that didn't involve having children. Isn't it strange how life takes you in such different directions sometimes, yet it always works out to teach you something or make you a better, stronger person?'

We tuck into our sweet delights and Sarah looks surprised to hear this.

'Were children not in your plans, then?' she asks. 'I have to admit when I got pregnant with Toby, my youngest, the shock nearly killed me and I still can't figure out how it happened but I wouldn't change it now for the world, of course.'

'I didn't plan to have one on my own,' I clarify. 'It's not that I'd said I would never have children at all, I just hadn't planned that far ahead I suppose. Life threw me a big challenge and it was the best thing that ever happened to me, but sometimes we only realise these things when we have to sit back and reflect on where we are, where we thought we'd be and how we got here.'

I hope I'm not being too deep and meaningful but I think Sarah is still interested in what I have to say.

'Yes, life certainly does take us in all sorts of directions,' she agrees with me. 'Even when it comes to relationships, yes? Like, when we are young and in love with being in love, we really do believe it will last forever, or when we make friends we think they will be friends for life and it doesn't always work out that way, but if someone told you that at the time, you'd never believe them.'

'Exactly.'

We sip our coffees and a few seconds of silence follow. I can't help but envy her as I notice her glance over at her daughter who is chatting away to Rosie without a care in the world. How I wish that Rosie was secure in her life like that with a healthy mum, a little brother and a loving dad to go home to every day. Horse-riding on the beach, shopping with her mum, planning birthday parties ... I lose my breath a little in self-pity and try to realise that none of this is Sarah's fault. Everyone has their own cross to bear, as my grandmother used to say.

'I do look back and cringe at some of the boys and men I thought I would spend the rest of my life with,' says Sarah with a smile. 'And then after searching the whole of Ireland and beyond, I ended up marrying my next-door neighbour and I couldn't be happier. I didn't see that one coming!'

She couldn't be happier ... stop it, Juliette. Stop. Maybe

some people do have life a lot easier. Maybe I'm just being bitter and jealous because it's not working out for me. We can't all find love and happily ever after with the boy next door, can we?

I happened to go a bit further afield to marry, but I don't want to share that part of my life right now with Sarah. I went to Cornwall to be precise and the pain of how it all turned out so wrong chokes me up and I can't even bring myself to talk of my own husband to this lovely lady.

Oh, Dan. My lonely, lost soul Dan, who is back in Birmingham battling and trying so hard to stay on the straight and narrow when it comes to his drinking, which has ripped the foundations out from our marriage and is tearing us both apart if we both could stop to admit it. Life, eh?

'I thought I was going to travel the world and then settle down in a place just like this,' I tell Sarah who is wiping cream from the sides of her mouth as she enjoys her éclair. 'When I first came here sixteen years ago, I didn't think it would be so long until I'd get the chance to return. I had visions of making my fortune or raising enough to buy a small property and moving somewhere like here where I'd walk and write and paint and do all sorts of beautiful relaxing things at peace by the sea.'

'That's so nice that you have come back after all these years,' she says. 'Was it summer time when you were here? And note how I use the term summer lightly. We tend to have all sorts of weather here no matter what month of the year it is, so hurray for today's burst of sunshine.'

'I was here in August ,' I tell her and I can't help but glance up at the window of the room I stayed in again as I remember it all. That window is like a magnet every time I go past it, urging me to look up and acknowledge its part in all of this.

'That would have been the summer after my first year at, university, I think ... most of my friends were away that summer, now that I think of it,' Sarah explains to me. 'A few of us went to Wildwood in New Jersey when we broke from uni and I think that Matt, Shelley's husband, was living in Dublin with his then-girlfriend. They broke up shortly after that summer though and then Shelley moved here, they fell head over heels in love and the rest is history.'

I smile at hearing Shelley's love story from her friend and I'm glad that my fleeting moment of envy has passed. I really do hope that Shelley finds peace and happiness again with Matt, who I sense she is having difficulties with at the moment as she struggles with her horrible grief and loss. It must be hard to be apart at such a difficult time.

'And so you never did find a place to live like this then?' Sarah asks me. 'Can I ask why? You don't have to tell me of course if you don't want to.'

I pause. I am not sure how much of my story to divulge to Sarah, or how much she really wants to hear.

'Well, no, I didn't ever get that far,' I tell her. 'My life didn't work out that way.'

'I'm sorry,' she says.

Goodness me, I must look sad and I don't mean to be sad.

'Oh no, you see, I found out I was expecting Rosie when I returned from here,' I explain. 'My life took a very different turn for me, that's all. I needed my family around me as I would be raising her alone but I always still had this hope of settling by the sea, maybe when Rosie left for university, or maybe when she put down roots of her own somewhere or hopefully, set off to travel the world. That was my plan, but my life still isn't really going according to plan now, is it?'

Sarah looks on with deep sadness. 'Are you sick, Juliette? I didn't like to pry earlier in your business, but—'

'The wig gave me away, didn't it?' I joke and Sarah looks at me in protest, but I shake my head to reassure her.

'No, I just—'

'I am very, very sick, yes. I am dying.'

Her hand goes to her mouth. I shouldn't have said that so bluntly, but it's the truth isn't it? And saying it aloud like that for the very first time is somewhat liberating.

'So I should probably just stop making plans and then I won't be disappointed,' I say, stirring the froth on my latte. 'Not that I want any sympathy, please don't get me wrong. We are here in Killara now to enjoy ourselves

237

and that's what I fully intend to do from now on in life, however long it lasts.'

I smile and shrug at Sarah whose hands slowly come back to the table. She has gone pale.

'How long do you think that might be?'

My throat dries up when I think about it.

'I'm not holding much hope for longer than a few months,' I say to her. 'Every day now is a bonus. I'd so love to see one more Christmas and maybe it will snow this year, just for me. I'd love to see just one more white Christmas.'

Sarah's face has frozen in shock and I'm sorry that I have brought her down like this. She looks over at Rosie and Teigan who are chatting animatedly about horses and boats and birthdays, of course. She looks at me, then she looks at her coffee, then she looks at me again.

'I honestly don't have any idea what to say to you, Juliette,' says Sarah, closing her eyes now. 'I'm so sorry to hear your news.'

'You don't have to say anything, honestly,' I tell her. 'You've been more than kind to us and I won't forget it. You have no idea how much it meant to us both yesterday to spend those precious moments on the beach together like that. It was a memory that I will cherish until my very final moments. I will never forget Rosie's face.'

I gulp now as my daughter's smiling face reflects in my memory.

'Thank you, Sarah,' I whisper.

'Look,' she says, biting her lip. 'I know you are only

around a few more days, so if there is anything I can help with to make your stay here as good as it can be, just let me know, please, I mean that.'

'Honestly, you have done more than enough, more than you might ever realise.'

'And I know you were joking earlier about Shelley being your tour guide,' continues Sarah, 'but I swear, you have helped her so much too in the past few days and I think she has really benefitted from your company. A lot more than *you* will ever know.'

Sarah wipes a stray tear from the inside of her eye.

'Gosh, really? I have? How?' I ask.

I am genuinely taken aback by this. I thought it was very much the other way around with Shelley and I. She is the one who has been helping us have a good time.

Sarah shakes her head and exhales as if she doesn't know where to start.

'Shelley has been ... look I don't want to talk behind my best friend's back, but she has almost disappeared since Lily died,' she explains to me. 'She's just ... been gone. And I've missed her company. We used to be like sisters. Meeting you and Rosie seems to have given her this magnificent lift. Your timing, as far as Shelley's concerned, was almost fateful and yesterday on the beach meant as much for me and Shelley as friends as it did for you and Rosie as mum and daughter.'

'My goodness, really?' My cynical view of this woman's perfect life has mellowed as I see the pain and gratitude in her eyes when she speaks about her friend. I feel better already at the very idea that I may have helped, even in the tiniest way, to ease Shelley's pain or to show her that life really is worth living – because of course I only realise how fragile it is now that mine is about to end.

'Yes, you really have sparked something off in her and I, for one, am so delighted to see it,' she continues. 'It's like my best friend is slowly coming back to life, like meeting you and Rosie has breathed some new life into her. She has been to the most devastating hell and back but it's only now that she's realizing that maybe, just maybe, she might be able to learn to live again, and maybe even love again too. Guilt free.'

She sips her coffee quickly as if she is trying to stop herself from saying too much more than she already has.

'I never even thought of it that way,' I say to Sarah, 'but maybe there was some big universal reason for us meeting. I do believe that everyone comes into our life for a reason, and if they leave, they leave for a reason.'

'Exactly,' agrees Sarah.

'I also believe that Rosie came into mine for a reason even though at the time it was the very last thing I expected,' I tell her. 'I didn't want to be a single mum and have a child to a man I didn't even know, who probably didn't even remember I existed. I thought when I had her that I would have a best friend for life, but that isn't working out too well, is it? All we can do at the end of the day is embrace what comes our way and have faith that somebody out there knows what it's all about and is taking us in the right direction.'

'My God, you must be terrified,' Sarah says to me. She has pushed the remainder of her chocolate éclair to the side now. 'Did you ever manage to tell Rosie's father about her? Does he know yet? You are so incredibly brave, Juliette.'

I shake my head and look out onto the harbour.

'I'm not brave at all, Sarah, I just don't have a choice unfortunately,' I tell her. 'And no, he never did get to know that she existed and that's going to sink in soon. He isn't here anymore unfortunately, so I really *don't* have a choice. I should have tracked him down at the time but now it's too late. I left it too late.'

'He isn't here?' asks Sarah with surprise. 'Do you mean here on earth or here in Killara?'

I can see her calculating years and dates and Rosie's age in her head.

'Both,' I tell here. 'He isn't here on earth and he isn't here in Killara anymore either.'

She puts down her coffee.

'You mean he was *from* Killara?' she exclaims. 'Well, if that's the case I must know him then. Who is he?'

I look over to my daughter to make sure she isn't listening in. I have nothing to lose now by telling Sarah who my one-night lover was. He is long gone and he wasn't even from here after all. What is there to keep secret anymore, apart from not letting Rosie know just yet, I can tell Sarah openly, can't I?

'His name was Pete, but he went by the nickname Skipper and I believe he was a good friend of Matt's,

Shelley's husband? He was a boatman and he's gone now, as you probably know. Gone from this earth as well as gone from Killara.'

Sarah's hands slowly come up to her face and she nods her head as it all slots into place.

'Oh yes,' she says, and then she shakes herself back to reality. 'God, yes, I knew him really, really well. Wow.'

She looks over at Rosie. Then back at me.

'Wow,' she says again. 'He was one of our gang for a short while many years ago. We were all so shocked and upset when he died. Bloody hell, Juliette. Who else knows about this?'

I take a deep breath.

'Absolutely no one around here apart from you and Shelley,' I tell her. 'I don't even know why I told you, Sarah, sorry if this is all too much. I probably shouldn't have told you.'

But Sarah is fascinated.

'And are you going to contact his family?' she asks. 'Do you even know where to start looking for them? Wasn't he from Waterford or somewhere that direction? Yes, Waterford, yes he was definitely from there.'

'Yes, he was apparently and no I have no idea how to contact his family,' I say to her, emphatically. 'I have no clue what I want to do next, Sarah. I might let sleeping dogs lie until I get home on Saturday, or else I might take my daughter for a walk today and tell her everything, as little as it is so far, that I know about him. I'm just not sure she can cope with all that baggage with what she already has ahead of her. Or maybe I'll write it in a letter for her to read much later, after I'm gone and she's old enough to digest it. I don't know, Sarah. I just can't get my head around it at all.'

Sarah sits back in her chair and folds her arms, still a look of wonder in her face. Then she leans forward again.

'You really don't know anything about him at all, do you?' she asks in a whisper.

'Nothing,' I say. 'Just his name and some fuzzy recollection of what he looked like perhaps and what happened that night all those years ago. And even that, as I say, is a little fuzzy as I'm not sure of how much of it I made up in some romantic memory and how much of it is true. It was quite a while ago after all.'

'Okay,' she says, pursing her lips in thought.

'Yes, I'm sure it really is going to be okay, I'll get over it and Rosie will muddle through,' I tell her. 'You look like you are thinking, Sarah. What are you thinking?'

Sarah smiles a little, a sympathetic smile.

'Look, I hope I'm not going to upset you but you are not going to believe this,' she says to me. 'Remember we were talking about old boyfriends earlier?'

'Yes,' I reply, not knowing where this conversation is going to.

'Well, back in the early days, Skipper was one of mine,' she says and now it's my turn to gasp.

'Jesus, I'm so sorry! I honestly had no idea!'

'No, no don't be silly!' she says quickly and she reaches

243

across and puts her hand on my arm. 'It was never serious, I swear. No hearts broken, I promise! It never even got past first base – he took me to the cinema in Galway and we kissed a bit out on his boat and that was it, end of. Like a teenage romance only we were a bit older than teenagers. But the only reason I'm telling you this, is not because we had some mad love story going on, but because ...'

She pauses.

'Go on,' I say to her.

'I'm telling you this because I am almost sure I have a photo of him somewhere in the attic of the B&B and I'm thinking maybe you would like it, for Rosie.'

I look across again. The window. The laughter. The lateness. The dark.

'You're kidding me,' I tell her. If only she knew that was where we spent the night together, in her mother's B&B where she may have a photo of him hidden somewhere in a box of old memories.

'I'm not kidding,' she says. 'Look, I'm not promising anything, but I'll have a search over the next few days and if I find it and you want it you can have it. You're here till Saturday, am I right?'

'Yes, Saturday,' I tell her and my eyes fill up at the thought of it. 'Sarah, I can't tell you how much it would mean to me to have a photo of Rosie's dad to leave with her. That's so special and so kind of you to look for it. Honestly, thank you.'

Sarah bites her lip.

'I'm so sorry your search for him didn't have a happy ending,' she says to me. 'He was a a real gem and I'll take the place apart over there until I find the photo. I'll do my very best to help you leave something behind for her. My very best. That I can promise.'

Now it's my turn to take Sarah's hand and give it a squeeze of appreciation. We both watch our daughters, who are still in full-blown conversation with little Teigan swinging her legs under her seat as she chats away with confidence. A photo of Rosie's dad would be so precious to have when I get around to telling her all about him. I feel a lump in my throat at the very idea of that conversation, so it won't be today. And it probably won't be tomorrow but when I do give it to her I want to make it a positive moment when she will finally see the man whose genes she shares and who might even look a bit like her and whose family might even learn to love her

Today, and every day while we are here, is going to be a good day. I hope so, anyway.

Chapter 18

Shelley

I arrive at *Lily Loves* fifteen minutes late and Betty, to say the least, has a face on her like a bulldog chewing a wasp.

'I'm ever so sorry, Betty! You should have just closed up and put a sign on the door,' I say to her. 'The traffic coming out of the city was insane for this time of the week and my phone battery died so I couldn't ring ahead. I'll make it up to you, I promise.'

Eliza hurries in behind me before Betty can open her mouth and she automatically takes over.

'Blame me, don't blame Shelley,' she says to Betty who already had her coat on when I arrived and is trying to get out the door. 'I insisted we went for a walk on the Prom and we lost track of time and then the traffic. Are you okay, Betty? You look like you've seen a ghost?'

I don't think that Betty and I have ever had a proper conversation about anything that didn't involve the shop so to see her now in such a fluster just because I am fifteen minutes late is a bit of a shocker. I'm more than glad to let Eliza, who's known her for years, take over. Betty was at our wedding as a guest of Eliza, she was even at Lily's christening and she never missed buying her a birthday present. And yet, apart from being much appreciative of her work in the shop, I realise I barely know the woman at all.

'I just need to go to town myself and get some stuff for my ...' she says, trailing off and straightening up a little, or should I say, calming down. 'It was busy today, Shelley. I've left the usual note for you explaining any sales and just a general overview of the morning.'

'Thank you,' I respond.

Eliza steps aside at last and lets the poor woman out, but as soon as she steps outside, she's back again.

'Shelley, before I go,' she says. 'Do you know a young girl, a teenager, dark hair, pretty but wears a lot of make up? She was looking for you.'

'Ah yes, that must be Rosie,' I say with a smile. 'Did she call in while you were here?'

Betty has that strange look about her again.

'She did,' she tells me. 'Is she a friend of yours? A relative of yours?'

'No, no she's here on holiday,' I explain. 'Any message from her? I'm sure she'll text me if she needs me for anything important. And now that I think of it, I'd better plug in my phone. She might have been trying to get me for something.'

I go behind the counter and do just that. Hearing that Rosie was looking for me gives a sense of urgency that I can't explain. Maybe it's the feeling of being needed by someone? The feeling of being able to give to someone something that comes with just being me?

'Here on holiday? Oh, is she?' says Betty and she glances at Eliza and then back to me as if she doesn't believe me. 'No, no message from her as such. She just said to tell you that she called to say hi and that was it. Off she left in a blaze of makeup and perfume that I didn't recognise.'

'Thank you, Betty,' I smile at my ever so courteous shop assistant as she makes her way outside again. I honestly have never known her to be so curious.

'And sorry again for being late!' shouts Eliza, then she mumbles under her breath to me. 'God forbid if she's late home to feed her bloody well cats. Honestly, was there any need for that look on her face? Is she always like that? You know, you think you know someone!'

'Never,' I say to my mother-in-law and I am telling the truth. 'She is never like that. She did look a bit shaken though, didn't she? I do hope she's okay and that I wasn't taking the mick by being late. I'd hate to have to come in here in the mornings now that I've discovered brunching and walking the Prom when the rest of the world is working.'

'And why would you when you don't have to?' asks Eliza. 'Take it easy, Shelley. You're not out of the woods just yet, love.'

Eliza tilts her head to the side and watches me as I fix clothes on the rails in my little boutique, the only haven where I can seem to occupy my mind completely. I feel her stare and the warmth of her smile on me as I go to the counter where I read down Betty's list of notes from the morning. Betty always writes down how many customers called in and at what time and she makes a note of what was sold even though I can tell all that by balancing my till receipts with stock.

Customer 1 – 9.35 am – browsed, didn't try on, didn't buy.

Customer 2 – 10.05 – bought scarf and green wrap dress, said she would be back for more. Said she would tweet about it also.

Customer 3 – came in as customer 2 was trying on. Bought denim jacket and said the smell reminded her of her father. Strange fish. Didn't like her.

Customer 4 – just before lunch, teenager, English accent. Not a customer after all. Asking for you.

And so it goes on, but then I freeze at what she has scribbled on a different piece of paper that I don't think she meant to leave behind, and my stomach goes sick.

'What is it?' asks Eliza, noticing my sudden change in mood. That woman could pick up energies from anywhere in the world and I'm not kidding.

'Nothing,' I say to her with a deep breath. I lean across the counter to cover Betty's note and I force a smile as my stomach rips into shreds. 'Nothing at all. Thank you so much for today, Eliza. It was just what I needed and

249

lots more. I had a great day, thank you so much. You're such a star to me.'

But Eliza is not one bit convinced.

'You know you can tell me anything, Shelley' she says, unconvinced. 'Is there something going on that's worrying you? Are you missing Matt? Did you have a row or something?'

I stand up straight and shake my head.

'No, no, I'm fine, I really am fine,' I tell her. 'Now run along or you'll be late for your committee meeting.'

She gasps as she remembers that she is meant to be at the Cancer Research Society AGM in ten minutes.

'And thank you again for today!' I call after her. 'I owe you lunch or dinner soon!'

She waves without looking back and mutters to me as she leaves but I have no idea what she is saying. Then she is gone in a blaze of perfume and positivity and I look down at Betty's note and try and make sense of it all, but I have no idea what it means. Or do I? No. I don't want to go backwards, I can't go backwards. I feel my breath shortening so I take out my phone and I call the first person I think of who can make me feel better.

I call Juliette and the second she answers, I scrunch up Betty's scribble and I throw it in the bin.

'Juliette, it's Shelley,' I say and I close my eyes when I hear the now familiar sound of her voice. 'What are you guys up to today?'

Juliette

It is so good to hear Shelley's voice and I can honestly say that she has perked up quite a bit, even on the phone, from the downbeat shell of a girl I only met a few days ago.

'Shelley! So lovely to hear from you. We have plans to go sailing soon around the cliffs with Leo, and I'm really looking forward to it, as is Rosie. How was your morning? I bet you were tired after yesterday.'

'I was tired to be honest but I was also feeling very energised and positive afterwards, especially today,' she says to me. 'So much so that you will never believe what I did today. I've been itching to tell you!'

I am intrigued. 'Go on?' I say to her.

'I actually pushed myself and went to Galway this morning with my mother-in-law,' she says. 'And we had a wonderful time shopping and brunching and people watching. I know to most people that's an everyday thing but I'm so out of touch with real life and I know that you'll understand how big a leap it was for me to do that.'

I take a deep breath. 'You're a champ,' I tell her. 'I'm so proud of you. Keep taking these baby steps, Shelley. I can see your glow is starting to return and we need to keep fanning those flames.'

Shelley's newfound positivity, as simple as it may sound to an outsider, is music to my ears. I shudder to think of what she must go through every morning when she wakes up, especially this week when her husband is gone.

'So, did you buy anything nice?' I ask her, looking at my nails as I speak and reminding myself that I really do need to take more care of my appearance. 'I'm hoping to take Rosie shopping tomorrow, all being well. I'm sure Galway was buzzing today, was it?'

'Of course it was,' says Shelley. 'It always is this time of year. It was nice to get away from here for a change of scenery, but ...'

I wait for her to continue.

'Are you there, Shelley?'

'Yes, yes I'm here,' she says much to my relief. 'Oh, there are no buts at all about a morning in Galway, Juliette. Just ignore me. It was lovely and it was nice to spend some time with Eliza. She's such a darling and makes me feel good from the inside out. I should really be in her company more. She's so different to my own mother and of course no one can ever take my mother's place, but she's got my back and I feel safe with her. I need to do things with her more often, for both of our sakes.'

I want to hug her and cheer her on even more. She has so much more to give to her life and she is finally starting to see that.

'That is so good to hear,' I tell her and I really mean it. I am sitting on a picnic bench across from the cottage watching the boats come in and out from their day's fishing as I wait for Rosie to get her stuff together and if Shelley hadn't called, I'd probably have ended up moping or weeping and feeling sorry for myself. I keep thinking, or should I say, worrying about Dan and wondering if it was a good idea to leave him out of this trip when I know it would have done him the world of good to get some time away from reality. If only he would get sober enough to make that decision easier.

'It's a pity you're at work, as it's such a beautiful day outside. I'm not sure this good spell is meant to last so I'm lapping it up while I can. Tell me, do you think you'll be busy all day?'

She pauses. 'I'm not sure, why?'

'I was going to suggest you pack up for the day and come and join us? You've had a great day, the sun is shining. I think you should come and have some more fun when the going is good.'

'You always have the best ideas, Juliette,' she tells me, brightening a little more. 'Life is too short for shit, isn't that what you told me the other day?'

I shrug and laugh in response. I can't remember if I did say that, but what's new there lately? According to Rosie, I've the worst memory ever, after all.

'I may have said that at some stage,' I say to Shelley with a giggle. 'I tend to spew out lots of little mottos now that I'm on death's door so don't feel the need to take all of them seriously.'

'I'm. going to finish up here right now,' Shelley announces. 'I'll put a note on the door and I'll go out and get some of that sunshine on my face. I am going

to miss you when you leave here you know that, Juliette!
You are like flames under my feet every morning, like
the push that I've needed for so long. I'll never forget
you for it.'

Well, I feel honoured at that and I remember Sarah's
words from earlier when she said we had helped Shelley
so much, then a wave of fear overcomes me when I think
of how she might be after we leave. She will never see
me again, yet I am not sure she is even thinking that
way. When I leave here, I will be leaving to die.

'You can come and join us if you want?' I suggest
again, wondering if she is wanting me to say what she
is already thinking and hoping that I can keep her spirits
up for a bit longer before I *do* go. 'I don't want to pressure you, but the invitation is there and you would be
very welcome. I think Rosie is your number one fan so
she would be delighted.'

I hear Shelley breathe in and out again. I breathe in
and out again. I am tired, more tired than I will ever
admit, and it's starting to gnaw at my bones and although
I've been denying it to myself, I am light-headed and
dizzy more often than I'm not these days.

'Ah, that would be such a perfect way to spend the
afternoon. Are you sure you don't mind?'

'Of course I don't mind!' I tell her. 'We'd both love to
have you come along!'

She asks me where I am right now and I explain my
exact location.

'I'm directly across from the cottage, sitting on a picnic

bench with the wind in my hair and looking like I haven't a care in the world,' I tell her, trying to force mind over matter. 'All I need is a glass of something bubbly and I'll be sorted.'

'Well if that's the case, don't move an inch and I'll join you very soon,' says Shelley. 'I'll just pop home and get changed and ... oh, I don't have my car with me today. Ah, maybe I'm being too spontaneous and irrational. I'll just—'

'Go!' I tell her. 'Walk up to the house now and drive back to me with whatever it is you need to take with you for the afternoon. Rosie is just starting to get ready so you know how long that will take and our excursion isn't due to take off for another twenty-five minutes. We have time. Don't change your mind! Go!'

'Perfect,' says Shelley. 'That's just what I needed to hear. I'm going.'

'That's it, Shelley,' I tell her. 'I want you to always remember something.'

She pauses. 'Of course? What is it?'

'Always make the most of the sunshine, in any way you can,' I tell her. 'I want you to promise me that when I leave here, you will always look for the sunshine even in your darkest days. Always look for the rainbow and you'll find it. Try not to focus on the dark.'

'I will, I promise,' whispers Shelley. 'You've made me realise that there is sunshine in every day if we open our eyes and look for it. You're an inspiration and I'll never forget you.'

When I'm gone, she means. She doesn't say it but I hear her finish the sentence in the silence. And then she hangs up the phone before I get a chance to say goodbye. I tilt my head back and up to the sun and I marvel at the warmth on my face, the brightness when I close my eyes. I'm feeling very tired today but I won't let it beat me. I won't let my sunshine days be over just yet.

Shelley and Leo, who is taking us out on his private boat, walk down the hill towards me together, chatting harmoniously, and I instantly realise that everyone knows everyone around here. This warmth of Irish village life is what I fell in love with all those years ago – the cama-raderie, the community spirit, the knowledge that help and support is only ever a little while away was what I had dreamed of experiencing in my own everyday life. And yes there are the gossips, the whispers and the 'do-gooders' but all in all, that security and simplicity of everyone knowing your name is something that always appealed to me over living in a large anonymous city where your neighbour is a stranger.

'Shelley tells me she'll be joining us,' says Leo with a hearty smile. 'You must be Juliette?'

I shake Leo's hand and his firm greeting almost takes my arm out of my socket but what else would I expect from a sailor like him. His arms are muscular and strong and his weather-beaten face is open and friendly. I like him instantly.

'Shelley, I am so freakin' excited!' says Rosie and to

my delight and surprise, Shelley puts her arm around my daughter. There is a glow around the people here and yes, they have suffered with loss and tragedy like any corner of the world, but I adore how they reach out to each other and to strangers and visitors alike. Seeing that Rosie can be loved by people like Shelley, who has only known her for a few days, reassures me that life for my daughter will indeed go on when I'm no longer here.

'You will love it,' says Shelley. 'This is Rosie, Leo. She's fallen in love with Killara, I think.'

She's fallen in love with Shelley, I want to say and I don't mean that in any way other than that my daughter is mesmerised by Shelley and all they have in common, not to mention her dog and her magnificent home and shop, and how she arranged for us both to go horse-riding yesterday plus how she has been a confidante since finding her on the sand dunes on Saturday.

'Well, we can't blame you for that, young lady,' says Leo and he gives me a wink and a smile. 'When people come to Killara on holiday, they always come back or else they simply stay, don't they Shelley?'

Shelley nods in agreement.

'I came here on holiday and I ended up staying forever,' says Shelley and a pang of remorse shoots at me like a dart. I wish I had done the same thing, now. I could have had such a beautiful, peaceful life by the sea just like I had always dreamed of and maybe, who knows, things would have worked out differently for me in many ways.

'I want to keep coming back here forever,' says Rosie,

linking both Shelley and I by the arm. 'I don't even want to think about going home. Mum, can we just stay here forever?'

I give her arm a squeeze. Forever is a long time, or so the saying goes but just how long is my forever? Days? Weeks? A few months? I wish so much that we could all press pause right now and make my forever last, to give me a chance of making sure she will be okay, to talk to her and tell her all the things that I need her to know before I go. Focus, I remind myself. Live in the present, not the past. No regrets. Sometimes though, it's not that easy.

'So, if you want to follow me further down the pier then, ladies,' says Leo, 'I'm going to be your captain, or your skipper if you like, on this very exclusive boat trip, and on today's excursion you will see, all being well, some of the Atlantic's finest landmarks and also some of its most exclusive wildlife.'

Rosie gives us both a squeeze now.

'Excited dot com!' she says to all three of us. 'This is going to be unreal!'

'And so you should be, young lady. Let's hope the puffins come out to play or maybe even a whale if we're lucky,' says Leo and I think my child is about to levitate with excitement.

'I have a feeling they will,' says Shelley. 'They normally like to peep out and say hello to new faces. I have a good feeling about today.'

I am still fluttering inside from when Leo used the

word 'skipper' but Shelley doesn't seem to have noticed. Maybe it's nerves, or maybe it's just sadness for the man who fathered my child, but I feel a bit sick right now, not to mention these dizzy spells, and if it wasn't for Rosie's enthusiasm and the fact that I had made such a big deal of today and this boat trip, I'd gladly sit this one out.

'Are you okay, Juliette?' Shelley asks me. 'You look a bit pale all of a sudden.'

'Oh don't tell me you're seasick already, Mum,' laughs Rosie, but I can see that she is worried inside. 'Mum?'

'I'm fine! Ship ahoy!' I say to both of them and I put both my thumbs up. Then we each take Leo's hand in turn and step on the boat, and follow his health and safety instructions as we put on our life jackets. A dull pain kicks in at the back of my head as we set sail but I don't want to ruin this moment by mentioning it. I'm fine. Maybe if I keep saying those two words out loud, I *will* actually be fine. But I am not of course and I will never be fine. This pain, has come on so strong today and the tiredness is exhausting me, and I'm not fine. I am scared. I am absolutely terrified. Please don't let this happen to me already. I'm not ready yet. I don't want to die, please don't let me die!

'I hope you've more sea-legs than your husband, Shelley,' says Leo and Shelley rolls her eyes at what is obviously a long running joke to the locals about Matt and his intolerance of all things boat-related.

'I'm like a child in a sweet shop,' says Shelley back to

him. 'This is one of my favourite things to do in the whole wide world. Let's go, Leo! Aye, aye captain!'

And at that we are off and I look behind as we sail out at speed onto the bay and leave Killara and all its colourful brightness in the distance, including Brannigan's with its green walls and its loaded memories.

I honestly don't feel so good but I cannot let this sickness take over me now. I close my eyes and let the speed of the wind and the splashes of the water waken my senses and I thank God for how good it is to be alive.

Shelley

'Rosie! Juliette! Look, the puffins!'

Rosie is practically Leo's best friend by now as we sail out onto the choppier waters, far from Killara and the stillness of the bay. The cliffs come into view and I do think that Rosie is going to jump out of her skin with excitement at the majestic sight and I look around to make sure that Juliette is taking everything in, but she doesn't seem to be enjoying it as much as her daughter, or as much as she herself believed she would.

'Juliette, you don't look well,' I say to her over the sound of the boat's motor and the spray that comes off the water. 'Are you cold? I should have said to you that it gets a bit nippy when you sail out this far.'

I sit beside her and look at her face which is more

ashen in colour than the usual shade of green that comes with seasickness.

'Ssh,' she says to me, nodding up towards Rosie who is bending Leo's ear with questions about puffins and whales and dolphins and the like. 'I don't want to ruin this for her. What an absolute treat on the eyes. It's amazing.'

I follow her eyeline up to the cliffs as Leo sails in as close as he can get to the famous Cliffs of Moher. Larger tour boats from County Clare sail ahead of us but Leo skirts in more intimately than they ever could and I marvel at how no matter how many times I have made this trip during my time in this part of the world, it always takes my breath away.

'It's the most beautiful country in the world,' says Juliette and she looks up in awe at the wondrous view. 'I always loved Ireland. I feel so at home here, isn't that strange?'

I look at her knowing exactly what she means. I've heard it so many times from tourists who come into my shop and who absorb everything about our homeland in a way that we locals never do, as we can often take it for granted.

'Juliette, a part of you will always be here, you know that,' I whisper to her and when I look into her eyes I can see that she is crying. I link her arm, just as Rosie did with us both earlier and she leans her tired head on my shoulder.

'I need to see Dan,' she says to me. 'I miss him.'

'Of course you do,' I say to my new, oh so brave friend. She has just a few more days in Killara and then she will be gone from here, then gone forever and I dread the thought of it, but something tells me that Juliette will never be far from me or from here. She has touched something within me, she has lit a spark inside me that has brought me to life and that won't just go away no when we're apart. I feel stronger for knowing her and I don't think that the part of her that is now within me will ever really go

'Look at Rosie, Juliette,' I whisper. 'Look at how this place suits her so well. There is a part of this place in her blood, can't you see it?'

Juliette nods and smiles through her tears as we both watch Rosie who can't decide if it's more important to watch through her own eyes what she is experiencing or via her phone as she snaps everything she wants to share with her friends.

'She is loving every moment of it and I have you to thank for so much of what she's experienced so far,' Juliette says. 'These are the days she will remember the most, I hope.'

'And there's more to come,' I say to her. 'Would you mind if I cook for you both tonight?'

Juliette's eyes widen in delight. 'At your place or ours? That would be a real treat!'

'I'll come to you if you don't mind,' I tell her. 'It's cosier and at least you can slip off to rest if you want to. I'll bring all the ingredients and cook a nice supper.'

'Deal,' says Juliette, and she leans her head on my shoulder again. I can tell she is slowing down by the look on her face. Something has changed, like her spark is slowly flickering. She looks tired, a little paler and the way she reaches out to me physically to lean on me or to just hold my hand as we sail along tells me that she is scared inside. I look out onto the water and fight back tears as the reality of losing Juliette when I have only just found her hits me properly for the first time. I need to help make her final days in Killara as comfortable and special as I can so that she knows how much I appreciate her. My next plan for them both needs to kick into place as soon as possible. I am excited and moved at the very thought of it.

I arrive as promised armed with a wicker basket full of local produce at Juliette's cottage later that evening and make my way to the kitchen, ordering Juliette to rest up on the sofa while Rosie and I get stuck into supper.

'Do you like spag bol?' I call into her. She is snuggled up under a fleecy throw in her pyjamas and Rosie, who is also in her pyjamas, is on cloud nine because as well as cooking up a storm in the kitchen we are also cooking up a plan of our own.

'It's my favourite dish ever,' shouts Juliette and Rosie gives me a high five. We have so got this.

'I told you it was her favourite,' she says to me. 'She loves anything Italian, especially the men, ha!'

'Good taste! So, did you think about what I asked you

earlier?' I ask as she chops onions beside me like the perfect little assistant.

'Yes, I have the playlist made,' she tells me in a whisper. 'It's all ready to go. I have Prince on there, some INXS, a few Meatloaf tracks and what was the other one you told me to find?'

'Wake Me Up Before You Go Go?' I suggest.

'That's the one,' she says. 'Yes, I just Googled '80s classics and most of what you thought Mum might like came up, so all I need now is the you-know-what and that was your part of the bargain.'

I smile at Rosie and signal at her to throw the onions into the pan and soon, with a touch of garlic and oregano, some salt, black pepper, green peppers and mushrooms as well as mince and tomato sauce, we are almost ready to serve – with spaghetti, a sprinkle of parmesan and a basil leaf on top.

'Voila!' I say to Rosie. 'Take that in to your mum.'

'That's French,' she corrects me and I shrug. What's a language blooper between friends?

We tuck in to our taste of Italy in front of the evening's soap operas and just after our food has settled and the plates almost licked after a day at sea, and when we are totally assured there is nothing more on the TV that catches our attention, Rosie makes her excuse to use the bathroom. I take this as my cue, just as we had arranged and when she comes back in, I am all ready for action.

'What the ...?'

Juliette looks confused and when Rosie presses play

on her iPod and Prince's 'Kiss' rocks through the living room, we are all in stitches laughing. Rosie is dressed in neon pink leggings, a 'Choose Life' t-shirt which I had kept from my days at roller discos in the north, obligatory yellow leg warmers and a Toyah Wilcox style spikey wig. She takes her mother's hands and gently pulls her up off the sofa.

'Come on, Mum!' shouts Rosie. 'This is another of your favourite things!'

'Man, I loved Prince!' shouts Juliette. 'Turn it up!'

And I do just that.

You don't have to be rich they sing at the top of their voices and as they dance, I take in the joy on their faces and my heart melts when they hold hands. Finally, I take notice of their feet as they dance together to the music, laughing and singing and dancing like no one is watching. The music booms through the air, leaving no room for any other sound and Juliette, as physically difficult as it seems to be after such a long day, is really giving it her all as she boogies along with her baby girl.

'Kiss!' they shout together and punch the air as if it was rehearsed, then Juliette pulls Rosie in for a hug. She gives her a big kiss on the cheek and Rosie does the same back.

Once again, I feel that old familiar twinge when I think that this could have been me with my own mother a few years into the past, or me and my Lily a few years into the future, if life wasn't so cruel. And life is being cruel here too, I remind myself. As happy as this moment is, every day I see them together will always be tinged with sadness at what is still to come.

The song choice moves on to some retro Madonna with 'Papa Don't Preach' and Juliette whoops with delight, then swaps her own wig with Rosie's more exciting version and they beckon me to join them with Juliette taking the TV remote control as her makeshift microphone.

'I had no idea what this song was about when it was released!' she bellows over the music. 'But I freakin' loved it!'

Rosie bops along beside me, enjoying every moment whether she knows the songs or not.

'Good job, DJ!' I mouth to her with a thumbs-up and she looks up at her mum who is totally lost in the music and I see the tears glisten in Rosie's eyes.

They are dancing together with sheer freedom, this dying woman in her pyjamas and a punk style wig and her teenage daughter who has totally jumped into character just to make her mother laugh and sing out loud.

She is seeing Juliette as a person in her own right now, and not just her dying mother. She is seeing a person with a past, with old memories that came before Rosie existed, a person with hopes and dreams that were formed before she was even born. I wish I had taken the time to recognise my own mother as just that.

But most of all I wished we had danced together just like Rosie and Juliette are doing right now here in front of me. And even better, I wish that someone would have captured it on camera so that I could treasure it forever, just like I have done for these two beautiful people who have done more for my healing than they will ever know. I hit record and catch every moment of it and I can't wait to see their faces when they look back on it. A perfect memory of happy times, for Rosie to hold on to and cherish forever and for Juliette to smile back on for however long she has left in this life.

Chapter 19

Juliette

WEDNESDAY

'It's just a headache; I really don't want any fuss, Helen,' I say to my sister.

'It's not just a headache, though is it!' she replies. 'Tell me the truth. When did this start? Yesterday? The day before? When?'

I knew she would panic.

'We're on holiday and I probably just got over-excited yesterday, wanting to make the boat trip special for Rosie, and it *was* special,' I say to Helen who has phoned to find me curled up in bed in the cottage with the blinds and curtains closed. Rosie has gone to take Merlin for a walk as was agreed with Shelley when she left us last night after our hilarious '80s disco, which was so much fun. As much as I don't want to admit it to anyone, the headache that started on the boat yesterday is now getting worse and it's scaring the life out of me.

'Should I ring Michael?' my sister asks me, her voice trembling with panic from across the Irish Sea. 'He could maybe arrange for a doctor there to see you. Oh, Jules this is a nightmare with you being so far away like this.'

'Don't say I told you so,' I warn her amicably. 'I don't need any lectures right now.'

'I won't lecture you but I am going out of my mind now with worry. How bad is the pain on a scale of one to ten?'

I can sense my sister's urgency but I really don't want to raise the alarm. It has to pass. It can't be happening so fast, not like this, not here, not now when I'm on my own with Rosie. I need to see Dan. I need to see Helen again and my mum and dad and my nephews. I can't just die here alone with my daughter, no, please don't make it happen like this. I'm terrified. Perhaps I'm over-reacting? Dr Michael said it wouldn't happen so fast, didn't he? He wouldn't have told me to go away for a few days otherwise. I can't be dying so quickly, no. It's just a bad day. I'm just having a bad day after all the excitement of being here.

'Seven right now, but let me see how I feel after a few hours' rest,' I tell my sister, adamant not to let this get to me or admit to her what might really be happening. 'It could just be seasickness and exhaustion. We've packed a lot in so far but I so wanted to take Rosie into Galway today and do some shopping. I just know that she would love to hear the buskers and buy some nice new clothes.

I can't ruin this for her, Helen, not now when she is enjoying herself so much. I've never seen her so animated and she's really taken to this place just as I hoped she would. She loves it.'

I can hear Helen's boys in the background and I get a pang of homesickness that is almost worse than the pain going through my weary mind. I long for Dan, for how he used to be when he was strong and caring and loving and able to cope with my down days, when my illness would take over and he'd have to down tools and tell me that I was going to be okay.

'But it's not just a headache that is going to go away after some rest, is it?' whispers Helen, her fear spilling out down the phone. 'It's not like you can take a painkiller and make it go away. You have a brain tumour. You have cancer. And let's not forget, you got a pretty big shock when your dreams of bumping into Skipper were well and truly scuppered.'

Helen, I know, wants to scream at me for coming here, for all sorts of reasons, but I am too tired to argue with her or protest at anything she has to say.

'Right,' she continues. 'I'm booking a flight and I'm coming over to you tonight, Juliette. Brian can take a few days off until you are strong enough to come home but you are not making that journey back here alone. Over my dead body.'

I sink into the pillow and close my eyes, my hand barely able to keep holding my phone to my ear. *Over my dead body, you mean.*

'Just let me sleep it off, please, and I will call you later,' I tell her, my voice slow and weary. 'I mean it, I'm going to fight this until Saturday morning and then I will take the ferry home as planned. Give me a few hours and I will be back on my feet and annoying you with more pictures of loveliness, of good times and magic memories for Rosie. Just another little while, please. Just let it pass.'

Helen keeps talking but I can't listen to her anymore. Her voice that was once so soothing and reassuring is now piercing my brain and sending shocks through every inch of my body. I have no idea what time of day it is but I need to keep my eyes closed. I manage to hang up the phone and I embrace the darkness and the silence at last. I need to sleep it off. I will be back on my feet in no time. I have to be. For Rosie. We are having such a good time and I can't leave her yet. Last night was so much fun, thanks to Shelley who has really come to life in helping us and I don't want this to end now. Please God, don't take me just yet. I have so much still to live for. Please, give me just a little more time with my girl.

Shelley

Betty was acting weird again when I came to take over in *Lily Loves* and she couldn't wait to get away from me, just like yesterday – but I'm not going to ask what her problem is. Maybe it's because I already know what she is thinking, or maybe it's time I let her go anyhow. I should be able to come into my place of work like other people do, at nine in the morning and take my lunchbreak and work until closing, just like I used to do before grief and its poison took over my very existence. I want Matt to be home already, for us to be taking the steps forward that he has urged me to for as long as I can remember now, and I want to be able to let him love me and for me to love him just as Lily would have liked us to.

Maybe we could start trying again for the family that we so crave, but the very thought of facing more disappointment through miscarriage, like we did before Lily, tears at my heart and my empty womb tells me no, begs me to please not go through that agony again.

I tend to my customers all afternoon on autopilot until Rosie bounds in through the door with Merlin on his lead and I want to tell her not to bring him into the shop as it wouldn't look well should he shake his fur and spray the clothes with the smell of wet dog. It is raining again in Killara but Rosie doesn't seem to mind at all and her cheeks are glowing having spent the entire afternoon outdoors with her favourite canine friend. She sits up on a high stool at the back of the shop and I chat to her from behind the counter.

'Have you checked in with your mum this afternoon?' I ask her, almost afraid of hearing her answer. I had waited last night until Juliette was asleep, and Rosie and I had spent some time chatting about boys and makeup and music before I slipped off and locked the door when she too was in bed. I promised her she could take Merlin today which has proven to be the perfect distraction for Juliette to get some rest and I fear that maybe the elation of the week so far and all that she has learnt about Skipper has taken its toll on her body, mind and soul. I, too, am feeling a dip in my mood but it's probably from seeing Juliette suffer so much and battle against what is inevitably coming her way.

'I popped by about an hour ago to check on her and she was fast asleep,' says Rosie. 'Aunty Helen rang me too to see if I'm okay and so did Dan but he sounded a bit tipsy as usual. I wish he would really wise up, Shelley. Mum needs him and so do I but all he seems to want is a bottle by his side instead of the woman who loves him most in the world. I'm never getting married. Ever.'

I want to put my hands over her ears and protect her from adult conversations and pressures and let her be the child that I was never allowed to be after my mother died.

'Rosie,' I say to her softly. 'As an only child, the burden of loss you are going to face is multiplied with all that you have ahead but I really hope you don't become hardened by life along the way. Dan is doing what he has to do at the moment to cope, and if your mum chose him and loves him like I know she does, I bet he is a good man despite his drinking?'

She shrugs and then smiles a bit.

'He's great fun, I suppose. Well, he used to be,' she whimpers. 'He used to make Mum laugh so much and

I swear when he comes into a room Mum really lights up. I used to be jealous at the start but then I got to love hearing them laugh their heads off at the silliest things. She's missing him a lot.'

'See?' I say to her. 'I'm not saying marriage is right for everyone, but in life I always think it's good to keep an open mind on absolutely everything thrown at you, no matter how hard it seems. I think meeting your mum and seeing how positively she embraces everyone and everything she meets has made me see that life is a lot easier when you look at the glass as half-full instead of half-empty, though at times it's hard to see if there's anything in the glass at all.'

I may have lost her somewhere in my metaphors as she is now checking her phone but if she even takes in some of what I have to say, I might feel that I have done right by Juliette in this conversation, and by Rosie too.

'When my mum died, I felt I had to grow up overnight and drift out into the big, bad world all alone,' I say to her. She puts down the phone. I've got her back.

'Were you scared too?'

'Petrified,' I tell her. 'Yes, I had my father to lean on but he wasn't much use for the first few years and he did the same as Dan is doing now. He drank to block out the reality of being left with a teenager who was full of questions and despair and that's how I eventually found myself here in Killara with my aunt who seemed to understand just a little bit more as to how to cope with me when he couldn't.'

Rosie looks panicked now. Oh no.

'I don't want to live with Aunty Helen, Shelley,' she says to me, shaking her head. 'It just won't be the same and even though she's really nice, she does things differently in her house.'

'She will look after you, I'm sure she will.'

'And I don't want to grow up overnight like you had to,' she continues. 'I want my mum. I want to hear her laugh with Dan again when I'm doing my homework in the kitchen and they are snuggled up on the sofa in the next room. I want to dance and be silly with her again just like we did last night in the cottage. I don't want Mum to die.'

I take a deep breath. What on earth do I say to that?

'You and Dan and Aunty Helen and everyone that knows your mum will come good because you won't have to grow up overnight like I did, wait and see,' I say to her. 'I bet Helen knows you inside and out and thinks the absolute world of you?'

She nods. 'I suppose she does. She says I'm the daughter she never had as a joke when the boys are getting on her nerves. I've sometimes told her things I couldn't tell Mum, just to get some advice.'

I see a tiny glimmer of hope in her eyes.

'Well, then?' I say. 'That's good you trust her like that. And do you talk to Dan in that way at all? Do you ever tell him things and trust him with your feelings like that?'

She shrugs and thinks.

'I suppose I do sometimes,' she says, 'though in a different way, I think. He sticks up for me always if I ever feel in trouble.'

'That's good!'

'Yes, not that I get into trouble much but you know what I mean – I mean when I am worried about something he reassures me, like once he went to my school because I was being bullied by a girl in the year above me and he spoke to the headteacher, demanding it never happened again. And it didn't.'

She sits up a little straighter when she tells me this and I feel better for her already.

'Oh Rosie, darling, you see? You have so many people who love and adore you,' I say to her. 'And on top of all that, your mum has given you the very best she can in every way so you can be the strong, independent young woman that I have no doubt you will be.'

'But she won't be able to guide me for much longer, will she?' she states.

I bite my lip. Do I be honest with Rosie that her mum is deteriorating? Do I try to prepare her for what is coming, but then again, how can I possibly do that? There is no preparation for grief when someone so young is getting ready to say goodbye. I think of my own mother and how the gaping hole of loss felt like someone had ripped out my very core and I couldn't breathe as I was so buckled with the shock even though I knew it was coming.

'Your mum will always guide you, Rosie,' I say to her.

'Not in the way she has been when you can see her and hear her every day, but she'll always be near you in a very special way. Look, I know it's not the same and it's the most awful thing in the whole world, but wait and see, when you need her you will feel her near you, I promise. I know that's what gets me through each day without my mum and Lily. I have a place I go to and if I close my eyes I can see them and it makes me feel just a little bit better.'

I realise this much more now when I think of my own loss. Call it an awakening, call it a moment of change or maybe it was seeing someone like Juliette stare death in the face but I have opened my mind and heart over the past few days and it has made me feel my loved ones so much nearer. I see how Juliette doesn't want to leave Rosie, and I know my mother didn't want to leave me, so how can she be very far away? She is with me in everything I do, she is guiding me and watching me and I now know that she is looking after Lily and urging me to make the most of my days here just like Juliette is before her time is up.

'I should probably go back and check in on her, shouldn't I?' says Rosie, fiddling with Merlin's lead in her hands. 'She's tired today and I hate watching her when she's so weak. I am so afraid of something happening ...'

She takes a tissue from her sleeve, dabs her nose and slides off the stool.

'I think that's a good idea, yes, plus I'm sure you're fed up by now with Merlin,' I say trying to lighten things a little. I'll call down on you both as soon as my shift is finished and I'll make you something nice to eat, how's that for a plan?'

'That'd be cool, yeah.'

'We could watch a movie, all three of us and let your mum just take it easy. She's done so much to make this holiday special and it has been special, hasn't it, Rosie?'

Rosie's lip begins to tremble and she doesn't notice how much Merlin is tugging at the lead, trying to get out of the restrictions of my little workplace. He starts to bark and as he does, Rosie gives into her emotion and lets her tears fall.

'It's been amazing because we found you and you've made me feel so much better and you make Mum feel better too,' she says. 'I just don't want it to end. Not yet. Not yet, Shelley.'

I look into her beautiful eyes and the fear in them takes my breath away. I know exactly what she means. She doesn't want this holiday to end because it means she will have to start preparing for life as she knows it to end.

'I can't help it, I'm so scared,' she sobs to me. 'I'm so scared that I'm going to have no one to turn to no matter how much Aunty Helen and Dan try. My grandparents are old and my Nanna is too sick to even worry about Mum. I lie in bed at night and worry that she might have the same sickness as Mum does and Aunty Helen has enough on her plate with her own family. Who's going to be there for me? I don't want my mum to die. Please God, don't let her die.'

I rush to Rosie's side and I put my arms around her and hold her tightly into my chest, then I let her cry and cry and cry and as she does so, I do too for Juliette and for this dear little girl that has so much loneliness and grief ahead of her.

'I know you're scared, baby,' I whisper to her. 'You don't want to lose your mum and your mum doesn't want to lose you. This is the most terrifying thing you will ever go through. You will be angry, you will be so angry that you want to tear the place down and run away and hide and scream and shout and you will see other girls with their mothers at all stages of their lives and you'll think 'why me? Why my mum?' It will burn you and it will kick you in the stomach and it will hit you like a ton of bricks just when you think the pain has gone. It will never go away, Rosie but if you can, and I know it's going to be really hard to think this way, just try and think of all this pain that you are going through as a big storm that happens every time you remember how much you love your mother.'

'What do you mean?'

'If you didn't love each other so, so much, the pain would be a lot less, wouldn't it?'

She shrugs. 'I suppose.'

'If you didn't care for her, you wouldn't feel this pain, so when you have a really hard day and all that anger and gut-wrenching pain takes over, see it as a sign of how much you really love each other and always will. It's like the floods after a storm, or the damage done by a hurricane. It's a sign of something so big that no one or nothing could control it. That's how much you love your mum and you will find that when you need her, she will be near, because she is in here.'

I put my hand on my heart.

'No one can ever take her away from there, Rosie. She will never, ever leave your heart and once you realise that, you will feel just a little bit better, day by day, week by week. You have a strong woman in your heart and that's where she will always stay.'

I have to look away when Rosie puts her own hand on her own heart and takes a big deep breath in and then out again.

'I feel her in here already,' she says. 'No one can ever take that away from me.'

'That's exactly it,' I say, fighting back tears. 'And you know if you ever need someone to talk to, I'm always just a phone call away.'

'Thanks Shelley. You've been so kind to us and I will definitely phone you lots and lots,' she sniffles. 'I dread when I can't walk in here and chat to you like this. I can't talk to anyone like I can talk to you.'

And now I do shed a tear. To think that this little girl feels even a little bit better by talking to me makes me fill up inside.

'Well, we have to make every moment count then, don't we? I know, why don't you walk up to my house and leave Merlin back there and by the time you walk back here, I'll be finished and we'll both go see your mum, how's that?' I suggest to her, thinking the responsibility of seeing to the dog might just distract her for a little while. Plus, Merlin is becoming irritable and restless and I can sense he has had quite enough of being out and about for one day. He is a home bird, old Merlin and we need to think of him too, if only to help ourselves.

Rosie nods to me as her tears subside and she pats the dog. I give her the key to my house and hold her hand for a moment.

'Take a big deep breath, Rosie,' I say to her. 'You're doing so well. Let's try and make the most of the next few days and keep having fun, eh?'

'Yes, yes I will,' she says. 'I am so glad we came here now. It's been the best time ever, mostly because of you.'

'And you've helped me too, don't forget. Now, when you get to the house, just open the door and let old Merlin in to the hallway and hopefully he won't follow you from the dog flap and you can make your escape back here,' I tell her. 'In fact, put him in the kitchen and that will give you enough breathing space to make your move because he loves being in there and by the time he notices you are gone, you'll be at the bottom of the driveway at least.'

Rosie takes the key from me and manages a smile.

'Oh, and here's the alarm code,' I remember. 'It's really simple. Hold him on the lead until you punch in the six numbers, and then walk him to the kitchen and you're done. Is that okay?'

She takes it all in.

'I feel like I'm in Mission Impossible with all those instructions,' she says and the way her little face lights up tugs at my heart until it's sore. 'It's one of our favourite movies. Mum just loves Tom Cruise.'

'Well, we might just have a good old Tom Cruise feast tonight then while your mum puts her feet up,' I suggest. 'I think that sounds good, don't you?'

I wipe away her tears with my thumbs and tilt her chin up, just as Matt does to me when I'm having a tough time coping with all that I have been dealt with. It always makes me feel better to have that physical touch and direct eye contact when I need to pull it together.

'I wish we could just stay here and it could always be like it has been since we met you,' she says to me and I shake my head slowly.

'I will always be here for you, Rosie,' I tell her. 'You're a special girl to me and I think you and I have become buddies, what do you think?'

'I'm afraid that we'll never see you again once we leave,' she says to me, and my heart warms up so much I feel it might burst that she might want to keep in touch. 'You know, after everything.'

'I have a feeling we'll keep in touch, so don't even think about that now,' I tell her. 'You know you can talk to me whenever you want and that's a promise. Now, go and let your other old pal there get home for a rest and I'll be waiting for you when you get back.'

'Thank you, Shelley,' she says to me, wiping fresh tears with the back of her hand.

'No, thank *you*, Rosie,' I whisper as I stand at the door and watch her make her way up the hill onto the outskirts of the village where my house stands on the highest point of Killara.

Rosie doesn't realise it, but I dread the day that she leaves here just as much as she does. I fear that if I don't see her again I might spiral back into that deep dark hole of grief and I can't even dare to think of going back there again. Juliette has given me tough love when I needed it to face the world again and see the good in people like Sarah and Leo. She's forced me to realise how I have been doing myself no favours by shutting the people out who really do care for me. She has shown me that, just like she has done, I am pushing the man I love away when all I really want to do is pull him closer. She has shown me the beauty of laughter and good food, of fresh air and of spontaneity, while her daughter has filled me up inside by just letting me be there for her as a shoulder to cry on when she needs it because we have so much pain in common.

Betty's scribbled piece of paper still lies scrunched up in the wastepaper bin so I take it out the back to the wheelie bin and drop it in, feeling relief at getting rid of it. I need to keep going forward, like my dad says, one day at a time.

I have just about enough time to call him before Rosie gets back here. I need to hear his voice to keep me going, one day at a time.

Juliette

'You're an angel, Shelley,' I say to my Florence Nightingale friend when she hands me a steaming bowl of tomato soup as I lie on the sofa, snug as a bug with a comfy blanket around me and my favourite pyjamas on. 'I could get used to your cooking. I hope I don't look too scary, do I?'

I have taken the liberty of not wearing my wig this evening as I can't bear it with the headache and it's making me itch. Shelley shakes her head.

'You look like Marilyn Monroe, wig or no wig,' she jokes. I must have told her my nickname for the wig at some stage. I can't remember. Oh God, there are so many things now that just slip in and out of my memory and it makes me lose my breath. Little things, like where I put something or something I said or didn't say. I don't want to forget the big things. I need my memories to keep me going on bad days like this.

It's like a winter's evening outside and I honestly don't know what I would do without Shelley here to keep us going and distract Rosie a little. They are setting up the living room for a movie night with the fire lit and Shelley has brought along some Tom Cruise DVDs which is so kind of her. She is such a sweetheart.

'So, what do you fancy then, first, Madame?' Shelley says to me. 'We have Top Gun for a bit of phwoar factor, Cocktail for some good old retro cheese, or the action of Mission Impossible which I believe to be one of your favourites. You choose?'

Rosie pulls the curtains closed and lights some scented candles (also supplied by Shelley) and I revel in the warmth of being looked after so well.

'I think some phwoar factor is what is needed right now,' I say to them both and Rosie rolls her eyes.

'I knew you were going to say that,' she says.

Of course she did, I laugh to myself. Teenagers know everything, don't they? How could I possibly forget that?

Shelley works out the DVD player and we snuggle down to watch the movie as I drink my soup and thank God for letting our paths cross in this way. There are reasons for everything in life, I really believe that more than ever now. I may have hit a roadblock with my search for Rosie's biological father and my dying wish that she might have some direct blood relative who would learn to love and look after her for me, but instead I have met a true friend in Shelley and I have a strong feeling that she will always look out for my little girl, even from afar.

She has fitted in with me and Rosie so easily, though we have only known each other for a few days. I can see her mending before my very eyes, not because I am doing anything in particular, but because she feels she is helping us and she is. Home-cooked meals, horse-riding on the beach, dancing to '80s cheesy pop and letting my daughter into her world by letting her walk Merlin, and talking to her about grief is more than I could ever have imagined I'd find in the kindness of a stranger. In turn, we are filling some sort of void in her life I think. She sees in Rosie the little girl she once was and she also sees the daughter she should have had in the future. And I hope that by making her face her own fears, by confronting those gossips, by going out for lunch, by talking to her old friends and just by getting out and about again, that I may be helping her too. But I am weakening fast and I don't know if I have much more to offer anyone in this life other than my very fragile presence. The painkillers are becoming less effective and I know it won't be long until I have to give in and see a doctor to help me manage this force that is eating me up inside and taking me further and further away from any quality of life. It is rapid, it is fearless and it is much stronger than I could have ever imagined. If I can just make it to Saturday so I can see Dan and Helen and my parents …

I finish my soup and set the bowl on the coffee table that Shelley has moved so it sits right beside me, within arm's reach. Then I settle down to watch Tom Cruise strut his stuff, but I barely get past the opening soundtrack when I drift off into a deep and badly-needed sleep.

Shelley

Matt calls me halfway through the movie, and with Juliette out for the count on the sofa, I slip out into the kitchen and close the door to chat to him. Rosie is on her phone as much as she is watching the movie so she hardly notices me as I go past her on my way.

'Hi honey,' he says to me. 'Sorry, were you asleep?'

I look at the time. It's only just gone nine in the evening.

'Gosh, no, not at all,' I say to him. 'I'm at the cottage with Juliette and Rosie. Oh, Matt she isn't so good today. I think our trip around the cliffs yesterday was just all too much, or maybe she's been struggling for a while and she's kept it quiet. I made her some soup and she's fast asleep now.'

I finally managed to tell Matt briefly about some of Juliette's backstory, last night after our boat trip. I told him how she'd come here looking for Skipper to tell him he had a daughter, and how I'd had to break the news to her.

'It's such a sad situation, really, isn't it?' he says to me. 'Imagine the thought of leaving your child alone in the world like that. Maybe Skipper's family will step in and get to know her when they find out. Like I said to you last night, Shell, I will do whatever I can when I get home to try work out a way to track them down.'

'That would be a good thing to do,' I say to my husband. 'It's such a pity they're going to be back in England when you get home. It would be so comforting to Juliette to hear that directly from you but I'll pass it all on when she's feeling a bit stronger. Maybe she just needed a day off. Even I'm exhausted from it all and I'm not the sick one.'

I keep my voice low in case Rosie can hear me but I'd

very much doubt it as she is too engrossed in her phone to listen, and the TV is up loud enough to drown out my voice.

'You need to take it easy too, Shelley,' Matt says to me. 'I know you're doing a wonderful job by reaching out to these people, but I'm afraid you might crash when they go and you don't have them to look after anymore. You need to look after you too, honey. I can't wait to get home to see you.'

I close my eyes and a deep longing to have him here hits me in the stomach.

'I really need you right now,' I say to my husband and his silence echoes his surprise. It has been so long since I have admitted how much I really do need him. 'I can't wait 'til you get home too.'

'We're going to be okay, aren't we Shelley?' he says to me. 'You know how much I love you. I hope I tell you that as often as you deserve to hear it and most of all, I hope I show you in what I do and say.'

I bite my lip and look to the ceiling, then exhale.

'I love you too, Matt,' I say and a tear rolls down my cheek. I can sense his overwhelming relief down the line and I sit there, relishing in the moment and the sheer joy of being able to feel my heart again. 'I love you so much.'

'You deserve good things, Shelley,' he whispers to me. 'I'm going to get some sleep now but I want you to know I'm so proud of you for looking after that little girl and her mum. You've come a long way this week. Our beautiful Lily is still with us, Shelley. She will always be our baby girl and you are the best mummy in the world.'

'Thank you, Matt,' I say, sniffling now as the tears flow. 'I'd better get back to Rosie and see Juliette to bed. You have no idea how much it means to hear you saying that I am a good mother. Thank you.'

'You will always be Lily's mother,' he says to me. 'She may not be with us in the way she used to, but it doesn't mean you aren't her mum and I am still very much her dad. I miss being her dad.'

'I know you do,' I say to him and when I close my eyes I see him with her like it used to be, how she'd snuggle in with him on the sofa in the evenings or on lazy Sundays and how she'd call for him in the night just as often as she did for me.

'You've come so far, Shell,' says Matt and his voice breaks a little. 'I love that we can talk about Lily now and maybe someday we can remember things she used to do that made us laugh and how she made our life so complete for the short time that we had her. It's good to talk about her, to remember her.'

'I can't wait to see you,' I whisper, cradling the phone and not wanting him to go. I am so ready now to love him again and to love the memories we have of our daughter instead of fearing them.

We take our time to hang up and I go back into the living room to find Rosie fast asleep just like her mum. I go to over to the armchair and turn down the TV, then I pull a fleecy throw around me and join them, closing my eyes. Maybe we are all just exhausted. Maybe Juliette is going to be okay after a good rest tonight. I won't leave her side until morning, until I know that she is strong enough to face another day.

Chapter 20

Juliette

THURSDAY

I feel like I have a hangover as I make my way to the kitchen where I find Shelley tidying away bits and pieces that have gathered over the past day or so. My legs are weak and there's a banging in my head, like someone is constantly knocking on a door within my skull, but I need to get up and face the day. I can't lie around forever, especially not when I'm here.

'Oh darling, did you stay here last night?' I ask her. 'You really are one in a million, Shelley. I'm sure you have much better things to be doing with your time than looking after us. I'm so sorry for yesterday.'

Shelley busies herself, wiping down worktops and filling the kettle.

'I can assure you that this is where I feel I should be right now, and it's the least I can do,' she says to me.

'Now, sit down and I'll get you a cuppa. How are you feeling? You look a bit brighter this morning. Did you have a good sleep?'

Her words of encouragement are endearing so I decide to go along with her observation.

'I'm a bit brighter, yes,' I tell her, but the sadness in my eyes won't lie. I sit down, slowly. 'It's not going to take me over just yet, Shelley. There is no way it's going to happen this fast. I have plans for today. I have plans for the rest of this holiday.'

'Do you need to see a doctor?' Shelley asks me. 'You look very frail, Juliette. I know you're in a lot more pain than you were yesterday and you don't have to try and hide it from me or from anyone. Please don't suffer in silence. I'm here for you.'

I shake my head.

'Yesterday was beautiful,' I tell her. 'The day before was also beautiful. Every day that I've been here with Rosie has been so wonderful and I don't want her last few days here to be spent watching me in bed with a doctor by my side. I simply won't let it happen.'

Shelley's hands are shaking as she pours a pot of tea.

'You can't play God, unfortunately, Juliette,' she says to me. 'If you need a doctor, I'll get you one. You can't pretend this isn't happening.'

'I'll pretend for as long as I can,' I say to her and she stops what she is doing and looks me right in the eye.

'You're a stubborn old gal, aren't you?' she says to me. 'Were you always this headstrong?'

I manage a laugh. Then I shrug and roll my eyes.

'I have been told that before a few times, yes,' I say to Shelley. 'You have summed me up pretty well, my friend but I'm not giving in until I have to. Not until I collapse. I'll keep standing until I can stand no more. I need to keep going for Rosie and to make this holiday what I intended it to be. Fun.'

Shelley takes a deep breath.

'Tell me what you have in mind for today then, Superwoman,' she says as she brings the teapot to the table. 'Seriously though, Juliette, don't push yourself physically if you're not up for it today. I'm sure Rosie will understand if you need another day's rest and I can look after her if you need me to. I could take her into Galway and do some shopping like you said she might enjoy?'

Her offer is very kind, but I need Rosie near me today and tomorrow and every day from now on. I may not have too many days left.

'Thank you so much, Shelley,' I say as she sets down tea cup and pours me some tea. She sits on the chair opposite with her own cup in her hand. 'I've had a wonderful few days here. I've tasted the most beautiful seafood and freshly baked desserts not to mention all the bubbly; I've felt a whirlwind of emotions run through my veins when I was on the back of that horse and I've seen the most magnificent sights as we sailed around the Cliffs of Moher. In fact, I've enjoyed every single moment, especially opening this cottage door every morning and smelling the sea on my doorstep.'

Shelley's eyes well up as she smiles across at me. 'You really do take it all in, don't you?' she says. 'You've helped me awaken each of my senses too and I can't thank you enough for that. I was dead inside before you came along. I really can't thank you enough.'

'Hearing you say that makes all this pain a lot more bearable, believe me,' I tell Shelley. 'I had a feeling that coming here would make some sort of difference even though I didn't really know how. I didn't get to meet Skipper, but I got to meet you instead and that has made it even more special than I could have anticipated. You're going to be okay, you know that Shelley? You have a great man who loves you, you live in the most beautiful place and you have wonderful friends. You have a lot to live for.'

'And you have made me see that I do,' she says to me. 'Rosie is a lucky girl to have had such a strong woman as her mentor in her early years. I know it's a cruel twist of fate to take that away from her now, but she has learned a lot from you. She's a lot like you, you know that, don't you?'

I nod and smile at Shelley. I've always loved when people saw similarities between me and my daughter.

'You have left a great legacy in her and, in a way, in me too. I will never, ever forget you for it.'

I see tears well up in Shelley's eyes and the fear of my death rippling through her as she looks at me.

'Then you'll have to see my mission through 'til the end,' I tell her. 'No backing out now, Shelley. You said I have awakened your senses. Well, I have one more of those senses that I want to make the most of.'

She looks intrigued and I can see her run through the five senses to see which one I have still to maximise.

'Sound?' she suggests and I nod.

'Correct,' I tell her, sipping my tea. 'Today I'd like to go to Brannigan's Bar and drink Guinness and listen to a traditional Irish music session and let the sounds of the fiddle and the bodhran and the whistle fill my soul. Do you think you could round up some people to play some music for me, or is that too much to ask at such short notice?'

Shelley is up on her feet and pulling out her phone already. I feel a shiver run through me as she takes on my request with such passion and determination. She is glowing as she speaks on the phone, and pacing the floor with excitement.

In moments, she is out of breath with adrenaline and excitement and she hangs up and smiles.

'Done,' she says. 'That's sorted. Now can I get you some breakfast?'

'You can be Superwoman too when you put your mind to it, can't you Shelley?' I say with a smile. 'I'd love some scrambled eggs, please.'

And at that she is rummaging in the fridge, ready for the challenge of feeding me. Shelley is a champion and I am glad I am making her see that in herself. She has made my last wish come true in the blink of an eye, because of how much people around here like to help each other and I am delighted to see her realise that again after hiding away for so long.

Meanwhile, my own time is ticking away and I can hear my throbbing head counting down the seconds, minutes, hours. I hold my head in my hands when I know that Shelley is not looking and I pray that I get through the next few days. I need to see a doctor very soon, but I want to hear the sweet sounds of live music first.

Shelley

I listen to the bacon sizzle on the pan as Juliette is in the shower and the smell of it makes my tummy rumble. My blood is pumping through my veins, and I'm determined to make this the best day ever for Juliette and so far so good, as I've pulled in my good old friend Dermot to arrange the biggest music session he can in Brannigan's. One thing about living in Killara is that music of all sorts is never too far away and we all love any excuse to get together for a singsong and some tunes. Who would have thought that I would be capable of this? Of taking the bull by the horns and getting stuck in to doing something for another person that involves making phone calls on a whim? I can't believe that I'm actually going to go to a pub this evening and listen to music. I am driven by my determination, and it overtakes any fears for Juliette's health but maybe it's because I can do absolutely nothing about that besides look out for her when she needs me. This is the only way I feel I can help.

I can't help but smile to myself in a congratulatory way when I hang up the phone. Mission accomplished. Dermot was delighted to hear from me and said he misses seeing my face around. I never thought that anyone might miss me and to hear that from old friends in the community makes me feel warm and fuzzy inside.

'What a rainy day again!' says Rosie, who comes into the kitchen bleary-eyed and still in her pyjamas. 'Oh, hello, did you sleep here last night?'

She looks at me, noticing that I am still in the same clothes.

'Yes, I was too lazy to walk home so I crashed on the sofa,' I tell her, which is partly true. I really stayed because I was afraid that Juliette might get worse during the night, and I slept with one eye open in case.

'Where's Mum?' she asks. 'She isn't in her room.'

'She's just in the shower. Do you like eggs?' I ask her and she mumbles a yes, scratching her head and opening the fridge, staring into it and then closing it with a sigh.

I watch her and my heart spins as this moment kicks in. It's like my future should have been, asking my teenage daughter something as simple as what she would like for breakfast as she skulks around in her pyjamas on a rainy summer morning. This should have been my life and I am so content in this position, being a mum. Why couldn't I have been a mum for longer? Why couldn't I have moments like this?

I flip the bacon and listen to the fresh burst of sizzling on the pan and then just as I am about to say something, I feel two arms wrap around my waist and I freeze, not wanting to let this moment go. I look down and see pink and white sleeves and two young hands clasp together as she gives me a hug from behind, her cheek resting on my back. I look at her hands.

Oh Lily, I think to myself. How I am missing you and what we could have had together. I had so much love to give you and now you have sent me this beautiful young girl and her mother to be my friends and to teach me how to love again. I know that you are so very near. I can love again and I thank you, Lily.

'Thank you, Shelley,' says Rosie, still holding on to me. 'Thank you so much for staying. Thank you for being here for me and my mum.'

The warmth of her hug and the closeness she feels to me fills me up inside.

'Is this a private party or can I join in too?'

I turn around to see Juliette in her bathrobe and, with light fluffy patches of damp hair on her balding head.

Rosie and I both open our arms and she comes to meet us, then the three of us hold each other with our eyes closed, our minds wandering to places where our hearts belong.

After work, I walk up the hill of Killara and over the winding roads that lead to my house up on the heights and the familiar sight of the lighthouse in front of me makes me smile. I popped in earlier to shower and change and despite the drizzling rain, I decided to walk to work without a raincoat or umbrella, as I want to keep feeling things, even things as simple as the rain on my face or the wind in my hair. I need reminding that I am alive and there is still so much to be alive for. I'm looking forward to the evening ahead and to catching up with people I've been avoiding for too long. Sarah and Tom are going to be there, as are many familiar faces from the village. The word has spread about this very special gathering to give Juliette an evening she will hold in her heart for the rest of her days.

I get to the top of my driveway but instead of going inside, I walk around the side of the house to the garden where Lily's apple tree stands and I stare at it for a while as the evening rain falls down, wets my cheeks and runs down my forehead.

'You're still with me, aren't you,' I whisper and I feel her near me, her little arms around my neck and that warm sensation of unconditional love that only a child can give you. I was reminded of it so much today when Rosie hugged me and thanked me for being there for her. I found Rosie on Lily's birthday and my life has changed for the better ever since, though I dread to see Juliette get sicker as the inevitable comes close to her.

I do believe that some people come into our lives sometimes and it's hard to explain, but we just fit, we just work. Maybe it's just luck, maybe it's fate, I don't know, but I do know that when it happens, it can fill you up with a reminder of what it is that makes the world go round. It's this feeling I have right now, whatever it is called. It's the feeling I get when I hear Matt's voice, or when I laugh with Sarah. It's the feeling I get when I smell the familiarity of Eliza's perfume when she walks in the room, or when I get a call from my dad. It's the feeling I get when I am around Juliette, or when I get a hug from Rosie. It's the feeling I get now when I remember my sweet Lily.

It's big, it's powerful but it's ever so simple as it's just the universe reminding me that the void that has been left in my life with the loss of my mother and my child can never be filled totally, but it can be patched over a bit, little by little, drip by drip. It reminds me that the people I have loved and lost are still here and that they live on within me. It reminds me of the lessons I learned from each of them. I have my mother's maternal way of loving and giving. I have the knowledge to reach out when I see someone in need, just as I learned from looking after Lily and being her mum. Sometimes things don't go our way but we need to keep on being kind to one another, to keep loving and giving. I need to give out love and then the universe makes sure I get it back in in bucket-loads, just as I have experienced in so many ways over the past few days.

I have seen deep pain in Juliette, but I have also seen a deeper love of life than I ever have before. The way she appreciates every single thing; the scent of a flower, a bend in the road, the smell of the sea, the taste of good food, the sound of music and laughter. I need to take care and absorb all of these things so that Lily and my dear mother can live on every day, through me.

So, I take a deep breath and I go inside my beautiful home via the side door that leads to the kitchen, then I go into the hallway where my dog meets me with his usual boundless energy.

'Come with me, Merlin,' I say to him and he wags his tail and follows. 'Come with me upstairs. There is something I need to do and I really could do with you by my side.'

Chapter 21

Juliette

'It's an evening for your new blue dress again, Mum,' says Rosie, as she applies my makeup in the bedroom. 'There's no way you can go to Brannigan's wearing your summer gear in that weather.'

She sticks false eyelashes onto my eyelids, much to my disapproval and insists on filling in my almost non-existent eyebrows and I have to admit, even though my patience is wearing thin with all this beautifying, it really is lovely to be pampered by Rosie in such close proximity, to watch her face as she concentrates on her work. It's just that I am not used to pruning and priming and all these fancy things.

'Are we nearly done yet?' I ask her, marvelling as I always do at the amount of brushes and tools she goes through for what normally takes me three minutes maximum. Tinted moisturiser and a quick flick of mascara is as much as I do these days but for some reason Rosie is insisting that I need to make an effort this evening.

'You are going to look a million dollars when I show you, so please let me finish,' she says. 'It will be worth the wait.'

We have spent the past two hours pampering ourselves and while it has been most enjoyable as I had a long soak in the bath, then had my nails painted a deep plum colour, fake tan applied and now this, I wonder why we have to go to so much effort when we're only walking across the road to the local pub to hear some traditional Irish music.

Rosie concentrates with such precision and I try to stop my feet from fidgeting and my mind racing with all the other things I could be doing right now. My headaches, although they have eased a little now that I am well-rested and laced with painkillers, are still very much there and the knocking sensation I felt earlier has now turned into a dull repetitive thud.

Rosie goes to the dressing table and brings over my old faithful friend 'Marilyn' and I help her fix it on my head, not wanting to offend her by suggesting I wear a headscarf instead to avoid any discomfort or itching later.

'Is that okay, Mum? You look amazing. Or is it too uncomfortable?' she asks, admiring her work of art but obviously seeing the doubt in my face.

'I was going to wear my multi-coloured headscarf, if I'm honest, love,' I confess to her. 'I know the wig probably looks much more glamorous and you have gone to all this effort but I can't cope with much around my head when this headache just won't shift.'

She fetches the headscarf with no fuss and gets me a mirror to fix it and I do a double take when I see how I look with my new lashes and brows and a fully made-up face that is tasteful and subtle and, for just a second or two, it makes me forget this demon in my head and the pain that it is causing.

'Ta da!' Rosie announces when the headscarf is in place and she holds the mirror out to give me a better look. 'What do you think?'

What do I think? I think so many things when I look at my reflection but I can't put them into words. I really can't speak. I think I might cry if I do try to talk and I am determined not to let her see me cry, no way. Not tonight. I think of my beautiful girl and how creative she is and how she sees the need to bring out the good in others just to make them feel better. She has so much ahead of her and she has so much talent to share in this world. If only I could see the amazing woman she is about to become.

'You don't like it, do you?' asks Rosie. 'Oh, it doesn't really matter, so don't think you're offending me and if it's too much you can fix it yourself or just do it your way. I knew I wasn't as good as Melissa. There's just something about the way she contours that I can't figure out, but—'

'Ssh!' I say to my baby girl and I pat the bed for her to come and sit beside me. And when she does I put my arm around her and she puts her head on my shoulder as we both look into the mirror together.

'Here we go,' she says, pulling a face. 'This is the bit when you tell me we look alike now that we both have make-up on and then lecture me for wearing too much sometimes, and how I don't need it because I have perfect skin and have no need for so much foundation?'

I shake my head and smile.

'No, I am certainly not going to lecture you about make up because I can see how much time and effort you go to,to learn about all your brushes and applications, and I think you are a real natural,' I tell her. 'Even better than Melissa and that's not me being biased. It's true.'

'Oh Mum, don't exaggerate,' Rosie says to me, lifting her head off my shoulder for just a second and then putting it back there. 'Melissa is way better. You don't have to pretend she isn't. I can live with it. I've accepted it by now.'

She leans into the mirror a little to wipe off a black dot that has made its way onto her cheekbone.

'I was going to tell you a story about when you were little, actually,' I tell her as she does so and I can see her dimples starting to show when she smiles, just as she always does when she hears stories from her past. 'You were just three or four years old and you got your hands on my brand new makeup collection and you came in to me from the bathroom with lipstick all over your tiny little rosebud mouth, your eyelids were a fetching shade of green and your cheeks were rosy and pink and I just couldn't believe it. You even had mascara on your eyelashes but you'd missed them a bit and you'd brush marks all under your eyes.'

'Oh no, I destroyed your makeup? You must have been so mad.'

'No, no, well, yes you did actually destroy my makeup but that's not my point,' I say to her. 'My point is that my first thought wasn't that you had destroyed my makeup or made a mess in the bathroom that I was going to have to clear up, but it was that you had put all the different products on the right places and you were so young that I knew you could only have learned how to do so by copying me. You had been watching me so closely and it made me fill right up with love that you were imitating me with such clarity. You really were like my little shadow.'

'Ah, that's so sweet. I must have been a really cute child,' she jokes and I can't help but agree, of course.

'You had the curliest brown hair and the cutest dimples and gorgeous green eyes that everyone remarked on when they saw you. You were always my little princess.'

'Were?' she jokes again. 'Past tense?'

'You *are*, sorry,' I say to her. 'You are my little princess, though you've grown quite a bit in height since then. I think I have a photo of the makeup incident in one of your albums in the attic. When we get home, I'll get it for you and I want you to look at that picture of that little girl and remember how proud you made your mum that day when you wrecked her makeup but filled her heart with a moment of magic that she's never forgotten.'

Rosie snuggles into me again and then she lifts her phone and takes a sneaky selfie of us both and I barely have time to pose.

'You rascal,' I tell her. 'Is it okay? Don't be sharing that with your friends before I see if it's okay!'

But instead of running and hiding the photo like she normally does when I say that, she shows me the photo of the two of us sat together just now, both looking fabulous and flawless – well, as fabulous and flawless as you can look with a headscarf on where you are meant to have long flowing locks, and I have to admit, it's a good one even if I wasn't quite ready.

'I'm going to get this photo printed when I get home,' she says to me and I sit back and look at her.

'Really?' I ask her. 'That one? Why?'

'Yes, and I'm going to frame it along with the picture you just told me about and when I look at it I'm going to remember the mother I had who loved me so much that she only ever saw the good side of things, even when I messed up.'

'Oh, Rosie.'

'And I'm going to see in her smile all the kindness and love and positivity that she brought not only to me but to everyone she met,' she continues. 'I'm going to remember her love of life and her appreciation of music and art, fashion, food and flowers and everything that adds a little sparkle to every day on this earth. I'm always going to remember that she made me the person I am and I will always try to make her proud of the person I will become as I grow up in the big bad world without her.'

Her lip is trembling and her voice sounds choked as she makes her speech, but she tilts her chin up in defiance and I have never been so proud of her as I am right now. Despite the rush of emotion, I daren't shed a tear and ruin her work of art on my face so I just pull her in close to me and we squeeze each other tight. When we let go I see the fear that she is trying to hide from me in her beautiful eyes. She already knows what is coming, but I need to make sure she fully understands.

'I don't think I have very long left, Rosie,' I whisper to my beautiful girl and now I can't help it as the tears flow. 'But you already know that, don't you? I'm not feeling great tonight if truth be told and yesterday was just awful. I'm doing my best to be brave, just like you are, but it's okay to cry if you have to. You don't ever have to hold back your tears, do you hear me?'

She sniffles and nods her head and then she looks right into my eyes.

'Don't be afraid of leaving me, Mum,' she says to me, shaking her head. 'You will always be a part of me no matter where you go, and I'll be a part of you. We don't have to be afraid because I'll always feel you near me and I'll just close my eyes and know you are right in here.'

She puts her hand on her heart and I feel like I am

crumbling to pieces inside. This fifteen-year-old girl who will be left with no parents to call her own is telling me not to be afraid of leaving her. She is the one who is going to be left to pick up the pieces and she doesn't want *me* to be afraid.

'I am totally blown away with what you have just said, darling but can I ask where in the world you got this strength from?' I ask my daughter who seems to have had some enlightenment all of a sudden. This was not what I was expecting at all and I am both shocked and delighted that she is able to look at it that way, if only for now and if only to make me feel a little bit better.

'I think that's how Shelley is starting to deal with losing Lily and her own mum,' she announces as if she is suddenly a psychologist or an expert on grief. 'I know it will take a long time but I think that I will one day be able to remember you in a way that helps me be a better person. If Shelley can get through it, so can I.'

She looks at her phone as a message comes through and she straightens herself up. It must be important, whoever it is as it seems to have distracted her.

'Get your blue dress on, Mum,' she says to me. 'We need to be over at Brannigan's for seven or Shelley will be wondering where we are.'

She gets up and puts her phone in her pocket and I get the feeling that whoever has just sent her a message, it's something she doesn't want to share as she looks all-consumed by it. Teenagers, eh?

'I'm sure Shelley doesn't expect us to be there on the

button,' I tell her, feeling the need to lie down again just for ten more minutes. I don't think I will last very long at the music session but I have to show my face after Shelley's arranged it all on my request, plus I am desperate to hear the music of Ireland that fills my soul so much every time I listen to it.

'Well, I think it would be rude if we just swanned in late like it didn't really matter,' she says to me, scolding me almost. 'I don't think it would be fair on Shelley.'

Shelley, Shelley, Shelley, I think to myself and smile. I will always be so grateful for how she has come into our lives just when we needed her, when Rosie needed someone to lean on and to talk to – someone who understood, in her own way, what Rosie was going through and what she had ahead. What on earth would we have done on this trip without her?

Shelley

I walk around the house and feel like the walls are giving me a hug as I have worked my ass off for the past two hours making it look and feel like a home again.

The elephant that Lily used to climb on is back in the hallway, the canvas from our travels in India is up on the wall in the dining room, our wedding picture takes centre stage in the living room and photos of our life and memories and, most importantly, of our baby daughter who brought so much joy and happiness in her three short years are in every single room and every place where she should be.

I have put candles out and little trinkets and ornaments that I had packed away back on worktops and windowsills, and lamp shades back onto the bare light bulbs that hung so lonely in different rooms and I have put lighting in corners and switched them all on and their glow warms me up inside.

I've put rugs down on the tiled and wooden floors and throws back over the settees and armchairs and a mirror here and there where they used to be – and now they no longer frighten me to walk past them and catch my reflection.

Merlin looks more comfortable than ever as he tries out each of the rugs and I kneel down on the floor beside him and snuggle into his furry coat.

'I'm home, Merlin,' I tell my forever faithful old friend. 'At last I think we can remember her properly and keep her a part of me and her dad and even of you. She is part of all of us and I'm going to embrace that from now on and feel her love in every room instead of fearing it. Everything is going to be alright now, Merlin. We're home again now.'

I take my time getting ready to go out and Matt talks me through how I am going to face up to meeting so many people I know in public, all at the same time, something I never thought I would be able to do again. I have set the phone on my dressing table and I have him on loudspeaker. I haven't told him about my domestic burst of activity because I want to surprise him with a welcome home surprise so I'm glad he hasn't video called like he sometimes does in the evenings. Even our bedroom is back to how it once was with pictures on our bedside table – one of the three of us the morning Lily was born on my side of the bed, and another of the two of us on the day of our engagement in New York City where he proposed on Broadway and almost took my breath away.

'It's only Brannigan's,' he reminds me, 'and it's a very kind gesture you have made to take the time to invite people along to make it special for your friend, so try not to overthink it. You're going to your local pub to listen to some music, that's all. You will love it, just you wait and see.'

'Oh, I wish you were here so much,' I tell him as I put in a pair of tiny silver earrings. I have chosen black jeans and a grey silk blouse from the shop to wear with heels and a biker jacket, that I picked up years ago in Covent Garden market and just had to keep it for myself. 'I hate walking into pubs on my own, even if it is just Brannigan's.'

'Is Sarah going to be there? And Tom?' he asks me and I know he really does wish he was here too. It has been ages since we all hooked up and after breaking the ice with Sarah, I am really looking forward to hearing more of what she has been up to.

'She texted to say she would do her best to find a babysitter and if so, they'll both come out, but it may be hard at short notice,' I explain to him, remembering the torment of finding a decent babysitter around here when you wanted to go out for an evening. 'If not, then she'll pop down herself for an hour to see Juliette. I can't believe they go home the day after tomorrow. I just hope Juliette doesn't get any worse. I didn't like how she looked earlier today when I left. She is exhausted.'

I stand back to look at my reflection and I wish I had some of Rosie's ability to apply makeup, especially when I'm preparing to deal with all the nudges and stares and whispers that will inevitably come my way.

'Maybe she won't be able to hang around too long,' says Matt, 'but you can't control any of that so just relax and do what you can do and be there for her. All she wants is to listen to some music, not a party, so you don't need to worry about who shows up and who doesn't. Dermot will make sure there are two or three musicians and the rest of the evening will fall into place naturally.'

Matt is right of course. It's only a few people sitting round a table playing Irish tunes and maybe singing the odd song. It's not a leaving party or a celebration or a sad farewell. Juliette wanted to hear some music. I called a friend who plays some music. I invited a couple who I have been friends with for years to come along. I really don't need to panic about anything. Anyone else who is there would have been there anyway and I'm not being fed to crocodiles. It's not even about me, after all, and for that I am delighted.

'I think I'm good to go,' I tell Matt and I now wish

he was on video so he could tell me if I look alright. 'I'll call you when I get back and tell you how it goes.'

'Don't be worrying about that, either,' says Matt. 'Just go and enjoy yourself and have a few drinks with your pals. I'm going to schmooze in the hotel restaurant with more of Bert's clients and then I'm hitting the hay early, but call me if you want of course. I'm just saying you don't have to. I want you to have fun, Shell. It's about time you did this and I am so, so proud of you.'

I feel my heart glow again and it makes me stand tall knowing that I love this man more than anything and that he has totally got my back in everything I do.

'We've come a long way,' I say to him before I hang up. 'I'm proud of you too, Matt and I ... well I want to thank you for not giving up on me. I think, after what we have come through and will continue to have to live with forever, that we can face anything this world throws at us. We are stronger than we think we are. Thank you for sticking with me and helping me get this far.'

'I think that anything else life throws at us will be a walk in the park compared to losing our daughter,' he tells me and I know that he is finding it so hard to have this conversation over the phone when we can't embrace or celebrate the love we have managed to hold on to throughout this living hell. 'Now, roll on Saturday when I'll get home and see my wife and show her in person how much I have missed her.'

I feel a flutter in my belly at the thought of lying beside him and holding him and touching his body like

I used to. We have a lot of catching up to do in that department and I can feel the hunger rise within me to make up for lost time.

'Maybe we can go dancing again soon,' he says to me, softly. 'Dinner, drinks and dancing, remember that was always your request when we needed a night out?'

I laugh like a giddy teenager at the memory of how excited we used to be when it was just the two of us, all dressed up and an evening of laughter and love stretched out ahead of us.

'And then we'd go home and have dessert,' I say to him and I can't help but wink at the thought. I make my way downstairs and put Merlin in the kitchen for the evening. I take a moment to look at Lily's smiling little cherub face from a photo in the hallway as I walk past.

'I am the happiest man in the world right now,' says Matt. 'I think I've got my wife back and I've fallen head over heels in love with her again.'

'I'm so in love with you too, Matt,' I tell my husband as I close the door on our beautiful house that is now beginning to feel like our home again. 'I always was. It just took a bit of self-love and selflessness to realise it.'

Chapter 22

Juliette

Rosie and I slip into a snug in Brannigan's and the musicians who have gathered don't notice us at all as they chat and drink and tune up their instruments. This settles me as I really didn't want anyone thinking I was planning some grand farewell. Planning ... I laugh when I think of how Helen and Rosie have always mocked how I made plans that I never saw through, but this time I seen them through and I am proud of myself for doing so.

'What would you like to drink, Mum?' Rosie asks me and a piercing pain hits the back of my head, like a rush of heat and a knifing sensation all at once. I try to focus.

'Sparkling water,' I croak and Rosie's face changes at my reaction.

'You don't have to do this if you don't want to. We can go right back across the road and get you into bed. Please don't think you have to stay for my sake.'

'There's Shelley,' I say as our friend spots us and Rosie lights up at her entrance. 'A slice of lime in my drink would be lovely, please darling, but just wait to see what Shelley wants first.'

'I'll just have the same,' she says, easily joining in with our conversation and I swear, I feel I have known this beautiful creature all my life. She slides into the booth beside me and I feel more at ease, trying to ignore the lingering pain and the thuds that are still going on in my head.

'Isn't this lovely,' I say to Shelley. 'Lucky you, knowing real musicians who play real instruments! We think it's great if we have a jukebox working down in our local and even at that, you'd be afraid to turn it up too loud in case it might drown out the horseracing on the telly.'

Shelley, I have to say, looks very pleased with herself and rightly so as she waves across at the three musicians who have now struck up a tune.

'That's Dermot on accordion,' she explains to me, 'and Mary on fiddle and I think the other guy on fiddle is called Brendan. Aren't they fab!'

I lean back onto the soft cushion and let the lilting music warm me up from my toes right up to my aching head and I take a moment to let it all sink in. The lilts and the rhythm and the ease of it all fills my soul just as I knew it would and I close my eyes for just a few seconds to make the most of it.

'I remember the last time I was here so clearly,' I say out loud, not really knowing why I feel the need to relive it all again to Shelley, who already knows how my story ends. 'This music takes me right back to all those years ago and I am the same carefree, gullible, free-spirited soul that I was at the age of twenty-five, when all I had to care about was how to get the next bus to wherever it wanted to take me, and whether my money would last before I got home.'

I open my eyes to see Rosie coming towards us, confidently holding each of our drinks as she approaches us, half-walking, half-dancing along to the rhythm of the tunes.

'I think you might have passed on your free spirit ways to your beautiful daughter,' Shelley says to me and I am delighted at the very thought.

'I forgot to ask Dean did he have any snacks,' she says to us and I look behind her to see the handsome barman who greeted us when we first arrived.

'Oh, snacks, of course,' I say to Rosie and she doesn't seem one bit bothered that I have caught her out. She just turns on her heels and makes her way back towards him.

'I'll have some crisps,' I say after her but of course she doesn't hear me and Shelley nudges me playfully.

'Dean is Sarah's nephew,' she explains to me. 'Hottest catch in town, so our Rosie has mighty good taste. He's way too old for her of course. Check me out, I sound like I'm her mother.'

'You're right, he is way too old!' I agree and Shelley and I glance at each other, each knowing what the other one is thinking and we don't even have to say it. But then I do.

'I know you've only known us for about five minutes,' I say to Shelley. 'But after I go, would you ever see your-self looking her up or just checking that she is okay? I probably shouldn't ask that or put you under such pres-sure but she looks up to you as someone who really does get her more than I ever could, and even knowing that you might keep in touch with her would make this trip all the more worthwhile despite my brick wall where her biological father is concerned.'

Shelley leans her head on my shoulder and links my arm.

'Rosie and I discussed this already,' she says to me. 'Believe me, you have nothing to worry about when it comes to that. I'd say before she leaves here on Saturday, Rosie and I will be planning her return visit as soon as she can fit it in around school and any other commit-ments she might have at home, or should I say, as soon as you allow her to come back.'

A shiver runs through me and I nod as I watch my teenage daughter flirt with Dean, her handsome holiday crush, at the same bar where I met the man who swept me off my feet and who unexpectedly let me bring her into this world. She flicks her hair back as she is speaking to Dean, her head tilted to the side and she throws her head back in laughter at whatever it is he's telling her. I am going to miss so much of her precious life. She reminds me so much of myself sometimes it frightens me.

Her sweet naivety, her feisty ways, her determination – I think she gets that all from me and I hope she hangs onto those traits for as long as she can. I often wonder what traits she has that might come from her father's genes. Maybe her sense of humour or her love of the great outdoors and animals comes from him? It kills me that she'll never really get to know what she has in common with him. He has missed out on so much that I have gained, through no fault of his own, but I am now set to miss even more.

Her next birthday, her face on Christmas Day when she opens her presents, her exam results, her career choices, her boyfriends, her lovers, her friends, her wedding day if she takes the plunge (I think she will one day), her babies, her hopes, her dreams, her ambitions, her fears. I am going to miss it all.

'She kind of belongs here, Juliette, doesn't she?' whispers Shelley.

'She fits in here, for sure, but then I always knew she would,' I tell my friend. 'I really fitted in here too when I first came. I'm glad that part of me can live on in her, I really am. That gives me great comfort, not to mention knowing that you will be here – and Merlin of course. She really has fallen in love with that dog.'

I feel Shelley grip my arm a little tighter and then she leans forward and sips her water.

'This might sound really ridiculous and I hope I'm not being insensitive,' she says over the music. 'But ... would you do the same for me? You know, after you go?'

We don't look at each other, but again I know exactly what she is thinking. Again, a shiver.

'If there is such a thing as heaven, and I truly believe there is,' I say to Shelley. 'I am going to seek out your precious Lily and hold her in my arms and make sure she is being looked after by her sweet grandma and I will look after them both, just for you. Deal?'

'Deal,' she says and a tear rolls down her face. She loses her breath a little. 'I can't tell you how much that means to me. Oh my goodness, thank you Juliette. But how will I know if you find them?' she asks me.

'Oh, you'll know,' I say to her. 'If your mother is anything like you, Shelley, I don't think I will have any trouble in finding them. I think we'll meet for sure and you will know, don't worry.'

'You're a special woman,' Shelley says to me as tears now run freely down her face. She dabs her eyes with a napkin and tries to control her breathing and I put my arm around her shoulder.

'I am running out of time,' I remind her, 'so I can only see the good in everyone and the good I can do before my time is up. I think if all of us knew our days were numbered, we just might make the world a kinder place.'

Rosie returns to the table with a look of the cat that got the cream, just in time to up the mood a little, but I'm glad that Shelley felt confident enough to say that to me. It's a pact we have made and I take great comfort in her being able to say how she feels.

'So, any nice, um, *snacks?*' I ask, noticing my daughter's hands are empty.

'There's only cheese and onion crisps and there's no way I'm going to eat those and have smelly breath for the rest of the evening,' says Rosie. 'And neither are you, Mum. No point looking like a movie star and smelling like you've halitosis, is there?'

Shelley and I both roll our eyes and laugh at Rosie's very straightforward logic.

'Aren't you having anything to drink yourself,' Shelley asks Rosie and the delight on Rosie's face is priceless.

'I forgot to get myself a drink,' she replies. 'O-M-G! I suppose I'll just have to go back up there again.'

'She'll be back here to visit us all in no time!' says Shelley as we watch my darling girl adapt her flirty pose at the bar again. She's a chip off the old block for sure.

'You could have trouble getting rid of her!' I tell Shelley and we both know that it's true. Rosie is perfectly at home around here after just five days. 'I imagine there'll be tears on Saturday when we're leaving.'

Shelley doesn't answer me. And once again, she doesn't have to. I know exactly what she is thinking.

Shelley

'You look amazing,' says Sarah when she joins our company, in a bit of a fluster. 'You both do. I love the blue on you, Juliette.'

'It's from a really hot boutique,' says Juliette.

'In England?'

'No! Right here. *Lily Loves*, of course,' says Juliette. 'I have to say this dress will always mean a lot to me after the week that we all have shared. Thank you, girls.'

Sarah grabs a stool, takes off her scarf and coat and sits down beside us.

'I swear, I thought I was never going to get away from my house tonight,' says Sarah. 'I need a gin and tonic. *Need*. Do you ever feel like you are talking to yourself when it comes to men? I honestly told him I was going out at seven o'clock and he swanned in just twenty minutes ago like he hasn't a care in the bloody world. If the shoe was on the other foot I'd have a lot to listen to.'

'Ah, I'm sure you wouldn't be without him,' I say to Sarah, playfully. 'Can't live with them, can't live without him. I have to admit I can't wait for Matt to come home now. I never thought I'd utter those words and I'm so glad I finally feel that way for him again. It's been a long, lonely three years. Horrible, really.'

I don't know why I'm opening up so much but it really feels so good to be able to chat like this to my very good friends who I trust impeccably with anything I have to say.

'I miss Dan, too,' says Juliette. 'How I wish he would just walk through that door and take me home and ... God, what I'd give to have my old life back.'

I can sense for the first time since I met her, a glimpse

of anger in Juliette when she realises just how much her life has changed due to her ill health.

'Don't think like that,' I say to her. 'Dan has his own battles going on but I'm sure he is going to be there for you, Juliette. Maybe not in the way he used to but he is still your husband and he knows you need him.'

Rosie comes back to the table sucking a straw from a glass full of cola and she perches on a stool in front of us.

'Teigan has not stopped talking about you – she thinks you're the best thing since sliced bread, Rosie,' says Sarah and Rosie's face lights up at the compliment. 'Rosie this, Rosie that. She says she wants you to be her babysitter, so if you ever come back here and need a job, I have one ready for you. Gosh, I would have paid a fortune just to escape a bit earlier this evening. Isn't it great to get out and look around you, even if it's only to Brannigan's?'

'I'd totally forgotten what it was like to socialise,' I say to the girls. 'And isn't it nice to feel your toes tapping and do something as simple as clap along to the music. I think I've become institutionalised, I really do but at last I'm beginning to see there is a big bad world out there for me.'

Sarah puts her arm loosely around me and quickly gives me a squeeze.

'It's good to have you back,' she says to me. 'You've turned a massive corner, Shell, and I think that Juliette has a lot to do with it. You really did come here at exactly the right time, Juliette.'

Juliette looks like she is miles away and I know she is longing for her husband right now. I can't even imagine the thoughts that must be going through her mind as she sits here in a place that holds so many ghosts and memories, watching her daughter who is bursting with life, hearing stories of how she could come back here without her, and longing to go back to the way things used to be. Juliette looks lost. She looks so afraid and alone.

'I'm going to get in some drinks,' says Sarah. 'Is everyone okay or can I get you something stronger?'

'I'll go to the bar for you if you want,' says Rosie. 'Dean said he can serve me alcohol as long as he sees me handing it over. I already checked.'

I notice Juliette force a smile at her daughter's enthusiasm to give us table service on our evening out.

'Okay then, tell that cheeky face up there to give his old aunt a gin and tonic,' Sarah says, handing Rosie some money. 'And tell him to be more generous with the ice than he normally is.'

'With pleasure,' says Rosie and off she skips, delighted to have a third errand up to the bar.

'If you want to go back to the cottage at any stage, just say,' I whisper to Juliette as Sarah checks in her handbag. 'Maybe you've heard enough music?'

'No, no, I'm fine,' Juliette says to me but I can see in her eyes that she is struggling. 'Sarah just got here and Rosie is having fun. I'll stay another little while. Not much longer, but a little while.'

She is pale and waxy looking and I notice that the dress is a bit looser on her than it was when she first tried it on last Saturday. Her hand trembles slightly as she reaches for her drink, then Sarah gets up from her seat and goes around the other side to sit next to her.

'Well now, just as I promised, I have something for you,' she says to Juliette, handing her a white envelope that looks like it has seen better days. 'You don't have to open it in here if you don't want to, but I know you wanted to have it.'

I look on, puzzled, as Juliette stares at the envelope in amazement. She looks across for Rosie who is in mid conversation again with Dean, delaying with the task of getting Sarah a drink, but maybe that's for the best right now.

Juliette opens the envelope and she takes out a picture of a young man with sandy brown hair, smiling blue eyes, bare-chested on the beach, looking right into the camera. It is Skipper and my heart gives a leap. I can't even imagine how Juliette must feel at seeing his face again.

Sarah watches on at Juliette who doesn't take her eyes off the photo.

'He was a handsome chap,' says Sarah. 'I know it's not much but it's the only one I have of him and I want you to keep it and give it to Rosie when you feel the time is right. Gosh, I remember where I was when I heard the news. His funeral was one of the saddest I ever did see. Sorry, I shouldn't even say that. Are you okay, Juliette?'

Still Juliette doesn't take her eyes of the picture and I notice her hands are shaking even more now. She glances at Sarah and then at me and then she puts the photo back into the envelope and sets it on the table.

'What's wrong?' I ask her. 'Oh, Juliette maybe this is all too much for you?'

'I feel a bit sick,' says Juliette, putting her hand to her face.

'Me and my big fat mouth,' says Sarah. 'I'm really so sorry. I should have handled that all more sensitively. It's totally my fault. I'm sorry.'

'No, no it's nothing to do with that at all,' says Juliette, her eyes still fixed on the envelope.

'Shelley, can you come here a second?' calls Rosie from the bar and I look at my friends and then back at Rosie and then back at them again.

Sarah shoots me a look that tells me to go to Rosie so I do what I am told and make my way to the bar. I'm scared right now. I don't know what is going on in Juliette's head or how sick she really is feeling but I don't like this feeling one bit. Sometimes I wish I could have just stayed numb forever.

Juliette

I watch Shelley go to my daughter who is showing her something on her phone to great delight and they glance at the door and the room begins to spin, reminding me of that drunken night when I was here before and the room was spinning then just the same. I feel drunk but of course I can't be. I blink and lift the envelope again. Then I take out the picture, stare at it some more and I put it back again.

'It's painful, I know it must be,' whispers Sarah. 'I thought I was doing the right thing by bringing the photo here tonight but my timing was off as usual. I'm always putting my foot in it, even my husband says so'

'No,' I tell her. 'That's not it at all. You meant well. It's not your fault, Sarah.'

I take a deep breath. The music is grating on my brain now. The accordion and the fiddle and the second fiddle, it all sounds like squeaky noise now – I wish they would just stop and be quiet. None of it sounds good anymore and my head is so sore. I need to get out of here fast. I can't take any more of these surprises and curveballs in my life. I can't take any more of this bar and this place and these people.

Then the door of the bar opens and in walk my sister and my husband and I really think I am going to faint.

'Dan?' I whisper.

'What's wrong, Juliette?' Sarah asks me. 'You really don't look very well. Do you want to go now?'

'Dan! Aunty Helen!' says Rosie. 'At last! Come and meet Shelley!'

'It's not him,' I say to Sarah, staring at the envelope at the table again.

'What?' asks Sarah, lifting the envelope like I have

made some mistake. 'This is Skipper, darling. This is the guy we knew as Skipper who used to come here on the boat each summer?'

I feel dizzy. Rosie is waving at me. I look back at the photo. It's a blur and it makes no sense. This is all a big mix-up.

'It's not him,' I repeat to her.

'Mum! Look who's here!'

'Are you sure this is Skipper?'

'I'm sure,' says Sarah. 'I have no doubts. It's him.'

The room begins to spin. I don't know what to think now.

'That may be the man known as Skipper in that photograph, Sarah,' I whisper to Shelley's friend. 'But it's not my Rosie's dad. I must have got this all very wrong or else the man I met lied about his name.'

'Why on earth would he lie?' asks Sarah. 'Juliette, are you okay? You look like—'

Sarah's words are muffled and blurred. I can't make out what she is saying because my head is spinning and everything is a whirl in front of me. So Skipper, or the man who told me his name was Skipper, is not dead at all?

I hear a familiar voice calling to me. It is Dan. Oh thank God for Dan!

'I'm here, Juliette,' he says. 'Let me help you and get some fresh air.'

'Helen?' I mumble.

I see my sister, her face riddled with concern. And then everything goes black.

Chapter 23

Shelley

FRIDAY

Betty calls me at 8.30am to say she isn't feeling so good and can't work today and I feel like someone has punched me in the heart for the second time in the past twelve hours. Last night was horrendous and the memories come flooding back of how Juliette had to be taken home by her sister and her husband and it all feels like one big nightmare.

'Have you heard anything?' Sarah asks me as I walk around my house in a daze, brushing my teeth as I talk to my best friend on the phone with Merlin following my every move.

'No, not a thing but I have to go and open the shop for the first time in ages and I don't know how I am going to deal with customers today.'

'What are you thinking?' asks Sarah as I walk past a

330

photo of Lily, and the hairs on the back of my neck stand to attention.

'I'm scared. I'm thinking a lot of things,' I tell her. 'I feel like I want to pack up and go to my dad and run away from it all.'

'Well do that then,' says Sarah. 'Tell Matt to meet you in Belfast tomorrow instead of him flying into Dublin and take some time out from your life. You're almost there, Shell. Maybe a bit of your dad's company would do you the world of good right now. You've looked after Juliette and Rosie so well for what probably feels like forever but you still need to think of you, no matter what happens to them.' I sit down on the edge of my sofa and I look out the window of the glass doors that lead onto my balcony and further onto the sea. Merlin curls up in behind me.

'I did think of that,' I say to her, 'but then I'm afraid to go too far in case something bad happens to Juliette. I can't just abandon them. I think Rosie is going to need me now more than ever.'

I lean back on the sofa and Merlin awkwardly makes his way onto my lap.

'I hate to think of what is going to become of that poor child,' says Sarah. 'Juliette is very sick, Shelley. You can't help that. You have to look after you now.'

'You sound like Matt,' I say to Sarah and I close my eyes, just wanting to get back into bed and forget about everything that happened so quickly last night.

Rosie had called me to the bar to tell me that she had

a grand surprise for her mum and she was relishing in how well Juliette looked with her head scarf and her make-up and her lovely blue dress but when Helen and Dan arrived, it turned into a living nightmare for us all.

'Mum, are you okay?' Rosie called when she saw how pale Juliette looked, and before we had time to introduce each other, Helen swept in and took over and demanded that Juliette be taken back to the cottage where she was going to call her doctor immediately and I have never felt so useless in all my life.

'The woman is terminally ill,' Sarah reminds me and I nod in acknowledgement. I should never have become so close to them in the first place. How naïve can one person be? Of course it was going to end badly. What did I expect? Annual holidays and social networking in between? Juliette is dying and I feel like I am dying now too. I need to go to work but I don't know if I can. I need to talk to Matt. I need him here with me because there is no way I can go and interrupt Juliette's family time now that she seems to have taken ten steps backwards.

'I need to get to work,' I say to Sarah, and Merlin shifts on my knee as if to say it's about time. 'Maybe if you're around you could pop in during the day? I don't know how I'm going to get through this. I feel so useless.'

'I feel so guilty,' says Sarah. 'At least you have work to distract you for a few hours. I just wish I had never brought that photo with me. But how was I to know it was the wrong person? I haven't slept wondering if the shock of that all was what triggered her to feel so faint and sick in the first place.'

'It wasn't the photo,' I say to Sarah. 'How could it have been? Juliette wasn't well yesterday either or when we took her out on the boat. Maybe that's what set it off. Maybe we're thinking of too many maybes.'

'Maybe she's just misremembering the way he looked,' says Sarah. 'Like, how can she have thought that was his name and been so wrong all this time?'

'Maybe he gave her the wrong name,' I suggest and my stomach flips at the thought. 'Have you ever thought of that?'

'No,' says Sarah. 'I haven't. What kind of man would do that?'

'Someone who was doing something he shouldn't have been doing? Look, I need to go and open the shop,' I tell her. 'Call me later. It's good to be back in touch again, isn't it?'

'Yes, it is,' says Sarah. 'Now, I'm wondering who the hell this man of Juliette's was. Are you sure you are okay?'

'I am okay,' I tell her, and I stand up but my legs are like jelly. 'I'm glad I have you, Sarah. I think I am going to really need you soon if that isn't too much bother.'

'You will always have me,' she tells me and I hang up knowing it's true. I am going to need her very soon and I know it.

Juliette

Dan sits on the side of my bed, his face grey with worry and enforced sobriety.

'I scared you all last night, didn't I?' I say to him but he doesn't reply. He just holds my hand. I can hear Helen and Rosie argue in the kitchen as to who left the lights on all night and I long to yell at them that it doesn't really bloody matter in the wider scale of things.

'I have so many things I need to say to you but where do I start?' asks Dan and I manage a smile and to shake my head ever so slightly. 'I have so much I want to say right now, Juliette.'

'You want to say that right now I'm the sexiest thing you've ever seen?' I suggest to him but he isn't really in the mood for jokes. He squeezes my hand as tears fill his eyes.

'Tell me about the night we met,' I say and that seems to raise a reaction.

'You've always loved that story,' he says to me and it is true. I have.

It wasn't a drunken night out, it wasn't a blind date, it wasn't an online dating agency or any such thing, it was by pure chance that we met and we have both always told our meeting story with great pride to anyone who would listen.

Dan takes a big breath and squeezes my hand again. His eyes are darker now, spilling over with despair and worry but his voice soothes me just like it has for the ten years that I have known and loved him.

'It was an evening in August and I was on a plane on my way back from Paris, feeling sorry for myself because I hated flying so much and I *really* hated flying alone,' he begins, and I almost mouth the words along with him, so familiar is this tale. 'I was terrified, in a middle seat and was cramped and uncomfortable with a wailing baby on one side and a snoring old man on the other side of me.'

I nod and close my eyes, smiling at the sound of his voice and the most beautiful story I have ever been told.

'Go on,' I say to him. 'And then you looked—'

'And then I looked in between the seats in front of me and I saw the most gorgeous woman I have ever seen in my whole life and she was talking to someone about not being afraid of flying,' he continues. 'I saw that it was just a little girl she was speaking to and in about three seconds. I realised I was being a big baby as the little girl was much braver than I was.'

I laugh at this bit, I always do.

'The little girl said to her, "Mummy I'm not afraid. I'll always be okay when I'm flying next to you" and I said to myself; what the hell am I afraid of when this child is being so brave in front of me? Me – a grown man, when there was a child in front of me seeing the world in such a different way? She had someone she loved beside her and she wasn't afraid and I realised, that's what life is all about. That is what we are here for. To have someone we love beside us when we need to feel safe and secure.'

I pause. I haven't heard this last bit before. I swallow. I wish I could speak out but I can't right now.

'Juliette, you have flown beside Rosie every day of her life, and not just since that first moment I met you both on that flight from Paris,' he says to me. 'I may have helped you with your bags from the overhead locker and we may have talked the whole way up the aisle as we shuffled along, and then again as we waited at the carousel and then when we swapped numbers and knew we would be meeting up within days, but she has always been your number one and you should be so proud of that. You have flown with her all this time and you always will.'

I inhale all of his familiarity as I lie here with my eyes closed, the sound of music from the kitchen drowning out my daughter and my sister's conversation and when I open my eyes and look at him, he is all that I want to believe in right now. Me and Rosie, flying together always.

'I know that I didn't give Rosie the gift of life,' he says to me, 'but you and Rosie gave the gift of her life to me and I will always stand by her side in whatever way I can.'

His greying hair by his temples, his piercing blue eyes torn with grief and despair clutch at my heart and I know that he means what he says no matter what.

'Just be there when she needs you,' I whisper to him. 'She will always need you, Dan.'

He smiles a little.

'I can't promise to fly with her like you can but I'll

always be her wingman if she ever needs me and I know she will in some way as she grows up to be just as amazing as her mum,' he tells me. 'I will always be by her side when she wants me to be.'

A tear rolls down his cheek and he leans over to me and kisses my own tears away.

'You didn't finish the story,' I say to him, my voice weak and as faint as my body feels right now.

'Well, that lady who talked to me all the way to the exit of the airport that night,' he continues. 'I told her before we left, that one day I would marry her and I did, and it was the best day of both of our lives, wasn't it, Juliette? You said to me that day you were the happiest woman in the world. And you looked like you were.'

I was,' I tell my husband. 'It will always be my happiest memory in the world. Thank you, Dan, for everything. You've been my wingman, you know that? Despite everything I always felt stronger when you were near.'

'I've let you down, Juliette,' he says to me and he breaks down and sobs like a baby. 'I'm so sorry about the past few weeks. I am so, so sorry.'

'Dan, no, you don't need to be,' I whisper to him. 'We needed some time away from each other. I know I'm not going to be here for much longer but you needed to see that the time we have left is so precious and I need you to be strong. I need you, Dan.'

His sobbing subsides and he holds my hand to his face.

'You have given me ten wonderful years of memories

that I will treasure forever,' he says to me. 'So many things, so many great times and so much love from your big, generous heart. That's what will keep me and Rosie going, Juliette. The love you gave to us will never die. And our love for you will go on forever and ever. We will talk about you every single day and we will love you every single day so you'll never be alone.'

I close my eyes again and I smile in the knowledge that my man is by my side. My best friend in the whole wide world; I am his wife and he is my very own wing man. I love him more than he will ever know.

Shelley

Rosie doesn't talk much when she arrives in the shop around lunchtime but I know what she is after. Her eyes are red and puffy and her hair is scrunched back off her face and she is without her signature make up. Instead she is pale and blotchy and looks like she needs a good chat.

'You want to go for a walk?' I say to her as she pretends to look through rails of clothes she isn't interested in. 'We can go and grab Merlin and take twenty minutes on the beach?'

'But it's your lunch break and you need to eat,' she tells me, not looking my way. 'You don't have to come too if you don't want to. I just needed to get out of the cottage and I didn't know where else to go. Aunty Helen is getting on my nerves already, Shelley. She is just freaking out and I can't cope with it right now.'

I know that feeling all too well.

'Come on,' I say to her. 'It's almost one o'clock and I've been here since nine which I'm not used to, so I'd love a bit of fresh air to blow off the cobwebs.'

'I can get the dog if you like?' she says to me. 'If you need to stay until one?'

'You're an angel,' I say to her and I give her the keys to the house. God, I am so going to miss her when she leaves tomorrow. 'You know the alarm code, yes?'

'Just as well I'm not a robber in disguise,' she jokes and off she goes to get her good old buddy while I close up the till.

Ten minutes later Rosie is back with the dog and we walk down to the beach together in silence. She sniffles a bit as she walks which helps me start up a conversation because I *really* do not know what to say now. There's no point telling her that everything is going to be okay because we both know that it really is not. There's no point in saying clichéd statements about time healing everything, because I am the one person who knows that it certainly does not.

'Are you getting a cold?' I ask her and she shakes her head.

'Allergies,' she tells me. 'I always sniffle and sneeze at this time of year but Mum normally gets me antihistamines. She forgot to pack them this time.'

'I can get you some on the way back,' I say to her and she doesn't reply. 'I used to suffer terribly with hayfever in summer. It sucks big time.'

'So does cancer,' says Rosie and we both stop in our tracks. She throws her arms around me and leans into me as she sobs and I just let her do so without any questions, without any words, because there is really no way to deal with this other than to let her lean on me and cry.

I look out onto the lighthouse as I rub her weary head and I ask my mum to give me the strength to get through this for Rosie. The thought of losing Juliette after knowing her only a week is almost killing me inside but this is not about me. It's about this darling teenage girl who seems to have taken a shine to me and is leaning on me for comfort so I can't get sad for me. I have to stay strong for her.

We slowly start to walk again along the sand and Merlin provides a nice distraction when he tugs at his lead and when Rosie lets him go we watch and laugh as he bounds straight for the water until we can only see his head as he paddles along.

'I hated this place when I first got here,' Rosie says to me. 'I don't know why but I didn't want to like it. I think I was jealous of my mum's enthusiasm for it. Like, I wanted her to focus all her attention on me and not be so consumed with happy memories of a place that existed in her life before I did.'

We sit on the sand dunes and look out at the sea.

'That's totally understandable,' I say to her. 'I can't say I was a big fan either when I first got here because for me it represented a change that I didn't want to face up to. I didn't want to come here and stay with my aunt. I wanted to be at home with my mum and dad and for things to be just like they used to be, but that was never going to happen. It is going to be very difficult for you, Rosie but all I can say is that if you ever need me, you only have to call no matter what time of day or night. I know I'm not your mother and no one will ever mean the same to you but I will always be your friend. And you have Dan as well. You really do seem close to him. You seemed happy to see him last night?'

She smiles when I mention Dan.

'Maybe Dan will go back to being the old Dan that I loved so much and not the Dan who has been totally unrecognizable lately,' she says. 'We used to fight like cat and dog for Mum's attention but as I got a little bit older I realised how much Mum loved him and needed him and I accepted that he is really a very cool person after all.'

'That's very mature of you,' I say to Rosie. 'It can't have been easy for you when you were used to having your mum all to yourself for so long.'

'I hate being an only child,' she says, looking at the sand now as she makes circles with her fingers. 'Like you said, if I had a sister or brother maybe I wouldn't feel so alone?'

She looks up at me with huge tear-filled eyes and I

put my arm around her and hold her close.

'I always wanted a big sister too,' I say to her. 'I watched my cousins grow up together and saw how they stuck together when times were tough like they were knitted from the same pattern. And then when I had my own daughter I realised the bond you have with blood relations really is like that. You are knitted together. It's totally unconditional. It's the best feeling in the world.'

I can feel myself spiralling backwards to that dark hole again when I think about the bond I had with Lily and how I will never get that back again, with anyone, and I don't want to let it happen right now. I need to stay positive. I need to help Rosie. I can't slip. I just can't.

'Do you ever think of your father?' I ask her, feeling that I can bring this up now that we know that Skipper wasn't Juliette's one-night stand after all.

Rosie looks up at me with wide eyes like I have asked her the million-dollar question she always wanted to answer.

'All the time,' she says. 'I don't bring it up to Mum or Dan but I always thought that someday we would find my real dad and I'd have a ready-made family who would fill in all these gaps I feel inside. Someone who wasn't just an aunt or a step-dad or a friend – someone who is connected to me for real, you know?'

I think of my own father and how despite his struggle in the earlier years after Mum died, and despite the miles between us I don't know how I would have coped this far without him.

'Your dad is out there somewhere,' I say to her. 'And I am going to help you find him, Rosie.'

'How? Where on earth would you start?'

'I have no idea, but I will do everything I can to help you find him and when he does find out about you, I really hope that he is going to love you so much,' I tell her. 'You are the most loveable young girl and you have given me so much in just a few days. Imagine what you could give him for the rest of his lifetime. You're an absolute joy and you deserve all the love in the world. You really do.'

'I write to him sometimes,' she says, letting the sand fall now between her fingers. 'Nothing important, just stuff I'm doing in case he ever does want to get to know me better. Everyday things like what I had for dinner and what I did at school and what songs I like. Just stuff.'

I gulp as I feel my heart tear in two.

'Do you think you will ever have any more children?' Rosie asks me and I take a deep breath. My womb aches at the thought.

'I don't think I can ever suffer any more losses, Rosie,' I say to her and it is true. 'I had four miscarriages before Lily came along. Four babies that I had pictured in my head and dreamed of filling our home with. Lily was my miracle baby but my heart cannot be broken again and neither can Matt's. I wanted so much to give him a baby but my heart is in pieces.'

'Four, wow,' she says to me. 'How can life be so cruel?

That's just so unfair, Shelley. That makes me very sad.'

'Me too, and yes, it is unfair,' I reply. 'But I am working so hard at focusing on what I have rather than what I don't have and I think if you look for it, there is a lot of goodness and kindness in the world. I am trying to mend my broken heart by deliberately looking for love in the world and I've witnessed so much kindness and goodness with you and your mum which has made me realise that I need to focus my energies on just that. What I have in my life, not what I don't have. I have love and I have kindness that I can give out and that is what I will continue to do from now on.'

Rosie picks up her phone and looks at it, scrolling through photos as she talks to me.

'I saw a picture of Lily when I was in your house getting Merlin,' she says to me. 'I hope you don't mind me saying, but your home looks so much prettier now that she's there with her little smiling face and all your happy memories on the walls. I love the elephant in the hallway too. It reminds me of Africa. Did you get that in Africa?'

I feel my palms go sweaty even though it is quite cold here on the beach. I can't find my voice at the thought of Lily's little smiling face. Rosie keeps scrolling through her phone and then she stops at a photo of ... oh my God has she taken a photo of my Lily on her phone? No, Rosie—

'Lily has exactly the same hair as I did when I was her age,' continues Rosie. 'Same colour and everything.

I know this is stupid but I thought at first glance that it was me. Do you think we look alike?'

She puts her phone screen towards me and my heart is racing now so fast and I feel dizzy and sick inside.

Betty's scribbles on that piece of paper come back to me. Just three words that had sent me into a spin but I had dismissed it as it just can't physically be the case. *Rosie? Lily? Matt?* She had written their three names together and scored through them with her pen but it was still eligible enough for me to read.

'Why is Lily on your phone?' I ask Rosie. I want to get mad at her for taking pictures of my daughter when she was in my home. Anger fizzles through my veins down to my fingertips at the thought of such intrusion. 'Rosie, you shouldn't have taken pictures of Lily when you—'

'No,' she laughs. 'I didn't take pictures of Lily, Shelley. That's what I'm saying. That's not Lily. That's me in the picture when I was three years old. It looks exactly like Lily, but it's not her. It's me.'

Juliette

'Rosie? Rosie is that you?'

Dan calls out when we hear the front door shut and I wait for Rosie to burst into the room with tales of Merlin and Shelley and all the wonderful things she may have got up to for the past hour or so – but she doesn't come in and she doesn't answer, and I am too weak and sore to even call for her.

'The doctor will be here again soon, love,' says Dan, patting my forehead with a damp cloth. 'She'll know for sure if you are able to travel and soon we'll have you home in your own bed and that should make you feel a little better, shouldn't it? I'll go and see how Rosie is.'

I love the thought of my own bed, or my own room where Dan and I shared so many memories, yet part of me doesn't want to move from this place as I feel so at peace listening to the water on the pier outside and the gulls overhead as I lie here becoming weaker and weaker and weaker. I'd happily just stay here in this room with its lemon walls and sash windows with the gentle breeze coming through the window moving the floral curtains so that they look like they are dancing. It's like a burst of sunshine, this little room and I feel quite dreamy lying here which is probably something to do with the medication the doctor pumped me with earlier this morning.

'She says she's fine,' says Dan when he comes back in to the room, 'but she told me that through her bedroom door so I don't know if she is fine or if she's climbing out the window to meet someone she shouldn't be, or drinking cider, or rolling a joint. Shall I tell her you want her to come in here?'

I lightly shake my head. My eyes are like half-moons and Dan seems to have grown a stubble since he left the room and came back in here again. I know that isn't possible but time is really slowing down and I think I could actually notice the grass growing right now if I watched it closely. That's the thing about being terminally ill. Your observations are so much sharper, like you don't want to miss a thing so nothing goes unnoticed. Things I used to fly past without a care in the world now *mean* the world to me. I will stop to watch a tiny spider crawl up the wall in this cottage and marvel at his tiny legs and how he can defy gravity when we humans can't. I will notice the brightness of a yellow dandelion and smile at the childhood memories that such a humble weed brings back, of days running through fields with my friends when all we ever seemed to do was be outdoors and life was just one big wonderland. I will stop to listen to a toddler chit-chatting to his mum or dad and be in awe at how in just two years a little person can pick up languages and understand conversations, yet still look at the world through such innocent eyes, untarnished, clean and pure.

Everything is magnified, everything is wonderful, everything feels almost new. I will watch my sister's face as she rubs tea tree oil into my feet at the end of the bed, her mind racing with a million things. I think of how she has left her husband and three boys at home to come here to be with me and how she is putting her fears to one side just to try and make me feel a little bit better. She tells me I am the strongest person I know even though I sometimes feel the opposite. That is love.

I am bald, bloated and my body is not much more than a shell, yet Dan looks at me like I am a princess and even though I pushed him away and told him never to come back as he hit the bottle to numb his pain, he has come back to me and he has sobered up enough to prop me up in these final stages. He is my soulmate. He was there with me when I was first diagnosed, when I screamed at the horror of it all and when I woke in the night in clammy sweats and terrors and he held me and rocked me as I wailed and cried, back to sleep. That is love.

Cancer has brought me to the depths of my being and made me realise exactly what is important in this polluted, toxic world we live in. All I believe in now, is love. When I was diagnosed, all the nonsense we worried about before felt like materialistic bullshit and the rushing from pillar to post like a busy fool just stopped. Priorities fell into place. What mattered most really did begin to matter most and it took cancer to make us all realise that there is really nothing in this world that should take first place in your life over the people you care most about. Yes, we need to work to pay bills and sometimes life throws us stresses and strains like the car breaking down or being late for an appointment or missing out on something you really wanted to do or see but seriously? Cut the bullshit, I have learned. Life is too short for shit. Live it, feel it, love it and do it now. Don't wait for your day in the sun. Make today that day. Make the most of every change that comes your way and mean it. Most of us go around on autopilot not really living, just merely existing. We count the hours on the clock to see one day through and then get up to do exactly the same thing again the next day without even questioning it. I want to leave this world a better place than when I found it, even if it is just for one person. I don't want to die in vain. I have no idea what I can do to achieve that, but I think that should be everyone's aim in life, to leave it just a little bit better because you were there.

'Juliette? Juliette, the doctor is here, honey.'

My sister's voice disrupts my train of thought and I realise that I have been dozing. I open my eyes slowly.

I don't think I am going to make it home.

Chapter 24

Shelley

I can't stop my hands from shaking so I put my phone on the kitchen table with the photo of Rosie as a young toddler staring back at me. I asked her to send it to me, trying my best not to relay my shock and my sense of wonder but I know the poor child was traumatised at my reaction.

'You should go home,' I told her. 'You need to go back to the cottage to your mum, I mean, and I'm going to go home too. I don't feel like walking right now, sorry Rosie. I don't feel very well right now.'

The look on her face was like I had punched her in the heart. Like I was a boyfriend telling her it was over without giving her the full story. Like I was dumping her and telling her to just go away so I didn't have to look at her.

I didn't mean to shove her away but I needed to be alone to absorb this, so I wrote her a text message to try and explain without letting her know of my real suspicion.

'*Rosie, I am so sorry, I was just a bit freaked at the resemblance to Lily, I write. It's happened before many times, even in people that bear no resemblance at all. I didn't mean to chase you away and I am sorry. I'll call to see you all later this evening. Please don't be scared. I'm always here for you xx*'

I press send and bring the photo of a young Rosie back onto my screen and I take the photo of Lily from the table in the hallway, then I sit them side by side. The hair is identical, there is no denying that, soft dark brown corkscrew curls. The eyes are so similar, their almond shape, their shade of green. The smile is so alike, the baby teeth, the cheeks, the dimples, but the eyes ... oh my God, the eyes. I can't breathe.

I lift my phone and call my mother-in-law, not knowing what it is exactly that I want to say but I need to show her this to see if I am finally losing my mind.

'Eliza? Eliza can you please come here?' I stammer. 'I need to show you something quickly.'

'Shelley, are you okay?' my mother in law asks in a panic. 'What on earth has happened, darling? Is it Matt? Are you okay?'

I never ring Eliza these days. I never ring anyone come to think of it but I need her to come and tell me that this is just another figment of my grieving imagination.

I feel sick. I can't leave the house, no way. I need to stay here until someone tells me I am imagining things.

I want to send the photo to Matt and for him to tell me no way, there is no big resemblance and not to be so silly but I can't let him see that I'm behaving like this again when he thinks I'm getting better. He'll be so disappointed and will definitely think I'm going insane if I'm off the mark on this.

'I'm out for lunch with Betty right now,' Eliza tells me. 'We're just in the village though so I can be with you in a few minutes. Sit tight, Shelley. I'll be right there.'

She hangs up and I realise that Betty was meant to be sick today, wasn't she? Why couldn't she come to work when she could clearly go out for lunch with Eliza? What the hell is going on?

My phone rings and the sing song ringtone makes me want to throw it outside over the balcony of our home, as far away from me as it can be. Matt's name is on the screen now but I can't talk to him when I am in this state. He will be gutted to see me acting like this again. They'll call the doctor for me again. I shouldn't have called Eliza. She will call the doctor and they will bring me in to hospital again and fill me full of medication so that I am even more numb than I been for three years.

He rings again. I still don't answer.

'Shelley? Shelley it's me, love?'

Eliza's high heels click across my tiled hallway as she lets herself in and when she comes into the kitchen, I know by her face that she already knows.

'You know, don't you?' I say to her. 'That's why you were out for lunch with Betty. She isn't sick at all. She couldn't face me again because she thought she might spill the beans. She practically wrote it down for me to find when she was working in my shop!'

'Shelley, Shelley, hush darling,' says Eliza. 'I have no idea what you are talking about. You need to sit down. Can I get you anything? Tea? A brandy?'

'I do not want a fucking brandy!' I scream at her. 'Look at this! Look!'

I push the phone under her nose and she takes a step back.

'Tell me I'm insane, tell me I need to stop this,' I say, barely able to string my words together. 'Who is that?' I ask her. 'Do you know who that child is?'

'Shelley, you're frightening me,' she says to me. 'Why are you asking me this? It's my granddaughter for goodness sake. I'd know those eyes anywhere.'

Her granddaughter! Oh my God. My blood runs cold.

I fall onto the nearest chair and I stare at the floor. I breathe in and out, in and out, in and out. I find my wedding ring. Something familiar. I touch it. I twist it. Can this be true? Is Eliza really seeing what I am seeing at last?

Eliza pulls a chair across beside me and puts her hand on my lap. She hands me back my phone.

'This isn't our Lily, is it?' she says, her face etched with worry.

I shake my head in response. 'No, no it isn't,' I mumble.

'It's that English girl, isn't it?' she whispers to me. 'The one you've been spending so much time with. The one whose mother is dying. What's her name again?'

'Rosie,' I say to her. 'Her name is Rosie, the same as my mother's name. How could you forget that? I told you that.'

'Rosie, of course,' says Eliza.

'It's Rosie in the picture,' I say to her. 'Not our Lily, and I think that Matt might be her biological father.'

We sit in silence for a few seconds. Eliza tries to speak, then stops. Then she tries again.

'Do you know this for sure?'

Again I shrug and shake my head. 'I don't know for sure at all,' I reply. 'I just needed to see if you could see the resemblance too but it doesn't add up. How can he be? It just doesn't add up. She said the man's name was Skipper.'

Eliza tilts her head and takes a deep breath.

'And have you spoken to Matt about this yet?' Eliza asks. 'Have you shown him this photo? You need to confirm this with him, before we all jump to conclusions that may not be true.'

I sniffle and wipe my tears and nose on the back of my sleeve. I am a mess. I must look an awful mess.

'I know I have to do that but I can't tell him on the phone when he's so far away,' I say to her. 'Juliette said his name was Skipper. He was a boatman. Matt knows nothing about boats. He didn't even live here that summer, so how could he be Rosie's biological father?'

'He—'

'He was in Dublin back then with his ex, Alicia, I

know every part of his life story, Eliza. They were practically engaged, he told me, but then things started to
go badly and they were arguing a lot and she called it
all off and put him out and he never saw her again. He
came back home to Killara and then the following
summer, that's when he met me, isn't that right? Isn't that
what happened?'

Eliza is fidgeting. Eliza never fidgets.

'I first got to know Betty through Alicia,' says Eliza.

'Betty?' I say to my mother-in-law. 'What the hell has
Betty got to do with this or Alicia? I don't give a shit
about Alicia or Betty. I'm talking about my husband ...'

Eliza puts her hand on my knee and hushes me. It
works.

'Betty came here from Limerick to visit us once with
Alicia and she loved it so much she came back and
stayed,' says Eliza. 'There must be something in the water
that brings people here to heal and live a happier life
and just stay. It happened with Betty. Alicia, Matt's ex, is
Betty's niece.'

I look up at Eliza, puzzled.

'What? Her niece? But why didn't anyone mention
that to me before?'

Eliza shrugs.

'Well, I didn't really ever find the opportunity to tell
you that and to be honest it has never really seemed very
important,' she says. 'Betty is just Betty to me now and
has been for many years. She's a really good friend and
when you needed someone to help out at the shop after

Lily, I knew she would be the right person for the job. It was never important that she was related to Alicia, not until now of course.'

'Until now? Why? Because of this?' I ask, afraid of the answer coming my way.

'Because back in the day, Alicia confided in Betty as to why she asked Matt to leave and why their relationship ended,' Eliza explains to me. 'And there are two sides to every story as we all know. Matt's, as it turns out, was a bit leaner than Alicia's version of events, let's say.'

My stomach is sick. I don't know if I want to hear any more but I have to.

'I didn't know this until today and Betty only told me to get it off her chest,' she continues. 'But Alicia ended things with Matt because he came home here to Killara for a weekend after a row they'd had. He'd got drunk and confessed to her afterwards that he'd had a very regretful one-night stand with an English girl who was passing through. Her name, Alicia thought, was Julie. But now it looks like it was your friend Juliette.'

My blood runs cold. So it is true then. It has to be true. I drop my phone onto my lap. I feel like I am looking at my life through a blurry lens. It looks like Matt has a daughter. He has a daughter that isn't Lily and who isn't mine.

'And Skipper?' I ask, my throat drying up with every breath.

'The name Skipper must have been a safe decoy for

him, I guess,' says Eliza. 'I'm thinking that he deliberately gave her the wrong name in case anyone would hear of it and in case Alicia would find out. They were a very well-known couple around here at the time so I'm not surprised he was trying to be incognito.'

My eyes dart around the kitchen, then to Eliza, then to the floor and then to the photo on my phone on my lap. I lift it and look at it closely again.

'Oh my God,' I whisper, my face crumpling as it all clicks into place.

'Darling, I am sure there are so many things going through your head right now,' Eliza says to me, 'but you have to remember that this happened before Matt even knew you so it doesn't bear on how he feels about you at all. This will be as big a shock to him as it is to you. Please don't act too irrationally over it. You have been doing so well and you can't let this take over your own wellbeing. It might not be a bad thing when it all sinks in. You're in shock. I'm in shock too.'

I want to punch someone. I want to scream and shout and kick and pull my hair out and make this all go away. I want my Lily back. I want to snuggle her in and hold her close and smell her innocent baby smell and wave at Matt from our front door as he arrives home from his trip and spend the evening in sheer bliss watching her toddle around our home as he catches my eye every time she does something cute or new. We'll smile at each other and for that split-second it'll be like the world stops because she is ours and we made her and no one will ever marvel at the things she does like we do. She is a part of me and Matt. I want her back. I need her back. I want my mum. Oh God, I want my mum.

Eliza goes to the kitchen and gets me a brandy and I down in it in one. The irony; the sheer cruelty of it all. Four times our babies died, then we had Lily and we only had her for three years until she was taken too. And now I find out that Matt already has what I have been trying to give him for all our married life and he doesn't even know she exists. And the most painful thing of all, yet maybe the most beautiful thing of all, is that I love her already. Despite my shock, I know that I love his little girl already.

Over an hour later when we have gone over it all until we have nothing more to analyse and share, Eliza agrees to leave me after much convincing that I am slowly letting the bombshell that Rosie is my husband's daughter sink in and a flurry of emotions go through my mind as I walk her to the door.

'I'm sorry if I startled you earlier when I called,' I say to her when she reaches her car. 'I didn't know what else to do. I had to tell someone and I was sure you would tell me I was imagining things, just like I was before when I thought I saw glimmers of Lily in other young girls.'

Eliza walks towards me.

'Shelley, I promised Matt that I would look out for you every step of the way while he is gone and even if

I hadn't made that pact with him, you know that you are my family and I would come to your aid at any time of day or night, you know I would.'

I do know this. Eliza has been a wonderful friend to me as well as being my mother-in-law and I know that a lot of people don't find that bond with the so called other woman in their husband's life.

'So Betty knew the moment she saw Rosie that she had to be related to Lily?' I say to her. 'That's mad. I didn't even see that myself. Well, I thought I did for a fleeting moment but—'

'Yes, Betty did the sums,' says Eliza. 'She did question the poor girl at first on why she was here, what age she was, who she was with, etc and then it clicked into place. She didn't mean any harm, love. This could eventually be something very positive for you and Matt, although it might not seem as such now. You must see some hope in all of this?'

'I don't know, maybe I will do one day,' I say to Eliza. 'Maybe when I get over this shock and when Matt does too, this might be the best thing that ever happened to us. And Rosie. Oh my God I haven't even thought about how she is going to feel about all this. Or Juliette. I haven't even gone to see Juliette yet today. I need to go to see her.'

I can't imagine how I am going to find the words to tell Juliette what I now know. Will she be happy? Relieved? Angry that Matt told her a lie all those years ago? And Rosie? Well, it means that she will be forever a part of our lives now which of course will always be a blessing, but how will she feel about my husband being her real father?

'Do you think I should tell her, Eliza? Juliette is dying and I don't want to shock or stress her. Oh, I wish I knew what to do.'

Eliza thinks for a moment.

'You know better than I do on that one,' says Eliza. 'But you did say one of her hopes was to find her daughter's father when she was here?'

I nod.

'She's afraid to leave Rosie all alone,' I tell Eliza. 'We made a pact that I would look out for her and that she would look out for Lily in heaven in return. Jesus, Eliza, Rosie is Lily's sister? She is your granddaughter too. How does that even make you feel? There is just so much to take in with it all.'

Eliza puts her hands to her face.

'You know I haven't even thought of that,' says Eliza. 'I was so caught up in how you were feeling about it all but wow, I have another granddaughter. Oh Shelley, I miss Lily so much! I miss her every single day of life, I really do!'

And for the first time in a very long time, the woman who has been my absolute rock, who has propped me up when I was falling and who mopped up my tears when I screamed and cried for mercy, is crying now on my shoulder for the loss we have both suffered and for this very strange second chance to live again.

I am going to talk to Juliette. I need to go right now and find out for sure if all our suspicions are true. My heart is thumping and my head is sore but I can't stop to overthink this. I am shaking with nerves and I am terrified and maybe a bit in shock still, but it's the least I can do. I must go and tell her right now before it's too late.

Chapter 25

Juliette

The clock is ticking in the room and rather than irritate me, I find it soothing as the hours pass by, minute by minute, second by second. Tick, tock, tick, tock, tick, tock, stop.

'Michael just called,' whispers my sister and I want to tell her to start speaking in a normal tone and not to hush round me like I am already dead.

'Did he call or did he whisper like he was already at my wake?' I ask Helen and she half-smiles, then she speaks normally.

'He has been talking to Dr McNeill, the lady who just left and who has been medicating you,' she explains to me. 'They have both agreed ... they have both agreed that it would be unwise to try and move you right now, Juliette. I'm really sorry but you won't be able to fly home today. I'm sorry.'

I think back to the days when Helen and I were teenagers and when our mother would be tearing her hair out in despair as we fought over everything from a pair of tights to a bottle of perfume to lipstick and boys, and how she always said that one day we would stop fighting and be the best of friends. Helen is truly my best friend in the world. My only sister. My mother, as always, was absolutely right.

'Mum and Dad are on their way here now,' she says to me. 'Dan is hiring a car for a few days so he can go and pick them up later tonight and we will just look after you and make sure you are as comfortable as you possibly can be.'

'Where's Rosie?' I murmur. Despite my joking with Helen about not whispering around me, it's as much as I can manage myself right now.

'She's in the kitchen,' Helen tells me. 'Your friend Shelley just popped by. I wasn't sure if you wanted any visitors so I asked Rosie to entertain her for now. She seems nice.'

'Shelley is a superstar,' I say to my sister. 'Rosie adores her. I was almost getting jealous at one stage as she was so enthralled by the woman and I couldn't compare to her with her shop and her dog and her big fancy house.'

Helen nods in understanding.

'Rosie knows what side her bread is buttered on' she reminds me. 'I can make an excuse if you want to? She did say not to disturb you on her behalf.'

'Would you cut the formalities, big sis and just let my friend come in for a chat please?' I say to Helen. 'I know you mean well but stop fussing. I'm going to be okay.'

I close my eyes and then I open them again to see Helen looking on at me, in wonder at what I just said.

'You are, aren't you?' she says to me and I manage a nod. 'I'll go and get Shelley. Let me know if it gets too much.'

'How?' I ask her. 'Not like I can ring a bell or anything, can I, Nurse?'

'No, but you could use a code word or something like we used to do when we were younger if I casually pop in to close the window or pull the curtains?'

I close my eyes again and smile.

'Gosh, we were always so close, weren't we Helen even if we didn't realise it when we were growing up?' I say to her. 'It's funny but I see a very similar easy connection between Rosie and Shelley just like that. Coming here was the best thing I have ever done, even though I didn't find the man I thought was Skipper. I'm glad I came for Rosie. I'm glad I came back for me.'

'That's the best thing I've heard all day,' says Helen. 'I'll go and get Shelley.'

Shelley

I have been shaking like a leaf until this very moment, yet now, as I sit on this chair beside Juliette's bed in this little cottage by the sea with its lemon and white interior and the cool breeze coming in off the water, I couldn't feel any more at peace if I wanted to.

All of my fears, all of my worries as I drove here with such dread have gone and all I can see is the beauty in Juliette's weary face as she lies in front of me like an angel with a smile that tells me she is very glad to see me.

'You do know when I first met you I thought you were a cold-hearted snobby little bitch,' she says to me through her cheekiest smile. 'It just goes to show, doesn't it?'

I shrug, able to take what she is saying on the chin. I'm sure she isn't the only person who has got that vibe from me lately.

'Never judge a book by its cover,' I say to her. 'Is that what you are going to say?'

'I was trying to think of an appropriate equally clichéd sports quote but it isn't coming to me fast enough,' she says. 'My old brain isn't what it used to be.'

She reaches out her hand and I take it like it's the most natural thing in the world to do. Two friends, one dying inside and longing to live in Juliette, one living inside and longing to die in me. At least that's the way I was before I met this wonderful, inspirational woman who has no idea of the great bond and connection we will always share, even beyond the grave.

I had practised on the way here what I would say to her but now none of my speeches or approaches seem appropriate.

'They wanted to take me home to England but it doesn't look like I'm ready to leave my beloved Killara just yet,' says Juliette, still holding my hand. 'I'm not ready to let go of it yet for some reason. I do believe there is a reason for everything in life, a time for everything. Even a time to die.'

I think of this cottage, empty without her when she does eventually go and it catches my breath.

'I don't want you to go,' I say, not knowing where my words are coming from. 'I don't know what I am going to do when you go, Juliette. I am going to miss you so much.'

She leans back into her pillow and looks at the ceiling.

'Forty, eh?' she whispers, shaking her head. 'I just about made it to forty and I'm grateful for every single day of my life and everything I experienced.'

But life isn't supposed to end when you're forty, I want to scream out loud. It's supposed to just begin, isn't that what they say?

'Promise me Shelley that when you turn forty, you will do something totally insane and equally wonderful and remember me when you are doing it,' Juliette says to me. 'Would you do that please? Something totally mental. Go crazy, even if it's just for one day.'

'Like what exactly?' I ask her, loving the idea already yet my heart is piercing with tiny pinprick pains at the thought of her being totally gone which she will be of course by then.

'I dunno,' she says, still staring at the ceiling. 'Jump

out of a bloody plane or something mad like that – with a parachute of course. Or go skinny dipping in the moonlight. Or hike through a jungle or desert or rainforest. Just do something that you think might push you, not a little, but a lot. Scare the shit out of yourself. Remember how good it feels to be young and alive and pinch yourself if you have to in order to make you realise how damn lucky you are to be alive.'

I only have five years to go until I turn forty so I'm sure I will come up with something between now and then.

'Okay, yes I will do that. I promise to scare the shit out of myself in your honour, Your Honour,' I joke and she looks directly at me, her face scrunched in disbelief.

'You better!'

'I will,' I promise. And then we sit in silence for a moment.

'You love to dance,' Juliette then whispers to me. 'I could see that in you. Do that more, Shelley, won't you? You don't have to wait till you're forty to dance. You don't have to wait another day to dance your socks off.'

'Every day is a disco, isn't that what you said?'

'Exactly,' she says with a smile. 'Dance with your husband in the kitchen again when he comes home tomorrow, just like you used to and remember how in love it makes you feel. Never stop dancing in the kitchen.'

Goosebumps rise on my arms and tears fill my eyes. I never told Juliette that I used to do that with Matt, did I, but it was always one of my favourite things to do.

'And keep doing things for others,' she tells me. 'Do something, just one little thing for someone every day and it will help you heal more than you know. Helping Rosie has helped you heal, I really believe that.'

I nod as my tears sting my eyes. No one will ever know how being kind to that little girl has helped me so much inside.

'And every now and then, when things are not going your way or when life throws you a shit storm, close your eyes and breathe and know that it will pass and you have two, and soon three, very strong guardian angels up above, who will keep the wind at your back, urging you to sail on through your life at ease,' says Juliette. 'Get back into your book club that you loved so much, cook more like you used to, see the funny side of everything where possible and never say no to something out of fear. Love is always bigger than fear, Shelley. You no longer have to be afraid of anything.'

A tear rolls down my cheek at the thought of losing this beautiful woman. She has given me so much over the past six days and now I have something to give back to her. Peace of mind like she has never known it before. It's my turn now. I am ready to tell her.

'I have something to show you,' I whisper, glancing at the door for fear of someone interrupting this moment. I take a photo from my handbag and I hand it to her. And as she looks at it, I wait. And I wait ...

And then she looks up at me, and back at the photo and then she drops the photo onto the bedcovers and puts her hands to her face and she cries and cries and cries as huge waves of relief and closure engulf her whole body.

She nods at me and smiles then takes my hand and kisses it.

'You found him,' she says. 'Yes, my darling, that's him and you found him. That's the man I thought was called Skipper. How did you find him, Shelley? Does he know about Rosie? What did he say? Oh God, you found him. You found him. What did he say?'

I pause. I was afraid she might ask me that but of course he didn't say anything because I haven't told him yet. I had to be sure before I said a word and before I saw her reaction, but now there is no question about it. Betty was right. Her calculations were exactly right. Rosie's father is not Skipper after all. It is Matt.

'I haven't told him yet, Juliette, but I will when I see him tomorrow.'

'Tomorrow?' she whispers and her weary eyes widen.

I close my eyes and then I breathe out.

'Remember ...' I whisper to Juliette. 'Remember you said you thought when you first met me that I was a cold-hearted bitch?'

Juliette wipes her eyes. 'Yes,' she says. 'Sorry about that because I was very wrong.'

'You don't have to be sorry,' I remind her. 'You said you were wrong, but in what way do you think were you wrong? I need to know what you think of me because I need you to know that I'm warm in my heart and I

369

have so much room for love. I can love Rosie.'

She looks so puzzled, but I need to do this right. 'Just say anything,' I ask her. 'Say what comes to your head.'

She ponders a moment and then she looks at me so sincerely.

'You have been a light in a very dark place for both me and my daughter, Shelley' she says to me. 'You make Rosie glow and you make her feel safe, like she is going to get through this because you have been where she is and you have managed to battle on through it no matter what. You have shown her just how brave the human spirit is and to me, that's very admirable indeed. You're like a walking angel and you have changed our lives for the better. You have changed my life for the better as I face my dying days.'

Wow. Well, I wasn't really expecting all of that and I'm floored, but I need to stay focused. I need to continue.

'Juliette, I promised I would look out for Rosie, didn't I, so you trust me with that?'

'You did,' she whispers. Her eyes are getting darker and heavier I notice. 'And of course, I trust you. In return, I am going to wrap my arms around your little girl and your darling mother when I see them in heaven. That's our deal, isn't it?'

'It is,' I agree. 'But Juliette, my part of the deal is going to be a lot stronger than I originally thought. Than *we* originally thought, after all.'

'How?' She looks at me tentatively, like she already knows what I am going to say.

I take the photo of Matt from the bedclothes and I look at it for a second, then I look at Juliette.

'It's Matt,' I whisper to her.

She gasps.

'Oh Shelley! Shelley, really?'

'Yes, really,' I say and a shiver runs through me as Juliette takes this in. 'Rosie is Matt's daughter.'

Juliette swallows hard, her weary mind battling now to make sense of this all.

'Please don't judge him, but he really shouldn't have been with you that night,' I explain. 'His relationship at the time was coming to an end and he said his name was Skipper in case anyone found out that he was messing around but I know that he's going to love Rosie as much as I do. And I do love her, Juliette. Are you okay?'

She inhales deeply and then her tired eyes look directly into mine.

'I knew we met for a reason,' she whispers to me and takes my hand in hers. 'I believe in fate, I really do. I was meant to come here and find you. I just knew it.'

I put her hand up to my cheek and I close my eyes for a few seconds to let this moment sink in.

'I knew it too when I saw Rosie,' I realise. 'I never could let anyone into my life since Lily died, and yet here was this stranger, this sad little girl who I clicked with the moment I saw her. I knew there was something special about her and now I know why. We are family now. I always hoped that my mother and Lily sent Rosie to me to help me see love again but now I really believe it.'

Juliette stares at me in disbelief but with a smile on her face. She is exhausted.

'You always said you would look out for her, didn't you?' she whispers.

'Yes, I did. But now I'm not going to only look *out* for your precious Rosie, Juliette,' I tell her, 'but Matt and I will look *after* her in every way we can if and when she wants us to. We will be there for her every step of the way for the rest of her life for as long as she needs us.'

Juliette goes a bit paler and she leans back again, sinking further into the pillow. Her eyes widen, then drop heavily again, and then she closes her eyes and a single tear drips down her cheek and on to her pillow.

'I found him,' she whispers. 'I finally found him. Oh Shelley, I don't know what to say right now. I – I honestly had no idea whatsoever and I hope you don't think I ever did. This is overwhelming. It's more than I ever could have imagined. So much more. But are you okay?'

I shake my head and put my hand on her arm. She feels a little cold to touch. She is weaker than she is letting on and I don't think I need to drag this out any further.

'You have nothing to worry about as far as I am concerned,' I reassure her. 'Rosie is Lily's sister, imagine that, Juliette? I have seen so much death and loss in my life and it almost killed me too, and although my first reaction was to think that this was life's cruel way of throwing me such irony, someone I just met showed me how to turn things around to a positive in every circumstance we face, and I choose to look on all of this as the most magnificent gift of all. This is not bad news for me and Matt, Juliette. This is the best thing that could have ever happened to us and I mean that from the bottom of my heart.'

'Thank you,' she mouths and I know it's my time to go and let her rest. 'Can I ask you a big favour, Shelley?'

I pause.

'Of course you can,' I tell her in sincerity. 'Anything at all.'

'Can you tell Rosie about her dad, about Matt, when the moment is right, Shelley?' she asks. 'I don't think I can break it to her at this stage.'

'Gosh, yes of course but are you sure you want it to come from me?'

She nods her head very slowly and licks her dry lips.

'I'm so weak and sick,' she says, 'but I trust you more than anyone else to tell her after I go and please make sure she knows that I'm so happy about it all. You've done so much for us this week and now you have, through an incredible twist of fate, made my dying wish come true. You've found my daughter's father and I know she will be loved so, so much. I can't ask for anything more. I am happy. I will go from this life very content and happy.'

Juliette closes her eyes and sobs, squeezing my hand as she does and I realise that I am crying too, tears of sadness, happiness and joy all in one.

'I am going to miss you so much, Juliette,' I tell her, gasping now for breath between my free-falling tears. 'You're an amazing friend, woman and mother and I will look after your baby girl so well knowing that you are with us every step of the way. Sleep now, Juliette. Sleep and know that everything is safe with Rosie. She will always be welcomed at our home with her new family in this place that you loved so well.'

But Juliette doesn't speak back to me anymore. Instead she just rests her weary soul and as she lies here in the silence of this room apart from the clock ticking and the rush of the sea outside, I slip away with my head bowed, hoping that I might one day see my very good friend again.

Now, I just need to break the news to my husband. Tomorrow can't come quick enough.

Juliette

I am drifting.

I am sailing along on what feels like a big fluffy cloud and it is taking me somewhere but I don't know where to. I see faces in the distance, familiar faces, waving to me, smiling and urging me to come to them, to keep sailing. They are like a magnetic force, pulling me along invisible rails on a one-way system and I feel that there is no going back. There is a woman, holding a little girl and their smiles warm my heart and make me go faster towards them.

'Mum!'

I hear Rosie behind me, calling me back. I try to turn back but I can't.

'Mum!' she calls again, louder this time and the faces in front of me fade away. When I slowly open my heavy, tired eyes, the room that was so bright and breezy when Shelley was here earlier is now dark and cosy and I see Rosie's face in the glow of my bedside lamp.

'Rosie, darling,' I say softly. 'You're here. Where's Dan?'

'He's fine, he's asleep,' she tells me. 'Aunty Helen is asleep on the armchair. She only left you moments ago, to be with Nan and Grandpa but I didn't want you to be alone in here.'

The worry on her face crushes my heart.

'You don't have to sit in a vigil for me,' I say to my only daughter. 'Did they sit for long? I didn't even know Nan and Grandpa had arrived.'

'They sat for a few hours. They talked to you but you couldn't hear them.'

'I must have been in a very deep sleep,' I whisper. 'I'm very tired, Rosie. You need to get some sleep too.'

'I tried and tried but I can't, Mummy' she says to me. 'I can't sleep because I'm frightened. I don't want to leave you alone. I don't want to be alone.'

Mummy.

She called me 'Mummy'. She hasn't called me that since she was about three years old, she hasn't woken me up frightened in the night since she reached double figures and my heart breaks for her.

I pat the bed beside me, just as I used to back then when she was so little and dependent and she crawls in beside me under the covers. She drapes her warm arms around me and I inhale her familiarity, my safe haven, my first true love. My daughter.

I think of Shelley and what she told me earlier about Matt and I wonder if it was all a dream. How can I even bring up what I now know to Rosie? I don't think I can right now. It would be too much for her to handle.

'Tell me what you were dreaming of,' says Rosie, taking me by surprise. 'You were almost singing in your sleep like you were having a really fun time. I shouldn't have woke you, I'm sorry.'

I close my eyes and in my mind I try to go back to the bright yellow glow and the safety of the drifting cloud but I can't. I can't place the faces I saw anymore. The feeling I had has subsided and even though I remember how good it felt at the time, nothing compares to lying here with my baby girl in my arms.

'I don't know where I was in my dreams, darling,' I say to Rosie. 'But I want you to promise me something when and if you ever get scared again at night, maybe when I'm no longer here to soothe you.'

'No, Mum,' she says, but I need her to know this. 'I can't think of you not being here.'

'I want you to remember something, darling,' I say to her. 'I want you to remember the day we spent on the beach horse-riding. I want you to picture my face and how I was so scared yet I did it, I totally did it and when I did I realised that I had nothing to be afraid of after all.'

'I said you were a superstar and I will always believe you are,' she whispers to me. 'I will always remember you as a superstar, my hero, my brave, beautiful mother.'

'And the songs we danced to here a few nights ago, I want you to turn them up in your head and when fear overcomes you, sing them out loud and remember how we laughed and danced and sang together,' I tell her. 'I'll be dancing beside you. Dancing and singing. You won't see me but you'll know I'm there.'

She snuggles closer to me and I can tell by her breathing that her fear is beginning to subside.

'I had no idea what I was going to do when you were born, you know,' I whisper into her hair. 'You were a fiery little bundle of energy and I was very alone and very afraid, yet as well as me teaching you the ways of the world in the best way I could for fifteen wonderful years, you taught me even more than I ever taught you, Rosie. You taught me the power of unconditional love, of the extremes that we will go to for the people we really love. Never let anything stand in the way of love, my darling. Always be kind, always be positive and always choose love.'

My voice is tired and I can feel myself drifting off to sleep again, just as Rosie is in my arms. She feels so peaceful beside me and I cherish this moment of silence and bliss, with only the sound of the clock ticking away my time and her breathing as she lies in my arms, clinging to me like she will never let go.

'I will never let you go, Rosie,' I whisper. 'You will never be alone. I will always watch over you.'

I see the faces again, calling to me, urging me to come their way to a place free of pain and worry, where no heartache or fear exists and I don't think I'll be able to turn back this time. The woman and the little girl, waving at me to keep going, another much older couple wrapped in each other's arms reassure me to come closer. A small crowd gathers and they do the same, faces from my past, faces that I know so well.

My eyes open and the pale yellow of the bedroom in this sweet little cottage blurs into the deep yellow of the light that is calling me in the distance. I am safe, I am happy, I am at peace.

'I'll sleep now, Rosie,' I whisper. 'I really need to sleep.'

My heavy eyes close again and the clock is ticking louder now, soothing me as the hours pass by, minute by minute, second by second.

Tick, tock; tick, tock; tick, tock ...

Stop.

Chapter 26

SATURDAY

I haven't slept a wink all night as I wait for Matt's key to turn in the door and announce his arrival home at last. He told me he would be here for nine yet it is almost ten and there is no sign of him yet but I know not to panic. He will be here soon, I am sure of that. I lie on the sofa, wrapped up in a cocoon with my duvet tucked around me and I'm ignoring the outside world as I ride these waves of mixed emotions as everything sinks in.

Since the call came through, I have been clutching my phone to my chest as I cry and Merlin whimpers on the floor beside me, sensing the devastation I am experiencing since I heard the news just moments ago.

I hear Matt's car in the driveway at last and I bury my head deeper into the duvet that is wrapped around me. I can't look at him even though I have been waiting for him all night long. I don't know where to start right now. There is too much to explain and I don't know where to begin.

Merlin's ears prick up when Matt's key turns and he bolts for the hallway, bouncing and barking with joy and I am pleased that at least one of us is able to give my husband the homecoming he so deserves.

'Shell?' I hear him call in the distance. 'Shell, I'm home. Where are you, love?'

I want to run to him, to fall into his arms and tell him how glad I am that he is here but I don't have the energy to move and I hate that he has to come home to see me so upset. I had visualised this moment for days now where I would be waiting for him with a big breakfast, with music on in the kitchen and I'd be casually dressed but looking quite fine and he'd wrap his arms around me and we'd dance and make love and make up for so much lost time.

He comes into the sitting room, still calling my name and when he sees my tear stained face, his look of joy and anticipation changes to one of despair and disappointment. This is not what he was expecting at all.

'You fixed the house up, Shell,' he says, and then he hunkers down beside me by the sofa. 'Has something happened to upset you? What's going on, love?'

I swallow hard.

'She's gone,' I whisper to my husband. 'My friend, Juliette, she died this morning, Matt. She died in her daughter's arms.'

'Oh, baby,' says Matt and he pulls me towards him where I sob into his chest for Juliette and the hole in my heart she has filled within me by her presence, and the hole she has left in her cruel untimely death.

'I need to go to see Rosie,' I sniffle, knowing that my darling husband must be so confused right now. When he left I was a mess, when he was gone I was making great progress and now that he is finally home, I am a wreck again but it's nothing, and at the same time it's everything, to do with him or Lily and my ongoing grief.

'Can I get you something?' he asks me. 'Some tea? Have you eaten yet?'

'No, it's okay, I can't think of food,' I mutter. 'I'm so sorry you have come home to see me like this but she made such a difference to me, Matt. She made me see how important it is to keep living and to keep loving and even though I knew she wouldn't be here forever, I already miss her so, so much.'

'She sounds like she was an amazing woman,' he says. 'She must have come into your life for a reason. I know I sound like my mother now being all 'serendipity' but maybe Eliza isn't so far off the mark after all.'

'She was amazing and she did come into my life for so many reasons,' I say to him, sitting up now and I close my eyes and see Juliette's face. She looks happy now. She is not physically weak anymore and her skin is glowing as she waves at me. I breathe in. I feel her strength and when I open my eyes, I hear her words of wisdom in my ear as she tells me not to ever push my husband away when all I really want to do is hold him closer.

'I love you, Matt,' I say to him and he swallows hard, then takes my hand and kisses it softly. 'I love you and I love what we have and all that we have worked for. We can still live, even though we miss Lily, and we can still laugh and we can still smile. Lily would want her mum and dad to smile. And most of all, we can still dance.'

Matt is lost for words. He just keeps kissing my hand and smiling and then he pulls me closer and this time I don't push him away.

'I have something to tell you, Matt,' I say to him and he looks right into my eyes. 'It's going to take a while to sink in, but I need to tell you this now. It's not bad news, believe me. It's a surprise, a big one, but it's not bad news, no way.'

He frowns but my smiles through my tears seem to reassure him and he wipes my tears with his thumbs like he has done so for so long.

'You have ...' I begin. Oh God how do I say this. 'You have a very beautiful daughter that you have never known about, Matt,' I tell him and his frown returns.

'What?'

I nod to him to tell him that it's really true.

'You have the most amazing daughter called Rosie,' I continue. 'She is fifteen and she looks a lot like you and she is the most beautiful creature, just like our Lily was, and I cannot wait for you to meet her. You never knew she existed but she's real and she's yours and she is so wonderful.'

Matt sits down on the sofa and stares at the floor, waiting for my words to sink in.

'I have seriously no idea what you are talking about, Shelley?' he says to me. 'Where did this all come from? What's going on? Are you okay?'

Am I okay? It's a question I have been asked so many times, but one that I definitely know the answer to now.

'Yes, I'm okay and we are all going to be okay, I promise,' I say to Matt. 'Some people are blessed with just one guardian angel, Matt, but I believe that I now have three and I'm going to be okay after all.'

'You're talking about this woman? And her daughter? I'm lost, Shelley? I have no idea what to take from all of this.'

'One summer in August, here in Killara, an English girl called Julie, or so you thought? You told her your name was Skipper?'

His eyes widen and his face drains of colour. I nod in acknowledgement.

'The summer I broke up with Alicia?'

'Now, you're with me?' I say to him. 'She had a baby, Matt, all on her own over in England and that baby is Rosie and you are going to love her. I already do. I can't wait for you to meet her. She is going to need her daddy so much and I will do my best to be a great friend to her, just as I promised her beautiful mother I would.'

Matt puts his head in his hands and I put my arm around him and lay my head on his shoulder.

I have a lot of explaining to do to my bewildered

husband, but I thank God that, unlike Juliette, we have plenty of time to do all the explaining that is needed and grow together, still taking one day at a time.

And I intend to use my time on this earth very wisely from now on, because I won't wait for tomorrow, or until I'm forty, or until I'm anything, or anywhere, anytime in the future.

I will believe every day when I wake up and feel healthy and well enough to do so, that life begins right now.

Right here, with me, right now.

Epilogue

Shelley

CHRISTMAS DAY, 5 MONTHS LATER

It's late in the evening and Matt is tipsy and half-asleep, Dan is tipsy and half-asleep, Eliza and my dad are having an argument over a game of Scrabble at the table while Juliette's parents look on not knowing what to say, desperately trying to interpret the mix of Irish accents that fill their side of the room.

Helen and Brian and her boys are helping themselves to leftovers in the kitchen, still wearing their paper hats from the crackers we pulled at the table earlier and Rosie and I are on the balcony sharing a blanket around our shoulders as we look out onto the black of the sea, the moody December sky and the only light we can see is the twinkle on the lighthouse in the distance.

'Did you have a nice day?' I ask her, knowing that whatever her reply, there is absolutely nothing more I could have done to make this Christmas as peaceful and perfect as I possibly could.

'Yes, it was beautiful, thank you,' she says and she looks right at me, her green eyes full of happiness and pain all rolled into one. 'Do you think she is watching us right now, Shelley? I really hope she's here in some way, enjoying the day as much as we all did. She loved Christmas, especially when it snowed.'

I close my eyes and try to feel her near me. I have my own hopes too. I hope that she has found my girl like she said she would. I hope she has found my mum too and that she will let me know, just like she said she would.

'I have no doubt she is watching our every move and trying to tell us what to do from away up there,' I say to Rosie. 'Bossing us around, making us laugh and pushing us to be the best we can be. I have no doubt.'

Rosie chuckles. 'I think you're right, she probably is,' she says. 'She loved Christmas so much. It's the one time of year that will always remind me of her, no matter how old I get. Christmas was her time. I think she'd be very happy to see how much fun we had today. Thank you for having us all over for dinner and presents and all the works. It means a lot and it was a great distraction from how we would have been otherwise, sitting round the table in Helen's and staring at an empty chair.'

'It means a lot to us too to have you all here, believe me, Rosie,' I say to her. 'We're family now so it's the least we can do. You and Matt have a lot of catching up to do and your mum didn't believe in wasting time, so neither should we.'

'We do have a lot to catch up on,' she says with a smile. 'That day when you found me on the sand dunes ... It seems now that it was all meant to be, doesn't it?'

'Maybe it was. Do you believe in angels, Rosie?' I ask her and she shrugs.

'I dunno. I would like to believe that something makes things happen for the greater good,' she says. 'I sometimes like to think of my mum as an angel now, looking out for me, making sure that I don't get too sad or lonely. She brought me here to you, after all.'

'She did,' I whisper. *Look out for the colour blue*, I remember Eliza telling me and I smile at the memory and how far we have all come.

'At least I know now where I get my geekiness from now,' says Rosie. 'Oh, I don't mean that in a bad way! No offence! Matt's not a geek at all, but you know what I mean.'

'None taken,' I say and I can't help but smirk. 'I know exactly what you mean. He's an architect and a stickler for detail so I suppose you could say he has a geeky side. You have so much to learn from each other, Rosie and it's going to be so much fun. I know you and Matt are going to get on very well.'

She leans her head on my shoulder.

'I gave him the letters today,' she says as we both stare out onto the sky that looks fluffy and grey now like it is about to burst. 'I've been writing them on and off for years now so I hope it makes it easier for him to understand where I'm from and some of the things that I like. You never know, maybe he'll be into some of the same things too.'

I smile at her sweetness. She is just a baby really with so much to learn.

'He'll enjoy every moment of getting to know you, Rosie,' I say to her. 'And I have so much to tell you about Lily, your little sister. Plus, we will always talk about your mum, you know that. She will always be a part of our family too. She is a big part of me and you.'

'She is,' nods Rosie. 'I just wish I could tell that she is safe wherever she is and that she is happy and with the people she loved up there. I wish I could just get a sign. Anything. I wish I just knew ...'

'It's going to snow,' says a voice from behind us and we turn around to see Eliza at our shoulders, looking out over our heads. She hands me a glass of bubbly and a soft drink to Rosie. 'A white Christmas at last. The weather man got it wrong again.'

'A white Christmas,' whispers Rosie and we sit together, the three of us and watch as snowflakes slowly fall around us.

'Shelley, I think my mum is alright after all,' Rosie says to me. 'She really wanted a white Christmas so I think that this might be the sign I've been looking for.'

'You do?' I say to Rosie and Eliza gives me a satisfied wink of approval. 'Well, that's something to celebrate then, Rosie, love. Come on, let's dance in the kitchen like no one is watching, even though we know that Juliette is here with us watching our every single move and always will be!'

'I think it's time we all danced in the kitchen,' says Eliza. 'I'll wake up the lads and we'll get this party started.'

'Yes, let's celebrate this wonderful white Christmas in this most magnificent place,' I say to Rosie and Eliza. 'Let's celebrate being alive and all that life has to offer. Nothing more, nothing less. Someone once told me that being alive is as good a reason to celebrate as any, don't you agree?'

'To today and the joy of being alive to enjoy it,' says Rosie. 'Every day is a disco. Every day is an adventure, and don't you ever forget it.'

We clink our glasses and wipe away our tears as we toast.

'I'll drink to that,' I say and my heart fills up with a rush of love as I savour this precious moment and then Rosie takes a photo as I raise my glass.

Now, that is one memory of Rosie that I will want to take with me forever. And we have so many more new memories together to come.

Acknowledgements

Huge thanks to each and every single reader who has contacted me over the past twelve months with touching and very moving messages of encouragement and support. Thank you for taking the time to not only read my work but to let me know your own personal stories of love, life and loss. Big thanks to all the book clubs especially Edel O'Neill and all the girls in the Page Turners group in Mid Ulster and the Sea Isle City girls who sent me a very sunny photo from their book club on the beach in New Jersey.

To all the bloggers who do such amazing work spreading lots of book love, especially those who hosted me on a recent tour (ANovelThoughtWithJess, ChickLitChloe, APageofFictionalLove and WithLoveForBooks) plus Alba in Bookland, Shaz Goodwin, Celeste McCreesh, Claire Bridle, Cliodhna Fullen, and Kaisha Holloway at The Writing Garnet whose review moved me to tears! Big high five to little Eva as well!

I have had so much support from the media so a big thanks to *Belfast Telegraph* (Gail Walker and Kerry McKittrick), *The Galway Advertiser* (Kernan Andrews and Declan Varley), *Sunday Life* (Martin Breen), *Irish News* (Jenny Greenaway), *Irish Times* (Jennifer O'Connell), BBC Radio Ulster (Kerry McLean and Vinny Hurrell), UTV Life (Pamela Ballantine) *Tyrone Courier* (Ian Greer), *Dungannon Herald* (Annamay McNally) and further afield thanks to the support of Chicago Irish Radio and to my buddy Nolan Rafferty and Jimmy Keane over there for finding me a place on the airwaves Stateside.

Staying that direction, I am so appreciative of the support of Sean Maguire and his beautiful wife Tanya plus Sean's extensive fan base, especially Stacy and Ana who really help to spread the word about my books in the USA. I am overwhelmed to have you on my side and for all your Tweets and shout outs! Also thanks in this regard to country singer Derek Ryan and Graeme Clark of Wet Wet Wet for sharing the love with your own fans. It means a lot.

I am very grateful to all the support from the people of Kinvara, Co Galway, so much so that this book, well, let's say the location might sound a little bit familiar though I have used some creative license on my descriptions and landmarks! Special thanks to Joe Byrne, to Ruth and all at Sexton's Bar, Helen Larrissey at Be Yourself Boutique, and to Karen Weekes, Jackie Veale and Mary Keogh for your friendship and warm welcomes every time we visit. Big thanks also to Siobhan at Ballybane

Library, Galway for hosting events and to the staff at Westside and Tuam Libraries for accommodating me to give reader talks this year. A special mention to the beautiful inside and out Maureen Browne for adding some magic to these events with her magical fiddle playing at short notice!

I am so thankful for the support from local bookshops especially Sheehy's in Cookstown who always pull out the stops to give my books a big send off. Thank you so much Madeline, TP and staff and to all who turn out every time and show so much support, especially my aunties – Mary, Eithna, Margaret, Bernadette and Kathleen, cousins, friends and school-friends Aideen, Kathy, Katrina, Roisin and Rosealla for popping by to say hello. Bug hugs to you all and to all my friends old and new who share the word on social media. Also to Angela Morgan for lending her gorgeous voice and Jim McKeown for always being a rock of support for big events when I need him and to Ciaran Campbell who never loses sight of a PR moment!

To Emily Ruston, my amazing editor who is an absolute pleasure to work with – I honestly can never thank you enough for how you continue to push me in the right direction. It is such an honour to work with you. Also a big shout out of thanks and love to Charlotte, Kim and all at HarperImpulse who I enjoy working with so much and I still pinch myself that I'm part of such a talented team.

Finally, to my precious family – my Dad Hugh, sisters

Vanessa, Rachel, Lynne, Rebecca, Niamh, my brother David, all my in-laws and the McKee clan especially Nanny Irene and my beautiful children Jordyn, Jade, Dualta, Adam and Sonny James who I am so proud of more and more every day.

This one's for Jim McKee, my best buddy, my partner in every walk of life and in loving memory of the two little babies we lost in recent times.

And to all who have lost a loved one, no matter at what age of stage in life or in what circumstances, I hope you find strength and blessings to keep going when you need it.